KILLED
IN ACTION

ALSO BY MICHAEL SLOAN

The Equalizer: A Novel

KILLED
IN ACTION

AN EQUALIZER NOVEL

MICHAEL SLOAN

ST. MARTIN'S PRESS
NEW YORK

KILLED IN ACTION: AN EQUALIZER NOVEL. Copyright © 2018 by Michael Sloan. All rights reserved. Printed in the United States of America. For information, address St. Martin's Press, 175 Fifth Avenue, New York, N.Y. 10010.

www.stmartins.com

Designed by Omar Chapa

The Library of Congress Cataloging-in-Publication Data is available upon request.

ISBN 978-1-250-09867-2 (hardcover)
ISBN 978-1-250-09868-9 (ebook)

Our books may be purchased in bulk for promotional, educational, or business use. Please contact your local bookseller or the Macmillan Corporate and Premium Sales Department at 1-800-221-7945, extension 5442, or by email at MacmillanSpecialMarkets@macmillan.com.

First Edition: January 2018

10 9 8 7 6 5 4 3 2 1

This book is dedicated to my wife, Melissa,

and to my children, Griffin and Piper.

ACKNOWLEDGMENTS

I want to thank my editor at St. Martin's Press, Michael Homler, for his wisdom, his insight, and his terrific suggestions. I would also like to thank his wonderful assistant at St. Martin's Press, Lauren Jablonski, for being so supportive and helpful. Two of the nicest people it has ever been my pleasure to work with. I want to thank Colonel Michael G. "Gunner" Rose (US Army, Ret.)—the *real-life Gunner!*—who spent over half of his thirty years in Special Operations Units. Gunner's attention to detail, his insight in the "wartorn" sequences, and his unflagging good humor were invaluable to me. *And* his character wound up being a major player in the book! I would like to thank my manager, Peter Meyer, and my entertainment attorney, Nick Gladden. To my dear friend, the late Edward Woodward, who played The Equalizer on CBS-TV with style, and, as always, to the superb Denzel Washington, for portraying McCall with Oscar-winning flair.

KILLED
IN ACTION

CHAPTER 1

The two gangbangers were throwing her between them like they were passing a football back and forth. They were Latino, but pale skinned, second-
or third-generation American, probably only seen Mexico in TV ads for
Puerto Vallarta. They were dressed in black baggy jeans, their asses hanging out the backs. He'd never seen the fashion statement in the youth of
today wearing jeans that way. They had on dark boxers. They were both
wearing crimson shirts, unbuttoned to their belts, one of them with enough
gold necklaces to make the black dude on that old TV show—what was his
name? Mr. T—jealous.

The young woman was in her early twenties, medium height, dark red
hair to her shoulders. She was wearing a white silk shirt, virtually see-
through. No bra. One of the gangbangers had ripped her shirt open, popping little turquoise buttons, exposing her large breasts, but really, he needn't
have bothered, they were clearly visible through the sheer fabric. She wore a
flared white short skirt, probably very chic, and high-heeled white pumps,
which looked like you could only walk a few feet in them before blisters
starting forming. That was another fashion trend he had never come to
grips with. What was the point of young women wearing shoes with heels
so high they'd give you a nosebleed? A Gucci Soho leather shoulder bag was
at her feet, rose beige with fine gold hardware on it. Over fifteen hundred
bucks if you got it at the Gucci store on Madison Avenue. Probably four
hundred in Chinatown. The young woman kept trying to reach down to her
bag, as if something were in there she desperately needed. But they weren't
letting her get anywhere near it.

Gangbanger #1 slapped her face. It brought a trickle of blood from her
nose. He tossed her back to his pal, who shoved her toward a brick wall.
She'd come from the art gallery along Essex Street. He'd seen elegant folks
through a big glass window, drinking champagne from fluted glasses, sam-
pling hors d'oeuvres from passing silver trays, moving around amid a

jumble of weird-looking sculptures and Art Deco pieces that probably cost more than the national debt. He hadn't noticed her in particular, but when she'd left, he'd noted that she'd hurried away down Essex Street to take a shortcut through this narrow alleyway.

Bad idea.

As she'd found out.

The young woman tried to pull her ripped shirt across her breasts, but the Latino boys had really done a number on it, and the fragments of her shirt were too shredded to properly close over them. The first gangbanger—he decided to think of him as *Manuel*—grabbed her faux Gucci bag and started to go through it. The second gangbanger—let's call him *Lopez*—held the young woman's shoulder tightly with one hand. He stayed back in the shadows, unseen by either the young woman or the gangbangers. He was glad when Manuel came up with her wallet, so he'd have a name for her.

"Megan Forrester," Manuel said, showing her driver's license to Lopez. He looked at her. "Pretty name."

He took a bunch of bills out of the wallet, dropped it back into the open Gucci bag, and kicked it toward her, as if contemptuously.

"Take the money," she pleaded. "Just let me go."

"You think we want to hurt you?" Lopez asked. "We just want to get to know you, Megan. See what you look like under those clothes. Why don't you help us out? Lift up your skirt."

She shook her head violently, her eyes darting around the alleyway.

If she saw him, it didn't register on her face.

Lopez took a knife out of his jacket pocket and flicked up a wicked nine-inch blade. "We haven't cut you yet. And we won't. Just show us what you got."

"No need for you to get hurt," Manuel said reasonably.

"Okay, okay," she gasped.

She reached down and pulled up her white skirt. It was so short she didn't have to pull it up high to reveal the white panties she was wearing.

"Pull them down," Lopez said. "We want you to do it for us."

She froze, her skirt hiked up, her hand trembling.

"Don't make me do it," Manuel said. "You show us what we want to see, we'll let you go." She didn't move. "Okay, I can do it."

"I'll do it! I'll do it!" She pulled down her panties. She tried to hold on to them, but they fell around her ankles.

"Natural redhead," Lopez said. "Nice. Let's see your ass."

She started to turn around.

"Keep your skirt hiked up," Manuel reminded her.

She nodded and turned fully around, facing the brick wall. Her bare behind was pale in the semidarkness.

The Equalizer decided this had gone far enough. Although, he had to admit, she had a dynamite ass. Megan turned back to face her attackers. Leaned one hand down, still holding up her skirt with the other, to grab her panties.

"We'll tell you when you can pull them up," Manuel said.

"What do you think?" Lopez said. "Should we let her go?"

"We'll fuck her first."

That was the last thing Manuel said.

The Equalizer sucker punched him in the side of the head, then sank a fist into his gut. He went down on his knees, vomiting onto the dirty concrete. The Equalizer kicked him in the face, sending him onto his side. Then he kicked him hard in the balls.

What happened next happened quickly.

Lopez whirled with the knife, still not quite seeing the figure in the deep shadows, and thrust forward blindly. The Equalizer grabbed his wrist, avoiding the blade, wrenched it up and down, and broke his wrist. Lopez howled. The Equalizer brought him down with three blows to his face, breaking his nose, shattering his left cheekbone, knocking out some teeth. The gangbanger sprawled onto the ground.

Megan pulled up her panties, dropped her skirt, knelt down, flailed a hand inside her Gucci bag, and came out with a Mace spray in a Bianchi Elite pouch.

Manuel had dragged himself up to his feet.

Megan sprayed the Mace right into his eyes.

He screamed and went back down on his knees.

Megan didn't wait to find out who her Good Samaritan was. She grabbed her Gucci bag, then kicked Manuel in the balls with the toe of her white pump. She pulled the shreds of her white shirt over her breasts and ran from the alleyway.

Neither of the Latinos were getting up. The Equalizer knelt down beside Lopez, whose wrist hung like a marionette's with a string cut, and took something out of the pocket of his overcoat.

It was a business card.

On it was the graphic of a figure standing in an alleyway in front of a black Jaguar car, gun in hand, the New York City skyline behind him. Above it were the words JUSTICE IS HERE. Beneath the silhouette of the figure were the words THE EQUALIZER.

He tucked the card into the breast pocket of Lopez's crimson shirt.

Then he straightened and looked over at Manuel. Lopez and Manuel, a matching set of degenerates. But they didn't quite match. He regretted he hadn't broken Manuel's arm. *He'd* been the one who'd ripped Megan's blouse open and fondled her breasts.

The Equalizer shrugged. *What the hell.*

He knelt down beside Manuel, gripped his arm, and broke it in two places.

He screamed, but didn't move.

The Equalizer straightened again, pocketed Lopez's switchblade, and looked down at the two thugs. They wouldn't be attacking another defenseless victim for quite a while. *Well,* he thought, *not so defenseless.* Megan had sprayed Mace into Manuel's eyes for five long seconds. Might have blinded him.

Justice done.

He heard the sound of police sirens getting closer. Megan must have called 911 on her smartphone. He didn't stay around to be thanked or congratulated. He melted back into the shadows, leaving Lopez and Manuel—or *whatever* their real names were—lying broken and bleeding on the alleyway concrete.

But it was *not* Robert McCall who walked out of that alleyway.

CHAPTER 2

Ten adversaries in the partially constructed office building.

His inward smile was fleeting.

He'd have to lower these odds.

The pounding rock music washed over Robert McCall in undulating waves. The sea of people on both sides was like an amorphous being, forming and re-forming, different faces and colors and movement. The overpowering aroma at the rave party was sweet and sickly. McCall pushed past a young man dancing by himself, dressed in lavender jeans, shirt to match, hair teased with violet curls, who was wearing enough Polo Red Intense to gag a lavatory attendant. But he was pretty damn good.

Huge potted plants with towering palm fronds were stationed every few feet across the ground floor. Standing beside one of them was Blake Cunningham. At least, McCall assumed that was who the young man in the elegant suit with the dirty-blond hair was. He held Emily Masden's shoulder tightly. A thin trickle of blood seeped from the young woman's mouth. Her low-cut black dress clung to her figure as if molded to it. She wore black stockings with their tops held up by silver suspenders that the skirt didn't come close to covering. She looked at Blake, startled by being backhanded. She looked around the open building space, with its many staircases up to other half-finished construction levels, as if she'd woken up from a nightmare. Laura, whom McCall had left with her back against one of the big steel supports holding up the second-floor partial ceiling, had said Emily was high. She was right. Emily's eyes were dilated and a bright sheen of perspiration glistened on her face and bare arms. She was having trouble catching her breath.

She was also disoriented and frightened.

McCall knew where the two men behind him had their guns tucked into the waistbands of their jeans. He'd noted that when they'd got up from the booth in the River Café at the Brooklyn docks half an hour ago. They'd nonchalantly buttoned their jackets, but he'd had the impression they'd *wanted* him to see the weapons. They were armed and dangerous.

And they were right behind him.

McCall stopped suddenly, as if to avoid stepping right into the path of Cologne Man, who probably wouldn't have noticed if he'd stomped on both his feet. McCall half turned, his hands darting out like a blur. When he turned back, both of the men's jackets were gaping open.

Both of their guns were gone.

McCall slid the two pistols, one a Smith & Wesson M&P 22 Compact, the other a Smith & Wesson Shield 9mm, into the side pockets of his jacket. The two young men stopped dead, confused. The three men coming down the steel staircase on McCall's right were too far away. They'd have to draw their weapons and shoot into the crowd, which would cause immediate pandemonium and bring the cops here.

McCall glanced up at the two men on the second level above him, leaning casually on the railing, their jackets open, revealing their Heckler & Koch 9mm pistols. Same problem. They'd have a better shot at him, but what would be their motivation? He was just threading his way through the dancing mayhem below. By the time he reached Emily and Blake Cunningham, McCall would be *under* the level of the balcony where the men were standing. To get a shot at him they'd have to lean way down and shoot virtually backward, which would be risky, and even a novice would know it was not a viable move. And McCall was certain none of these young thugs were professional gunmen honing their craft.

That left the two young men moving quickly through the partygoers on McCall's left. One of them wasn't carrying a weapon. But his partner had a subcompact Glock 26 already in his hand. McCall turned a half step to his left and grabbed the second man's hand.

One second the gun was in his hand.

Then it wasn't.

McCall dropped the Glock 26 into one of the big palm-frond tubs.

McCall moved up behind Emily and jerked her out of Blake Cunningham's grasp.

Then he slapped her hard across the face.

"What the hell do you think you're doing?" McCall demanded. He squeezed her face with his hand. "Did you take something?" He looked over at Blake Cunningham, who had taken a step back. "Who is this?"

"I'm her boyfriend. Who are *you*?"

"I'm her father. What is she on? Quaaludes, or mollys—whatever the hell *they* are—or cocaine?"

McCall grabbed Emily's right arm, twisting it around so he could see the veins. She had been so stunned by being slapped by a complete stranger that she hadn't moved. Now she tried to twist out of his grasp, but it was like a steel trap.

"I don't know what she's on, *if* she's on anything," Blake said evenly.

He glanced over McCall's shoulder and give the barest shake of his head. Telling the college thugs behind McCall to back off. Blake could handle this. He did the same subtle head flick to his right, moving back the two on that side. McCall didn't appear to notice it.

"You said you're her boyfriend?" McCall's tone was still loud and accusatory.

Blake Cunningham only raised his voice a little, so that it carried just above the cacophony of the party. McCall thought Cunningham probably kept his voice well modulated at all times. Part of the hip young stockbroker image. He was wearing a Giorgio Armani Soho black wool-and-silk pinstripe suit, a Versace black-and-gold silk shirt, and black loafers with no socks, and a pair of Fendi 411 Aviator sunglasses rested on the top button of his shirt.

"I suppose saying Emily is my girlfriend could be debatable. We broke up and I haven't seen her in a week. I thought I might find her here," he added with an apologetic shrug. "This is the kind of party she likes to go to. How long has it been since you've seen your daughter?"

"Two months, if it's any of your business."

Emily looked up at McCall as if trying to focus through the smoky haze, most of it inside her head. "You're hurting my arm."

"I'm taking you out of here," McCall said.

Again, Blake's soft, insinuating voice: "What if she doesn't want to go with you?"

"I'm her father. She doesn't get a choice."

"She's twenty-two years old. That gives her the choice. You can't make her do anything she doesn't want to do."

Emily was still staring at McCall. She said almost tentatively, "You're not—"

McCall swung round on her. "Your mother's been sick with worry. How could you do this to her? Stop phoning, stop communicating? You know how much money it's cost me to fly out to New York to come and get you? I look at you, Emily, dressed like a slut, and I don't know you. You're not the daughter I raised. Who else are you sleeping with?" Back to Blake: "You don't think you're the only one, do you?" Back to Emily: "You want to stay here, take some more drugs, fry your brains, grope this degenerate, go ahead. I won't stop you."

He let go of her arm.

Emily continued to stare at him, but now it was with some kind of bleary realization. She looked from him to Blake Cunningham.

"I have to go with him, Blake. He's my dad."

Blake raised his hands as if in surrender. "Sure, take her out of here. She'll come back and find me. She always does."

Blake smirked and nodded a little more openly at the young men behind McCall. McCall assumed they took the hint and were fading back into the party. He kept his eyes on Blake. He wanted to knock that smirk off his face, but would good old self-righteous Dad, the CPA from Stillwater, Minnesota, haul off and slug him?

Probably not.

McCall spun Emily around and marched her away. He could feel

Blake's eyes boring into his back. The seven men who'd crowded McCall on both sides had disappeared. McCall had a firm grip on Emily's arm, but not as tight as before. She looked up at him. Her eyes were more focused now.

"They'll just come for me again. They'll take me away from you."

"No, they won't."

"You don't know them."

McCall ignored that. "What did you take?"

"One of the girls dragged me into the ladies' room. I snorted some stuff she put on her wrist. I felt icy. Warm, then cold."

"Your pupils are large and you're sweating. You look like you could be running a fever. How fast is your heart beating?"

"Real fast," she whispered. "What was it I took?"

"Cocaine. You know the girl who gave it to you?"

"Yeah. Her name's Lucy. A friend of Blake's. She told me I had to 'look right.' I changed into this dress. Put on suspenders and black stockings. Blake likes those. I made up my face. Black tears. The kind you cry inside."

Then her body convulsed as she began to sob. McCall held her tighter, gently pushing their way through to where he had left Laura.

"You're going to be all right, Emily."

"Who the hell are you?"

"Someone who's trying to help you."

"Why the fuck should you care about me?"

"I don't. But your mother does."

"You don't know my mother."

"Not well."

"What are you talking about?"

"Your mother's here."

Emily choked back the sobs, looking up at him. "My mom? She would never follow me to New York!"

"She was frantic with worry about you. With good reason."

"Where is she?"

McCall guided her around a raucous group drinking at one of the larger tables. Laura Masden stood exactly where McCall had left her five minutes before, looking out anxiously through the crowd. She hadn't seen them yet.

McCall pointed Laura out. "There's your mom."

Emily wrenched out of McCall's grasp so unexpectedly that he hadn't been ready for it.

"That's *not* my mother," Emily said in a fierce whisper.

McCall was stunned. Several moments of the past hour spun through his mind. Amid the crank calls he had received after putting his ad in the classified section of *The New York Times* and on the internet—*Gotta Problem? Odds Against You? Call the Equalizer*—there'd been a desperate voice-mail message from a woman saying her name was Laura Masden. When he'd called her back, she'd asked him if he was "the Equalizer." Hearing the name spoken out loud by a real client had given him pause, but McCall had said, "Yes. You have a problem?"

He'd spotted her, elegant and frightened, sitting alone at a booth at the River Café in Brooklyn, overlooking the East River, nursing an apple martini. He'd slipped into the booth opposite her and said, "Hello, Laura, my name is Robert McCall. What's your problem?" She had seemed a little disconcerted by his less than effusive greeting, but her sincerity about finding her daughter had been compelling.

"It's my daughter Emily. She's twenty-two. She's always been a difficult child, but she's not into drugs or alcohol. She's a dreamer. She wants to make a difference in the world."

"Why did she come to New York?"

"She was accepted at the Art Institute of New York City. Media arts. After being at the college one month, she dropped out. And disappeared."

Laura had described Emily's boyfriend, Blake Cunningham. He had told Laura that he'd broken up with her daughter and had practically thrown Laura out. Before that happened, Laura had heard Blake mention this address. McCall remembered how Laura had fought off the tears brimming in her eyes when speaking of her daughter.

"I'm going to find your daughter," he had told her. "If she's in danger . . ."

"You'll equalize those odds?" she had asked, smiling through her tears.

"Yes. I will."

He thought of their arrival at the rave party and how Laura had spotted Emily dancing and how her voice had broken when she'd seen her.

"She's changed her hair color. It doesn't even look like Emily, but that's her."

McCall had instructed Laura to put her back against the pillar and wait for him. That he would bring her daughter to her.

He pointed out Laura again, thinking perhaps Emily had looked at the wrong person.

"Right there, the woman in the gray suit with the black Dior coat, standing at that pillar."

"I *know* what my mother looks like. Duh. That is *not* my mom."

McCall suddenly wanted to get Emily out of there before Laura—or *whoever* she was—turned and looked in their direction.

"This way," he said tersely.

He guided Emily back to one of the many side entrances to the abandoned building. Party wranglers wearing obscene burn masks, like bizarre Walmart greeters, were ushering more people in. McCall looked over to where Blake Cunningham had been standing.

He had gone.

So had his college chums on the ground floor. Behind him, the woman calling herself Laura Masden was becoming impatient. She starting pushing through the crowd toward where she'd seen McCall disappear.

McCall hustled Emily to a doorway half-hidden behind one of the steel staircases. One of the grotesque burn masks stepped forward to stop them.

"No one goes out this way."

McCall shoved him to one side. Burn Mask looked like he was considering doing something about that, then thought better of it. McCall pushed Emily out through the door into the night. He noted that it had started to rain pretty heavily.

McCall looked behind him to make sure Blake Cunningham or any of his pals weren't following them. They weren't. When he turned back into the street, Emily had disappeared.

CHAPTER 3

The street was deserted, but McCall caught a flash of movement to his left. An old theater was nestled on the corner about ten yards up from the Whitehall subway station constructed of red brick. The theater was derelict, with scaffolding along the east side. The scaffolding looked like it had gone up just after World War II ended. Moonlight had picked up the bright suspenders flashing on Emily's legs as she ran through the theater's front door.

McCall ran across to the theater. Faded letters just under the second-floor windows read MERCURY THEATER. On what was left of a marquee that had been added to the façade at some point was, in slim unlit neon, CREST with the C missing. McCall hoped that wasn't an ironic message for him. Obviously the theater had been turned into a cinema at some point. Probably ran XXX-rated movies in the eighties, before it became as easy to find porn on the internet as your favorite lasagne recipe.

McCall jogged over to a big blue Dumpster, took the two Smith & Wesson pistols he'd appropriated, and tossed them inside. Then he moved back to the theater's front door. He noted a rusted padlock on it was broken. Probably a safe haven on cold nights for the homeless. The door groaned on blackened hinges as he pushed it open.

Inside, the lobby was the quiet of the dead. Dust particles hung in the air like a translucent fog. Rectangular glass frames were on one wall, most of them empty, but a couple of old theater posters were left. The city had turned the movie house *back* into a theater again for a while. The dates on the two theatrical posters were from the early 2000s. In one, the Mercury Theater was proud to present the US stage première of a thriller titled *Underground*, and depicted was a London Underground subway car trapped in a tunnel, with the words *12 Passengers on a Subway Journey into Hell*. The name above the play title was Raymond Burr. If McCall was put under oath, he would have to confess he liked watching TV reruns of *Perry Mason*. Next to this poster was one of a rustic cabin in a misty forest clearing, a scantily clad young woman running from it, with the demonic face of a cat superimposed over the woods. Above that was the title: *Catspaw—A new stage thriller by Robert L. McCullough*. It starred Greg Evigan and a New York cast McCall had never heard of. He thought wryly that this theater was about as off-off-Broadway as you could get and still be in New York.

He stopped and listened. There were small scuttling sounds. Probably rats. Cockroaches made no sound. He heard nothing else. He moved over to a heavy door with small stained-glass panels depicting a knight in green armor slaying a dragon and pushed it open.

Inside the actual theater, the quiet continued. Rows of faded onetime plush red seats were along both sides of a center aisle. The seating capacity was about 350. The stage was empty. A work light stage-right provided a harsh illumination. A ripped red curtain was lying stage-left, never to rise on a performance again. Two ornate boxes were above the stage on either side. As McCall walked down the center aisle, he glanced up. A mezzanine with ten rows of seats was above him.

She came at him from out of the gloom.

She'd picked up a sixteen-inch nail from some construction debris and stabbed it at his face. He grabbed her wrist and twisted it, just enough for her to yelp and drop the nail. He threw her over his shoulder, her black dress riding up over her hips above the stocking tops and silver suspenders. She beat her fists on his back. He didn't react. He reached row G, near the stage, and dumped her down into the first seat. She stared up defiantly, then dropped her eyes, as if just now realizing her dress was up to the level of her black panties. She pulled the dress down, but it didn't cover the stocking tops and suspenders. It wasn't supposed to. Her breath came out in ragged gasps. Her chest was heaving. McCall stood above her, allowing her to calm down, to get oxygen back into her lungs.

She finally said, "You pretended to be me my dad. You dragged me over to some woman who is *not* my mom. You're one of Blake's asshole cronies."

"If that were true, I wouldn't have taken you out of there."

"You were taking me to them."

"They didn't expect you to come out of that side entrance. Take a couple of deep breaths. I'm not going to hurt you, Emily."

She nodded. Her breathing was less labored. She was coming down from her high. "How bad is the withdrawal going to be?"

"Depends on how much you took. You mind if I sit down?"

She moved over into the next seat.

McCall sat down beside her. "We can't stay in here."

She looked at the empty stage. "I don't think the curtain's going up anytime soon."

"They may search for you. This is an obvious place to hide."

"I wasn't thinking. I just wanted to get away."

"This will be fine for a few minutes."

"I don't have to talk to you."

"I can take you back to the party. Lots of people to talk to there."

She shook her head violently, then suddenly reached down and undid the suspenders on both stockings. She rolled them down her legs and pulled them off. Screwed them up into balls and threw them into the row in front. She lifted up her black dress, undid the suspender belt, and tossed it after the stockings. Then she demurely pulled the dress down as far on her calves as it would go. Her breathing had regulated. She looked back at him.

"What do you want to know?"

"Your mother—the woman impersonating your mother—said you'd

come to Manhattan because you'd been accepted by the New York City Art Institute. Is that true?"

"Yeah. When I was six, I drew fairies and goblins and dragons for a 'Sticker Fairy Calendar' my mom was going to get published. It never happened." Emily shrugged again. She did that a lot. "But the pictures were pretty good for a six-year-old."

"Why did you drop out of your art course?"

"I got bored. I just wanted an excuse . . ."

"To leave home?"

"Yeah. You don't know my *real* mom."

"Describe her to me."

"Thin, very pale, blond hair, but stringy, you know, like she never washes it? Her face is kinda pinched all the time, like she's smelling something bad. Her eyes were always kind, but they had this haunted look in them. She does the best she can," Emily added, as if defensively. "She's bipolar, you know? Gigantic mood swings. One day she's chipper about school stuff and my dad being gone all the time, two days later she's a raving lunatic."

"Tell me about your dad."

Emily smiled. "You couldn't have got him more wrong. He's an archaeologist. Always off on some dig somewhere in Central America or Africa or some Arab caves. Looking for old bones and fossils or whatever the fuck it is they look for to try and discover secrets about people who've been dead for centuries. In 2014 he went to Huamparán, somewhere in Peru, on a dig for the University of Paris. Excavating that site and the areas around Huari and Royal Inca Road. I guess there was more cool stuff to find, because they asked him to go back again. He's been there almost six months. Discovering little pieces of broken pottery, that's what gets his dick hard."

She frowned and shook her head, as if the thought of her dad's penis was pretty inappropriate. She looked again at McCall. "My dad would *never* be aggressive like you were with Blake. He'd be reasonable and soft-spoken, but he would have dragged me out of there, too."

"He loves his daughter."

"Yeah, sure."

"And I'm sure your mother also loves you."

"*She* didn't leave small-town Americana to come and look for her daughter who'd been missing for three weeks."

"Maybe she sent someone else in her place."

A shrug. "Yeah, maybe." A beat, then: "I'm sorry I attacked you."

"I'll get over it. How did you hook up with Blake Cunningham?"

"At a cocktail bash at one of the artist's galleries whose work was on display at the Art Institute. Blake was mesmerizing, those blue eyes. I've never seen eyes so cornflower blue on a guy before. Have you?"

McCall thought of his friend Granny, with his piercing ice-cold blue eyes. He wondered how Granny was faring on the North Korean covert operation that he'd organized with Mickey Kostmayer. It was a dangerous mission.

"Just one guy," McCall said.

"Blake stunned me with his personality at first. Like, wow, being kicked right in the gut. He introduced me to his college friends. Most of them are in their last year at Columbia, but a few of them have graduated and are already on Wall Street making a gazillion bucks. I got caught up in a very intoxicating lifestyle. But I knew there was something wrong. Blake wanted to fuck me, and I wanted him to, but he kept his distance. He and his friends are into something—something dangerous and disgusting, but it's making them very rich."

"What is it?"

"I don't know. They were all very careful not to say anything when I was around."

"Something illegal?"

"More than that. It's dark. It scared me."

"How's your memory?"

"Pretty good."

McCall told her his cell phone number, the one on his second Equalizer iPhone. She repeated it and nodded.

"You won't forget it?"

"No, but why would I call you?"

"Just a precaution."

She nodded again, then touched his arm. "Thank you for saving me," she whispered.

Now the tears welled up in her eyes. She looked away to the stage, as if she were seeing some performance in her mind.

"I went to seven musicals in the first month I was here in Manhattan. *Wicked*—that was the best. Really funny and made your spirits soar. You like musicals? You look more like a *Death of a Salesman* kind of a guy."

"I like musicals."

"What's your favorite?"

"Les Misérables."

"I don't even know your name."

McCall didn't answer. He wasn't listening to her any longer. He had heard a sound, one Emily certainly hadn't heard. He squeezed her shoulder.

"What is it?"

"Someone came in here," he said softly. "Could be a homeless person. I'd say there are a lot of them who use this place. Especially when it's raining."

She turned around and looked back into the gloom.

"I don't see anyone."

"Don't move from this seat. Hunker down a little, so you can't be seen from the back of the theater."

She did as she was told. McCall stood and moved up the center aisle. He looked back and couldn't see Emily's figure in the seat, even though he knew she was still there.

No one was in any of the seats. McCall reached the end of the last row, row W, and took a step out into the darkness of the narrow corridor at the back. Reflected in the stained-glass panels he saw a shadow flicker in the illumination of the work light from the stage.

He whirled to his left.

It was one of the two young men from the River Café. His fist was aimed at McCall's throat, looking to sucker punch him as he stepped out into the corridor. McCall ducked under the punch and brought the assailant to his knees with a shot to his solar plexus. He grabbed the young man's wavy black hair and slammed his face down against his knee. He heard the sickening crack as his jawbone fractured.

He didn't sense the other River Café man until it was too late.

He got an arm around McCall's throat and hauled him back.

The thought flashed through McCall's mind that it was a good thing he'd relieved these guys of their Smith & Wesson guns at the rave party. He'd be very dead if they'd still had them handy.

McCall fell to one knee. He had the lapels of the second thug's coat in both hands and pulled him forward. He hit the floor hard.

Just as the first young man was coming up for air.

McCall kicked him in his broken jaw. He toppled to one side, moaning. McCall grabbed the second young man around the throat, thought briefly about snapping his neck, but they hadn't actually attempted to kill him. They were pissed that McCall had taken their guns away from them. McCall could understand that. It was embarrassing.

McCall slammed his knee into the young thug's back. He writhed and tried to reach back for McCall's face. McCall exerted more pressure around the thug's throat and he slumped forward. McCall set him down gently onto the threadbare carpet.

The first River Café thug had long ago lost interest in the fight. He was holding his jaw with both hands as if afraid it was going to come apart. McCall didn't need to do anything more to him or his partner. They weren't going anywhere.

But it was time to get Emily out of there.

McCall ran back down the center aisle to row G, knowing he would not see Emily's figure until he reached it.

She was gone.

A scuffling sound snapped McCall's head up. He caught a glimpse of two shadowy figures in the mezzanine, the work light barely reaching them. Emily was struggling in the grasp of one of Blake's college pals. McCall edged down the row of seats, ran through the aisle doorway, and took the stairs two at a time. The stairs led right out onto the mezzanine. McCall ran up the right-hand aisle. Both figures were gone. A gunshot echoed and a bullet splintered the wall an inch from McCall's face. He ducked down as two more bullets struck a seat in front of him with resounding thuds. McCall waited. A third bullet would have come right away. It didn't. The assailant was trying to get away.

And maybe Emily was not being a model prisoner.

In his mind's eye McCall could see her struggling in the assailant's grasp, kicking him, trying to rip at his face with her long black-tipped fingernails.

McCall moved down a row of seats to the mezzanine center aisle, crouching down fast. There was no movement ahead of him, but there was sound.

Something scraping.

A window being pulled up.

McCall ran up the aisle stairs to the narrow corridor at the back of the mezzanine. Two doors were there, one of them open. Beyond was a small office, the furniture and empty bookcases covered with dust and grime.

The second-floor window was open.

The assailant was dragging Emily out through it onto a wide plank on the scaffolding. She bit down into the assailant's hand. He snarled and swung around, but McCall was through the open window by then. He grabbed Emily and thrust her behind him. In the same fluid movement he executed a front snap kick that sent the assailant reeling. It was raining steadily now, and the man slipped and fell hard on the plank.

It caused Emily to stumble and fall.

McCall whirled and grabbed her arm.

Her body tumbled off the plank into the void.

McCall held on to her with one hand. Her weight felt like it was going to wrench his arm right out of its socket. He knelt on the slippery plank, grabbed her with his other hand, and started to pull her up.

In his peripheral vision he saw her assailant scrambling to his feet.

Emily's right hand slipped out of McCall's left and she screamed.

He caught her wrist again

For two agonizing seconds Emily dangled over the concrete below.

The assailant steadied himself, grabbed for the gun in his belt.

McCall hauled Emily back up onto the scaffolding plank. He hurled her down behind him, turned, and kicked the gun out of the assailant's hand. Then he barreled right into him. The assailant sailed off the scaffolding to the ground below. He hit the concrete with a sickening thud. It split part of his head open.

McCall was drenched now. He turned carefully as the plank wobbled and saw Emily crawling back through the open window. He went after her, but an arm closed around his throat from behind and he was hauled backward.

He'd recognized the first assailant on the scaffolding plank as one of the men who'd strolled casually down the steel staircase at the rave party. McCall jabbed an elbow into the second assailant's kidney in three fast strikes, weakening the grip around his throat. He threw his thumbs back into the man's face, plunging them into his eyes. He howled in rage.

The hold around McCall's throat came apart.

McCall turned and executed a *Shuto-uchi* knife-hand strike to the assailant's throat. He fell to his knees, his hands over his eyes. Blood seeped through his fingers. The man's face was a horror mask. But he grabbed McCall's left leg, trying to topple him off the unsteady plank.

McCall picked him up and threw him off the scaffolding. He fell with a cry right beside his friend, twisted and broken, unmoving.

McCall had felt the bulge of a gun in the second assailant's pocket. He wondered fleetingly why the man hadn't used it. Maybe *he'd* been told to take McCall alive. To find out what he knew about Blake Cunningham and his operation.

Which was absolutely nothing.

McCall looked down at the two dead men.

On the steel staircase at the rave party there had been *three* of them.

McCall ran back to the open office window. He slipped on the wet wooden plank and had to grab hold of the windowsill to stop himself from pitching out into the darkness to join the others. He steadied himself, then stepped through the open window.

Emily was not inside the office.

She wasn't in the mezzanine.

McCall ran down to the front row of the mezzanine and looked down into the orchestra seats. He couldn't see her. He edged his way across one of the mezzanine rows to the right-hand aisle, ran down the staircase, and burst out into the main part of the theater. He took out his Glock 19, which he hadn't had to use as yet, and ran up the center aisle. When he got to the corridor behind the orchestra seats, he saw that both of the River Café assailants were gone. He threw open the theater doors and ran through the lobby.

Rain sheeted across the narrow boulevard outside. Both of the dead assailants were no longer lying under the scaffolding. McCall ran across the street. He pulled on the half-completed building's side door, but it was locked from the inside. McCall pocketed the Glock and ran around to the back. The cacophony of sound was overpowering. They'd cranked up the decibel level of the music even higher. Perhaps there hadn't been enough people whose ears were bleeding. McCall moved through the partygoers, looking for Emily. There was no sign of her. No sign of Blake Cunningham or any of his asshole cronies either. And no sign of the woman who had told McCall she was Emily's mother, Laura Masden.

McCall stopped, the lights and the people and the music all fusing into a violent mosaic in his mind. He felt completely impotent. The victim was gone, his client was gone, and the bad guys were gone.

So much for his first case as the Equalizer.

CHAPTER 4

McCall sat at an outdoor table of the Starbucks on West Sixty-Fourth Street waiting for her to arrive. The memory of the rave party and the old Mercury Theater had been tumbling through his mind. The deaths of the two men below the scaffolding had never been reported. He had not heard again from the woman who had called herself Laura Masden—and maybe she *was* Laura Masden, and Emily had been lying. He had not heard from Emily. He had not run into Blake Cunningham, although he hadn't gone out of his way to track him down at his Morgan Stanley office at Rockefeller Center. But the strongest memory of that night was Emily turning to McCall in her row G seat in the abandoned theater and whispering, "Thank you for saving me."

Except he hadn't.

McCall saw the two of them walking down Sixty-Fourth Street toward him. They might have looked like a strange couple if they hadn't been in New York. The pale young woman was Candy Annie, in her midtwenties, with a stunning figure and red hair, which cascaded down onto her shoulders. She was wearing a sheer white blouse and a long beige diaphanous skirt and pink Reeboks. Sunlight shone through the blouse and skirt. McCall was relieved to see she was wearing underwear, not something she chose to do every day. She was wearing a Vans Realm backpack in a floral pattern, pretty roses all over it. She also carried a battered suitcase that looked like it might have survived the *Titanic*. On the sidewalk, pedestrians were listening to music on their headphones, texting on their smartphones, or just hustling to make their appointments. Candy Annie didn't see any of it. She was completely focused on the Starbucks at the corner of Broadway and West Sixty-Fourth.

Walking beside her was a tall, wafer-thin African-American dressed in black jeans, a torn NYU T-shirt, and brown workman's boots. Somehow the old clothes didn't take a sense of elegance away from his skeletal figure. A young guy in khaki pants and a blue blazer ran up to him and asked him something. McCall wondered whether the young guy thought the old black man might be Morgan Freeman. He'd been mistaken for him before. He shook his head, with an almost apologetic shrug, and kept on walking.

Unlike his young female companion, Jackson T. Foozelman took in every detail of the busy streets on both sides of Broadway. He shook his head, as if still amazed by the kaleidoscope of humanity, the rush of the traffic, the colors, sights, and sounds.

McCall stood up as they reached his Starbucks table. "You look radiant, Candy Annie."

"I'm scared to death," she whispered.

"But she's here," Jackson T. Foozelman said. "I never thought I'd live to see the day. She's got everything she needs. Didn't leave much behind. Well, you don't go into the tunnels with much, you don't leave them with much."

"What will happen to her living space?"

"I already got it rented out to Gina. She's a big I'll-crush-you-with-these-boobs-when-I-hug-you kind of a gal. She's got two small kids and has been waiting for the day Candy Annie moved out."

"She's been living over in the Amtrak tunnel with the Mole People, and the kids were getting sick," Candy Annie said. "It's warmer at my place."

McCall could see Candy Annie's place in his mind, a seventeen-foot niche in a subterranean tunnel. It had furniture, a couch and chairs, a bright patchwork Norman Rockwell quilt on her bed, a TV set circa the 1990s, with stacks of DVDs beside it, a working sink, a toilet, a small shower stall. It might have been a nicer apartment than most NYU students get, except for the location.

"Did that guy in the blue blazer think you were Morgan Freeman?" McCall asked Fooz.

He grinned. "Sure did. Usually I say yes and scrawl an autograph, but this was too momentous an occasion to dally with strangers."

McCall understood. Candy Annie had lived down in the subway tunnels below Manhattan since she was sixteen. She never talked about her parents, if they were still alive. She never talked about siblings. Her only friends were the Subs, the subterranean people who populated the miles of subway tunnels. Some areas were like corrugated parks, some with artificial turf laid down, all of it surreal, like the human race had been forced down into the sewers after a terrible apocalyptic war aboveground. But there was tranquillity down in the tunnels, and no one had to pay for rent or parking or go anywhere except to the Upworld on occasion for food and supplies.

But it had been no place for a young woman with a keen mind and soaring spirit. McCall had started walking the tunnels with Jackson T. Foozelman a year before, usually discussing Sir Arthur Conan Doyle's Sherlock Holmes. McCall had met Candy Annie and had been immediately impressed by her passion for living. He'd tried for months to persuade her to give up her life below the streets and come and live in the Upworld again. She had stubbornly refused. Then one night McCall had received a call on his Equalizer cell phone. He'd been surprised to hear Fooz's voice.

All he'd said was, "She's ready."

McCall hadn't been certain that Candy Annie would come. For some reason his mind had gone to his favorite scene in one of the original *Star Trek* movies, where, after Spock's death, Kirk had said to the assembled crew of the Starship *Enterprise*, "Spock said there are always . . . possibilities."

Fooz gently took the old suitcase out of Candy Annie's death grip and set it down beside the wrought-iron table. She shrugged off the backpack and dropped it to the ground. Now she looked across Broadway as if seeing it for the first time. A young man in a suit and tie roller-skated by and gave Candy Annie a wave.

"Why did he wave at me?"

"'Cause you're a babe," Fooz said. "Better get used to it."

Candy Annie looked at Robert McCall and shook her head. "I don't think I can do this."

Fooz turned her around and held on to her arms with both of his thin, gnarled hands. "Sure, you can! You can do anything you damn well please, because this is the US of A. You're going to make a success of living in the Upworld. I know it. So does Mr. McCall."

Candy Annie pulled out of the old black man's grasp and turned to McCall. "Are you going to equalize my odds?" she asked in an almost ironic tone. "Fooz showed me your ad."

"He said the odds were against you. I said I'd do something about that."

"But can you really?"

McCall thought about Emily and Blake Cunningham and the bogus Laura Masden. "I can try. Mostly it will be up to you."

Candy Annie nodded vigorously, as if her decision hadn't been made until that very moment. Now the tears came fast as she turned back to Fooz.

"I can never thank you enough for all you've done for me."

She hugged him fiercely. Fooz let her go and looked at her with damp eyes. His voice had a croaky rasp to it, but then, it did most of the time.

"Take care of yourself." He looked over at McCall. "Don't send her back."

Fooz walked down Sixty-Fourth Street with a brisker stride. He crossed Broadway, and Candy Annie watched him disappear. Then she looked back at McCall.

"I can't sit here."

They walked into Central Park from the Sixty-Fifth Street entrance. Bicyclists whizzed by, tapping their bike bells; rollerbladers and skateboarders weaved in and out. There were joggers, young women and businessmen strolling with sandwiches and coffees from Starbucks and Dunkin' Donuts and dogs being walked and kids being pushed in baby carriages and the hot dog and pretzel vendors on either side. Candy Annie looked around, not with trepidation now, but with a kind of excited wonder.

McCall cut across a wide expanse of grass down to where the chess tables were. He knew that Granny would not be sitting at his usual table. One of the chess players that Granny beat a lot—which is to say Granny allowed him to win an occasional game to preserve the man's self-esteem—waved McCall over. He was a big guy with a weather-beaten face, chiseled as if out of red sandstone, with close-cropped brown hair, wearing dark jeans, Adidas Solar Boost yellow-and-black running shoes, and a black *Doctor Who* T-shirt that said DON'T BLINK and had a picture of a stone statue on it. It meant nothing to McCall, but Candy Annie broke into a big smile.

"*Doctor Who!*" she said to the chess player. "The Angels! They move when you blink. Scariest *Doctor Who* aliens *ever*. How do you like the current doctor? I loved Matt Smith, but this Scots guy is kind of cranky and terrific."

"I like him, too. My name's Mike Gammon."

Candy Annie shook his outstretched hand. "Candy Annie." He seemed surprised and she shrugged. "I like candy."

Gammon looked at McCall. "I haven't seen Granny in a month. It's not like him to miss our tournaments."

"He went out of town."

The big man slowly nodded, as if he understood.

"My friend Annie is new to this neighborhood," McCall said. "If she needed some help, and I'm not around, I had told her to come and find Granny."

"But now *he's* not around."

"So I thought I'd introduce her to you."

"So I'd have her back?"

"Something like that."

"I could be a bad guy."

"You're not."

"How do you know that?"

"Granny likes you. He doesn't like bad guys. He told me you're an ex-cop."

"Homicide, Sixtieth Precinct, Brooklyn South." He looked at Candy Annie and indicated the chessboard, whose pieces were *Game of Thrones* characters. "Know how to play?"

"Sure."

"I'm always up for a challenge." Gammon glanced at McCall. "You get word on Granny, let me know, okay?"

McCall nodded, and he and Candy Annie moved away from the chess tables. They walked through the trees in silence, then she said, "He was nice, but you *will* be here for me, won't you, Mr. McCall? I don't think I can do this without you."

"I'll be here. Just creating options."

"Your friend 'Granny'—he's someone close to you?"

"No one's close to me."

"But he's a friend?"

"He can be."

"Tell me about your other friends."

"There aren't any. But I'm taking you to the apartment of a colleague. He's as close to a friend as I'll get."

He watched them walk away from the chess tables through the magnifying lenses of the small pair of binoculars. He had picked them up at Manhattan Pawn on Rivington near Essex Street for five bucks. He'd told the proprietor he needed them for his lifesaving work and had got a discount. Close up, Robert McCall didn't look imposing or threatening. Really kind of ordinary. Which was a little disappointing. But the babe with him was pretty hot.

He lowered the glasses and smiled.

Who knew the Equalizer had a sweet girlfriend?

CHAPTER 5

Kostmayer's apartment was on the second floor of a four-story walk-up on Fifty-Fourth and Second Avenue. Kostmayer had given McCall a key and told him to think of it as an alternate safe house if he ever needed one. The front door opened into a small living room with a kitchenette. McCall was surprised to find the walls were all pale sandalwood. There was a couch and two armchairs in a Pueblo motif, a Navajo rug on the floor, and Frederic Remington paintings on the walls. A forty-inch flatscreen TV was on one wall, and two floor-to-ceiling bookcases were filled with paperbacks and big coffee-table-type books on the Southwest, along with some exquisite Indian pottery. Against another wall was a wooden ladder like the kind the Mexican soldiers climbed to get up onto the ramparts of the Alamo. It was as if Kostmayer had taken this furnished apartment from Taos, New Mexico, and transplanted it into a New York City brownstone. And he might have. McCall had no idea of Kostmayer's background.

The place was absolutely spotless.

McCall set down Candy Annie's backpack and battered suitcase.

Candy Annie opened a door that led to a pale-oak bedroom, with an old-fashioned four-poster canopy bed, a chestnut Mission rocking chair, and a cedar oak dresser with more pottery and Indian crafts on top of it. Beside the bed was a red-tiled bathroom. McCall noted a framed Frederic Remington engraved image from *Harper's Weekly* over the bed titled *I Am Ready—I Will Go,* with a scene of soldiers on a field, receiving orders. McCall thought it apropos. Mickey Kostmayer was ready and willing to go wherever he was ordered, and do what had to be done.

McCall stepped into the kitchenette and opened the refrigerator. It was stocked for a family of twelve. So was the freezer. He walked out into the main living area to meet up with Candy Annie.

"You won't starve for the next week."

"Is this guy a cowboy?"

"It has been said," McCall agreed wryly. "I've never been to his apartment before."

"He's not living here?"

"He's out of the country."

"When is he coming back?"

"It could be several weeks. I'll find you a permanent place, but this will do for now. If you like it."

"I *love* it! But you're sure it's okay with your friend—I mean, your colleague—for me to stay here?"

"I've told him about you. Mickey will be fine with it."

"Because you've saved his life more than once?"

It felt like an odd thing for her to say, but then again, maybe it wasn't. She was smart and canny for a girl who'd spent the last ten years underground. She'd helped him plant a bug on Borislav Kirov, a vicious Chechen nightclub boss whom McCall had been forced to kill. Candy Annie was fearless. But she was also overwhelmed. She looked around the living room again, then back at McCall, as if trying to make up her mind about something. Sunlight from the two windows overlooking Second Avenue was streaming through her sheer blouse. McCall almost sighed.

"When did you take off your bra?" he asked, like a scolding father.

"I don't like it. It chafes my breasts."

She took a deep breath and walked toward him, unbuttoning her blouse as she did so.

"Annie, what are you doing?"

"I have nothing to give you but myself. And, really, I don't even have any experience in that. I only had sex once down in the tunnels, and that was a very long time ago. I enjoyed it, but I don't think I did it very well. It was over very fast."

"That probably wasn't your fault. Annie . . ."

She stopped right in front of him. Her blouse was unbuttoned all the way now. She put McCall's hands gently on her exposed breasts.

"Let me try to thank you," she said softly.

McCall would have been tempted if it had been anyone else but Candy Annie. He slipped his hands off her breasts and gently buttoned up her shirt.

Tears suddenly brimmed in her eyes.

"You don't want me?"

"Friends don't take advantage of each other."

"It would be exciting. And wonderful."

"It would be both of those things. But not with me."

"Because you're old enough to be my father?"

McCall thought of his young Czech "angel" Andel, with whom he'd spent a night in Prague. She had also dismissed their age difference. But this was different. Candy Annie was arousing, in a sweet, almost innocent way, but it wasn't going to happen.

"I'm here to be a friend. That's all I can be to you."

She nodded, as if she understood. "Because you're too damaged right now."

"If you want to put it that way."

She threw her arms around him. "I'm not angry. Or embarrassed. Or hurt. Because you told me all things are possible, right?" She broke the embrace and smiled at him through her tears. "And here I am, in your colleague's apartment, starting my new life. How cool is that?"

"Very cool. The next order of business is to find you a job."

That thought hit Candy Annie like a physical force. She stepped away from him, squeezing her hands together.

"What kind of a job?"

"I'll come up with some ideas." He wrote something down on a sheet of paper. "This is my cell phone number. Call it whenever you need to, day or night. Tomorrow we'll get you a smartphone of your own."

She made a rueful face. "I probably won't be smart enough to use it."

"Sure, you will."

Candy Annie noticed a picture on the mantelpiece. There was only one. Mickey Kostmayer was standing with his arm around the shoulders of a young brunette woman in front of the La Casa Sena restaurant in Santa Fe, New Mexico. The brunette looked relaxed and happy, but Kostmayer's smile was forced. Candy Annie picked up the photograph.

"Is this your colleague?"

"That's him."

"Who is the young woman with him?"

"I don't know."

"Where is he now?"

"I don't know," McCall said.

Kostmayer lay on the concrete floor in utter darkness. He was alone in the cell, which was unusual—normally six or eight North Korean prisoners were incarcerated with him. He had lost twenty pounds and was suffering from hypothermia. At least he wasn't hanging in the shackles on the wall, where he'd been forced to spend at least twelve hours a day. He welcomed the respite. He knew the reason. The North Korean prison guards were regrouping. They'd been embarrassed by the raid led by Kostmayer and

Granny. Kostmayer's band of mercenaries had been overpowered and killed, and Kostmayer and Granny had been captured. They'd been taken, along with the remaining Korean men, women, and children, to this new camp, but it was derelict. It would not be long before they were moved to a newer, stronger camp. But he and Granny had got over one hundred souls out, most of them entire families. They'd been picked up in three large AVIC AC391 Chinese helicopters and flown over the border into China. Kostmayer counted that as a victory.

He winced as he turned over. Every breath he took seared pain through his lungs. He felt alternately hot and cold and wondered if he'd contracted pneumonia. There was no doctor at the prison facility—at least, not for any of the prisoners. Many of them died of starvation and illness and torture. Kostmayer had lost touch with Granny. The North Korean prison guards had separated them right away. He thought they'd taken Granny out and had simply shot him. But he had no real intel.

Kostmayer's mind drifted to Robert McCall. He'd seen his ad before he'd left New York. It had made him smile. If anyone could help ordinary people with nowhere else to turn, it was McCall. *The Equalizer.* Kostmayer liked the name McCall had chosen. But it wouldn't do Kostmayer any good. *His* odds couldn't be equalized.

Not even McCall could get him out of this place.

Kostmayer had one way out. It wouldn't come today. Or tomorrow. But soon, because the North Korean prison guards would have to move the prisoners and shut down the camp before there was an official inspection. Kostmayer had heard them talking about it. That was where he'd heard that Granny was dead. They didn't know he spoke Korean. He had one chance of escape—and he had to be strong enough to take it when the time came.

CHAPTER 6

The RPG burst into the outdoor marketplace with blinding intensity, but for a split second everything he'd been looking at remained etched on his retinas. Tiers of colorful fruits and vegetables in big wooden carts. Multicolored grains in round wooden barrels. Metal and copper pots and pans stacked fifteen feet on either side of a halal meat market. Glittering necklaces were stretched out on wooden tables covered with white sheets. Acres of silks were laid out on the cobblestones. Carpets standing upright on stands eighteen feet high. He'd noted little oddities here and there: a vendor's stall of ancient Singer sewing machines; chickens hanging from metal hooks next to delicate cages of birds—babblers, nightingales, sandpipers, even one peregrine falcon; twisted bicycles with oversize wheels, all flat, lying discarded. The narrow marketplace in Al Tabqah was crowded with Syrian villagers, men in white Didashah one-piece robes, some of them talking on Apple iPhone 6s, women in abayas with tightly pinned hijab scarves covering their hair and neck, mostly in black, but here and there a splash of blue and red. Kids were tearing around the vendor stalls and tables dressed in jeans, T-shirts or dress shirts, hoodies and Windbreakers, Nikes or bare feet. The air was filled with bargaining and cajoling, scolding, and heated dissension over cost and quality and freshness.

All of it lingered for that split second—

And then it was gone in an instant.

The blast from the RPG turned all of it into a searing white frame.

The shock of the blast hit him with physical force. It was followed by assault-rifle fire. Captain Josh Coleman, US Army, heaved over the fruit cart he'd been standing behind. He was in his early twenties, with an almost angelic face, but a seasoned veteran. He heard shouts of *"Daesh!"* from the villagers. Bullets splintered along the cart. One of them grazed Josh's forehead, spitting blood down into his eyes. He carried an M4 SOPMOD Block II rifle. He fired it at the enemy before a hand grabbed his shoulder and hauled him down to the ground.

There were at least twenty insurgents, most of them in black, all of them wearing what looked like close-fitting gray skullcaps on their heads and gray material wrapped around their faces, leaving only their eyes exposed. They had jumped out of two stolen US Army Humvees and a Ural-4320 off-road truck, all flying the black insurgent flag. The Jihadists carried AK-47-M assault rifles. They fired indiscriminately into the panicked villagers, bullets exploding through merchants and women, children gunned down without mercy.

Three Sham 2 armored cars and one Sham 1 armored truck had already driven into the other side of the market square. Rebel Syrian troops poured out of them, firing on the insurgents with their own Hungarian assault rifles. The Jihadists were caught by surprise, firing back. Two of them threw hand grenades. Josh recognized them as RGD-5s, which propelled 350 fragments over a five-meter kill radius. Explosions erupted through the crowd, slaughtering more innocents. The Rebels fired two of their own RPGs. The first one just missed the Ural truck, but the second scored a direct hit on one of the commandeered Humvees. It sailed up into the air, turning almost gracefully before crashing down again, twisted and smoking. An NSV machine gun opened up from the Ural truck, scattering more of the villagers and the Rebel troops.

Colonel Michael G. Ralston still had hold of Josh's right shoulder. Ralston was in his late forties, black hair shot through with gray, a lean man with compassionate eyes. Both of them were dressed in Army multipatterned camouflage. Both had allowed their beards to grow while in Syria. The colonel was also armed. He made a gesture to Josh with his hand: *Slow down your breathing.* Josh nodded. There was no question that Gunner had saved his life. If you're in the Army, and your initials are M.G., you were called Machine Gun. In Ralston's case, it had been shortened to Gunner. The nickname had started at The Citadel and continued through his active service career, into his work in antiterrorism, and had followed him here with a US Army contingent sent to Syria to advise the Rebel army in their fight against the Insurgents.

More gunfire ripped through the burned-cordite air. Gunner motioned toward the doorway to one of the wooden fruit shops. He held up the fingers of his right hand and counted them off—

In four, three, two, one—

They ran, firing their M4 rifles as they scrambled for the safety of the doorway. They made it inside and dove to the ground as more bullets exploded through the space for the window. There was no glass. The American officers crawled to the windowsill and fired again at the Insurgent patrol, which was itself scrambling to get out of multiple lines of fire. The Syrian Rebels surged through the decimated square, stepping over the bodies of the villagers.

Five members of the US observation unit—which numbered twelve Army personnel altogether, including Gunner's XO, who was a chief warrant officer, and nine NCOs—had not been in the market square at the time of the attack. They were assisting a small UN contingent in the neighboring village of Alhora. The rest of the US unit here in Al Tabqah would have fallen back to the Syrian BTR-152 armored personal carrier that had brought them to the village.

Captain Josh Coleman looked out into the marketplace. Most of the vendors' stalls had been lacerated with bullets. Fruits, vegetables, spices, jewelery, pieces of wicker baskets were strewn among the corpses. The acres of silk were bloodstained. Birds from splintered cages were flying above the carnage. The villagers still alive stirred and tried to crawl away or get up and run. Some of them were missing limbs. The children who'd survived were kneeling right where they'd stopped, too scared to move.

Josh aimed his rifle at the retreating Insurgents. Gunner put a strong hand on his arm.

"Let the Rebels force them back. That's what we've trained them for."

A flash of movement near one of the shattered carts caught Josh's attention.

A little girl, probably six or seven, had popped up from a mound of bodies and started to run. She was wearing a red shirt and old Levi's jeans and might as well have had a target on her back.

Bullets kicked up the ground around her.

Josh was out the fruit-shop doorway and running through the market before Gunner could stop him. Josh fired his rifle, taking out one of the Jihadists. A Rebel soldier took out two more. When Josh reached the little girl, she flinched. He hugged her to him and looked down. A woman in her thirties, presumably her mother, was dead. Her father stirred, but he was missing an arm and blood was pumping out of the stump of his shoulder. Josh couldn't get to him. Too risky with the child in his arms. And the father would be dead within seconds.

Josh gripped the little girl tightly. "You run with me, okay?"

He wasn't sure she understood English, but she stared at him with big wide eyes and nodded. Bent low, shielding her with his body, Josh ran back toward the fruit shop. Gunner was in the doorway, firing his assault rifle. Behind Josh more units of Syrian Rebels were pouring into the square. Josh made it to the doorway. Gunner pushed him and the little girl inside, fired one more burst, then followed them. Josh sat the little girl down on a bunch of empty fruit sacks, piled up four feet, and took her hands.

"You stay here with us. Don't go outside. Okay?"

She nodded. Josh ran back to the window opening with Gunner.

"We should have had intel on that Jihadist patrol. The area was supposed to be clear."

"Shit happens," Gunner said with no inflection in his voice, but Josh knew him well enough to hear the suppressed anger in it. "We'd better get your head seen to. I've got an emergency trauma dressing and surgical tape in my kit."

Something on the edge of the market square caught Josh's eye.

One of the Jihadists was being hauled up into the second comman-deered US Humvee. Something about him was *familiar*. Josh stared through the drifting smoke. The Insurgent's head had been grazed by a bullet and he'd torn off his gray balaclava and face-covering cloth.

He turned in profile.

The breath seemed to go out of Josh's body, like someone had stepped hard on his chest. The Humvee turned in a choking cloud of dust and drove away with the Ural truck. They left behind the hulk of the first burning Humvee and fifteen of the Jihadists lying dead on the western edge of the marketplace.

Josh's reaction hadn't been lost on Gunner. "You recognized one of them?"

Josh nodded. "Can't be sure. One of the guys on our terrorist list. Means he didn't die in that air strike last Sunday. I'll show you the photo-graph when we get back to base."

All firing had ceased. Silence settled for a moment over the decimated marketplace like a damp shroud. Then shouting and wailing could be heard as more Al Tabqah villagers were on their feet, running to relatives and friends, digging out those still alive. The Syrian Rebel troops were helping. None of the Sham vehicles had gone chasing after the Insurgents. They knew better than to do that. They'd be outnumbered by the time they had over-taken them.

A woman came through the doorway of the fruit shop. Her black abaya was covered in blood, but obviously it was not hers. The little girl flew into her arms. Josh had looked at the wrong woman lying dead on the cobble-stones. *This* was the little girl's mother.

"Take the moment," Gunner said quietly. "There aren't enough of them."

Josh looked at the mother and daughter, holding on to each other fiercely in the bright doorway, the deadly slaughter laid out beyond them.

He realized, somewhat ironically, that he might be a little late calling *his* mother.

CHAPTER 7

McCall picked up a cruising cab on Second Avenue and dialed Kostmayer's cell phone. It rang three times, then Kostmayer's voice came on: "Hey. This is Mickey. Either I'm not here or I don't want to talk to you. Leave a message." Typical Kostmayer. There was a beep, but McCall didn't leave a message. He hadn't expected a call back, but he'd hoped for a text, a coded email, a whisper within the intelligence community about the North Korean mission. There'd been nothing.

He didn't like it.

The cab pulled up in front of the Liberty Belle Hotel on Sixty-Sixth Street. It had once been a grand old lady with marble skirts that flared out for half the block. Now the paint had faded, the gilt was tarnished, and more stone had been chipped away as if some super-rodents were nibbling at it. Sam Kinney had added the slim neon saying LIBERTY BELLE HOTEL complete with the crack down its side. McCall thought it cheapened the place. All the hotel needed now was Tom Bodett waiting in one of the rooms to leave the light on for you.

McCall got out of the cab and paid the driver as his cell phone rang. Not his usual iPhone, but the second one he carried with the Equalizer number.

"Yes?"

"Is this the Equalizer?" The woman's voice was strong and didn't have the melodious delirium of some of the women who had dialed his number. He could pretty well tell the crank calls in the first few syllables.

"Yes. Tell me your problem."

Her words came out in a rush. "My name is Linda Hathaway. I live in an apartment building in the East Village. My daughter is three years old and she's suffering and no one will help me. I don't want to go into details on the phone. Would you come over here?"

In what McCall thought of ironically as his *spy* days, this would have been an obvious trap. But he was out of that life now.

At least, that's what he told himself.

"Where's your apartment located?"

She gave him the address, a building on Tenth Street just below Tompkins Square Park. McCall assured her he would get there as soon as he could and pushed through the doors of the hotel. When he'd first walked into the tarnished elegance of the Liberty Belle Hotel, it had been deserted. Kost-mayer had called it a mausoleum. And it *did* have the feel of an old movie set in which Clark Gable or Spencer Tracy would have stepped out of the old cage elevator—replaced now with a modern one—to find Jean Harlow or Katharine Hepburn waiting for them on one of the ornate couches. Mc-Call glanced at the New York watercolors on the walls and thought they'd faded a little more into misty obscurity. But the woodwork still gleamed, along with the brass fixtures, and McCall decided that Sam Kinney must have the Turkish carpet cleaned daily.

Today the lobby was hopping. Two girls were behind the reception counter dealing with guests. He knew one of them, a petite brunette named Chloe, midtwenties, efficient, always smiling, except when she'd been running alongside the EMTs' gurney when Sam Kinney had been oozing blood from a bullet wound in his shoulder and his right eye had been hang-ing out of its socket. The other girl was a tall, languid blonde named Lisa, or so it said on her rectangular silver name badge. Both of them wore the uni-form of the Liberty Belle Hotel: gray slacks, pale blue shirts, and blue blaz-ers. A crowd of people were waiting to check in, looking tired; probably from Europe, a long flight after one or two connections. A South American couple in their fifties were seated, poring over a map of Manhattan. A younger couple with British accents were jubilantly showing some New York friends tickets they'd scored for *Phantom of the Opera*. A bellman in his for-ties, Vinnie, as Irish as a Killarney sunset, was pushing a brass luggage cart from the elevator toward the front doors. He acknowledged McCall with a wave.

McCall liked it when the lobby had energy and life.

He hadn't seen her yet.

But Sam Kinney had seen him. The old spy—probably in his seventies, McCall had decided, but he could have been anywhere between sixty and death—came around the reception counter. He shuffled a little, but McCall was never sure how much of that was real and how much of it was an act he liked to put on. He also wore the Liberty Belle Hotel uniform. He no longer wore a patch over his right eye, but it had an odd sheen to it where it had been damaged. He had about 30 percent vision in it now. A reward for try-ing to stop a Chechen assassination group from killing McCall.

Sam gripped McCall's arm and demanded, "Where have you been?"

"I meant to leave you a note with all of my appointments for the day, Sam, but you're so busy I didn't want to distract you from your guests."

"Sure, crack wise, I like looking out for you."

"No one looks out for me, Sam. What's on your mind?"

"You got a visitor. She's standing over there by the big palm. Gotta water that. It's starting to look as limp as my dick."

"I'll treasure that imagery all day."

McCall found the woman Sam Kinney was indicating. She was seated in an overstuffed armchair, dressed in a gray business suit, a lilac shirt, expensive shoes but with low heels, carrying a thin leather briefcase with her initials CB on it. She'd changed it from CM. She looked to be in her late thirties, even though McCall knew she was ten years older than that. Her blond hair was cut short. Her green eyes could be laughing or like chips of glittering ice. Right now, it was the latter. She looked sleek and sophisticated and gorgeous.

But then, McCall's ex-wife had always looked good to him.

Cassie Blake took out her iPhone, looking at the time, impatient. She hadn't seen McCall yet.

"Better go talk to her before she calls the cops," Sam advised, "and has you dragged out of here. That might look bad to my hotel guests."

"What did she say to you?"

"Just that she had to see you. I know she's some kind of a hotshot lawyer."

"She's an assistant district attorney for New York."

"Maybe it's for leaving a trail of dead men across the city. Which I'm grateful for. Or I wouldn't be standing here. You seen Brahms lately?"

"No."

"They moved Hilda from the Cancer Care Center at Boston Medical back to Sloan Kettering here in the city. Brahms says she's doing much better, but I didn't like the tone of his voice. You get to be an old spook, you know when someone is lying to you." Sam nodded at Cassie, who was now talking on her iPhone. "Weren't you married to her once?"

McCall knew that Sam had known this all along, but just nodded.

"How'd you let a babe like that slip through your fingers?"

McCall didn't answer and moved through the crowded lobby. She spotted him halfway across. She wrapped up her phone call and dropped the iPhone into the jacket pocket of her suit.

"You need to come with me, Robert." Cassie was clearly controlling her anger.

"Is Scott all right?"

"Scott's fine. This isn't about our son. Or us. There *is* no us anymore, but there used to be, and that's the only reason I'm not dragging you down to the Seventh Precinct." Then the terseness seeped out of her a little. "That and the fact you saved Scott's life." She looked around at the bustling lobby. "You really live here now?"

"I had to give up my apartment."

"Can you come with me?"

"Sure."

McCall followed his ex-wife out of the hotel. She stepped off the curb, put her fingers to her lips, and whistled. It would have shamed the doorman at the Plaza. A cab pulled over. McCall climbed into the back. Cassie said something to the cabbie and slid in beside him. She slammed the door and the cab took off.

"So how's your new job going?" Her voice had a sardonic edge.

"What job would that be?"

"Come on, Robert, I read *The New York Times* from cover to cover every morning, including the classified ads, and I've been known to surf the internet on occasion. 'Got a problem? Odds against you? Call the Equalizer.' When did you get all cute and schmaltzy on me?"

"Nothing romantic or precious about it. It's a service. If you're in trouble, you call me. I'll see if I can help. How did you know it was me?"

"*The Equalizer.* That's the legend on that Peacemaker Cavalry Colt revolver you always wanted."

"The legend on it says *Colt Frontier Six-Shooter.*"

"On the other side of the barrel. Something about 'Don't be afraid of any man, no matter what his size, when danger threatens, I will equalize'— or something like that. How much do you charge for this service of yours?"

"Nothing."

"You've become independently wealthy in the last ten years?"

"I don't need to charge clients."

She shook her head. "*Clients?* You've got to be kidding me. Are you really buying into the hype you've created?"

He ignored that. "Where are we going?"

"Bellevue."

CHAPTER 8

Seven people were clustered outside the intensive care unit. Two of them were uniformed NYPD officers. Two were Hispanic women, one in her late thirties, McCall judged, the other in her early forties, who held the hand of a five-year-old boy. Near them was a young blonde in her twenties with a canvas bag slung over her shoulder that had NYPD—CSI UNIT stenciled on it. She was waiting patiently. A man in his late thirties was talking quietly to the younger of the Hispanic women. He wore a dark suit with a thin red-striped tie, black shoes; all he needed was a trench coat. McCall knew at once he was a police detective. He had that capable, been-there-before atti-tude, but without the world-weary cynicism. He was tall, with close-cropped salt-and-pepper hair, high cheekbones, deep-set gray eyes. He had a low, husky voice that McCall doubted got raised often.

The younger Hispanic women glanced up as McCall and Cassie en-tered. Her voice cut through the murmured calm of the ward. "Is that *him*?"

In the next instant she was flying at McCall, her long red nails aiming for his eyes. One of the uniformed officers grabbed her, holding her back.

The detective stepped forward and caught her arm. "Mrs. Reyes, let me handle this."

"He tried to murder my boy!" she screamed. "He broke his nose and his cheekbone! God knows how many teeth he knocked out. Julio's face is all caved in!"

"I got this, Sofia," the detective said. Then, more gently: "All right?"

She tried to catch her breath, which was coming out it fitful gasps. She nodded. The uniformed officer let her go. McCall had not flinched.

"You need to go to the waiting area," the detective told her. "A nurse will come and find you as soon as there's news on your son."

The uniformed officer guided Sofia Reyes down the ward.

"I'll go with her." Cassie followed the mother and the cop down the ward. The older Hispanic woman, whose name was Anita Delgado, let go of her son's hand and stepped forward. Her reaction was the polar opposite from Sofia Reyes's: calm, low-key, and more intensely filled with pain.

"You sprayed my son Alejandro in the eyes with Mace," she said to Mc-Call. "He's blinded. He has a concussion and his right arm is broken in two places. What kind of an animal are you? You say you do this in the name of justice, Mr. *Equalizer*?"

She had taken three steps right up to McCall.

And spit in his face.

The second uniform jumped forward, but she waved a hand at him.

"I am going to be with Sofia."

McCall wiped the spittle from his cheek with a handkerchief. The Hispanic woman held out her hand and the five-year-old boy rushed over. The second uniform escorted them out of the ward.

The detective pulled back his jacket, showing his blue CITY OF NEW YORK POLICE—DETECTIVE badge pinned to his belt, with the numeral 7 in gold beneath the shield.

"Detective First Grade Steve Lansing, Seventh Precinct. And you're Robert McCall. The Equalizer." McCall didn't respond. "You've been operating out there on the streets of our precinct for a few weeks. We didn't know who you were, but we'd seen the card before. These aren't the only gangbangers you've roughed up. But you almost killed these guys."

"It wasn't me."

Detective Lansing turned to the CSI. "Show him the card, Catelyn."

Catelyn pulled on skintight surgeon's gloves, took out a small polyethylene bag from her canvas bag, removed a business card, and extended it. "Don't touch it!"

McCall looked at the gray card. He saw the graphic of the shadowy figure in the alleyway, dark and ominous, no recognizable features, standing in front of a Jaguar, a gun in hand, the New York City skyline behind him. The words JUSTICE IS HERE were above the graphic of the figure, and beneath it, THE EQUALIZER.

"My colleague wants to take a sample of your DNA, Mr. McCall," Detective Lansing said. "See if it matches the DNA on this card."

"It won't."

"Then you have no objection to her doing a DNA swab? Right here and now?"

"No."

The CSI tech unhooked the canvas bag from her shoulder, returned the gray card to its protective polyethylene bag, and took out a simple Q-tip. McCall opened his mouth and she swabbed his gums, then slid the Q-tip into a protective plastic sheath.

"Thank you, Catelyn," Detective Lansing said.

The blonde nodded as she pulled off the gloves, repacked her bag, hoisted it over her shoulder, and walked away.

"There's a waiting room on the next floor where we can talk," Lansing said.

"I'd rather walk."

They moved down the ward and pushed through some double doors, which led out to a bank of elevators.

"I deal with ADA Cassie Blake a lot. She was the one who came to me saying she believed this Equalizer was her ex-husband. When Julio and Alejandro were brought into the ER last night the attending physician found your card in Julio Reyes's shirt pocket and called the Seventh Precinct."

"I don't give out cards."

"But you *do* advertise as a vigilante known as the Equalizer?"

"I help people when no one else will. That's doesn't mean I'm a vigilante."

"So you do everything by the book? You come across an illegal situation, you let the authorities handle it?"

"Not exactly," McCall murmured.

"I don't care how you justify your actions, as far as the NYPD and ADA Blake are concerned, you're a civilian taking the law into his own hands. That's *against* the law. Are we clear?"

"Am I under arrest, Detective Lansing?"

McCall and Lansing descended the concrete staircase, their voices echoing.

"No. But don't leave New York until we're certain that both of these young men are going to make it out of ICU. We know you didn't spray Mace into Alejandro's eyes. That was the victim they were intending to rape, Megan Forrester. She gave her statement at the precinct last night and came here and ID'd both of her attackers."

They reached the first floor and pushed through a door into an antiseptic corridor. A male nurse in scrubs pushed a gurney past them in which a frail old man lay with an IV dripping life into his desiccated body.

"Who are these young men?" McCall asked.

"They belong to a street gang on the Lower East Side called the White Jaguars. Both of them are lower than pond scum. They would have raped and maybe killed Megan Forrester, except *someone* intervened. That Good Samaritan probably saved her life, but these two thugs were almost beaten to death. That isn't going to happen again on my turf."

They reached the main lobby.

"These hoodlums may be lowlifes, but they have rights," Detective

Lansing said. "You can't violate them." McCall waited. There'd be more. Lansing glanced away, sighed a little. "Look, sometimes I wish there *was* a guardian angel out there on the streets, helping us out. But I can't condone it. Do you understand?"

"Yes."

"If your DNA test comes back negative, we'll go on looking for this guy."

"He'll stay in the shadows. You won't find him."

"But you will?"

"I have ways of working that the police can't use. I don't worry about rules."

"You just break them."

"I don't break *my* rules."

Lansing took a card out of his jacket pocket and handed it to McCall. "You catch up with this Equalizer wannabe, call me at the precinct, or at my personal cell number on the back."

"If I find him, I'll let you know."

"Will he still be breathing?"

"Possibly."

McCall walked out of the hospital.

Cassie Blake was waiting for him at the curb.

"I don't think you beat those two Latino boys half to death," she said quietly. "It's not your style. I called for an Uber car. I can drop you off at the Liberty Belle Hotel."

"I'm going somewhere else."

"Equalizer business?" McCall didn't respond to the sarcasm. "Your new persona is going to get you arrested or killed."

A town car pulled up. Cassie got into the back without another word, and the cab took off into heavy traffic. McCall thought about the two youths attacking Megan Forrester. He would have stopped them from raping or killing her, but it would have been on *his* terms. He was going to find out who this vigilante was and stop him.

Before more people got hurt in his name.

Helen Coleman stared at the gun.

At least it wasn't pointed at *her*.

An attractive brunette in her early sixties, she appeared to have stopped aging at forty. Some laugh lines were around her hazel eyes, but they seemed to blend right in. Her hair was long and cascaded onto her shoulders. She never put it up. She thought it gave her a unkempt, carefree look, which worked well when dealing with diplomats from 193 member nations and government bureaucratic cretins. She was dressed in a Christian Dior fuchsia-pink textured wool blazer jacket and skirt. She had a spectacular figure, which she kept under wraps for the most part, in deference to her position. She worked for the under-secretary-general for humanitarian affairs and United Nations emergency relief coordinator. She cared passionately about the job. Which was good, because it was all-consuming. She had divorced her first husband almost thirty years before, and her second one ten years before. She had two sons and a daughter. She had a handful of good friends she didn't see much. She was just too busy.

She never ate at the UN cafeteria in the Secretariat Building, even though the views across the East River were spectacular. She liked sitting on a bench outside the visitors' center with a boxed lunch she always made for herself before she left her beautiful colonial house on the banks of the Navesink River in Red Bank, New Jersey. It took just over an hour for her early-morning commuter train to pull into Penn Station in Manhattan, and she could be at her desk in the Secretariat Building by eight thirty. Today her sandwich was a tuna melt on rye, with a small green salad and an almonds and chocolate Balance energy bar. As usual, plenty of tourists were surging from the security entrance out onto the grounds. Helen liked being among them. They were the people she was trying to protect in the world.

The gun stood on a raised pedestal: a giant Colt Python .357 Magnum revolver with the barrel tied into a knot and pointing up harmlessly at the sky. It had been created by the late Swedish sculptor Carl Fredrik Reuterswärd, inspired by the shooting death of his friend John Lennon. Luxembourg had offered it to the UN in 1988. Helen watched a tall Chinese teenager reach up and put his hand around the trigger of the sculpted weapon as if he could fire it. His friends took pictures on their smartphones.

Perhaps its nonviolence message isn't getting through to everyone, she thought wryly.

She unwrapped her tuna melt. Her LG smartphone vibrated on her lap. For some reason she thought of the one Jay Leno joke she remembered from his *Tonight Show* days: "They did a recent survey and twenty-four percent of women said they would answer their cell phones during sex." Pause. "The other seventy-six percent just kept it on vibrate." Then, over the laughter: "Now, folks, folks . . ."

Helen picked up the phone. Josh had promised he would call her at 12:20 EST sharp. It would be seven hours ahead in Syria, 7:20 p.m.

He was a little late.

Josh's face brightened on the LED screen. He had his iPad propped up on a desk in some big, drab room. Army personnel were around him. She noted a big white chalkboard with data she couldn't read and blue criss-crossed arrows. Above it were pinned up grainy surveillance photos of Jihadist terrorists. Josh was holding a small black-and-white photograph in his hands. He looked strained, his uniform disheveled, but he smiled and said, "Hey, Mom."

"What happened?" she asked immediately.

"We were assisting a YPG militia unit at a village called Al Tabqah. We needed to evacuate the villagers, but we got hit by a Jihadist patrol."

"How many causalities?"

"Twenty-six villagers, fourteen fatalities, the rest badly wounded. My forehead got grazed by a bullet, which is no doubt what you're staring at, but you know how hardheaded I am. Barely left a scratch."

"Where are you now?"

"We're headquartered in a team house in Ar Raqqah."

Colonel Michael G. Ralston crowded into the frame on the LG screen. "Hey, Helen." He smiled. "You look beautiful."

"I thought you had my son's back, Gunner."

"He did," Josh said. "If he hadn't hauled me behind an overturned fruit cart in the marketplace, that bullet would have done more than leave a scar."

"It was pretty intense for a few minutes," Gunner admitted. "The enemy patrol was taken by surprise. They had no idea a Syrian Rebel force was at the village."

"And what were *you* doing there? You're supposed to be *observing*."

Gunner's wide smile flashed again, but no part of it was in his eyes. "We *were* observing. Close to."

Josh handed Gunner the photograph.

"Is that our guy?" Gunner asked him.

"I'd say so."

Gunner nodded, looked back at the iPad. "I'll let you chat to your son, Helen. We've got an AAR meeting in five."

He moved away. Murmured voices continued in the background. Helen was glad she couldn't hear what was being discussed. Her entire world revolved around the concept of peace. Seeing the reality of war—especially when it involved her oldest son—jarred her.

"You found a terrorist you've been looking for?" she asked Josh.

"I can't be a hundred percent certain. We'd been told he was killed in one of the Turkish air strikes. But he was alive and well two hours ago."

"You're really all right?"

"Fine. I called to see how *you* are."

"Up to my ass in alligators. There was an exodus of thousands of refugees, mainly women and children, from villages in North Darfur this week. They're being sheltered at our UNAMID base in Um Baru. I'm dealing with the local authorities, but they don't give a fuck about human rights violations."

Josh said chidingly, "Language, Mom."

"Yeah, I know. There's been a complete failure by the Darfur government to take initiatives against endemic impunity."

"That's why you work for the UN. To try and instill a sense of morality into them."

"Yeah, right," Helen said. "So far all I've done this morning is shout and cajole and threaten."

"Sounds like a good start. But you're okay?"

"I went off my meds two days ago and I've been jumpy and skittish and not sleeping well."

"Why did you do that?"

"I was getting terrible headaches. My head is a little better today, until I saw that bullet graze on your forehead."

"No big deal. Have you heard from Tom?"

"Not this week. Your brother has got a test on his Arabic culture and it's giving him fits."

"But he's still in Istanbul?"

"Of course. He's cramming like he was back here at NYU for a math test."

"Do you have a phone number you can reach him on? I want to wish him good luck."

"Sure, I'll text it to you when we hang up."

Gunner stepped back into the frame of the LG screen. "Gotta take him away, Helen," he said apologetically.

"Okay. Call me tomorrow at the same time, Josh. Promise?"

"If I can. Go back on your meds or you're in trouble. Bye, Mom."

The image of her oldest son disappeared from the screen. That he was so far away, *within* Jihadist territory, scared the hell out of her. But there wasn't a damn thing she could do about it.

Helen dropped the phone into her Dior jacket, took another bite of her sandwich, and looked over again at the nonviolence symbol of the huge knotted gun.

If only it *really* meant something.

CHAPTER 9

McCall walked up to a four-story redbrick apartment building on the corner of Tenth and Avenue C. An iron fire escape came down from the fourth floor with balconies of wrought-iron filigree to the second floor, where a final ladder could be lowered down to the street. Ten limestone steps led up to a wooden apartment door. Two big concrete pots of flowering shrubbery rested on either side of the stairs, but the plants had wilted and died about the same time the Pittsburgh Pirates won their last World Series. Sixteen black garbage bags had been lined up outside the building at the curb. They were ripped, and part of the trash had spilled out onto the sidewalk.

McCall climbed the steps. The front door was unlocked. He stepped into a narrow hallway that smelled of cat piss, disinfectant, and stale pizza. There was no elevator. He climbed the stairs to the second floor and knocked on the door of apartment 2B. He could hear a television faintly playing. Footsteps ran to the door, a shadow darkened over the keyhole, then four dead bolts were thrown back and the door opened. The sound of the TV show magnified—a lot of scary, thundering music.

In the doorway stood a faded blonde in her midthirties, not unattractive, but a little gaunt, with bright green eyes and full lips. Her hair was piled up on her head. She wore a black New York City skyline sweatshirt over gray sweatpants and blue sandals.

"You must be the Equalizer." She caught her breath. "No one else looking like you would come knocking on my door. I'm Linda Hathaway. Please come in." McCall stepped into the hallway of the apartment. "I can't call you Mr. Equalizer."

"My name is Robert McCall."

"I just got my daughter back from day care and the babysitter will be here in less than an hour, so I'm a little rushed."

"You work nights?"

"Yeah, and the weekends. Come with me, please."

She indicated a door off the narrow hallway. McCall followed her through it into a large living room, nicely, if inexpensively, furnished. The carpet was strewn with toys and a blue Thomas the Tank Engine & Friends train was derailed around big yellow tracks. A three-year-old blond moppet was sitting on the floor in front a flatscreen TV watching a cartoon. In it a purple dog in a dark cave was cowering away from a huge wolf with prominently featured teeth.

The little girl looked up at McCall. "His name is Courage the Cowardly Dog, but he's not really cowardly, he's very brave."

"I allow her an hour on the Cartoon Network before I have to go to work," Linda said.

"Where's that?"

"A diner in Chelsea. The New York Minute?" Linda shook her head when he didn't respond. "Not the kind of place you'd go to. There's so much grease in the kitchen I'm surprised the place hasn't burned to the ground." She suddenly smiled. "Wow, I'd be *fired* in a New York minute if my boss heard me say that."

"I won't tell him."

"I suddenly feel very foolish having called you. I don't think there's a thing in the world you could do to help me . . . but I'm at my wit's end and . . . I just don't know what to do."

"What's your problem?"

"Gemma, come over here, okay, honey? Just for a minute."

Gemma reluctantly tore herself away from Courage the Cowardly Dog and got up and walked over to them. She was wearing a pretty sunflower dress, her feet bare.

McCall could see the problem immediately.

Red, angry bites were on the little girl's face and up and down her arms. "They're *rat* bites," Linda said. "I took her to the ER this morning. They put some antiseptic cream on the bites, said the inflammation will die down by the weekend, but it takes forever for them to fade away."

"This has happened to her before?"

"Twice." Linda tousled her daughter's hair. "Okay, thanks, honey."

Gemma ran back to her place on the floor and watched her program.

She noticed with a frown that Thomas the Tank Engine had toppled over and set him back up on the yellow tracks.

"Let's talk in the kitchen, if that's okay," Linda said.

McCall followed her into a bright kitchen with old appliances and worn-out cabinets. Linda put together dinners for the babysitter to put into the microwave for her and Gemma.

"I put out rat poison, but you've got to be so careful with a three-year-old around. I've actually killed four big rats in the last six months—and I mean *huge,* like they were out of some horror movie—and threw them into the garbage, but they keep coming back."

"Did you report it to your super?"

"He's a fat, lazy slob who watches more television during the day than Gemma does, probably the same channel, and smells like a brewery. He says he's put out traps, but I've never seen them."

"Who owns the building?"

"I don't know, some CEO of some big corporation. I think he owns a bunch of apartment buildings in Manhattan and Queens. I went to city hall and signed a formal complaint, and they did nothing. No one's going to do a damn thing just because my brat got some rat bites." Linda stopped making her dinners and turned to McCall. Now tears were brimming in her eyes. "But my daughter's suffering. Those bites sting. I have to check under her bed every night and show her there are no rats under there the size of fat raccoons. I've talked to other people in the building, and they're sympathetic, but they all have their own problems in this place." She went back to her macaroni-and-cheese plates and ham sandwiches.

"You're a single mom?"

"How could you tell? Do we have an aura about us?"

"No family picture in the living room. No husband you turned to."

"He left me right after Gemma was born. Good riddance, but it's been tough."

"Would you allow me to take pictures of those bites on Gemma's face and arms?"

"Okay."

Linda hustled back into the living room. McCall took out his iPhone and followed her.

"Gemma, honey, stand up for a minute and stand very still," Linda said. "Mr. McCall is going to take some photos of those awful bites."

Gemma jumped up and stood awkwardly, like she was in a fashion photographer's studio and didn't like it. McCall took several pictures of her face and both of her arms with his iPhone. Linda raised Gemma's sundress up a little so he could take pictures of the bites on her legs. He checked the photos and put the iPhone away.

"I need to leave and you need to finish getting dinner ready."

Linda Hathaway escorted McCall down the hallway and opened the apartment door. She searched his face with her bright green eyes. "I don't know a damn thing about you."

"All you need to know is that I'm going to help you."

"Why should you care? And don't say, 'Someone has to.'"

McCall smiled. "Someone *does* have to. Put out more rat traps. Keep reassuring your daughter by looking under her bed at night. I've got this." He stepped out into the dim corridor.

Linda caught his arm, turning him back. "Do you really?"

"Yes. I'll be in touch with you, Linda."

As she closed the door, there was a cry from her daughter, but McCall didn't think she'd been attacked by another huge rat. He thought Courage the Cowardly Dog was probably fighting for his life.

McCall didn't know what he expected to find in the alleyway. Detective Lansing had allowed him to read Megan Forrester's police report, but the lights from Essex Street barely permeated the concrete tunnel. If this had been a black-and-white 1940s detective movie starring Bogie or Robert Mitchum, McCall might have found a dropped matchbook from a ritzy bar with a name or a phone number written on the inside.

There was no matchbook.

A shadow moved to his right.

McCall whirled to see a young man stumbling out of a back doorway to one of the buildings. He was wearing dark jeans, a gray hoodie over a green Polo shirt, and black Adidas Cosmic Boost running shoes so old they looked to be unraveling. McCall grabbed the man's arm before he could bolt. The hoodie fell back to show straggly dark hair shot through with a little gray, a narrow face, and a pathetic scrawl of beard. He had small hoop earrings in both ears and a ring pierced over his top lip. He stank of sweat, sweetened with a little Old Kentucky bourbon. But it was his eyes and eyebrows that chilled your blood. The eyes were so pale blue as to almost disappear into their sockets. The eyebrows were like a fine white powder you could just blow away. McCall figured the melanin pigments for brown, black, and yellow colorations were missing. But not all of the albino characteristics were there. His eyes were red rimmed, as if he'd been crying, but that may have been a permanent condition. When he spoke, his voice was hoarse.

"I didn't see anything! I was asleep! I woke up when she ran away. They deserved what you did to them!"

"I thought you said you didn't see it." When he didn't respond, McCall shook him like a rag doll. "What *did* you see?"

"Two gang guys. They were lying on the ground."

McCall dragged him to the doorway. He noted it went back six feet to an old door that didn't look as if it had been opened in this century. A can of Sprite and a big cardboard box and some newspapers were crammed into the space. Also an L.L. Bean backpack with a Gideon Bible poking out of the top.

"This is where you sleep?" McCall asked in a gentler tone.

The young man nodded emphatically. "My spot! Isaac's spot! Everyone knows. They leave me alone. I don't hurt anyone. I don't bother anyone. 'The sacrifices of God are a broken spirit; a broken and contrite heart, O God, you will not despise.'"

"You think I'm the man who beat up those two gang guys?"

Tears formed in Isaac's eyes, but they seemed like alien beings there, unable to fall down his pale face. "Sure, I know it was you!"

"What makes you think so? You saw my face?" Isaac shook his head emphatically. "Then why do you think it was *me*?"

"You look the same. Same height, same build. Same hair. Same coat."

"*Same coat?*"

Isaac nodded again. McCall let him go. He didn't bolt. Just shuffled from one foot to the other, his breathing ragged, sniffing like he had a bad cold or had snorted something.

"You mean this coat is the same style and color?"

"*Same* coat, man. You're trying to trick me. Then you'll break my arm and punch me in the face. 'Who so sheddeth man's blood, by man shall his blood be shed.'"

"Genesis nine:six."

A big smile creased Isaac's face. "You know your Bible, sir!"

"I didn't beat up those gang members. The attacker won't come after you if you didn't see his face. Were you in that doorway in the shadows the whole time?"

"Yes! Isaac's spot!" He suddenly looked a little guilty. He reached into the pocket of his hoodie and came out with some turquoise buttons. "These came flying off her shirt when one of the guys ripped it open. Exposed her breasts. They were very big. She was embarrassed. I thought the buttons might be worth something. Took them over to Gems on Houston Street. You know, the pawn place? Weren't worth shit." Isaac spilled the mother-of-pearl buttons into McCall's palm. "Maybe you can take them back to her?"

"Sure." McCall dropped the turquoise buttons into his coat pocket. "What more you can tell me about him, Isaac? Was he white, black, Latino? The way he walked, the way he moved? Anything?"

Isaac shook his head vehemently. "I didn't leave my spot. Isaac's spot."

"How old are you?"

"Maybe twenty-six. Can I go now?"

"Go where?"

He shrugged. "Somewhere for a handout. A kind word." He suddenly grinned. "A shot of bourbon."

"You don't need to sleep in a doorway, Isaac. I live at a hotel where there are a lot of empty rooms. I'll see you get some food and a bed and maybe that shot of whiskey."

Isaac shook his head, stumbling away from McCall. "I'm not worth you trying to save me." He picked up his backpack and stuffed the Bible down into it. "'And fear not them which kill the body, but are not able to kill the soul: but rather fear him which is able to destroy both body and soul, in hell.'" He turned. "You know it?"

"Matthew ten:twenty-eight."

Isaac gave McCall a thumbs-up. He shrugged on the backpack and moved quickly down the alleyway until he was swallowed up in its darkness.

McCall said softly, "'He will wipe away every tear from their eyes, and death shall be no more, neither shall there be mourning, no crying, nor pain anymore.' Revelation twenty-one:four."

He thought about Serena Johanssen and Elena Petrov. Two women he'd loved. Both lost to him. He looked at the place where Isaac had disappeared. The homeless man had been too frightened to move from his spot—Isaac's spot—during the attack on Megan Forrester. But something in his watery eyes told McCall there was more Isaac could have said.

McCall walked over to the brick wall Megan had been thrown up against by Julio and Alejandro. He'd noticed something sparkling on the ground beneath it. He kicked away a Mars-bar wrapper, knelt down, and picked up a diamond earring. It glittered in the light. It wasn't something you picked up at Gems pawnshop. It might have flown from Megan's ear when one of the gangbangers had hit her. McCall dropped the earring into his coat pocket to join the turquoise buttons. Maybe a clue, maybe not.

He was no closer to finding this Equalizer wannabe.

McCall found Brahms the next morning seated on a bench in St. Catherine's Park a block down from the Memorial Sloan Kettering Cancer Center. His real name was Chaim Mendleman, but he'd been called Brahms because of his love—make that *addiction*—to the Maestro's music since the age of six. He always reminded McCall of Jerry Stiller, the actor who played George Costanza's dad on *Seinfeld*. Some mothers holding on to their baby carriages were conferring together on life's secrets. A group of preteens were shooting hoops. People cut through the park to get to First Avenue.

Brahms didn't look at McCall, but at his surroundings. "You know the layout of this park mimics the Santa Maria Minerva church in Rome where the remains of St. Catherine are buried? That flagpole represents the altar, the play areas are the pews, and even those elephant sprinklers are an adaptation of the sculpture in front of the Roman church."

"I didn't know that."

McCall thought Brahms had aged twenty years in the last two months. His eyes had dark pouches under them, the lines cutting even deeper into his already craggy face. His gray hair stuck out in all directions. McCall doubted Brahms had ever seen a comb he liked. His voice was still vibrant and rich, but it felt like he was holding back a tide of emotions.

"How's Hilda doing?"

"She has good days and bad days. Yesterday was a good day. Her eyes were bright and she had this mischievous smile on her face. She reminded me of that Princess cruise we took when the ship lost power in the Mediterranean for two days and all of us passengers bonded like we were on the *Titanic*, except we didn't sink, and I was like the tour director signing people up for shuffleboard tournaments and swimming competitions and giving away prizes to couples who could prove they'd had sex in a very inappropriate place somewhere on the ship." Brahms smiled at the memory. "Hilda and I won."

"How is she today?"

"Not a good day so far. I was hoping she could come home at the end of the week, but her doctors say she's going to need to stay at Sloan Kettering for another month. I'd be worried about the expense, except someone paid for all of her medical treatments. The check was signed *W. Mays*. You still think Willie Mays is the greatest baseball player of all time? I'd give that accolade to Ty Cobb. Sure, he was a mean SOB, but he only batted under .300 once in his career, and that was his first season, and he stole home base when he was forty-two! Hilda doesn't know who signed the check, or she'd make me drag you into her hospital room for a big hug."

"Did Mary tell you?"

"No. Did you think I wouldn't recognize your handwriting?"

"How is Mary?"

"I've promoted her to senior vice president of internal affairs at Manhattan Electronics."

"Which means?"

"She's looking after the store when I'm here."

The store was an electronics shop on Lexington and Fifty-Second that could kindly be called Dickensian. McCall thought of Brahms's twentysomething assistant, gorgeous and petite and sophisticated with a knockout figure in her distinctive dark Diane von Furstenberg tortoiseshell glasses. McCall and Brahms had discussed whether Mary would keep on her Diane von Furstenberg tortoiseshell glasses when making love. Brahms had given up the debate as too disturbing. McCall knew that Mary wore *only* her Diane von Furstenberg glasses when having sex, but he only knew that because she had told him so.

Brahms handed McCall something bulky, but not heavy, in a brown envelope.

"Here's what you asked for. Do I want to know what you're going to do with it?"

"Probably not."

McCall put the envelope into his coat pocket.

"You heard anything about Mickey Kostmayer?" Brahms asked.

"I thought you didn't like him."

"He's brash and reckless, but I was like that once. I know he went on some clandestine rescue mission. Either for The Company or freelance. There's nothing on the spook network or Sam Kinney would have heard."

"I can't reach Kostmayer."

"Did Granny go with him?"

"Yes."

"Not the same as being with you, but close. Call Control. He'll know what's happened to them."

McCall stood up. "I may just do that. Give Hilda my love."

Brahms nodded and stared back into the park. But now he was far away. Maybe walking with his wife down a Manhattan street on the East Side, holding hands, content and happy with no words necessary.

CHAPTER 10

McCall liked Langan's Irish Pub and Restaurant. He'd been to the Langan's Brasserie in London many times. It had been opened in 1976 by Irish restaurateur Peter Langan, Chef Richard Shepherd, CBE, and Sir Michael Caine. McCall had made a phone call to Sir Michael, whom he'd once done a favor for, who was still a friend—Michael Caine made friends for life—and a day later Candy Annie was working as a waitress in the Langan's on West Forty-Seventh just off Seventh Avenue and above Times Square. The interior was cosy: warm wood, a long bar, small tables. The alcove McCall sat in was surrounded by framed photos of celebrities, sports figures, and politicians. McCall noted a large picture of Michael Caine on one wall. Waitresses in black silk shirts with loosely knotted patterned ties, stylish black jeans, and white aprons were moving back and forth with accomplished ease. It didn't take McCall long to spot Candy Annie. She had just dropped a plate of leaf spinach with a clatter and was on her hands and knees cleaning it up. Two other waitresses and a bartender were helping her, trying to soothe her nerves. They had this. Candy Annie grabbed two plates of food and carried them to a table where a young couple waited. She apologized for the delay and told them the spinach would be coming right up. She turned, saw McCall, and hurried over to him. She was both frustrated and exhilarated.

"How do these servers carry *three* plates? I tried to juggle the spinach in the crook of my arm. Total disaster. But the people are so nice! I'm *loving* it here." McCall glanced down at her chest. "I've got my bra on! I swear! You can just see it through this black shirt."

"I want you to take it off."

That gave her pause. She lowered her voice and her eyes sparkled. "You want to take me up on my prior offer?"

"That would make my day, but, no. I want someone distracted. And I need you to do something you used to be very good at."

She stared at him a moment, then she got it. "You mean like at Danil Gershon's funeral?"

"Like that. I already cleared the time off with your boss. I'm an old friend of *his* boss."

"When do we need to go?"

"Right now."

The Garden Restaurant in the lobby of the Four Seasons Hotel on Fifty-Seventh Street had been turned into a buffet area for the stockbrokers' meeting. The elegant space with its tall trees was packed with men and women in casual chic, all of them wearing plastic name badges on their lapels. Long buffet tables had been set out, replacing the usual tables for hotel guests and their friends, with every kind of hors d'oeuvres imaginable. Glasses of champagne and white wine were being handed out by waiters and waitresses passing among the crowd. McCall figured at some point the conference would transfer to the FIFTY7 ballroom, where there'd be slide shows featuring trading securities and hedge-fund data, and by then it would be impossible to get to Blake Cunningham. But at the Garden Restaurant the financial conference was just warming up.

McCall had surreptitiously swiped a badge from the table where you signed in and had slipped it to Candy Annie, who was wearing her Langan's outfit, minus the tie and apron. And her bra. McCall had given her a package, which she'd slipped into the one item he'd bought for her new stockbroker role—a Michael Kors satchel bag in burgundy. He'd told her to be careful. She'd looked at him like *Hey, pal, I used to do this for a living when I was sixteen in the Upworld*—which didn't make him feel any less uneasy. She'd winked at McCall and had then climbed up the left-hand staircase into the slightly raised restaurant level.

A lot of hugging and shaking hands and raucous conversation were going on. McCall had no trouble finding Blake Cunningham in the midst of it all. He was wearing a Calvin Klein khaki linen suit, white shirt, and a George Neale paisley tie. Blake probably had a hundred different expensive outfits that he rotated, but McCall was *certain* Blake always had one accessory with him.

His Fendi 411 aviator sunglasses.

They hung on the front of Blake's shirt. He was standing with some

Morgan Stanley colleagues near one of the buffet tables. McCall watched Candy Annie threading her way through the tightly packed crowd as if she were in a hurry. She turned to edge her way past one of the waiters with a tray of champagne, and McCall got a good front view. Candy Annie's black silk shirt from Langan's was sheer, but to add to the desired effect she had unbuttoned three buttons. Her cleavage had already turned a few heads— both men's and women's.

Blake Cunningham turned toward her,

Candy Annie looked behind her, tripped over the shoes of one of Blake's companions, and hit Blake with unexpected force. She clutched at Blake's shirt for balance, inadvertently pulling off his Fendi 411 aviator sunglasses as both of them hit the floor. Candy Annie was cursing and sputtering apologies. Blake was laughing. And looking right down her open shirt at her breasts. She grabbed his fallen sunglasses as he helped her back up to her feet. She handed him his sunglasses and apologized some more.

But the Fendi 411 aviator sunglasses *weren't* the ones that had dropped to the floor. They were the ones that Brahms had made up for McCall with a tiny tracking device concealed in one of the frames. It was as good a bait and switch as the one McCall had seen her perform at the Green-Wood Cemetery in Brooklyn at Danil Gershon's funeral, when she'd switched Boris Kirov's lighter for one with a tracking device.

Candy Annie started to move away, but Blake caught her arm. McCall couldn't hear what he was saying in the overall ambience, but it was something like *Let me get you a glass of champagne.* He looked at her lapel badge. *I see you're with Charles Schwab.* But Candy Annie kept up the charade of having to find someone and moved past Blake. He grinned at his colleagues. McCall lip-read his next remark: *Did you see the rack on that babe?*

Then McCall suddenly moved over to the right-hand stairs leading up to the Garden Restaurant. A figure was standing amid the crowd watching the corporate movers and shakers. She was dressed in designer jeans, a blue blouse, and a short brown leather Dior jacket. She had a black leather Giorgio Armani mini-shoulder-bag over her shoulder. Her hair was no longer auburn, but a light brown. But there was no mistaking her face.

McCall took hold of her arm.

The woman who'd posed as Laura Masden froze.

"We need to talk," McCall said softly.

He waited until he saw Candy Annie walk out the front entrance of the Four Seasons, buttoning up her black waitress shirt, mission accomplished.

Then McCall shoved the young woman out of a side entrance. They walked up Fifty-Seventh Street in silence, past Fendi and Dior and Chanel, then turned onto Fifth Avenue. McCall wasn't holding her arm any longer, but he didn't think she'd bolt.

She seemed almost relieved to see him again. "My name is Tara Langley. I'm a private detective in Minneapolis. Laura Masden lives in New Brighton, a nice slice of the American dream about six miles outside the city. She came to me distraught with worry about her daughter Emily, who'd dropped out of her Media Arts classes at the Art Institute in New York. Emily hadn't answered her cell phone in ten days."

"Why didn't her mother come here herself?"

"Bipolar. It took her two days just to get up the courage to find me in the big city. Her husband is an archaeologist, away on some Inca dig site in Peru, and Laura hasn't even contacted him yet to let him know their daughter is missing. So I came to the Big Apple and liaised with a slick PI firm here. I'm used to working alone with a thermos of Starbucks Cinnamon Dolce Frappuccino and my Glock 27 Gen4. They worked hard, but they're expensive, and once Laura Masden sent a picture of the postcard Emily supposedly sent from San Francisco, they thought she was a runaway. End of story. End of case."

"But you didn't believe that?"

"Something bothered me, so I tracked down the one lead I had, Emily's stockbroker boyfriend, Blake Cunningham. I followed him around for three days. He didn't lead me to Emily. He did screw three different blondes on three different nights. Nothing illegal in that, except that they were *barely* legal, and I wanted to go back to my hotel and take a shower just *thinking* about it."

"So then you confronted Blake at his Morgan Stanley offices?"

"Yeah. Very meek and mild, Emily's desperate mom. He got pissed off and threw me out."

"Why did you call me?"

"I'd noticed your ad a couple of nights before on the internet. The Equalizer. How cool is that? Was there *really* a guy out there who could help people in trouble? Be still my heart. I needed backup if I was going to find out where that address was that Blake muttered into his iPhone."

"Why didn't you tell me the truth at the River Café?"

"I needed to know if you were for real and not some kind of weird Manhattan escort service. I didn't know if I could trust you."

"What makes you think you can now?"

"Gut feeling."

"You gave an Academy Award–winning performance as the tearful Laura Masden."

"Yeah, Meryl, eat your heart out. You walked into that mêlée at the rave party and I never saw you again. Or Emily. Tell me what happened."

McCall told her, from the moment he pulled Emily away from Blake Cunningham, to her insisting that Tara was not her mother, to their quiet talk in the abandoned Mercury Theater, to her disappearance.

"Two dead guys lying outside a onetime porno theater," Tara said, "and two guys badly beaten up inside. That's a headline the *New York Post* would pounce on. Blake Cunningham must have some real clout to get that cleaned up."

"Where have you been?"

"I went home. Cats to feed, bills to pay, a mom I needed to visit in her assisted-living facility. But I kept seeing Emily's face on that dance floor. Pale and frightened and so lost. I may not have really been her mother, but it clutched at my heart."

They'd reached the Grand Army Plaza Circle and crossed over to Central Park South.

"Are the hot dogs as good in New York as they say they are?"

McCall bought her one. She had everything on it and ate it as if she hadn't eaten for a week. "That was a sweet bait and switch you had done on Blake," she said between mouthfuls of hot dog. "Who's the babe?"

"A friend who did me a favor. She has nothing to do with Emily Masden or Blake Cunningham."

"Great-looking chick. I wanted to do her myself."

McCall glanced sideways at Tara. She ate her hot dog without expression, but he thought he saw amusement in her eyes.

"I'm helping her out."

"Equalizing the odds against her?"

"If you want to put it that way."

"I figure it was the sunglasses that got switched, but I couldn't be sure. What's in the *new* Fendi 411s?"

"A tracking device."

"Wow. Cool." She finished her hot dog and turned to him. "So what's our next move?"

"*We?*"

All levity had left her eyes now. "You killed two men, maimed two others, and let our sweet, if fucked-up, young victim get kidnapped. I figure that doesn't happen to you a lot. If ever. *Are* you going to equalize the odds for me?"

"I didn't do a very good job at the Mercury Theater."

She put a hand on his arm. It sent a jolt of electricity right through him. A sexual awakening he hadn't felt in a long time. He looked at her face, no more Laura Masden tears, no hesitant speech. He hadn't bothered to look at her figure in the River Café that night. It rivaled Candy Annie's for curves, with longer legs, and Tara gave new meaning to the term *bedroom eyes*.

"If you didn't want to find Emily Masden," she said, "you wouldn't have tracked Blake to his financial convention or planted a bug on him. You must have the receiver."

McCall took a receiver out of his pocket. It was about the size of a chewing-gum package. He handed it to her. "You can track him. I have a lunch date at the Russian Tea Room."

"Sounds ritzy."

"You carry cards with you?"

"I like the one with a machine gun on it and myself naked in silhouette, but I forgot to bring those. I have the plain old ones that say *Tara Langley, Private Investigations*."

She took out a small silver case, removed a card, and handed it to McCall. He wrote on the back of it and handed it back to her. "This is my cell number. I'm pretty sure Blake will be at that conference at the Four Seasons all day."

"Good. I can get wasted at the Ty Bar and listen to New Yorkers solve all the world's problems. I'll call you if Blake leaves and goes anywhere interesting. He's into something, Mr. McCall. Something very serious."

"That's what Emily said. And you can call me Robert."

He started to walk away down Central Park South.

"Does this mean we're partners?" she called after him.

"If you have a problem, call me," he said over his shoulder.

Tara sighed. "You could cause me all sorts of problems," she murmured.

CHAPTER II

Dr. Patrick Cross was bone tired. He'd been on duty since 4:00 a.m. He'd just finished giving his last patient, a thirteen-year-old boy who had contracted one of the four strains of the Ebola virus, *Bundibugyo*, an injection of immunoglobulin. The blood plasma proteins and antibodies in the gamma globulin would boost the boy's immune system, but only temporarily. There *was* no vaccine. The boy had contracted the disease from hugging his mother. She had been dead two days later. Dwe, that was the boy's name—Dr. Cross thought it meant "elephant" in Grebo—had become sick ten days after that. He was a big, strapping boy, or he had been. The disease was eating away at him like, well, a disease. This new outbreak in Liberia had come several months after the World Health Organization had declared Liberia, and the Monrovia area, Ebola-free. Dr. Cross had already completed one tour of duty with Doctors Without Borders, or Médecins Sans Frontières, as it was known all over Africa and Europe, the year before. They had asked him to return. Usually the tour of duty was a minimum of nine months, but they'd agreed to his insistence on six months.

Dr. Cross went into the changing room and took off the yellow protective scrubs, the white hood and goggles, and blue surgeon's gloves. Beneath them he wore jeans and a T-shirt, which was soaked through. He looked at his face in the mirror. Long and angular, with pale blue eyes, his blond hair bleached in the sun. The strain of trying to help these infected townspeople was evident in his eyes.

And, of course, his secret work.

Dr. Cross walked out of the big white tent into the blazing sunlight. The temperature had to be over one hundred degrees. The compound had six large white tents where the infected villagers from the village of Nedowein, just outside Monrovia's International Airport, were isolated. Blue barricades were up amid the narrow, twisting lanes to each of the quarantine tents. The compound was fenced off and surrounded by jungle. Soldiers from the Armed Forces of Liberia were at the gates. The civil war in Liberia had ended over ten years before, but there'd been pockets of rebel activity recently, and the AFL force was there for the protection of the doctors and nurses as well as the villagers. The guards had never searched Dr. Cross's Land Rover when he'd driven it out through the main gates.

But there was always a first time.

Dr. Cross carried a briefcase of files and a Puma ProCat black tote bag in which he kept slides, medical equipment, including his stethoscope, and a blue Medicool vial cooler and protection case into which his vials fit snugly. He didn't like carrying the cooler into and out of the compound, but he had no choice. He couldn't just leave it in the offices. The vials needed to be refrigerated. He could have put a lock on the refrigerator in the kitchen area, but that might have raised suspicions. So he just carried the cooler back and forth with him. *That* raised no suspicions. He was working with medicines and highly volatile agents, and sometimes he took his work back with him. He was staying at the Mamba Point Hotel on United Nations Drive by the ocean, where there was a refrigerator.

Dr. Cross put the tote bag and the briefcase into the back of his white Land Rover, fired it up, and drove to the closed gates. One of the AFL officers smiled and waved him through. Dr. Cross drove out of the compound, down the jungle road, and finally into Monrovia. He made a pit stop at his Mamba Point Hotel room, fit the Medicool vial cooler and protection case into the refrigerator there, and then drove to the Palm Hotel on the corner of Broad and Randall Streets in the city center.

The lights were muted inside the Bamboo Bar in the hotel. Western music played—Lady Gaga saying she was "born this way." Dr. Cross recognized a couple of the other doctors from Médecins Sans Frontières sitting up at the bar. They acknowledged him, but didn't wave him over. Cross was known as a loner who liked his space. He collapsed into one of the big cane chairs at one of the tables. A waiter brought him his usual drink: a Green Hornet, a variation on the classic stinger. Cross liked brandy with green crème de menthe, shaken and poured into a cocktail glass with no ice. He glanced up at the plasma TV that was hung over the bar. It was running CNN. There was no sound, but it was all about the fighting in Syria and Iraq. Cross had no interest in it. That was a physical war, with bloodshed and atrocities, wounds that were inflicted from *without*. In the war Dr. Cross was fighting, the wounds were insidiously inflicted from *within*. You knew who the enemy was—in this case, Ebola—but not how to destroy it.

A figure detached itself from the end of the bar and moved to Dr. Cross's table. She was an MSF nurse named Ann Crosby, who'd shed her green scrubs and was dressed in a denim shirt and skirt, sandals on her feet, a silver cross at her throat. She was petite, just over five-one, in her early thirties, with bright blue eyes and brown hair cut across her forehead in pageboy bangs. She'd told him she was bringing the fifties back, but subtly.

It was a kinder, gentler time when innocents weren't being slaughtered in the name of religion and little boys like Dwe weren't dying of a disease just because they had hugged their mothers. Ann was somewhat waiflike, but not model skinny. Her breasts pressed hard enough against her shirt for the nipples to protrude. Not that Dr. Cross was looking, of course.

Ann Crosby sat down in the big cane chair opposite Cross, looking tired herself.

"Long day?" he asked.

"Two-in-the-morning-to-three-p.m. shift. We've initiated a mass inoculation for measles. Fifty villagers today. Five more cases in the past two days. I looked for you at the compound, but you weren't around. I thought Scott Pelley of *60 Minutes* had corralled you for another interview."

Sixty Minutes had been following up on a story they'd televised a couple of seasons ago about the Ebola disease. Cross smiled. "I think *you're* the one he wants to interview next. I told him what a fantastic nurse you are and how much you've given to Doctors Without Borders."

It was Ann's turn to smile. "You're biased."

He was. He adored her. "Still enjoying this work?"

"Hundred-plus degrees, eighty percent humidity, sudden heavy rains that drench you in seconds, ten-o'clock curfew when you're confined to the compound, long toilet drops, and bucket showers by candlelight. What's not to love?"

"I heard there was some excitement this morning."

"Because I'm an OR nurse and an anesthetist I got called in to assist in an emergency appendectomy. Dr. Millford almost didn't diagnose it in time." She leaned across and took Cross's hand. "How is your work going?"

Cross lowered his voice. "I'm getting *so* close. But my stomach ties up in knots every time I drive through the compound gates with those vials in my protection cooler."

"Leave the cooler at the compound."

"I don't dare do that and run the risk that some MSF nurse—no offense—will open the refrigerator looking for a sample and find it."

"But you're working on an Ebola *cure*!"

"Not sanctioned and not funded. It's dangerous and volatile because of having to use part of the Ebola virus strain. I'd be fired from Doctors Without Borders and could face criminal prosecution."

His voice had an edge. They'd discussed this before.

"But you've got all of the research data to back up your work!"

"I haven't made enough of a serious breakthrough to sanction the tests."

"But you *are* close, right?"

"I believe so."

She squeezed his hand. "I'm very proud of you."

"You can be proud of me when the vaccine is endorsed by the CDC and it saves one person having contracted Ebola."

He squeezed her hand back, then their hands parted quickly. No one knew of their relationship, and it would be frowned upon at Doctors Without Borders. Romances were for civilization, and out here, in the frontier of third-world poverty and despair, all of them had to be focused completely on their lifesaving work.

Dr. Cross glanced up at the TV screen over the bar. The scene behind the CNN anchor had shifted to an area in Syria. An overturned US Humvee was on the side of a dusty road, black smoke pouring out of it. Syrian Rebel troops were milling around, the footage captured on a handheld cell phone.

Dr. Cross nodded at the TV screen. "That's what's newsworthy. US Army personnel sticking their nose in where we're not wanted. They get killed and the American public is outraged. But here, in this desperate corner of the world, with an epidemic that could potentially wipe out millions, let's keep it quiet. Don't want to alarm folks."

Ann Crosby reached out again and closed her hand over his. Her expression of concern tried to reassure him that it was all going to be okay.

But he knew better.

Whenever McCall entered the Russian Tea Room on West Fifty-Seventh Street, he felt like he was walking into a Fabergé egg. The décor was all gold, with red booths along two walls and tables with white tablecloths. The stained-glass ceiling, in blue and yellow, was gorgeous. McCall glanced over at the girl at the coat check, where Madonna had once worked, to see if he could spot the next Material Girl, but this one looked more like a runway model, with thick purple eye shadow and cheekbones that could slice carrots. The restaurant had gone through some tough times, had closed for four years, but had reopened again in 2006. McCall had been there on its reopening night.

The RTR was packed for lunch. Norman Rosemont was sitting in one of the red booths with two men and a woman. The older man was in his fifties, wearing a red polka-dot bow tie. He looked like he owned the Bank of America. The younger man was obviously Rosemont's assistant, fresh faced, eager to please. The woman was in her forties, stylishly dressed. She had a husky voice that reminded McCall of Lauren Bacall, whom she somewhat resembled at that age. They were all listening intently to their host.

Norman Rosemont was a big man, also midfifties, immaculately dressed in a Hugo Boss gray windowpane wool suit with a Turnbull & Asser blue dress shirt. McCall recognized him from various TV appearances, where he'd been opening a new Manhattan skyscraper or debating the economy on Fox News.

Their main course had just been served. The banker was having *kulebyaka*—salmon, mushrooms, onions, and vegetables in pastry with cabbage—the woman executive was nibbling at sevruga one-ounce caviar, Rosemont's assistant had ordered *vareniki*, which was Russian-style ravioli, and Rosemont was digging into *côtelette à la Kiev*, not worrying that the herb butter stuffed into the breaded chicken breast squirted out across the table every time he stabbed his fork into it. The banker was laughing at something Rosemont had said. The female executive smiled tolerantly, but the story had obviously been a little off-color. Rosemont's assistant chuckled and remained poised for more iPhone notes.

McCall reached the booth. "Norman Rosemont?"

The corporate CEO looked up at him quizzically. "That usually precedes being served with divorce papers, and my wife was *very* friendly this morning before I left home." Rosemont grinned at his guests to see if they were amused—the banker chuckled and the woman executive looked frosty. Rosemont returned his attention to Robert McCall. "Or am I under arrest?"

"I'm not serving you papers and I'm not a cop."

"You can see I'm in the middle of a lunch meeting. If you need to make an appointment, you can contact my assistant, Mark, here."

"I don't need an appointment."

Rosemont played to the table again, being magnanimous. "Can I do something for you, sir?"

"Not for me."

McCall placed four eight-by-ten photographs on the table. One was a full shot of Gemma Hathaway standing in her living room, the red marks on her face and arms looking like mosquito bites. Two pictures were close-ups of the bites on her arms and legs. The last picture was a close-up of her face.

"This little girl is covered in rat bites," McCall said.

"And why should I give a rat's ass about that?"

Rosemont glanced around the table to see if his play on words had had an effect. The banker grinned and took another mouthful of *kulebyaka*. The female executive set down her fork, looking at the photographs with some concern. Mark, ever the faithful assistant, wouldn't have cared if the photos had been body parts that had been discovered in Rosemont's office.

"This little girl and her mother live in a building you own in the East Village."

"What do you want me to do about it?"

"Move your tenants out, bring in exterminators, move your tenants back in when it's safe for them to live in their apartments. Or have the building condemned."

Rosemont made a face to the banker as if to say, *Is this guy for real?*

McCall said, "Why don't you look at the pictures, Mr. Rosemont? They tell a more eloquent story than whatever anecdote you're regaling your guests with."

Norman Rosemont had *not,* in fact, looked at the pictures. Nor did he when he nodded curtly to Mark, who scooped them up and handed them back to McCall.

"They're not my concern."

"Do you want to know *which* of your apartment buildings the Hathaways live in?"

"I do not. If your tenant friend has a beef about her building—"

"She's not my friend."

"Girlfriend, sister, whatever. Have her take it to the proper authorities."

"Linda Hathaway tried that. She went down to city hall and filed a formal complaint. Nothing was done."

"Obviously they found no merit in it. Now, I'd like to have my lunch meeting with these good people without further interruption. Or do I have to call the cops?"

McCall put the pictures back into his jacket pocket. "No need for that." He looked around the table. "I apologize for disturbing you."

"Not at all," the female executive said.

McCall looked back at Norman Rosemont and smiled. "Have a good day."

McCall headed back through the RTR. Rosemont shook his head and went back to his chicken Kiev. The banker went back to his *kulebyaka*. The female executive looked after McCall, having not picked up her fork, as if she had lost her appetite.

Helen Coleman moved back the curtain at her living-room window when she heard the sound of the car pulling up. Twilight was wrapping the front lawn and trees of her colonial house in dusky violet colors. The vehicle was a black Lincoln town car. Three military men got out, all in dress uniforms. One was a two-star general, the second an Army colonel, and she thought the third man was an Army chaplain. She didn't know them, but she knew why they were here. For a moment she just stood paralyzed. The three somber men walked up the flagstone path to her porch.

Helen Coleman allowed the hot tears to roll down her face as she walked into the hallway to open her front door to the news of her older son's death.

CHAPTER 12

The Equalizer sat on a park bench in the playground in Sara D. Roosevelt Park. He was watching some teenagers playing a pickup game of basketball. He remembered back to another afternoon when kids like these were shooting hoops, throwing passes, and just having a grand old time. The Equalizer had two older brothers, Zachary and Caleb, whom he idolized. Zachary had been seventeen on that summer day. Caleb would have been twenty. The Equalizer himself had been sixteen. But Zachary had allowed the Equalizer to play basketball with his friends on that day. Zachary had actually *motioned* to him to get into the game.

"Let's see if the runt can show us some good moves!"

Zach's friends had all hooted derisively, but they'd let him join them. It had been an unexpected and thrilling moment. The bigger kids had shoved him around and stolen the basketball from him every time, but he hadn't cared. He was playing right alongside his big bro Zach, who tried to look out for him, but the Equalizer was such a nerd in those days, awkward moves and flailing arms. He didn't get many passes thrown to him, but it didn't matter, it had felt *so good*.

He didn't see the black Dodge Intrepid pull up on the road right outside the playground. It had idled there for three seconds, more than enough time for the teenage gang members inside to pump seven bullets into Zachary's body. The Equalizer had been standing right there beside his brother when he fell. Blood had spurted like fountains. He had collapsed to his knees, cradling Zachary's head, not knowing what to do. He remembered screaming, "Get help!" But no one had moved. He heard the squealing tires as the Dodge Intrepid sped away.

Then the other kids had pulled him off his dead brother. His legs had been rubber. He looked after the Dodge Intrepid, but he could not have identified any of the killers. He knew Zach had belonged to a gang called the White Jaguars. The Equalizer had always been enthralled by street gangs. They had such *cool names:* Lower East Side Dragons, the Assassins, Cut Throat Crew. The Equalizer had learned later that it *had* been the White Jaguars who had murdered his brother. But Zach had not been their target. It was his older brother Caleb against whom the White Jaguars had a grudge. He once had a chance to join them when he was younger and had refused. Caleb had not wanted anything to do with *any* of the street gangs. He was older than his other two brothers and was going to law school. But the White Jaguars had sent a message that afternoon to Caleb. *No one* ever walked away from their gang.

The cops finally arrived. None of the other high school kids had been hurt. The bullets had only been for Zach. The cops would investigate, sure, but it was just another drive-by shooting in a tough neighborhood. By that time, the Equalizer had been dragged away by his mom.

For years after that he would be harassed by gang members. Not just by the White Jaguars, but by *other* gang members, too. He remembered once being cornered by a street gang called Dead Man Walking in his neighborhood and had thought he was going to be beaten senseless. But they had just bloodied his nose. And always with the same taunt: "Hey, Pussy." He had allowed his brother Zach to get killed. He had done nothing to stop it. The name had stuck to him. He remembered at school kids whispering when he walked past, "Hey, Pussy, what's up?" But he always just kept on walking, his head bowed.

Now the Equalizer sat once again in Sara Roosevelt Park, on the same park bench, watching teenagers playing a pickup game of basketball, feeling good about himself. He thought about rescuing Megan Forrester in that alleyway in Essex Street and kicking the shit out of the two gangbangers who had tried to rape her. He wasn't sure if they were members of the White Jaguars gang or not. It didn't matter. He had sent his *own* message to the

White Jaguars or any other gang who preyed upon the innocent in this city. They had been warned. The Equalizer was here. He patrolled these mean streets now.

And *no one* would ever call him Pussy again.

McCall had expected the Dolls nightclub façade to have changed now that it had been taken over by Samuel Clemens, a Fort Worth used-car salesman. McCall wondered if he'd see a neon bucking bronco below the DOLLS sign, which would have been changed to COWGIRLS. But the same cascade of silver dolls spilled over the entrance. The usual line of people were waiting outside, and the same burly African-American bouncer was playing God as to who went in. Without a word, he beckoned McCall to enter.

A young man at the front of the line said nastily, "Why's that guy so special?"

"Don't know," the bouncer said with a voice like spring rain. "Just is."

The silver décor inside the nightclub hadn't changed. Cocktail wait-resses in their silk shirts and tailored slacks glided around the small tables, the dance floor was packed, and more politicians and businessmen and attorneys waited at the bar for their turn to dance with one of the Dolls' hostesses. When Borislav Kirov had run the club, the word *hostess* had been a euphemism for beautiful young women who would have sex with VIP clients for blackmail purposes in the small rooms up on the second floor. Music still pounded at earsplitting decibels. The same young Chechen DJ, a big guy with wild black hair, was spinning the records.

A soft touch on McCall's arm turned him around.

He only knew her first name—Melody. She was in her early twenties with beautiful blue eyes and porcelain skin that almost glowed. She wore a shimmering blue dress, showing a good amount of cleavage and legs, but not too much. Her blond hair floated over her shoulders like a golden shroud. McCall had encountered her in Dolls when he'd been trying to even the odds against her Russian friend Katia Rossovkaya. McCall had been forced to kill Katia's ex-husband, Alexei Berezovsky, an old enemy, who had been running an elite assassination ring. Melody looked radiant tonight, a far cry from the tense and frightened young woman he'd first met. Things at the nightclub were better now. At least, McCall hoped they were. Other-wise he'd have to have another friendly chat with Davy Crockett about this here Texican hoedown.

"Mr. McCall!" Melody's voice was as lyrical as he remembered it.

"Katia told me your *real* name! She's off tonight. Actually, she and her daughter have gone to Walt Disney World in Florida for four days. I'm so jealous! But she deserves a vacation after everything that happened to her."

"You know everything that happened?"

"Not the details, except Katia said you saved her life. And Natalya's. Everything here at the club has changed. No more special clients wanting . . ." Melody shook her head and actually blushed. "I'm still so ashamed that you saw me in one of those upstairs rooms with that guy and I was, you know, *naked*. He was some foreign diplomat. Bakar Daudov would have killed me if I hadn't gone upstairs with him. But you know what? Mr. Daudov hasn't set foot in this club in over a month!"

McCall knew that because he'd killed Daudov when the Chechen enforcer had attacked him in his old apartment. But he just nodded. "He won't be coming back here."

"Not ever?"

"No."

"All those rooms upstairs were torn out and a really cool bar was put in, the Watering Hole. I think Mr. Clemens could have come up with a classier name, but we get *real* VIPs up there now, and none of the hostesses have to do anything but dance."

"That's good to hear."

"I'll let Katia know you were in when she comes back to work."

"I'm not here to see Katia, Melody. I need to talk to you."

She looked surprised. The DJ cranked up another song—Taylor Swift knowing her lover was trouble. Melody glared over at the DJ booth.

"Too loud, Abuse!" The DJ just grinned and waved at her. Melody turned back to McCall. "Such an asshole. Forgive my language. His name is Abusaid. We all call him Abuse. He likes young girls, and when I say young, I mean jailbait. The rumor is between twelve and sixteen years old."

"Do you have proof of that?"

"No. But I'll bet there's a ton of kiddie porn on his computer."

McCall made a mental note of that. They sat down at a vacant table in the lounge area. Melody looked expectant. "What can I help you with?"

"A young Wall Street stockbroker named Blake Cunningham. In his twenties, Tom Cruise looks when he was that age, rich, arrogant, with all of the warmth of a cobra. And I'd say just as deadly. I believe he kidnapped a young woman from a party a month ago."

"Kidnapped. Wow. Shouldn't you get in touch with the FBI?"

"It's on me to find her."

"What can *I* do?"

"Tell me your full name."

"Melody Fairbrother."

"Where are you from?"

"Lake Geneva. *Not* in Switzerland! It's a little town about sixty miles southwest of Milwaukee."

"Can you play the naïve Lake Geneva girl in the Big Apple looking for love and excitement?"

"That's what I came here for," Melody said a little sadly. "The naïveté didn't last very long."

"How good an actress are you?"

"Good enough to fool an egocentric stockbroker."

"Blake Cunningham is dangerous. You need to understand that."

"Okay."

"He's the only lead I have to finding this missing girl."

"What's her name?"

"Emily Masden."

"You're sure she's been kidnapped?"

"No. But it's the only scenario that makes sense."

"So you'd be using me as bait." It was a statement, not a question.

"Yes."

"Bring it on. After all you did for Katia, for all of us here at Dolls, you think I'm going to turn you down?"

"You don't owe me a thing. Neither does Katia."

"That's for us to decide. What do you want me to do?"

"Meet up with Blake. Somewhere with a lot of other people. I'll let you know when. Can you leave Dolls at short notice?"

"Oh, sure, I could twist Mr. Clemens around my finger."

"Wherever the meeting takes place, I'll have your back. There'll be at least two others watching you at all times."

"When do I meet this Mr. Wonderful?"

"Soon." McCall stood and looked down at her. "You don't have to do this for me, Melody."

She smiled, the kind of smile that would curl your toes. Along with her figure. "Yeah, I do."

"Remember, no matter how charming Blake is . . ."

"Cobra. Got it."

She jumped up and gave McCall a hug, then moved away to dance with a waiting customer. McCall hadn't wanted to involve Melody, but he was out of options. He couldn't use Candy Annie again, Blake would recognize her immediately. He couldn't use Tara because she reeked of street smarts and she was too *old*. McCall had the feeling that Blake Cunningham liked his conquests young. Maybe not as young as the DJ Abusaid, but a girl like Melody from mid-Americana who was *this* gorgeous? Blake wouldn't be able to resist.

Now McCall just had to keep her alive.

Helen Coleman sat at an antique desk in her home office. She had mixed herself a Tom Collins, which she sipped with trembling hands. She was on the internet trying to find out something more on the recent US Army personnel deaths in Syria, but there's wasn't anything other than what she'd already been told.

Something was wrong.

The thought sounded so ridiculous in her mind. Of *course* something was *wrong*! Her son had been killed. But it wasn't that stark, terrible fact that was nagging at her. The two-star general had been evasive about the circumstances of Josh's death. If Helen heard the words "highly classified" one more time, she'd scream. The colonel had told her that no one in the US observation team had been in frontline conflict, but that her son had been involved in a skirmish in a Syrian village and had been killed. Captain Josh Coleman was a hero. His body would be flown home for burial at Arlington National Cemetery—but not right away. The general had had no explanation for the delay. The chaplain had offered her spiritual support. The three Army officers had walked back down the path, their burden lifted, her burden of grief just beginning.

Helen hadn't been able to reach Gunner. She'd even called Josh's satellite phone, what the hell, and predictably got no answer. It gnawed at her. She'd been around the Pentagon long enough to know when the truth was being withheld. She might be a high-ranking UN official, but here she was just a mother of a fallen soldier who needed to deal with her grief.

She remembered something she'd seen on the internet about a month ago. She got on Google and typed in *Equalizer*. It took her to a personal ad:

Gotta problem?—Odds against you?—Call the Equalizer.

There was a phone number to call. She wrote it down on a piece of scrap paper on her desk. But she didn't dial it. Not yet. She took another swallow of the Tom Collins, letting the sweet taste of gin and lemon juice, sugar and club soda, calm her. The Equalizer was probably some conspiracy theorist who'd love to get dirt on the Pentagon.

If her son was dead, *no one* could equalize those odds.

CHAPTER 13

Beauregard "Bo" Ellsworth was six-foot-four, kind of good-looking if you found John Wayne good-looking, barrel chested with a close-cropped beard, a *real* man his five-year-old nephew liked to call him, because he hunted and fished and got into barroom brawls, although he'd told his nephew that was *not* something he was proud of. Bo had no children of his own; his wife had left him years before after one of his drunken tirades. Something else Bo was not proud of. But he wasn't a loner. He had stalwart friends who went back to his high school days. He'd wanted to enlist in the Marines, but an inner-ear problem had killed that dream. Bo considered himself a patriot. He believed in the Constitution and the freedoms the forefathers had so carefully worked out to make this new United States of America great. He had been seven years old on September 11, 2001. He'd never got the horror of those images out of his mind. Alan Jackson, the country-and-western singer, wrote a beautiful song about that terrible day titled "Where Were You When the World Stopped Turning?" The lyric that haunted Bo was *Did you burst out with pride / For the red, white, and blue / And the heroes who died / Just doin' what they do?* Not trying to be heroes, just doing their jobs as firemen or cops or just folks caught in the nightmare trying to save their coworkers.

Bo had formed the Texas Minutemen Militia when he was twenty-two. It had started with six members—himself, his best friend, Randy Wyatt; Jeremiah Buchanan, who worked for him; Big Teddy Danfield, who ran Bo's plant; and Bo's two cousins Steve and Kyle. Now the TMM numbered sixty, spread out across his hometown, Boerne, San Antonio, Austin, Dallas, and Houston. They were ready at a moment's notice to defend their state and their fellow Texans. Hell, their fellow *Americans,* didn't matter where they lived. That's what Bo and two of his minutemen were doing outside the Marine Corps recruiting office at 3837 Binz Engleman Road here in San Antonio. Dutifully standing guard in their TMM uniforms, beige and gray with insignia on their lapels. No ranks on their sleeves. Everyone was the *same* rank, a minuteman. Of course there were senior officers, that was manda-tory for discipline. Bo was the ranking officer at this location.

They all carried Bushmaster M4 assault rifles. They were also armed with Smith & Wesson M&P Shield 9mm pistols in holsters on their hips. They could have had their handguns concealed, but what was the point of that when they were hefting M4s? Although Bo *did* have the carry licenses for all of their weapons in the glove compartment of his black Ford Explorer XLT SUV in the parking lot.

Bo had members of the Texas Minutemen Militia at three other loca-tions today in San Antonio, in Kerrville, and a unit in Houston. Two days earlier the US Marine location in Atlanta, Georgia, had been packed with uniformed marines for some kind of an informal seminar. One lone-wolf gunman—a Muslim US citizen formerly from Yemen—had opened up on the office with a Russian AK-47 assault rifle. It had been a bloodbath. Seven marines killed, twenty injured, two of them critically. The usual outrage had been expressed by the White House, with lots of debates about violence and gun control on Fox News, folks who'd never even *picked up* a firearm pon-tificating on the pros and cons of issuing gun licenses and protecting the homeland. Texas governor Perry had initiated the Castle Doctrine in 2007, so that folks "lawfully occupying a dwelling" could use deadly force on a home invasion by *anyone* who unlawfully entered with force. But that did not protect their armed forces. The Atlanta shooter had been killed by police when they'd found him taking a piss at the side of a country road outside the city. Others out there were just like him, paranoid or crazy or brainwashed by the Jihadist ads on the internet, which were produced with the slickness of a Madison Avenue ad campaign. After all of the talk and debates and rhetoric, *nothing* was really going to stop such an atrocity from happening again.

Unless someone like Bo Ellsworth and his Texas Minutemen Militia stepped up to the plate. So he'd deployed twelve of his militia to four US Marine recruitment offices throughout Texas. They were prepared to stand guard all day for a week, maybe longer.

It was the least they could do.

Bo glanced over in the general direction of the Alamo. The Alamo Mis-sion security forces had recently arrested a Japanese tourist who'd cut his initials into one of the memorial walls with a penknife. He'd received a hefty fine and a slap on the wrist. A hundred and fifty years ago he'd have been dragged out to a tree and hung for defacing a shrine like that.

The Marine recruitment officer had come out at ten past nine and assured Bo that this kind of protection, albeit appreciated, was not needed. Bo had told him it was very much needed, no trouble at all, and if the TMM had been deployed at the Marine recruiting office in Atlanta, the tragedy there would not have occurred.

Bo wasn't surprised when the Feds arrived.

They pulled up into the west parking lot in three black sedans. Two men got out of each car. They all wore the FBI uniform, dark suits, muted ties; all were in their twenties, except for one guy in his midthirties. He was obviously the senior man and took the lead walking over to the Marine recruiting office. The other agents fanned out until they were facing Bo's other two minutemen. They didn't register the arrival of the Feds with even a flicker of interest or emotion. Bo thought they'd make good beefeaters, those British soldiers in fancy dress who stood outside Buckingham Palace in London and ignored the tourists who took selfies or kicked their shins, or the young women who unbuttoned their shirts to catch their eye.

The leading Fed displayed his ID and picture as he walked up to Bo. "FBI special agent Todd Blakemore, sir. May I ask you what you're doing here?"

"Protection detail."

"You and your friends—"

"They're not friends, they're members of the Texas Minutemen Militia."

"We're aware of your radical military organization, Mr. Ellsworth."

"Nothing radical about it. We're patriots, doing a job *you* should be doing."

"You're carrying assault rifles."

"We're issued with Bushmaster M4A rifles. The *A* in that stands for 'Armalite,' *not* assault. The 2015 Texas legislature allows concealed-handgun-permit holders to carry firearms openly."

"Firearms are prohibited from being carried or displayed in front of post offices, federal courts, offices of the FBI, IRS, Justice Department, USDA, the Department of Energy, and the FDA," Special Agent Blakemore said. "That provision is covered by federal statutes that supersede state law."

"This is a recruiting office and not a federal building."

"Folks see men carrying assault rifles—excuse me, *Armalite* rifles—with handguns clearly visible in holsters, dressed in military uniforms, taking up positions in an outdoor mall that could cause public alarm.

It has the potential to exacerbate an already volatile situation. You need to order your men to stand down."

Bo took a deep breath. This was *so wrong.* "We're under attack. By those Jihadists slaughtering innocent people in the Middle East. They get sympathizers and crazies here at home all fired up. We need to make a stand against them. That's our constitutional right."

"I know what it says in the Constitution," Agent Blakemore told Bo.

"Lieutenant General Bradley said, 'The enemy is underground.' As Americans, we can't stay underground. We've got to be *visible.* We've got to let the enemy know who we are, *where* we are, and that we're ready to fight."

"If I can't persuade you to stand down," Blakemore said reasonably, "the next thing you and your militiamen will see is a SWAT team arrive in this parking lot with twenty cop cars and Homeland Security backing them up. So, I say again, with all due respect for your rights and your patriot gesture, have your Texas minutemen stand down."

Bo heard the sarcasm in the words "Texas minutemen," but he lowered his M4. He made a hand motion, which Agent Todd Blakemore did not follow, but the other two minutemen also lowered their assault rifles. Some kind of a secret *stand down* signal, Blakemore thought. *Boy, these guys are scary.* But he just said, "You need to leave now, sir. Have yourselves a pleasant day."

Blakemore walked back to his Dodge Magnum company car, his agents following. But they didn't actually climb into their vehicles. They waited. Bo gave his men another hand signal, which was basically *retreat,* even though they were only going to climb into his Ford Explorer and drive away.

Bo was seething inside.

What this country needed was a major wake-up call.

He knew they were going to rob the mom-and-pop grocery store as soon as the three men walked into it. He had that sixth sense you developed when you did the job he did. It was all about body language. You probably wouldn't notice if you weren't looking for it, but he was a pro and knew the signs. The thugs were all white guys in their midtwenties, dressed in jeans, dark hoodies, and Reebok Ventilator neon casuals in yellow, blue, and black.

The Equalizer was at the back of the store picking up some Oreo cookies. When he was in a store like this, he always gave a thought to his older brother Caleb. Eight years after his brother Zachary had been gunned down by the White Jaguars, Caleb had been killed in a convenience-store robbery over in SoHo. Caleb had run in to grab some Christmas lights for their mom's tree, which had been in dire need of new strands. Caleb had been about to take the New York City bar exam. His dream had been to practice law somewhere right there in their neighborhood. He was already a civic leader in the community and becoming a real champion for the rights of the people. The SoHo convenience store had been robbed by two guys who took sixty bucks out of the cash register. Caleb had tried to stop them when they threatened the Asian proprietor and had been killed for his trouble.

The Equalizer had that very afternoon been to the Cedar Grove Cemetery in Flushing, New York, where both of his brothers were buried. He'd left fresh flowers on their graves. He talked to Caleb most often when he was in the graveyard. His older brother had understood that the Lower East Side needed a hero. Hell, *all* of the neighborhoods around there needed one, from Hell's Kitchen down to the Financial District. Someone who would fight for the oppressed, right their wrongs, keep them safe.

The Equalizer had just taken a quart of 2 percent milk out of the refrigerated section, which he now put back, stuck the Oreo cookies into the pocket of his big overcoat, and strolled over to where a coffeemaker stood on a table near the counter for the benefit of the customers. That was because Thug #2—he kept them in the order he'd seen them enter the store—had moved right beside it. His jacket was slightly open, a Glock 34 9mm in his belt. Thug #1 stayed in the doorway of the store, blocking anyone else from coming in. Thug #3 was on his way to the counter, behind which the Muslim-refugee grocery-store manager was stacking lottery tickets. He spoke little English, but rattled off a torrent of some foreign language into his cell phone all day.

The Equalizer picked up the coffeepot and poured black coffee into a styrofoam cup. He noted his favorite young Hispanic girl was behind the cash register. He thought her name was Raquel, a hottie with a great smile. She was ringing up some purchases for an old guy he'd seen around the neighborhood. The Equalizer shifted his gaze. A big guy in jeans and a Windbreaker was over by the Lay's potato chips freestanding display. Two black teenagers were bopping to whatever rap music was blasting in their earpods, checking out, of all things, the fruit aisle.

Thug #3 pulled a Ruger 9mm pistol from his pocket and waved it in the manager's face. "Give me all the money in the register! All the lottery tickets!" The manager just stared at him, paralyzed. "Do it *now*!"

The shouted demand had almost a touch of desperation.

The manager started grabbing the various lottery tickets from their stand.

The Equalizer turned and threw the scalding-hot coffee into Thug #2's face, then smashed the coffeepot against the side of his head. It shattered as he fell, spilling glass shards and what was left of the hot coffee down his face. The Equalizer crouched beside him, grabbing the Glock out of his belt.

In the doorway, Thug #1 pulled out another Glock 34. The Equalizer dragged Thug #2 up to shield his body. Thug #1 fired, and two bullets struck his pal in the back. The Equalizer fired, but even though Thug #1 was a pretty big target, he missed. The glass exploded in the door behind him.

Then several things happened simultaneously.

The guy in the Windbreaker at the Lay's potato chips drew a Sig P226 from a holster on his hip. The thought flashed through the Equalizer's mind—*Off-duty cop*. Thug #3, panicked by the gunfire, fired on the cop, who was Dirty Harry and fired a split-second quicker. Thug #3 kicked around and fell to the floor. Blood spurted from the off-duty cop's right leg. He went down hard to the floor, taking the Lay's potato-chip stand with him.

Raquel ran around the end of the counter from her cash register.

The Equalizer fired again on Thug #1. This time he didn't miss. The man took the bullet in the chest, firing as he was flung back against the shattered door. His bullet struck the fleeing cashier. She fell to her knees with a cry and grabbed her chest, blood gushing through her fingers. The two black teenagers pulled their earpods out of their ears and just stood there like they were watching a movie. The old man ran out of the store, stepping over the body of Thug #1. The manager grabbed his cell phone and dialed 911.

The Equalizer didn't have much time.

He felt for a pulse at Thug #2's throat. Dead. He ran over to where Thug #1 lay moaning in the doorway, picked up his fallen Glock 34, and put it into his overcoat pocket. He moved up to the counter where Thug #3 lay unmoving. The undercover cop had gone for a head shot. Pretty good shooting. The Equalizer picked up Thug #3's fallen gun and stuck it into his other overcoat pocket. He looked over at Raquel. Her blouse had come apart and blood ran over her breasts. He had spent a lot of time admiring her chest. Too bad having to see it like this.

He ran over to where the off-duty cop lay on the floor and knelt beside him. Bags of Lay's potato chips lay scattered around him. The Equalizer pulled off his own belt and tied it around the cop's leg as a tourniquet, cinching it tightly. The belt couldn't be traced back to him. He'd picked it up at a thrift shop in SoHo for a buck. The cop raised up a little to look at him. The Equalizer pulled the collar of his overcoat up around his face. He couldn't let the authorities know who he really was. That's why superheroes had secret identities—they needed to be *secret*! But the cop's eyes weren't focusing. The Equalizer snapped his fingers at the two black teenagers, who ran to his side. He motioned for the first kid to press his palms against the wound in the cop's thigh. The kid nodded, got it. The Equalizer didn't want to talk to them so they could describe his voice later. He thrust the second kid down beside the first one. The second kid got it, too. They'd take turns.

The Equalizer straightened and looked over the deadly scene. Good thing he'd been there—no knowing how badly these three assholes would have shot up the grocery store if he hadn't intervened. He sauntered over to the counter. The manager had just finished his 911 call. He looked at the Equalizer almost in awe. The Equalizer nodded. He took the two guns out of his overcoat pockets and dropped them onto the counter. He decided to keep Thug #2's Glock 34. He took out one of his new Equalizer cards with the figure's silhouette holding a gun in front of the Jag below the NYC skyline and set it down on the counter beside the confiscated weapons.

Then he knelt down beside Raquel. She looked up at him with fear and pain in her eyes. He squeezed her shoulder. "You're going to be okay," he said softly. "Paramedics are on their way."

She nodded. Grateful. He stood, knowing it wouldn't make any difference when the EMTs got there. She was dying. You got used to collateral damage when you did the job he did, but it was too bad. She should have stayed behind her cash register.

He heard sirens faintly in the distance, getting closer.

The Equalizer glanced around once more at the carnage, then walked out of the grocery store into the night.

CHAPTER 14

She'd awakened him at four in the morning and apologized for calling so early. McCall had told her the time didn't matter. It was just before 5:00 a.m. when he sat down at one of the metal tables under a red umbrella in front of the NYPD booth in Times Square. It was a little chilly and he was wearing his dark overcoat. To one side a huge neon American flag was lit up on a billboard, while others had commercials for a new Ferrari and a new Chanel fragrance. He was always amazed at how crowded Times Square was at this hour of the morning. He spotted Helen Coleman striding toward him. She had described herself on the phone. She was dressed in an elegant tailored Donatella Versace herringbone gray suit and carried a Tory Burch tote in light blue over one shoulder. An attractive woman in her early sixties, she had brown hair tumbled around her shoulders. He hadn't given her a description of himself, but she walked right up to his table and sat down. Closer to, he could see she had been doing a lot of crying. But she held her emotions in check. All she'd told him on the phone was her name and that she worked for the UN.

"Helen, my name is Robert McCall. What's your problem?"

If she was disoriented by the abrupt greeting, she didn't show it. She took a thin manila envelope out of her tote bag and slid it across the table.

"My son is Captain Josh Coleman. He's with the US Army Observation Unit in Syria advising the Syrian Army in their fight against the Jihadists. He was killed two days ago in a skirmish in a Syrian village. A two-star general, a colonel, and an Army chaplain came to my door to tell me he'd been killed."

McCall glanced through the slim file. Brahms always said that McCall "worked miracles," but he wasn't bringing Helen's son back from the dead. There could only be one reason she had called him.

"You didn't believe the Army officers."

"I won't say that. But . . . something's not right. I spent all day yesterday trying to get answers from the Pentagon. I used every bit of influence I have, which is considerable, and got stonewalled. No one will give me any details of what happened." She took out a small bottle of pills from her tote bag and swallowed one of them with no water. "I'm on medication. Sorry. I have a friend in the Army, a colonel, they call him Gunner. He hasn't returned any of my voice mails or emails, which is unheard of. He wouldn't ignore me like this unless he doesn't have a choice."

"What does your husband say about this?"

"Married twice, divorced twice. First time was a big fucking mistake. Second time I was the one who fucked up. Sorry. My son was always picking me up on my language."

McCall closed the file and sighed. "Mrs. Coleman . . ."

"Please call me Helen. I know what you're going to say. This is just my own desperate plea for this nightmare *not* to be happening. Isn't that the second stage in the cycle? Pain and grief? I'm past that stage, but not to acceptance. Josh might be a prisoner of the Jihadists—maybe there's a prisoner exchange in the works—maybe Josh is going to be used as a bargaining tool in some high-level covert mission. I know that I'm clutching at emotional straws, but I believe that maybe, just *maybe,* my son is alive and the Army is covering it up."

"Why would they do that?"

"I don't know. But I need proof that my son is dead. Or proof that he's still alive." She took a breath, the words having finally run out. She regarded McCall frankly. "Were you once Special Forces?"

"Not exactly."

"But you worked for some kind of clandestine organization in our government. Black ops, some splinter spy group. Would that be close?"

"Why would you think that?"

"Something about you. Can you help me?"

McCall spotted him jogging down Seventh Avenue from uptown. He'd also spotted McCall and changed direction. McCall looked back at Helen Coleman.

"I'll help you."

It looked as if a great weight had been lifted off Helen's shoulders. Her body relaxed, just a little, and she nodded. "Thank you. I don't know what you charge as a fee . . ."

"I don't charge clients."

"Wow. No shit. Sorry."

She stood up. Jimmy jogged over to the table. Helen smiled at McCall. Not a hundred-watt light-up-Broadway smile, but the best she could manage in the circumstances.

"Your next Equalizer client?"

McCall didn't detect any irony in her words.

"An old colleague. I'll be in touch with you, Helen."

She nodded again and walked away from the table. Jimmy jogged gently in place. He was slight in stature, just under five-ten, a sharp face with luminous eyes. He wore a dark green running suit and his usual orange Nikes.

"I saw your ad in *The New York Times.* You may not have friends, McCall, but at least now you have *clients.*" Jimmy looked after Helen Coleman, who disappeared down the stairs into the Forty-Second Street/Times Square subway station. "Can you equalize her odds?"

There was no irony in Jimmy's words, either.

"I don't know," McCall said.

Jimmy sat down in the chair Helen had vacated. "I haven't seen Granny at his chess table on any of my runs in a month." He glanced at his GPS Epson running watch, checking his time, distance, and pace. "I went by Mickey Kostmayer's apartment yesterday. A lovely young woman is living there. His girlfriend?"

"No."

"Who is she?"

"A friend of mine."

"I thought we'd agreed you have no friends."

"An acquaintance. She's going to stay at Kostmayer's until I can find her a permanent apartment."

"She's from out of town?"

"No, she's lived in Manhattan all her life. But not aboveground."

"I won't ask. I can't get a squeak off the spook network about Kostmayer and Granny. Not even from Sam Kinney, and he hears birds fart in Central Park. I'm worried."

"I'll talk to Control. Find out what's happened to them. How's the security business?"

"People still want to be protected. You didn't ask me to stop by to chat about my work. You always want something. It's one of your more endearing qualities."

"Not everyone finds it so endearing," McCall said wryly. He took a photograph of Norman Rosemont out of his overcoat pocket and handed it to Jimmy. "You know this guy?"

"Sure. Big real-estate tycoon. Always on the news. Got a loud mouth."

"I need to know his daily routine. Where he goes, what deals he's making, what lawsuits he's involved in."

Jimmy nodded, folded the picture, put it into the inside pocket of his lightweight running jacket, and stood. He looked down at McCall, a little sadly.

"Sarah says the invitation for dinner one night is still open."

"I'll have to pass. But thank her for me."

"You can't isolate yourself forever, McCall. Someone has to come to your funeral and throw a white rose on your grave. I'll get you Norman Rosemont's schedule and the highlights of his corporate life by tomorrow night. Let me know if Control has intel on Kostmayer and Granny."

Jimmy jogged away, heading downtown.

Maybe Cassie would toss a white rose on my grave one day, McCall thought.

Then again, maybe not.

A silver Nissan Sentra pulled up, a red light pulsing in the passenger-side window. Detective Steve Lansing got out and walked over to McCall's table.

"Are you having me followed?" McCall asked.

"Come with me."

The grocery store was now a crime scene. One of the uniforms pulled back the yellow police tape to let Detective Lansing and McCall in. More uniformed cops were inside and a forensic team. McCall recognized Catelyn, in her NYPD—CSI UNIT jacket, kneeling beside an overturned Lay's potato-chip stand. She was bagging one of the spilled potato-chip packages strewn around it. A Middle Eastern man in his forties—obviously the grocery-store manager—was talking animatedly to a somewhat heavyset detective with kind eyes in a craggy face. Probably Lansing's partner. The manager stopped his torrent of words and backed away.

He thinks he recognizes me, McCall thought.

Not good.

Lansing led McCall to an office at the back. Another detective, mid-twenties whose blue jacket read NYPD TECH, sat at a computer. On the monitor was a still frame from a high angle on the interior of the grocery store.

"One surveillance camera, at the back," Detective Lansing said. McCall had noted it on their walk through the store. "We loaded in the tape. If 'the Equalizer' had just let the robbery play out, no one would have got hurt. But you had to be a hero."

Lansing motioned to the NYPD tech, who hit a key. Grainy black-and-white footage rolled. A figure wearing *exactly the same overcoat* as McCall threw coffee into the face of one of the thugs. He smashed the coffeepot against the side of the thug's head, bringing him to the ground. Then the shooting started. Six seconds later it was all over. There was no clear frontal shot of the figure in the dark overcoat. He'd known where the camera was and had kept his back to it.

"Who's the guy at the Lay's potato chips who fired?" McCall asked.

"Off-duty cop. He shot the perp at the counter. Probably saved everyone else's life. The officer is going to be okay. You applied a tourniquet around his leg wound using your belt, stopped him from bleeding out. But there was nothing you could do for the girl."

"I'm still wearing my belt."

Lansing ignored that. "You left this behind on the counter, your good deed done for the night."

He showed McCall another of the *Justice Is Here* cards with the words *The Equalizer* below it, in a polyethylene bag. On the computer screen, the figure in the overcoat stepped over the body of the thug in the doorway and out into the street. The NYPD tech froze the frame.

"Same height, same build, same hair color, *same* coat," Lansing said. "Where were you two hours ago?"

"Asleep in my hotel suite."

"Anyone with you?"

"No."

"The off-duty cop is in good shape, but he probably never saw you. You didn't talk to anyone but the cashier, and she was dead before the EMTs got there. The perp in the doorway came out of the OR at Bellevue twenty minutes ago. If I put you in a lineup, what are the odds he'll swear *you're* the guy who shot him?"

"Pretty high. But the body language is wrong." McCall said to the police tech, "Run it back to where the figure is standing with the coffeepot in his hand. Right before he smashes it into the guy's head."

The tech ran the surveillance tape back, then froze it.

McCall leaned in. "You can just see a little of his profile."

"Not enough to recognize him," Lansing said.

"No, but look there, at his right ear." To the tech: "Can you blow up that frame?"

"I can zoom in on it."

The tech hit a computer key and the camera zoomed in on the figure's profile, turned away from the camera.

"Look at his ear," McCall said. "There's a hole in the lobe for an earring. Now look at my right ear. I've never had a piercing there."

Detective Lansing sighed. "I already did. That's not you on the screen. I was hoping if you saw him, you might know him."

"I don't."

The police tech killed the image. McCall and Lansing moved back through the grocery store out into the street. Lansing took McCall's arm. "I know you're looking for this Equalizer wannabe."

"Three people in that grocery store are dead. That's on me. It's in *my* name."

"Don't take this vigilante down. Let me do my job. *That's* justice."

McCall nodded and walked away.

"Yeah, right," Lansing said softly.

Across the street, he watched Robert McCall walk away from the crime scene. From the back, in their overcoats, they would have looked *identical*. But he felt no strength in this man. Just because he'd advertised as the Equalizer—a white knight ready to do battle for those with nowhere else to turn—that didn't make him a *real* hero. *Anyone* could put an ad like that in the papers and on the internet. But then you had to *follow through*. You had to be the real deal. And *he* was. He hoped Robert McCall wasn't claiming responsibility for what had happened in the grocery store, getting all of the glory.

The Equalizer stepped back into the doorway of a Chubbies pizza-and-chicken place and pulled the overcoat a little tighter around himself in the cold.

He might just have to do something about McCall.

CHAPTER 15

Only four people in the world had Control's private cell phone number: the president of the United States, the head of the Joint Chiefs of Staff, Control's wife, and Robert McCall. Control was the one person who would know what had happened to Granny and Mickey Kostmayer in North Korea. McCall had called Control several times, but there had been no answer. More than that, the automated voice had said the number had been discontinued and there was no new number.

McCall walked into the nondescript building in Virginia, one of six in a rural complex surrounded by trees, right off the highway. No company names were displayed on any of them. In the bland marble lobby McCall approached a desk and was immediately given a badge with his name on it. He was still a *shadow operative* as far as Harvey, the African-American uniformed security officer, was concerned. He'd been on the front reception desk since Desert Storm and knew all of The Company operatives by sight.

But when McCall stepped into the elevator with another security officer, Harvey picked up the phone at his desk.

McCall walked down the corridor on the sixth floor. He knew an operations room was behind one of the doors, with fifty analysts working at their computer stations, digital maps of the world with hot spots glowing in red on big screens. The security officer opened the far door with a key on his belt and ushered McCall inside.

There were three small offices. McCall walked to the center one. He had expected to see Emma Marshall, Control's assistant, sitting at her desk, looking up at him with amused eyes, her blouse always partially unbuttoned, her attitude somewhere between British irony and caustic observation. She had once told him she knew he fancied her, and he'd never denied it, but he had the feeling she thought the intern who delivered the mail, the NRA lobbyist she had been dating, and probably Control himself wanted to get her knickers off.

But Emma wasn't sitting behind her desk outside Control's office.

The young woman there was around thirty, wearing a crisp business suit, long blond hair piled up on her head. She was attractive, but with an Ice Maiden frost to her demeanor. McCall had never seen her before. She smiled at him, but the smile was the Cheshire cat's and would disappear as soon as he'd moved out of her sight.

"Mr. McCall. Welcome back."

"Where's Control's assistant?"

"There was a young woman working at this desk until a month ago. I believe she returned to England. My name is Samantha Gregson. People call me Sam."

McCall moved past her desk.

"You have to have an appointment with—"

"I don't need an appointment to see Control." McCall pushed open the door to Control's office.

It wasn't exactly as McCall remembered it from the last time he had been there. The desk had been to his left—now it was beneath the window in front of him. The shades were up, spilling sunlight across the room. Control had always kept his office like a shadowy nook in some corner of an apocalyptic bunker. A thin green putting strip was on the plush carpet with the hole up on a raised plastic cup at the end. The putter lay to one side. Control didn't need to practice his putting: he had a 4 handicap.

The man standing at the bright window, talking on his cell phone, turned in surprise at McCall's entrance. But he waved him in without hesitation, murmured something into the phone, then dropped it onto the desk.

"Do close the door behind you."

McCall closed it. "This is Control's office."

"That's correct. *My* office. Even a shadow operative needs to let me know he's in the building before he barges in, Robert."

"Don't call me by my first name. We don't know each other."

"Yes, we do," the man said quietly.

He was tall, six-foot-five at least, his wavy black hair streaked with gray. Probably in his midfifties, McCall judged, not an athlete, but not a couch potato. His hands were calloused, so he didn't spend every day behind his desk. Although that didn't mean he ventured into the field. He was dressed as Control would have been, in a dark blue three-piece suit, a red tie with small chess pieces on it, a gold watch, gold cuff links, and a thin gold bracelet on his left wrist, which Control would not have worn.

He came around the untidy desk with his hand outstretched. "Matthew Goddard."

McCall didn't shake hands.

"Why don't you sit down, Robert. You've been away from the fold for a very long time. We have a great deal to talk about."

"The only person I want to talk to is Control."

"I *am* the designated Control at this time. There are others within The Company, and we *do* rotate depending on security, tactical, and health issues, but I have been the Control of this division for some time."

"How long?"

"Two years now."

"Then why haven't you been *my* Control in the field?"

Goddard moved back behind his desk. "I *was* your Control in the field, Mr. McCall, whether you were made aware of that or not. I don't know who you dealt with directly, old son. Do you have this Control's real name? Perhaps I can find out if he's ever worked for this intelligence unit."

"Not many people know his real name."

"But, surely, it will be on record, if he worked here."

McCall felt as if he had walked into a wall. "I was controlled by a man six-foot-one, always immaculately dressed, who wore a distinctive cologne he purchased in the only store that sold it, in Mayfair, London, was ruthless and expedient, but dealt out compassion and wisdom in small doses, and even a couple of well-chosen observations on the human condition on occasion. He worked in this building, in *this office,* for years. His assistant was a saucy London girl who sat at that outer-office desk, and he drinks only very fine Scotch."

Goddard shrugged almost apologetically. "That description doesn't fit anyone who's ever worked here, to my knowledge. Please sit down, Robert. You were a very valuable asset to this Company. An indispensable elitist who would not sacrifice his principles. I know you resigned under difficult circumstances. You felt The Company had betrayed you. But what are you doing with your life? We know you left Bentley's restaurant in SoHo in Manhattan. To be a bartender somewhere else? Or is there a new profession you've chosen? Whatever it is, your skills are being wasted, old son." Goddard leaned forward, his voice vibrant with suppressed urgency. "We need you, Robert. Your country needs you."

McCall just stared at him, then threw open the door.

"Does being the Equalizer really mean something to you?" Goddard had to raise his voice just a little. "Or was that reaching out for some kind of meaning in your life?"

McCall wanted to slam the door, but closed it gently behind him.

At her desk, Samantha looked up at him with glacial eyes. "I did tell you you needed an appointment. Control is very busy today. A lot of hot spots have blown up on the board."

McCall ignored her as he dropped his badge onto her desk and walked out of the office complex. The security officer was waiting to escort him downstairs.

Matthew Goddard opened the door to his office. "Put a tail on him. Make sure it's someone bloody good, because McCall's the best."

Samantha picked up the phone on her desk.

Three McMansions closed off a cul-de-sac in a quiet Arlington neighborhood. All three were two stories with an attic and a long front porch. The architecture of the middle home was modern farmhouse. An overturned bicycle with training wheels was on the front lawn, a skateboard on the porch. Rosemary pines were on one side, separating the house from the one on the left. Seventy-foot butternut trees completely obscured the house on the right. The gravel driveway went straight up to a big garage. McCall had never been to Control's house before, but he'd seen a photograph of it on Control's desk with his old boss standing on the flagstone path with his arm around his fifteen-year-old daughter, Kerry, and his seventeen-year-old daughter, Megan. McCall knew he'd been followed from The Company, but he hadn't shaken the tail. If he brought them right to Control's house, that was fine with him. He figured they were parked somewhere up the street.

McCall got out of his rented Volvo and walked up the flagstone path. Grass strips were on either side of it. On the right-hand strip, McCall noted the grass was trampled down at either end. The front door opened just as McCall climbed up onto the porch. An attractive blonde stepped out, in her midfifties, but with effective use of Botox she looked closer to forty and was probably incapable of wrinkling her brow. She was small and compact, in a cream tracksuit with jewelery and freckles and Reebok ZPumps. Control's wife, whom McCall had met once, was a Brazilian beauty in her fifties with jet-black hair. Behind the small blonde McCall could see a hallway. A large Wimbledon tennis picture took up one wall, with some oblong discolorations on either side of it. He noted a few towels on a chair and some cardboard under a table where mail had been tossed. He could see into a kitchen with a gleaming KitchenAid French-door refrigerator and gas-range convection oven.

The blonde looked surprised to see him. "Can I help you?"

"I'm looking for James Cameron." McCall thought this was the first time he'd ever spoken Control's real name out loud.

"I'm sorry, I don't know who that is."

"He lives here with his wife, Jenny, and two teenage children, his daughters, Kerry and Megan."

"I'm afraid you have the wrong address."

"This is the right address."

The compact blonde forced a tolerant smile onto her face. She leaned down and picked up the skateboard.

"We're the Peterson family, Tom and Marsha. I have to get my youngest son to the dentist right now."

"May I ask how long have you've lived here?"

"Fourteen years. Your friend does not reside in this house. You've obviously been misinformed."

"Sorry to have troubled you."

"No trouble." She closed the door without quite slamming it.

McCall heard her voice shouting, "Get in the car, Evan! We're late!"

McCall walked down the flagstone path. The door of the garage rumbled up. A moment later a red Ford Explorer pulled out, Marsha Peterson at the wheel. A young blond boy was buckled into the backseat. McCall continued walking back toward his rented Volvo. The Explorer drove out of the cul-de-sac and disappeared. McCall stepped through the butternut trees onto the property to the right. It had exactly the same driveway, same grass strips on both sides, the house painted a dark blue with light blue trim. McCall walked up onto the porch and rang the doorbell. He had to ring it a second time before the door finally opened. A tall brunette in her late thirties stood on the threshold. She was wearing jeans, a white shirt, no shoes, and a painting smock with smears of red-violet and green, yellow, white, and deep purple on it. She held a couple of paintbrushes in her hand and also looked surprised to find a stranger on her doorstep.

"I'm sorry to disturb you. Especially if you're painting."

"No problem!" She was a little breathless, having run to get the door. "I'm painting a landscape of the trees in our backyard. We've got such beautiful Muskogee crape trees, a flowering dogwood, some tulip poplars, and even a Dynamite crape myrtle, and when I say *Dynamite,* that's its actual name! Are you here to see my husband?"

"No, I was looking for James Cameron. He lives next door?"

"The Petersons live next door."

"You know how long they've been there?"

"Oh, since God was a pup." She turned and raised her voice. "David, honey, how long have the Petersons lived next door to us? Ten years?"

There was the scrape of a chair, then a dark-haired man, also in his thirties, with a close-cropped beard, dressed in a suit and tie, walked down the corridor from the back.

"At least ten years," he said, looking at McCall curiously. "I just saw Marsha Peterson pull out in her SUV."

McCall ignored him, looking at the man's wife. "So you've seen the Peterson children grow up?"

"Oh, yeah! I gave Marsha her baby shower for Evan, that's their six-year-old. Gary, their teenage son, is at American University in DC."

"Not much time to use his skateboard, I guess. I noticed it on the porch."

"Oh, no, he skateboards up and down that driveway all weekend! Drives us crazy!"

"Who were you looking for?" David asked, a little more pointedly.

His wife turned to him before McCall could respond. "Someone named James Cameron. Do you know that name, hon?"

"Never heard it before."

"I'm Candace Jameson, by the way," she said, turning back to McCall. "I won't shake your hand as I've managed to get paint on my fingers, my smock, probably on my ass, everywhere except on my canvas!"

David glanced at her, as if mildly scandalized.

"How long have you lived here?" McCall asked.

"Sixteen years," Candace said. "Before the Petersons moved in, there was a couple next door, Ginny and Paul, very sweet people, *Dinks*, double income no kids; they moved out and Tom and Marsha moved in with their son Gary, he was four then. Evan came later and was a real surprise, if you know what I mean! A New Year's Eve baby!"

David glanced disapprovingly at his wife again, then looked back at McCall. "You could talk to the Andersons on the other side of the cul-de-sac. They've been here the longest, twenty years I believe."

"So you're all pretty friendly?"

"In a neighbors kind of way," Candace said. "Barbecues on Labor Day weekends, block parties, charity drives. Marsha and I go to the same tennis club. What was the name of your friend again?"

"He's not my friend. Used to be my boss. I must have the wrong address for him. Thanks for your time."

"Not at all." Candace dazzled him with a smile.

Her husband just waited for McCall to leave.

McCall walked over to his rented Volvo, slid behind the wheel, and pulled away from the cul-de-sac.

They'd all been lying.

The Wimbledon tennis picture in the hallway of Control's house had been hung a little off center. The oblong discolorations showed that *other* pictures had been hung there that had been hastily removed. The towels on the chair and pieces of cardboard were used to move furniture around. The appliances McCall had seen through the doorway in the kitchen had been brand-new. And he knew the house had electric cookers, not gas. The bicycle that was overturned in the driveway had training wheels on it. No self-respecting six-year-old would ride a bike with training wheels. The skateboard carefully discarded on the porch was brand-new. If the Petersons' college son still skateboarded up and down the driveway every weekend, the board would have been scuffed up on the edges. Control had told McCall that he parked his Mercedes S-Class sedan on the grass strip on the right of the driveway because so much furniture and boxes and junk were in the garage. That's why the grass where he'd parked it in the center was not damped down.

The next-door neighbors, Candace and David, had been the best. Candace was painting the trees in her backyard. A Dynamite crape myrtle was a deep red color, not the red-violet that was smeared on her painting smock. Her flowering dogwood leaves did not have white blossoms in the autumn, which would have turned red by now. McCall had seen enough Muskogee crape trees to know the blooms were lavender, not deep purple, and the tulip poplar's blooms were gold, not yellow. The smock and the paintbrushes were props. McCall doubted if Candace had ever painted anything more than a wall in her house—which wasn't the one he'd met her in. As for her husband, David, he was packing a 9mm Smith & Wesson compact pistol. His suit jacket had been unbuttoned, and the holster was far back on his hip, but the way the jacket hung on him, McCall had noted the butt of the gun. Since Candace had suggested McCall talk to the "Andersons" in the house on the other side of Control's, he figured they would also be plants.

He felt a chill flood through him. It was one thing for The Company to make Control disappear. It was another for them to make it appear as if *he never existed*.

CHAPTER 16

McCall's iPhone vibrated. He looked at the caller ID and pulled over. He glanced up in the rearview mirror. He didn't see the following car, but he knew they'd have also pulled over.

"This is McCall."

He could barely hear Tara Langley's voice over the pounding music behind it.

"I'm at another of those rave parties. It's in a warehouse down at the Bowery. I followed Blake Cunningham here. If he follows his usual MO, he'll be here for a couple of hours, checking out the babes. This is the first time he's deviated from his mind-numbingly boring routine. Where are you?"

"In Virginia."

"I picked up Melody at Dolls and brought her here, but I haven't let her go inside yet. I need more backup and you're too far away."

"I'll get the backup there. I can be with you in just over an hour."

"So you *do* have a superhero suit under your clothes with a cape."

McCall had to smile. "What's the address of the warehouse?"

Tara gave it to him. He described Mike Gammon to her, hung up, and called Gammon. He got him on the third ring and told him what he needed. McCall expected to have to explain what was happening, but Gammon just asked for the rave party address and Melody's description. Then he hung up. McCall called one more number, then pulled away from the side of the road, and this time he did lose the tailing car.

Hayden Vallance met him at a small airfield on Wakefield Street near Arlington. He had a Citation Mustang private jet waiting on the tarmac. He didn't ask McCall any questions either. He hadn't when he'd flown McCall to Prague some weeks before, where McCall had stopped an assassin from killing the secretary of state and, as a bonus, the president of the United States. Vallance was a mercenary who'd been recommended by Granny. McCall buckled himself into the passenger seat. Vallance stepped into the cockpit and taxied down the tarmac. He flew McCall to Teterboro Airport in Bergen County, New Jersey. Only when he stopped taxiing and brought down the steps for McCall did Vallance ask, "Any word on Granny?"

"No. I'm working on it."

Vallance nodded. McCall took a helicopter to the East Thirty-Fourth Street helicopter terminal. Jimmy was waiting for him in his silver Lexus.

McCall gave him the address of the warehouse. "Thanks for picking me up."

"It's been a slow night." Jimmy drove and tapped into his iPad affixed to the dash. "Norman Rosemont, worth about two billion, lives in a penthouse apartment on Central Park South. His wife, Angie, left him six months ago. They've kept the split quiet. Three grown-up children: the daughter is an actress in Los Angeles, she's on *Game of Thrones*, cool role; two grown-up sons, both in business, one in Chicago, the other in Miami. No one calls Dad a lot. Rosemont has had a couple of girlfriends, but nothing that lasts beyond the kiss, grope, and *hasta la vista* stage. Kind of a sad guy, for all of his millions."

"Not as sad as the tenants in his slum buildings. I may need you as a chauffeur again."

"Anytime."

There was no more to say. There never was with McCall. Jimmy dropped him at the warehouse in the Bowery. McCall could hear the faint pounding of the rock music. The warehouse looked like it had been erected at the same time Five Points was the center of New York. He followed a stretch limo around to the back, where the music vibrated loudly through three open entrances. Late teens scrambled out of the back of the limo, the guys in tuxes with carnations in their buttonholes, the girls wearing short dresses. They were greeted by the rave party bodyguards. This time, instead of hideous burn masks, they were wearing dead president's masks. Nixon, Ford, and LBJ seemed to be the favorites. McCall didn't think it was an improvement. He followed the teenagers into the prom from hell. Inside were open spaces, broken up by tall plants and some Chinese screens. This time, big LED screens were everywhere, pulsating with psychedelic colors synchronized to the music. The old warehouse had three levels, all of them packed with revelers.

McCall spotted Melody standing at a table with Blake Cunningham. She was dressed in one of the shimmering blue dresses she wore at Dolls. She had a glass of champagne in one hand and appeared to be completely at ease. Blake was dressed in an Armani black Tonal Pindot wool suit with a mauve shirt, from which his 411 aviator sunglasses hung. He was doing the heavy verbal lifting. He was charming, nothing at all like the cobra McCall had promised Melody. But his eyes told a different story. They stripped Melody of her dress, then of her underwear, then of her skin, and examined the bones and tissues and nerves beneath. It was the look of a predator.

There was a tug on McCall's arm. Tara Langley put a glass of merlot into McCall's hand. She raised her own glass to her lips. "Just for appearances sake. If you stand around at a party like this without a drink, they toss you out."

"How long did it take Blake to pick up on Melody?"

"Five minutes tops. She looked a little lost, first time in New York, and her date didn't show. Blake stepped right in. Are you *sure* this nightclub dancer of yours is from a small town in the Midwest? She's got all of the innocence and naïveté, but she's wrapping our Wolf of Wall Street around her little finger."

"She tells me she's good at that."

"There's no sign of Blake's college thugs. He appears to be working solo tonight."

"Where's Mike Gammon?"

"In his Toyota Prius at the side entrance to the warehouse. If Blake tries to take Melody out that way, he'll be waiting." Tara looked at McCall's face. "You think Emily Masden's dead, don't you?"

"You haven't seen her with Blake since I put the bug on him. I haven't heard a word from her."

"You didn't answer my question."

"I don't know the answer. Did you report in to Emily's mother?"

"Yeah, I told her I was getting closer to finding her daughter. Told her not to give up hope."

"But you have?"

"Not when I'm with you."

Something had caught McCall's eye. A stooped young man in a green Army coat stood at one of the buffet tables. He wore a black hoodie, torn jeans, faded black Adidas, and wore small loop earrings in both ears. Mc-Call caught just a glimpse of the scraggly dark hair and the pale eyes without eyebrows. Isaac had helped himself to two plates piled high with hors d'oeuvres. He was stuffing them into the pockets of his coat.

"I need to talk to that guy."

Tara followed his gaze. "He's a little creepy. That's the third plate of food he's helped himself to."

"His name's Isaac. He's homeless."

"Why should you care?"

"He may have information I need."

"About Emily?"

"No." He looked back over at Melody and Blake. "If he starts to leave with her . . ."

"I've got the receiver you gave me. If she gets into his car, I'll be right behind them with Mike. I also gave Melody my cell phone number. I could take Blake down without breaking a nail, which is good, as I just got Cross My Heart Sinful Red put on them, but your friend Gammon looks like he chews concrete and shits bricks."

"He's an ex–Brooklyn cop. Make sure you don't lose sight of Melody."

McCall pushed through the crowd toward where Isaac stood near one of the entrances. Richard Nixon had just let in a young couple and appeared to be leering at the girl, although to be fair, that was probably the mask. LBJ grabbed another girl's ass as she passed and she giggled. McCall moved right up to Isaac and touched his arm.

The young man jumped as if he'd been electrocuted. "Hey, hi there, yeah, wow, you come to shindigs like this?"

"Obviously you do."

"Sure, man, I keep track of these parties. Free booze, free food. I can usually get a week's good eating out of one of them."

"You left your alleyway before I could ask you any more questions."

"Nothing more to say."

"I think you know the guy who beat up those gangbangers."

A sudden haunted look was in Isaac's eyes. He tried to make his voice casual. "What makes you think so?"

"Experience. So you can tell me right now, or I can take you outside and beat the information out of you." McCall thought that was a tad overly dramatic, but it was the kind of threat Isaac would respond to.

Isaac nodded, his face screwed up as if in pain. "I might have something for you."

"What is it?"

"Maybe a name."

"Whose name?"

At that moment a fairly inebriated blonde dropped a tray of champagne glasses. Isaac took the opportunity to bolt from the table, grabbing more hors d'oeuvres to stuff into his coat pockets. McCall started after him, then turned. Tara mouthed the words, *I got this*. McCall turned back in time to see Isaac push his way to one of the open entrances out of the warehouse.

McCall went outside after him. It was misting rain. He saw Isaac's running figure turn off Clinton Street into an alleyway between two more warehouses. McCall heard the homeless man suddenly cry out, then the sound of his body hitting the ground. McCall ran into the alleyway. Four men were gathered around Isaac on the ground. They were white, dressed in heavy coats, dark jeans, all of them wearing black hoodies. Two of them were kicking Isaac in the ribs. A third was dragging off Isaac's Army coat and taking the food out of the pockets. The fourth had an Army boot pressed down against Isaac's throat to keep him on the ground. It wasn't necessary. Isaac had curled up into a fetal position, his hands covering his face, whimpering.

The two men who'd been trying to break Isaac's ribs turned as McCall ran forward. They were big. The one closest to McCall noted his age and broke into a smile that revealed several teeth missing. He grabbed for McCall's coat. McCall knocked out several more of his teeth with one punch and kicked his legs out from under him. The second mugger picked up a length of pipe lying beside a row of old-fashioned metal trash cans. McCall disarmed him in two moves and slammed the pipe into his right knee, hard enough to bring him down, but not to shatter the kneecap. The mugger who'd been going through Isaac's coat lunged for McCall. McCall picked up one of the trash-can lids, smashed it into the mugger's face, then executed a knife-hand strike to his throat. He started gasping for breath. McCall threw him bodily into the trash cans.

The fourth mugger took his foot off Isaac's throat. A knife blade in his hand caught the oblique light in the alleyway. It flashed for McCall's throat.

Robert McCall hesitated.

For a split second he saw Anita Delgado standing outside the ICU at Bellevue. "What kind of animal are you?" she'd asked him. Her son would never be able to see again. "Is *that* the kind of justice you're dispensing, Mr. *Equalizer?*"

McCall shut her out and twisted his head away from the knife.

Too late.

The blade sliced across the side of his neck, spurting blood. McCall ignored the sudden pain. He grabbed the mugger's knife hand, got in two quick shots to his kidneys, and wrenched his right wrist at the same time. The knife spun out of his hand and clattered onto the concrete. McCall kicked him in the balls and threw him also into the trash cans. He hit the concrete and rolled over into the same fetal position as Isaac.

None of the muggers got to their feet.

McCall put a hand to his neck. His fingers came away sticky with blood. He took out a handkerchief, pressed it against the knife wound, and knelt down. Isaac's eyes were closed tight. He was still whimpering, anticipating the next kick to his ribs. McCall took hold of his shoulders.

"Isaac! It's okay! Open your eyes!"

The homeless man blinked in the fine drizzle, looking up at McCall. He stopped whimpering and McCall literally dragged him up to his feet. He swayed, but remained upright.

"I'm going to get you to an ER. You may have some broken ribs."

Isaac shook his head, mumbling, "No hospital."

McCall picked up Isaac's Army coat and handed it to him. Enough food was still in the bulging pockets for at least a three-day feast. Isaac shrugged on the coat, looking at the men lying beside the trash cans.

"Do you know them?"

Isaac shook his head. His voice was raspy and choked with pain. "'A proud look, a lying tongue, and hands that shed innocent blood.' Proverbs six:seventeen."

"You had a name for me! The man who beat up those gangbangers."

Isaac looked back at McCall and smiled. "The way you beat up *these* guys." Then he frowned, concerned. "Your neck is bleeding."

McCall shook him. "The *name*, Isaac!"

Isaac blinked and nodded. "We call him DM. Demolition Man. He's like a crime fighter. Patrols the streets. Calls himself something else now."

McCall let Isaac go. "The Equalizer."

"Yeah, that's it. New name, same dude. He's a badass."

Another subliminal memory assailed McCall. He was sitting in his new digs at the Liberty Belle Hotel, after he'd placed his ad, listening to fifteen phone messages. He remembered a low, husky voice: *Hey, Equalizer, I'm DM—Demolition Man. I protect the streets of Manhattan. I patrol the area between . . .*

McCall had moved on to the next voice message.

He looked back at Isaac. "What do you know about this—"

Isaac's eyes widened. McCall sensed the attack in the same moment. He whirled to see the first mugger he'd thrown into the trash cans coming at him with the knife he'd picked up from the cement. McCall sidestepped the blade and took the knife right out of the mugger's hand. McCall threw his arm around the man's throat, holding him in a viselike grip. He thought of breaking his neck, but then thought about Sofia Reyes and Anita Delgado. Instead he applied pressure until the mugger stopped writhing and lost consciousness. McCall dropped him to the ground. None of the others came to his aid. McCall walked over to the crumbling brick wall behind the trash cans, jammed the knife blade into a crevice, and snapped it off. Then he turned back.

Isaac was gone.

CHAPTER 17

President Carter welcomed McCall back to the rave party. So not *all* dead presidents. The bleeding on McCall's neck had stopped, but the bloodred knife scar was vivid and ugly. He pushed through the revelers toward the table where he'd seen Melody standing with Blake Cunningham. They were gone. So was Tara Langley. McCall made his way to the side exit guarded by

President Bill Clinton. He graciously stepped aside to let McCall pass. Mc-Call had always liked him. Outside it was still drizzling. No Toyota Prius was parked at the curb. McCall could only hope that meant Mike Gammon and Tara had followed Blake and Melody when they'd left.

A silver Lexus pulled up. Jimmy purred down the driver's window. "I didn't like the look of this place. Decided to stick around. I was worried you might get sexually assaulted by some babe in a Lady Gaga outfit."

"Spock says . . ." McCall murmured. He slid into the passenger seat.

Jimmy pulled away from the curb. "Spock says what?"

"There are always possibilities. When she's away from her Lady Gaga alter ego, I have a feeling Stefani Germanotta is a very sweet Italian girl."

Jimmy looked closer at him. "What happened to your neck?"

"I got distracted. Drop me off at the corner of Forty-Second and Lex."

"What's there, besides Grand Central?"

"I need to visit an old friend."

The silence in the car was thick. McCall was worried about Melody. He didn't like not knowing where she was. He checked his iPhone. No text from Tara. Fifteen minutes later Jimmy pulled over to the corner of Lexington and Forty-Second.

"Can you wait for me?" McCall asked.

"I live to serve."

McCall got out and walked up Forty-Second Street. Jimmy's iPhone beeped. A text message from his wife: *Bring home wine, eggs, and cereal.* When he looked up, McCall had vanished.

McCall climbed down the iron ladder. He knew the manhole cover at this location was not secured tightly, but even so, it took him a few moments to slide it to one side and back again. He jumped down from the bottom of the ladder into the sewer tunnel. Rusting red pipes and two newer blue ones stretched away into darkness in both directions. Work lights cast a pale radiance. McCall wasn't sure he'd know the way from here, but he had a blueprint in his mind. He transversed an old subway tunnel, climbed up a two-foot wall to a familiar iron door that led into the vaulted space that had the mural of the Williamsburg Bridge with the little girl and her mother in a vast field of daisies. McCall noted that the golden retriever had finally been painted at the little girl's feet. Probably Fooz's work.

It only took McCall twenty minutes to find his place. The wide tunnel niche was decorated like a Victorian parlor straight out of a *Strand Magazine* illustration of a Sherlock Holmes story. The rolltop desk had empty minibottles of vodka and gin strewn across it. All of the Victorian Chloe Amore table lamps were off. The large circa-1995 TV was on, showing one of the new *Sherlock* TV episodes with no sound. Fooz was sitting bleary eyed on his Lucinda sleigh bed. He had a syringe in his hand, a piece of plastic tubing wound around his forearm, and was about to plunge the needle into his vein.

McCall slapped the syringe out of the old black man's hands and unwrapped the plastic tubing. He slapped Fooz across the face to bring him closer to clarity. His eyes cleared a little.

"Mr. McCall," he mumbled, barely forming the two words.

"It's bad enough you drink yourself into a stupor!" McCall shouted at him. "Now you're going to shoot heroin into your body?"

"It's the damn rush," the old man whispered. "Ain't gettin' it with the booze no more." He flinched, as if expecting McCall to hit him again.

McCall shook him instead. "What the hell's the matter with you? You've been down in these tunnels forty years. What's different now?"

"Loneliness. Didn't realize I'd miss Candy Annie as much as I do. She was like a daughter to me, forget the skin color. Got other friends down here, but I don't see much of 'em. It's a big neighborhood," he added ironically. "When I sit here for too long, sometimes the monster comes out of its cage."

McCall let go of him. "What were you going to take?"

"Fella called it a Blue Velvet."

"You know what that is?"

"No, sir."

"Elixir terpin hydrate with codeine and tripelennamine. It's a weak heroin substitute."

"He told me it was the real deal."

"It's bad enough. You ever shoot up before?"

"No, sir."

McCall picked up the syringe and smashed it against the low coffee table. "You want to OD in this sewer tunnel under the streets, don't do it on my time. I need your help. Do I have to stay here to sober you up?"

"No, sir. I'll be right as rain. What can I do for you?"

"I need Morgan Freeman."

"He ain't available. Guess you got me."

McCall told him what he wanted. The flicker of the TV screen played across Fooz's face. McCall wasn't sure Fooz had even heard him. McCall got to his feet and left the old black man to struggle with his demons. It *was* a lonely struggle. McCall knew that only too well. He retraced his steps back to the iron ladder and climbed up to Forty-Second Street. If anyone took any notice of him popping up from a manhole cover, no one reacted. These were New Yorkers. McCall walked quickly to where Jimmy was now parked beside a fire hydrant and slid into the passenger seat.

"Where'd you go?" Then Jimmy looked at McCall's face and decided not to press it. "Where to, boss?"

"You know where Brahms's Manhattan Electronics is?"

"Sure, I stop by once in a while to see how the old spy is doing. I hear his wife is real sick."

"She is."

"Is she going to make it?"

"I don't know. I need to talk to Brahms."

"I can drop you."

Jimmy pulled out into traffic.

Helen Coleman was sitting at the desk in her home office talking to her son Tom, via Skype, when her cell phone beeped to let her know she had a text. It was seven hours later in Istanbul, which made it the middle of the night, but Tom was burning the midnight oil for his studies. He was eight years younger than Josh, with a thin face, wild brown hair, brilliant green eyes, and an academic intensity that had brought him straight As all through high school. He was studying Arabic at the Istanbul Sehir University, specifically at its School of Islamic Studies. He'd always been an emotional child. At eighteen, he was more balanced, but Helen could see it was hard for him to contain his grief. Tom had idolized his older brother.

"I'm coming home on the first flight I can get," he told his mother.

Helen shook her head. "I haven't heard back from the Pentagon. There's some kind of a delay in bringing back"—she paused, almost unable to say the terrible words—"Josh's remains."

"But they *have* them, right? I mean, they *know* he was killed, right?"

"That's what the two-star general told me. But the colonel who accompanied him wasn't his CO in the field."

"What are you saying?"

Helen sighed. "Just that it was odd. There's no need for you to interrupt your studies to fly back yet."

"I'm not going to let you deal with this alone, Helen." Tom had called his mother Helen since he'd been four years old. At first it had startled his parents, but then they'd accepted it, and now it was as much of an endearment as *Mother*. "They *are* going to bury him in Arlington National Cemetery, right?"

"Yes, with full military honors. They're awarding him the Purple Heart and the Silver Star posthumously."

Her son lost his battle. Big tears rolled down his cheeks. "I have to get through my midterm exams." He brushed away the tears with an impatient hand. "They'll be done on Friday. Then I'm coming home."

Her cell phone beeped at her. "Fuck this thing!" she exclaimed.

Tom said automatically, "Language, Helen," and smiled through his tears.

"I'm expecting a text from work."

"Don't they ever leave you alone?"

"It's the UN, honey. One hundred and ninety-three nations. One of them is always threatening to kick the shit out of another one."

She picked her phone up and looked at the caller ID.

Her entire body stiffened.

She set the phone down and looked back at the laptop screen.

"I've got to go, Tommy. We'll Skype again tomorrow, okay?"

"Okay. Be strong. That's what Josh would want. Save the tears for the funeral."

"I will if you will."

Tom smiled ruefully as two more tears ran down his cheeks. "Yeah, just follow my lead. Talk to you tomorrow, Helen."

Tom's face faded from the laptop screen. Helen picked up her cell phone and tapped into the text. When she read it, her sense of sudden elation—of sudden *hope*—was replaced with bewilderment.

She searched her desk until she found the piece of paper with Robert McCall's phone number on it.

McCall sat with Brahms in his darkened office at the back of Manhattan Electronics. He could hear the small sounds of items in the store being moved around. The store was closed, but Mary was doing some stocktaking. McCall thought she used every excuse she could think of to be close to her boss for a comforting word while his wife lay critically ill in hospital. Brahms was working on his desktop computer, fingers flying over the keys, writing some kind of algorithm. Mary stepped into the office. She was dressed in a tight black skirt and beige blouse that clung to her petite and quite spectacular figure. She wore her dark Diane von Furstenberg tortoise-shell glasses even though it was gloomy in the store.

"I don't want to throw out an heirloom," Mary said, "but do we *really* need to keep an eight-track player with AM/FM radio on a bottom shelf?"

"Belongs to Hilda," he said without looking up from the screen.

"Going right back." Mary smiled at McCall and disappeared.

"She loves you like a father," McCall said.

"Hilda couldn't have children," Brahms said softly, as if responding to a question that McCall hadn't asked. He sat back. "Done. Seven o'clock tomorrow morning your man Norman Rosemont will be off-line."

"Thanks, Brahms."

McCall's iPhone on the table vibrated. He looked at the caller ID and picked up.

"This is Robert McCall."

Helen asked, "Can you meet me at our table in Times Square in twenty minutes?"

Times Square was jammed with people. McCall watched Helen Coleman stride through them with her usual purposeful demeanor. Something about her was immensely likable. Even in her grief her warmth shone through. At least, it did to McCall.

She sat down at the table. "What have you been able to find out?"

"Nothing yet. The one contact I had that could have told me the truth about the circumstances of your son's death has vanished. Literally into thin air. You've got something?"

Helen took out her cell phone and double-tapped the LED screen into life. "I got a text from Josh's satellite phone half an hour ago. But I don't know what it means."

McCall picked up the phone and looked at the text.

He knew exactly what it meant. "This doesn't mean Josh is alive."

"I know that. Someone else could have picked up his phone. But how? It would be in the safekeeping of the Army. And why send *me* a text?" She leaned forward and gripped McCall's arm. "Unless it *was* Josh who sent it. A message he wanted only *me* to see."

McCall turned the phone around and tapped the screen.

On it was displayed *35° 45′ 00.60″ N—38° 22′ 56.60″ E.*

"It's the latitude and longitude of a location."

"Do you know where?"

McCall accessed the internet and found the coordinates.

"Syria. It's close to the coordinates of Aleppo."

"But if it *is* from Josh, why is he sending it to me?"

"Because he doesn't want anyone else to know where he is. Or he'd have sent it to the Pentagon, or to your colonel friend, what was his name again?"

"Colonel Michael G. Ralston; everyone calls him Gunner."

"And you still haven't been able to get in touch with Gunner?"

"He hasn't called me back, and he's one of the good guys."

"He may be under orders not to get in touch with you. And he may not know the truth."

"What could that truth be?" Helen squeezed McCall's arm, not quite cutting off all circulation. "Can you find out?"

"Only by going there."

She let him go, shaking her head. "You don't work for the UN for as long as I have, liaising with the Pentagon, and not know the guidelines. If that location is in Syria, they'd never let you get anywhere near it."

"I won't be asking their permission."

She stared at him. "You would really fly to Syria to try to find my son?"

"Yes."

"Fuck, yeah. Language, sorry. When can you go?"

"I have some arrangements to make first. Send this text to my phone."

Helen sent him the coordinates.

"Who else knows about this?"

"I was on Skype with my other son, Tom, earlier tonight. He's eighteen, studying Arabic at the Sehir University in Istanbul. The text came through while I was talking to him."

"Did you tell him what it was?"

"No, I thought it was from the UN. I haven't showed this to anyone but you."

"Keep it to yourself. I'll call you. But don't get your hopes up. These could be rerouted coordinates from someone else or a kid picking up Josh's satellite phone and playing around."

Helen pocketed her cell phone. She reached out and clasped McCall's hand. "Josh *is* alive. I can feel it. And that's not just a mother's intuition. It's something deeper than that. Find him for me, Mr. McCall. *Please*."

Then she let go of his hand, stood up, and strode away.

McCall lost her in the crowd.

CHAPTER 18

McCall walked into the lobby of the Liberty Belle Hotel. Chloe was behind the reception counter dealing patiently with a florid guest who said "Honey!" to her like he was ordering it. Sam Kinney came around the counter and walked over to McCall.

"Hey, what happened to your neck? Cut yourself shaving?"

McCall ignored that. "I need you to do a job for me. Probably take a day to set up. Can you take time away from the hotel?"

"Sure. You gonna let me know what this is all about, if I'm gonna get shot at again, or will it all be a fun surprise?"

"I'll brief you when the time comes."

"I look forward. There's *another* babe here to see you. This one wouldn't wait in the lobby. I let her into your suite. I figure you'd either shout at me or tip me."

McCall moved into the elevator and ascended.

"You're very welcome," Sam Kinney said.

McCall entered his seventeenth-floor suite. The lights were out in the living room, but the curtains at the big windows were open. A square of light was coming from the bedroom. McCall heard the small, thrumming sound of a hairdryer. He touched the Mark Newman sculpture of the naked sea nymph walking an eel on a leash as he walked past it. Kostmayer's favorite. McCall entered the bedroom.

The far bedside table lamp was on. Tara's clothes were strewn casually on top of the bed. Light spilled from the bathroom through the open doorway, where the sound of the hairdryer was louder. Then it snapped off. Tara walked out into the bedroom. She was wearing one of McCall's dress blue shirts, one button in the middle holding it together. The swell of her breasts threatened to pop it. Her long legs glowed in the shadows. Her hair was still a little damp. She smiled at him.

"I decided to take a shower while I waited for you. I wanted to get rid of the smell of pot smoke and red wine and too many sweaty people crowded into that big space."

"Where's Melody?"

Tara looked at him appraisingly. "A fairly attractive woman, maybe eight on a one-to-ten scale, steps out of your bathroom clad only in one of your shirts and you want to talk shop. Okay. Melody left with Blake

Cunningham not long after you ran out of the place. He called her a cab and took her home to her apartment building on Eighth Avenue and Jane Street. He walked her to her front door. He was the consummate gentleman. Got a big good-night kiss out of her and that was it. She walked inside and he hailed another cab and was gone. I watched the lights come on in her third-floor apartment. I waited with Mike Gammon in his car for another forty-five minutes. The lights went out in Melody's apartment. Blake did not come back. I asked Mike to drop me off here at the Liberty Belle. I tried to call you, but you didn't pick up your cell."

"I was in the subway tunnels below the streets. There's no cell coverage down there."

"The subway tunnels? Sure, why not? I thought I'd have to bribe the hotel manager to get up to your suite, but he liked the idea of my waiting in here. He thinks you need to get laid."

"He worries about the national debt, too."

She saw the thin livid knife scar across his neck. She moved right up to him and her fingers gently traced it. He winced a little.

"Sorry. What happened? I hope the other guy is in an ER somewhere fighting for his life."

"Isaac got jumped by some muggers. I chased them away."

"How did you let one of them get close enough to cut you?"

"I was careless."

"Did you get the information you needed from Isaac?"

"I got a name. It's something."

"Since I'm almost naked, you could at least take off your coat."

She unbuttoned McCall's jacket. As she slid it off and tossed it onto the bed, she noted the heaviness of the gun in one pocket.

Then she looked up into his eyes. "Are you going to make me do all the heavy lifting?"

McCall unbuttoned the single button on the blue shirt. Tara shrugged it off onto the floor. She moved naked into his arms and kissed him. He kissed her back. She broke the embrace and stepped back to give him a better look at her body.

If the bathroom door hadn't been open, he wouldn't have seen it.

The barest shadow moved across the steamy mirror.

McCall shoved Tara to the floor. The sound of the gunshot was deafening. The bullet missed McCall's ear by an inch. It hit the one lamp that was on, shattering it. Tara dragged McCall's jacket off the bed and threw it to him. McCall caught it, took out the Glock 19, and moved to the bedroom doorway. He just caught sight of the front door swinging shut.

McCall ran across the suite and threw open the door. The elevator door was closing. McCall ran down the seventeen flights of stairs, taking some of them two at a time. He reached the ground level and ran down the short corridor to the lobby.

It was deserted.

McCall ran out onto Sixty-Sixth Street. There was no sign of the shooter. McCall put the Glock into his pocket and walked back inside the hotel. Chloe was behind the reception counter now.

"Did you see anyone in the lobby? Ten minutes ago he would have walked to the elevator. A minute ago he would have run from the elevator through the lobby to the street."

"I didn't see anyone, Mr. McCall. I had to leave the desk for a few minutes. Is something wrong?"

"Everything's fine."

"Should I call Sam?"

"He needs his beauty sleep."

McCall took the elevator up to the seventeenth floor. When he walked back into his suite, Tara was dressed and waiting for him in the living room. She had a glass of brandy in her hand.

"I helped myself."

"You can pour one for me."

But she didn't. McCall nodded. *Nothing like being shot at to break the spell of the moment.*

"Did you get a glimpse of him?"

"He was long gone by the time I got outside."

"One of Blake's college buddies?"

"Blake doesn't know who I am or where I live. He still thinks I'm Emily's father, who probably went home to the Midwest a month ago."

"So you have no idea who just tried to kill you? I doubt that bullet was meant for me. The only people who hate me are my landlord and my accountant."

"I have an idea who it was."

Tara threw back the brandy in one swallow. She picked up her leather jacket from the couch and shrugged it on.

"I'll check up on Blake on the receiver. Find out where he is. Probably at home. I'll continue to follow him tomorrow morning. If anything breaks, I'll call you."

No mention of the kiss or the naked encounter. McCall doubted she was embarrassed by it. It just wasn't part of the night any longer. But Tara did smile reassuringly at him.

"We're going to find Emily," she said with quiet determination.

Then she left him alone in his suite.

Norman Rosemont liked getting to his office early in the morning. He put a sheaf of documents into his Coughlin leather attaché case on his desk. He could have scanned them and sent them to Chicago, but he liked to have the hard copies with him. Soon he'd have a 29 percent merger with Webstar Telecommunications that would net him a cool $17 million. Not bad for a day trip to the Windy City. *Trump that!* he thought. He was grinning as he fired up his desktop computer.

The grin froze on his face like a rictus smile on a Halloween pumpkin.

His array of desktop icons were gone. In their place was a death's-head skull, bright orange in the empty eye sockets. A little ironic tune played Brahms's Three Motets for Four and Eight-Part Chorus a cappella, *Ach, arme Welt,* not that Rosemont recognized it. Beneath the eerie death's-head appeared the English translation: *Ah, Shallow World.*

Above the skull were the words, in bright orange, YOU'VE BEEN HACKED.

Rosemont hit various computer keys, but nothing happened. He unplugged his computer, plugged it in again, typed in his password, and the same sepulchral skull mocked him. He crossed the office and threw open his door. His assistant Mark leapt to his feet. Rosemont could see the *same* death's-head skull was on *his* computer screen.

"This is on all of the computers, sir."

"Get the tech guys in here right now!" Rosemont shouted. "I haven't got time for this crap. I've got to catch a plane to Chicago. If our own techs can't get past whatever firewalls this asshole has put up, call that specialist company we talked to a few months ago, what was their name?"

"Cyber Solutions, sir."

"Yeah, them." Rosemont strode back to his desk and slammed shut his briefcase. "Damn good thing I've got the merger contracts right in here." He picked up his briefcase and stalked back to his open office door. "Get the Uber car here now! Make sure this hacker is *off* our company systems by the time I get back into the city tonight."

"I'll take care of it, Mr. Rosemont."

Rosemont strode to the main reception area and a bank of elevators. Mark picked up the phone on his desk and dialed the limo company. He stared at the menacing death's-head on his screen, which played some classical composer's tune that was as jarring as fingernails down a blackboard. He could see some nerdy hacker putting in an ironic musical riff from the Grateful Dead or Armageddon or Black Sabbath.

But who the hell composed *Ach, arme Welt*?

When McCall walked into Bentley's Bar & Grill it felt like he was visiting an old friend. The place was packed for lunch. Two of the servers came hurrying over and gave McCall a hug. Gina, an actress with sorrowful eyes, said, "You're back," like Arnold in *The Terminator*. Amanda, looking as sepulchral as ever, her hair a raven red today, said, "You're back," but it conveyed the idea that she'd like to take McCall back to her place and ravage his body. Brahms had decided her place was a coffin in a crypt in some Manhattan church.

Sherry, the ebullient Asian hostess, ran over. "It's *so* good to see you, Bobby! Tell me you want your old job back!"

McCall smiled. He had taken a bartending job at Bentley's after he'd quit The Company and disappeared off the radar. Andrew Ladd, the young head bartender, had taught him how to mix drinks with style. No one at Bentley's had anything to do with his other life of betrayal and duplicity and death. They were just happy to see him again.

Hayden Vallance was waiting for McCall at the bar. He motioned for another greyhound, which Andrew Ladd brought over. When he saw McCall, he smiled with genuine affection.

"Great to see you, Bobby."

"How's your play coming along?"

"I'm reworking the second act. You know, we could use a hand behind the bar."

"Some other time, Laddie," McCall said. "But if you're really short-handed, I may have someone for you."

"If it's your recommendation, they're in."

Amanda set a tray of empty glasses right beside Hayden Vallance and did four hand signals for Laddie before she rushed off. McCall slid onto a barstool and translated for Vallance. "Sex on the Beach, Bloody Mary, and two vodka gimlets."

"You used to bartend here?"

"For about a year."

"I guess it was as good a place as any to disappear."

McCall slid across a piece of paper to Vallance. "These are the coordinates. I need you to fly me there, no questions asked."

"Did I ask questions the last time we went abroad?"

"No, you didn't. But this location is trickier to get in and out. What's your usual fee?"

"Fifty K."

Laddie set Amanda's drinks order onto a new tray. She came back, grabbed the tray, looked Vallance over, gave him a seductive smile, and moved back into the fray.

"Don't even think about it," McCall said. "She's very high maintenance."

"Can't be higher than my first wife. She was a USAR drill sergeant in an Echo Company. You breathed the wrong way and she had you drop and give her fifty."

Vallance opened the piece of paper, looked at the coordinates, closed it. "If it was anyone else, I'd charge double my fee. But not for you, McCall."

"Getting into the country may be easier than getting out."

"Fifty K gets you to those coordinates on a one-way ticket. Getting to an extraction point is on you."

"I figured."

Vallance drank the second greyhound and slid off the barstool. "I've been asked to go to Uzbekistan. The OSCE Office for Human Rights have accused the government there of unlawful termination of human life and denying citizens freedom of assembly and expression. A rebel faction needs some serious players."

"So you're still a mercenary for hire?"

"I like to think of myself as a gunfighter getting a telegraph to go to Deadwood."

"How long will it take you to arrange the transport?"

"A couple of days. I'll call you."

Vallance walked out of Bentley's.

Laddie leaned across the bar. "Someone from your old life?"

"A reminder of why I left it," McCall said quietly.

Then he thought again about Emily Masden, frightened and alone somewhere in the city, *if* she was still alive, and realized he hadn't left it very far.

Norman Rosemont walked out of the terminal at JFK at 8:05 p.m., clutching his leather briefcase with the documents in it, all signed, sealed, and delivered. He should have been on cloud nine. But his computer system's being hacked had robbed all of the triumph from the day. He'd made six frustrating calls from Chicago back to his office to discover that his tech guys, *and* the tech guys from Cyber Solutions, had all failed miserably. All of his computers still had the same grinning death's-head on them. He was royally pissed. His company had already lost God knew how many millions in one day with all of his systems off-line.

He hadn't been sure which flight he was going to take back to New York, so he hadn't ordered a car. Normally he'd have gone to the Russian Tea Room for a celebration with some babe from an escort service, but he didn't feel like celebrating. Then he noted a stretch limo at the curb and a chauffeur in a black suit carrying a sign that read MR. NORMAN ROSEMONT. Rosemont frowned. He walked over to the chauffeur.

"I'm Norman Rosemont. Who ordered this?"

"Compliments of Mr. Jim Sterling, sir."

Rosemont almost smiled. Jim Sterling was the CEO of Webstar Telecommunications, which had merged this afternoon with Rosemont's subsidiary Digital Communications Network. The chauffeur opened the back door.

"Mr. Sterling has also provided you with some company, sir."

Now Rosemont *did* smile. This was a welcome surprise. He slid into the back of the limo. The chauffeur slid behind the wheel and pulled away from the curb.

In the back Rosemont found a gorgeous babe in her twenties, petite but with a spectacular figure, dressed in a long black cocktail dress showing a lot of cleavage. A slit up one side revealed a tantalizing expanse of bare leg. A small jeweled bag was beside her. She was holding a glass of champagne, which she handed to him. She had on Diane von Furstenberg tortoiseshell glasses. She took them off, revealing gorgeous brown eyes, and smiled at him. It was enough for Rosemont to get an immediate hard-on.

"Where to, sir?" Jimmy asked.

"Russian Tea Room. Can you raise up the partition?"

"Sure thing, sir."

Jimmy raised the window, shutting off the back of the limo.

Mary looked at Rosemont with frank appraisal. "Mr. Sterling tells me you like to play a lot of kinky games."

She leaned in and kissed him. There was a lot of tongue action on Rosemont's part. He plunged his hand down into her cleavage, grabbing hold of her bare right breast, no room for a bra in this dress, and squeezed her nipple hard. Mary gave a little gasp, unbuckled his belt, and reached in for him. Now it was his turn to shudder. She broke the embrace and whispered in his ear, "Take off your shoes."

Rosemont leaned down, starting to untie his right shoelace.

Mary took a hypodermic syringe out of her jeweled bag and stabbed him in the neck, pressing the sedative into his vein.

Norman Rosemont shuddered again, this time with an icy cold, and the world fled away until all that was left was utter darkness.

CHAPTER 19

They made love as fiercely as they ever had, but with poignancy this time. They both knew it would be their last in Monrovia. Dr. Patrick Cross climaxed and Ann Crosby shuddered as the ecstasy swept through her. Cross rolled off Ann's body. Both of them were perspiring freely in the humidity. Cross ran his hand lightly over Ann's right hip. His fingers strayed across her buttocks.

She snuggled closer to him. "You know what I was just thinking about?"

"What a fantastic lover I am and how you can't get enough of me?"

She smiled. "That's what I *should* have been thinking about. I was worrying about lopinavir/ectonairre."

"The HIV medicine? How romantic."

"Dr. Ryan had a meltdown Thursday about what's happening in South Africa. He said AbbVie markets LPV/r and are very protective of their product. There *are* generic versions of the drug, but patients are being turned away from hospitals in Johannesburg and told to purchase LPV/r on the private market, which they can't afford."

"Dr. Ryan always has some cause to champion," Dr. Cross said.

"People are going to die."

"We save the lives we can."

"But *you* can do more than that. You can save *thousands* of lives. That's why your project is so important. Do you have the vials ready to take with you?"

"I'm all set. I'm just afraid of being stopped at the airport."

"No one's going to search your med kit. You're with Doctors Without Borders, for God's sake. You're taking samples home to Atlanta to deliver to the CDC headquarters for further analysis. You're going to make a break-through, Patrick. You're going to change the lives of so many people." Then she whispered, "I don't want you to leave."

He stroked her brown hair, tracing his fingers over her forehead, disturbing her pageboy bangs.

"I can't delay going home. There's nothing Dr. Ryan would like more than for me to extend my tour. But I have responsibilities."

"Will you tell your wife about us?"

The question kicked Dr. Cross in the stomach, even though he'd been expecting it.

Ann hugged him closer.

"I'm sorry," she whispered again. "I shouldn't have asked you that."

"Of course you should have. It's an issue I need to resolve. When do you fly back to South Carolina?"

"In two weeks, but Dr. Ryan is lobbying for me to join the contingent flying out to northwest Pakistan after that 7.8 quake on Tuesday. Survivors are being treated, but it's really in the aftermath that the Red Cross needs help. They're talking about taking over the emergency room at the Timengara Hospital to be able to deal with the number of injured. They need every MSF nurse they can get."

"What did you tell him?"

"That I'd consider it. But if I go to Pakistan, that'll add six months to my tour. And who knows what will happen to us then? You'll have had another six months to patch things up with Beth."

"She knows the marriage is over. We just don't talk about it. When do you have to give Ryan an answer?"

"By this afternoon." Then Ann said softly, "I love you, Patrick."

She reached down for him, getting the erection she wanted within seconds. He stroked her right breast and smiled up at her.

"I love you, too," he whispered.

He kissed her and rolled back on top of her.

Then he put his hands around her throat and strangled her.

Her eyes bulged, first in utter surprise, then it terror. She writhed, trying to scratch at his eyes, but his grip was strong and her struggling only lasted a few seconds. Her body went limp and her hands fell back to the sheet. He looked down at her face, her bright blue eyes staring sightlessly up at the fan that sluggishly rotated the hot air around at the ceiling. Gently he closed her eyes.

He got dressed and wrapped her in a blanket that was kept in a closet, as if any guest would ever need one in the heat. He carried her down a back staircase into the parking lot of the hotel. It was deserted. There were no surveillance cameras here. He slid her into the back of his Land Rover and covered her with an old tarpaulin. He drove out of Monrovia into the tropical rain forest, following a GPS unit on the dash, to where a dirt track led deeper into the jungle. He'd already dug a shallow grave and covered it over with dirt and leaves. He stopped the Land Rover, surrounded by densely packed trees. The jungle was moist and damp and oppressive. He caught a glimpse of a Diana monkey swinging through the branches of one of the thirty-foot trees. Otherwise it was silent, or as silent as the jungle ever was. He hauled Ann's body out of the back of the Land Rover and dropped her into the grave. Then he covered her up again with dirt and foliage. The chances of anyone finding her were remote.

He stood for a moment over Ann's grave. He hadn't wanted to do it. He *had* loved her, in his way. But he wasn't going to leave his wife and family. At least, not yet. And she knew too much about his secret work.

But still, he thought, it *was* a damn shame.

Then he climbed back into the Land Rover, turned it around, and drove back to Monrovia.

Sunlight was streaming through a grimy window when Norman Rosemont woke up the next morning. He was lying naked in a queen-size bed in a shabby bedroom. It contained a dresser, a cane chair, and two bedside tables with functional lamps. The furniture looked like it had been delivered from a secondhand store in some forlorn part of Queens. Rosemont felt groggy. He didn't know what that babe in the back of the limo had injected him with, but it had left him with a pounding headache. He'd been kidnapped. He assumed for ransom. Or maybe for revenge? Some personal indiscretion against someone's ex-girlfriend or daughter or sister? For a moment Rosemont lay very still, listening. He could hear nothing.

He tried to stand, but started wheezing. Then he saw his inhaler on a bedside table and grabbed it. He pressed two puffs into his mouth, and his breathing regulated. He got to his feet and staggered into a bathroom, hitting the light. The mirror over the sink was spotted with black. He used the toilet and checked the shower. A large yellow ring was around the plug and it smelled to high heaven.

Rosemont walked back into the bedroom, feeling self-conscious about being naked. He saw the trousers of his Hugo Boss suit folded neatly on the cane chair, a new pair of boxers and black socks folded on top. His black oxford dress shoes were underneath. Rosemont felt the pockets of his pants, assuming they'd be empty, but his wallet was still there and all of his credit cards. He put on the underwear, socks, and trousers. He cautiously opened the bedroom door and walked into a small living room. The furniture was threadbare. He walked into the kitchen. The appliances looked like they'd been installed when *I Love Lucy* was the number one show on television. He was surprised to find the refrigerator was well stocked. He glanced down suddenly and saw two cockroaches skittering across the worn linoleum. Rosemont shuddered and went back into the bedroom and the bathroom. He took a whore's bath, soap and hot water under his armpits; he wasn't going to set foot in that shower. He dried off, found a new Turnbull & Asser shirt in the closet, pink with a white collar and cuffs, and stepped into his oxford shoes. He walked across the grungy living room to the front door. He looked through the keyhole, but no guard was posted outside. He stepped out into the corridor. There was no elevator. Before he could take two steps toward a door marked STAIRS, the door to apartment 4A opened with a flourish.

Sam Kinney stepped out.

"Hey, new neighbor!" he said cheerily. "Welcome to the building!"

"I am *not* your neighbor," Rosemont snapped.

His fear had been replaced by mounting anger. Whoever had played this practical joke on him was going to be sorry.

"You're the new tenant in apartment 4B, right?" Sam said, ignoring Rosemont's retort. "Hey, would you like to come in for a cup of coffee? It's instant, but Maxwell House, come on, good to the last drop."

Rosemont ignored the invitation, opening the door to the stairs.

"Maybe tomorrow morning," Sam said affably.

"I will *not* be coming back here!" Rosemont said curtly.

"Hey, it ain't such a bad place! You'll get used to it!"

Rosemont slammed the door behind him. Sam walked to one of the bright living-room windows in *his* new apartment. After a moment he saw Rosemont run down the limestone steps outside the building and hail a passing yellow cab.

Sam grinned. "Have a great day."

Melody met McCall at the Rock Café beside the Rockefeller Center skating rink. It was her favorite place in the city. Through the window she watched the skaters whirling and passing each other like an intricate ballet being performed for the benefit of the lunch crowd. It had a festive feeling to it with the golden Prometheus statue keeping a benevolent eye on the skaters. The restaurant was jammed. Melody was sitting at the last table against the windows. McCall slid into the chair opposite her. She was totally caught up in the interplay between the skaters.

"I love coming here. It's a joyous place."

"Why's that?"

"I grew up in Lake Geneva. I used to hike the shore path around the lake all the time. I liked to go to the Racine Art Museum to see the displays of exquisite jewelery and ceramics and glass. I'd sail on the lake with my friends. It was tranquil and exhilarating. But the longer I lived there, the more convinced I became that I had to get away from that place. I didn't know what to expect coming to the Big Apple, but it's so . . . *thriving*! All the people and the traffic and the *energy*! I love it!"

"So being a dancer at Dolls hasn't taken the gloss out of your rose-colored glasses?"

Melody looked back at him and smiled. It would have warmed McCall's heart, assuming he had one, and Kostmayer had once said the jury was still out on that.

"It was tough sometimes," Melody admitted, "watching the avarice and sexual intensity in the club. But that's all changed now. Thanks to you."

"What happens at Dolls nightclub has nothing to do with me."

"Sure it does. Katia told me how you came to her rescue. And mine, too. Between Mr. Clemens being the new owner and Barney, our gentle giant who protects the door, it's a great place to be. It's when I *leave* the club that the cynicism of the city seeps into my soul. If I let it."

"Tell me about your dates with Blake Cunningham."

"He's funny, gentlemanly, very smart, and absolutely the predator you warned me about. But he hasn't made a single move on me that I couldn't handle."

"When are you seeing him next?"

"Today for lunch. But it won't be here at the skating rink. Blake likes to go to the really ritzy places. And I have my new BFF, Tara, shadowing me whenever we go out."

"She'll stick close to you. You'll be safe with her."

That gave Melody pause. "Where will you be?"

"I have to go out of the city for a while."

"How long will you be gone?"

"Maybe a few days. Will you be all right until I get back?"

"Sure, I'm a big girl, despite the Lake Geneva naïveté. You don't need to worry about me." She reached over and took his hand. "But I'm glad you do."

"Don't underestimate Blake. That girl I told you about, Emily Masden, is still missing."

Melody had not relinquished McCall's hand, but it was a warming touch, not fearful. "I'll be careful, Mr. McCall. I promise."

"You can probably break down and call me Robert."

"Okay."

Melody leaned across the table and kissed McCall gently on the lips. Then she leaned back, as if suddenly embarrassed. "I really wasn't going to do that."

"I'm glad you did. Where are you meeting Blake?"

"At my apartment."

"Don't let him talk you into going up there for a drink before lunch."

She scoffed. "Lake Geneva girls don't do that. Strong values are instilled in daughters from a young age. But *you're* invited for a drink whenever you want."

"I'll keep that in mind." He stood up.

"Just come back soon."

"I will. Can I take you somewhere?"

"No. I'll just watch the skaters. It's very zen." Melody looked up at him with a smile that was still in her eyes. "You won't forget that kiss, will you?"

"Probably not."

"Conversation to be continued."

Melody looked back out at the skaters. McCall hesitated a moment, but there was nothing more to say. He didn't like leaving Melody alone, but he had another client. He had a sense memory of Helen Coleman in Times Square, also clutching his hand, talking about her son Josh, saying, *Find him for me, Mr. McCall. Please.* The odds were long, but McCall had to take the shot. Melody had a handle on Blake. And Tara was keeping a close watch on her.

McCall moved away from Melody's table.

Blake Cunningham stood at the bar area at the back of the Rock Café, a crush of tourists waiting for tables blocking him from sight. Blake watched McCall walk out a side door, skirting the skating rink. Blake gave him a few minutes. He was amazed that Emily Masden's dad was still in New York looking for his daughter. If this man *was* her father? Two of Blake's college buddies had been killed after the rave party, thrown off a scaffolding on an old run-down theater. Two others had been beaten up, but they had survived. The ones who survived hadn't been able to describe their assailant. Could it *really* be this old guy?

Blake looked at the place where he'd lost McCall in the crowd. He thought he might have been some friend of Melody's, maybe even a sexual partner. But how did he *know* Melody? *Or* Emily? Too much of a coincidence, but it didn't matter. He was someone Blake could handle. Maybe he was a regular at Dolls nightclub. One of Melody's low-life dance partners who might be obsessed with her. Maybe she had agreed to meet him at the Rockefeller Rink to get rid of him. Blake carried the fantasy a little further. If this creep didn't leave Melody alone, Blake would take care of him.

Blake had plans for Melody.

He pushed through the crowd to Melody's table. She looked up, a little startled.

"Hey! Hi, there! I thought we were going to meet outside my apartment building?"

Blake slid into the chair that McCall had vacated. "I got out of Morgan Stanley early. Some crisis meeting I don't need to be at. I know you like to come to Rockefeller Center and watch the skaters. Not that it's any of my business, but who was the guy you were with?"

Melody shrugged, like it was no big deal. "Some guy who comes into Dolls. I have coffee with him sometimes. He's harmless." She dazzled Blake with a smile. "I'm glad to see you."

"I'm glad to see you too, babe."

Yeah, Blake thought, *I have great plans for this little cunt.*

CHAPTER 20

Norman Rosemont strode through his office complex two hours late, clutching a Starbucks Caffè Americano and a blueberry scone in a bag.

His assistant, Mark, jumped to his feet. "I tried reaching you all evening, sir!"

"I wasn't reachable." Then Rosemont decided to spin that into a night's conquest. "I got lucky. What the hell's being done about this hacker?"

"I've got two more technicians from Cyber Solutions working on it in your office right now, sir. And Jerry Chandler is waiting for you."

Jerry Chandler was Rosemont's CFO, a compact man in his fifties, a bundle of energy who paced even when there was nothing to pace about. A young tech was sitting at Rosemont's desk working on his computer, a second tech working on another laptop. They barely glanced up when Rosemont entered.

Jerry Chandler stopped pacing. "This is serious shit, Norman. I called you half the night."

"Found myself in a strange apartment." Rosemont winked. It wasn't a lie. He looked at the tech at his desk. "You got a solution yet?"

"I've never seen firewalls like it."

"Can you kick this virus *off* my system?" Rosemont demanded.

The second tech glanced up from his laptop. "It's an algorithm we've never encountered before."

"Then you're no good to me." Rosemont wanted Dumb and Dumber out of his office. "Come back with an answer."

The two young techs left. Rosemont collapsed at his desk. His headache was hammering even worse.

Jerry Chandler continued to pace. "Every one of our systems is down at every company worldwide. I just got off the phone with Mr. Ling in Hong Kong, who was screaming at me. We can't do business. We're losing millions of dollars a day, and that's conservative. We've got to get back online."

"I'm open to suggestions, Jerry."

From outside the office there was a small commotion. For a moment Rosemont's spirits soared. Maybe the two tech guys had had a sudden *eureka!* moment and were coming back. But it was an elegant African-American who walked into Rosemont's office.

Jackson T. Foozelman was dressed in a Kenneth Cole gray suit with a silver watch chain and wearing a pair of Cole Haan wingtip oxfords. His face was scrubbed clean, his eyes bright, and a waft of Armani Di Gio aftershave filled the office.

"Who the hell are you?" Rosemont demanded.

Mark appeared in the doorway. "He just walked right past me, Mr. Rosemont!"

Rosemont waved Mark away with a disdainful hand. He looked at the visitor. "I'm not taking any meetings this morning, sir."

"I think you'll want to meet with me, Mr. Rosemont." Fooz stuck out his hand. "Jackson T. Foozelman. At your service, sir."

Rosemont did not shake hands.

He thought the man looked a little like Morgan Freeman.

"And what service are you offering me, Mr. Foozelman, before I call security and have you thrown out of the building?"

"I represent the person responsible for hacking into your computer systems. I understand they're off-line at all of your company offices around the world. That can't be good for business. But my client is prepared to remove the virus from your systems on the following condition."

Rosemont took out his checkbook and tossed it onto the desk.

"Norman, you're not going to give in to this blackmail!" Chandler exclaimed. The CFO looked as if he were going to burst a blood vessel.

"How much?" Rosemont demanded.

"It's not a monetary transaction, sir. I understand you own a number of apartment buildings in the tristate area."

"What of it?"

"I believe you woke up this morning in an apartment in one of those buildings in the East Village. My client wants you to live in that building, in *that* apartment, for two weeks. You can bring whatever personal belongings you want from your penthouse apartment overlooking Central Park, but *no* furniture. Once you've moved into your new digs, you can't return to your own apartment for anything at all. That's the one hard-and-fast rule."

"What the hell is this crap? I wouldn't even consider your outrageous proposition."

"Not *my* proposition, sir," Fooz said patiently. "I's just the messenger here, boss."

"Who *is* this client of yours?" Rosemont demanded as his blood pressure rose and the little man with the big hammer started pounding in his head again.

"He likes to stay anonymous." Then Fooz added ironically to himself, "'Course, puttin' an ad in the paper and on the internet don't help that none."

"Who put your *client* up to this? Jim Sterling at Webstar Telecommunications?" *Maybe he wants to sweeten the merger deal,* Rosemont thought bitterly.

"Don't know that name. My client kinda made this up all by his lonesome. I understand it's not such a bad building if you don't mind the rats and the cockroaches. At the end of two weeks, if you've stayed in your new apartment, the virus on your computers will be lifted."

"How do I know if I went through with this insane charade the virus will be taken away?"

"My client always keeps his word, sir," Fooz said with dignity.

Jerry Chandler fretted over to Rosemont's desk. "Maybe you *should* consider this, Norman. Better than the company going under."

Rosemont looked at Mark, who was still hovering in the doorway. "Call security!" he snapped. "I want this man arrested."

"Time for me to go," Fooz murmured. Then his voice lost its soft, mocking tone. "You spend a couple of weeks in that apartment building like the rest of the folks there, Mr. Rosemont. See how that works for you."

Fooz turned on his heel.

"Tell security to follow him!" Rosemont shouted at his assistant. "Find out where he goes!"

Mark jumped to his desk and picked up the phone.

Outside the Fifth Avenue skyscraper, Fooz was still smiling to himself. That security detail might find it a little tough to follow him where he was going.

Three minutes later he had disappeared down the iron ladder from the manhole cover on Fifty-Third Street into the labyrinth of subway and sewer tunnels beneath the Manhattan streets that he'd called home for over forty years.

Hayden Vallance had only needed twenty-four hours to set up McCall's clandestine trip. McCall took a flight from LaGuardia to Washington, DC, then took a cab to Wakefield Municipal Airport in Virginia. This time Vallance was standing on the tarmac beside a Global 6000 VistaJet.

"Does just under six thousand nautical miles," the mercenary said. "Max speed five hundred and ninety mph. Fifteen-passenger capacity, so it'll be a little lonely in there, but plush. Galley is stocked with chilled champagne and gourmet food."

"No copilot?"

"If I have a heart attack, you can take over, right?"

McCall nodded. "Where do we refuel?"

"Budapest, then Somalia. Then I'll land at the Aleppo airport in Syria."

"Your flight plan has been approved?"

"ARTCC confirmed with Washington Center. All but the Aleppo part. HCMK, that's the airport in Somalia, is supposed to be my destination. I got all of the equipment you asked for on board. Last chance to change your mind."

"Let's do this."

McCall slept fitfully while the Bombardier Global 6000 Vista 9H-VJJ climbed to forty-one thousand feet and leveled off to an average speed of 860 kph. The Vista had been configured for night travel, and McCall could vaguely smell the smoky ambience of Santal on the leather seats. His dream was fragmented, but the face of Matthew Goddard swam into and out of focus. His aquiline features and his deep-set eyes had murder in them. McCall knew that Goddard was somehow responsible for Control's kidnapping. *If* he *had* been kidnapped and wasn't lying in a grave in the Virginia countryside. Control had warned McCall when he'd quit that a high-stakes game was being played at The Company. Control had hinted of the identity of a mole. McCall saw himself walking down the grassy knoll from the World War II memorials in Yaroslavl shouting at Control about Serena Johanssen's death, the wind whipping at them from the Volga River. McCall had said, *I resign.* Then men were hacking at Control with knives. One of them was Goddard. Something glittered on his right hand. Something sinister. Then Goddard pushed McCall into the wind and the darkness and it was a long way down.

McCall felt a touch on his shoulder and then a knife blade was in his hand.

Hayden Vallance didn't flinch. McCall focused on him, then slid the tactical six-inch Black Tiger throwing knife back into its sheath and swung his feet to the jet's floor.

"Where are we?"

"I refueled in HCMK Kisimayu Airport. We're in Syria, twenty minutes from the coordinates."

"What's the visibility?"

"Low cloud cover. Sporadic moonlight. You're going to free-fall into darkness."

McCall rose and moved to where Vallance had spread McCall's gear out across two of the couches. He was carrying a commercial tandem sky-diving rig designed to hold the weight of two people, but he would be jumping alone. He would be taking weapons and first-aid gear, a timetable of the trains in the region, a radio, and the two six-inch Black Tiger throwing knives. He had a modified Aquatimer automatic chronometer tuned to the coordinates.

Vallance helped McCall into the chute. "I see the tandem includes a little drogue chute. Pretty sporty."

"Ensures stability in free fall until I push the rip cord. Then it'll deploy a large canopy about double the size of the small one. Check the backpack."

"Radio check, sheaf of maps check, trauma kit with a small amount of pain drugs, including Toradol and a small amount of morphine with an IV drip and antinausea medication. Canadian passport, stamped, the paperwork shows you're an NG volunteer. Not sure that's going to fly."

"It explains why I'm carrying a med bag and a drug kit with me."

"You're driving a 2006 Hyundai Avante sedan that would not even make it to the outskirts of Aleppo. You were hit by an Insurgent patrol and your vehicle was shot up. I'll buy that. Until a Jihadist patrol surrounds and searches you, wanting to know why you are out this far."

"I'll improvise. Check the weapons."

"M70 ABM milled AK-47 underfolding rifle. Original Yugo parts kits and a US-milled receiver and barrel for increased accuracy. Yugo grenade-launching ladder sight and bayonet lug. Nice touch. Two four-pack thirty-round AK-47 mags, 762-by-39, AK fixed-stock modification. AK-47 bullet button and mag lock. Ti-rant 9mm silencer suppressor. Bulgarian Makarov 9-by-18 MAK PM semi pistol with a leather brown holster. Two Black Tiger throwing knives. You're carrying two pairs of EES Profile NVG Foliage Green, three-times magnification, 37 mm objective up to 100 yards. Steiner 10-by-50 M50 LRF binoculars. Also two packs of four signal flares. You're set."

McCall hoisted the backpack into a more comfortable position. The skydiving rig was a little snug, but it was the best Vallance could come up with in time.

"In the zippered pocket you'll find a SanDisk Cruzer Glide USB flash drive," McCall said. "Take it out." Vallance unzipped the pocket and took out the small flash drive. "When you plug it into your laptop, it will transfer fifty thousand into your personal account. If you want to verify the transaction, you've got time to do it before we get to the drop point."

"I'll get around to it. Once you're airborne, we're done. I'm not coming back for you."

"That's our deal. How long?"

"Less than eight minutes."

Vallance climbed back into the cockpit. McCall sat on the forward couch and waited. The Global VistaJet started a descent, but it was so gradual McCall was hardly aware of it. He was running on epinephrine in massive doses. His adrenaline had been enhanced to increase his heart rate, pulse rate, blood circulation, breathing, and carbohydrate metabolism, and it raised his blood levels of glucose and lipids. Every emotional response he was feeling had a behavioral component.

He was keenly aware that he was jumping to nowhere.

Vallance came out of the cockpit.

"We're below the ceiling of the clouds, light gusting winds, the moon is out, but it's retreating into and out of shadow. I've got you about one mile from the target area. I'm going to open the cockpit door. We're at three thousand feet."

McCall and Vallance moved to the cockpit door. Now Vallance hesitated. McCall had been expecting it.

"This is a mistake, McCall. When did Helen Coleman hear from her son? Forty-eight hours ago? She has no idea if he's even *at* these coordinates. He could have moved his location. He may be wounded. The Insurgents have been searching for him. Maybe they found him. Maybe they cut his throat. There are atrocities we can't rectify."

"I'm not looking for vindication. I'm here to find one soldier."

"That soldier is long gone. Granny would say you're talking to a voice that's only in your head."

"Granny only listens to one voice. That got him into a North Korean prison camp. And he's not here. You are."

Vallance looked down at his own chronometer. "Ninety seconds."

He released the door. Wind howled through it.

"Go easy, McCall. Nothing out there but night."

Vallance held up his hand in the cockpit. McCall looked down at the rocky terrain below. He caught sight of railway tracks in the distance.

The moon came out of the clouds again, bathing the scene in a malevolent pale glow.

Vallance counted down, "Four, three, two, one, zero."

McCall parachuted from the VistaJet and realized they were being fired on.

CHAPTER 21

Vallance took evasive action. He threw the VistaJet down into a screaming spiral and then righted it again. McCall plummeted into the opaque sky and spotted the ZU-23-2 Soviet Union antiaircraft autocannon pounding shells up into the clouds. Above him the streamlined jet was climbing higher. McCall couldn't see from his position, but he was sure Vallance had closed the steps into the aircraft. A few seconds later it was swallowed up into the cloud cover. But that didn't stop the Jihadist fighters from firing on it from their position along Highway 6, somewhere north of Ar Raqqah and west of Aleppo. McCall thought it was unusual for insurgent activities to be mounted at night, but he knew that Syria's Kurdish Democratic Union Party had targeted Islamic State positions near the Syrian Kurdish town of Kobani.

McCall drifted from his position amid the high clouds until he saw a BTR-50 armored personnel carrier below on the highway. A DShK 1938 12.7×108mm heavy machine gun was firing up at the VistaJet, but the barrage had been hastily mounted. Another of the vehicles, a Ural-4320 off-road, had been stripped of everything. Two of the Jihadists were in the blackened shell, one of them holding a shoulder-mounted rocket launcher— man-portable air-defense systems, or MANPADs, as McCall knew them— manufactured in Bulgaria. They were also firing up at the Global VistaJet but Vallance had maintained his maneuvers until the jet was a speck in the dark canopy before it disappeared altogether.

McCall had seventeen seconds to reach the ground before the Insurgents turned their firepower on him. He pulled the drogue out of its pouch at the bottom of the BOC and let it go. It pulled out the seven-to-ten-foot nylon bridle. McCall released the pin to the D-bag, and the tension that pulled out the main chute stretched. The wind inflated the cells of the canopy. It was as black as night. McCall looked at the small drogue chute, judging how it was unfolding. He knew he could go from 120 mph to 10 mph if it was opened instantaneously. But Vallance had packed the chute expertly, using the slider to hold the lines together. McCall caught hold of the two toggles and started steering the main parachute to the landing site.

The machine gun stopped its barrage into the night sky.

McCall caught a break.

The moon slid back beneath its cloud cover, and instantly the terrain was shadowed in violet. McCall worked the chute to compensate for where he was heading. He'd had to change his game plan. He was too close to Highway 6 now. He needed to get into the rocky scrub hugging this part of the terrain. He wasn't worried about the Insurgents spotting him. He was descending rapidly and all their eyes were skyward. McCall heard the two military vehicles start up again. He knew they were already radioing to find the jet's position. It was not a military aircraft, but it had clearly strayed from its flight path. Vallance would be heading back to Aleppo's airport. The Insurgents would not be looking for a clandestine drop this far south.

If the cloud cover held.

He was coming in too fast.

It only needed one of the Insurgent patrols to see the barest movement in the billowing canvas in their peripheral vision for them to call a halt on the highway. McCall judged the terrain that rushed up at him. He tried to maneuver to a ravine that cut diagonally near the highway. He hit the uneven ground and badly twisted his left ankle as he skidded over the bracken, but managed to stay upright. He came to a lurching halt. He gathered the black chute around him and limped down into a gully that would hide it from the highway. He packed the chute into the crevices in the ravine and listened.

He was waiting for the vehicles on Highway 6 to turn around and come back.

McCall took out the Makarov semiautomatic from his backpack and slid one of the mags into it. He took aim on the road he could barely glimpse and waited. But the sounds of the Jihadist engines were dying away. The Insurgents could be heading off Highway 6 to Bab al Salama on the Syrian-Turkish border. They would find refuge there. The intel McCall had gleaned from Vallance had fighters from the Lebanese Shiite Muslim group Hezbollah tightening the noose around the Insurgents fleeing Aleppo.

But he would wait another twenty minutes.

The wind was blowing sand across the gully. McCall lowered the

Makarov pistol. He limped to the backpack, pain searing now through his left leg. He didn't have time to find out if the ankle was sprained or only twisted. He didn't think it was broken. If it was, he was finished. He checked the chronometer on his right wrist. He estimated his position from the coordinates to be two miles along Highway 6 and below it about another three miles. He hadn't seen any identifying markings or buildings. Nothing was out here but desolation and destruction.

The signal from the coordinates was strong. But that didn't mean anyone was *sending* out those coordinates. Vallance's words came back to him: *He could have moved his location. He may be wounded. The Insurgents have been searching for him.*

But the coordinates glowed on the dial of the chronometer.

McCall weighted down the black chute with rocks. When he'd finished, you couldn't have found it in daylight even if you'd been searching the gully. McCall sat down on a rock and painfully took off his left boot and heavy sock. His left ankle was badly swollen, but it had not discolored yet. He put it down as a painful sprain. He put one of the bandages from the med kit around the ankle and wound it tightly. He put back on the woolen sock and manipulated his left ankle down and tied the ankle boot. He hoisted the backpack onto his shoulders. He paused long enough at the mouth of the ravine to listen once more. Just the wind moaning and wailing. There was no longer the sound of the Insurgents' vehicles.

McCall climbed out of the ravine and made his way toward where he knew Highway 6 would be. When he came to it, it had taken him the best part of an hour, that's how far he'd been off course. The highway glowed in the moonlight, pocked with blast debris, reaching in both directions. McCall used his compass, checked the coordinates one more time, then started walking. He kept to Highway 6 as a reference point. Silvery moonlight sporadically brought out light and deep shadows. He was favoring his bandaged ankle, and walking on it was more difficult than he'd anticipated. He could absorb the pain of a flat-out run if necessary, but the terrain gave him little cover.

Then he heard the sounds of vehicles coming for him.

McCall ran to the other side of Highway 6 where a small track led off toward the south. He scrambled down the rugged channel and found some shelter amid the jagged boulders. He'd been lucky; there was little jumbled terrain at this point on Highway 6.

On the sliver of cloudy highway were two Sham I armored pickup trucks used by the Syrian Rebel Army. McCall took the NVG night goggles out of his backpack and put them on. Now he could read the script on the vehicles, assigning them to the Syriac Military Council, which was against the Assad government and the Islamic State of Iraq. The two vehicles turned into a growing sandstorm toward the Turkish border. McCall climbed back onto the glowing strip of Highway 6. The Syrian Rebel Army vehicles had been swallowed whole, as if they'd been devoured by some demon. McCall picked up his pace. He checked the chronometer on his wrist.

The coordinates were closer.

The wind had kicked up again. Sand was gusting across Highway 6 in undulating waves. McCall trudged against the blasting squall. It brought his vision down to a scant few feet in either direction. Little granules of sand scourged his face. He descended down a road as it fell precipitously away from the highway, skirting a bombed-out wall that had fallen finally to a handful of stones. He climbed down another half mile.

McCall was out of the sandstorm now and heading out into a wilderness that was a green matte through his night goggles. Nothing moved in it. He looked like an alien being, covered with grime and grit, stumbling down the road under a brilliant cluster of stars. He consulted the GPS tracker and the coordinates on the chronometer.

McCall stopped in the middle of nowhere.

Highway 6 was behind him, maybe four miles, but with no identification marks. He might have been a hundred miles from any kind of traffic. In front of him were the silhouettes of a couple of buildings, one a hut, the other an old carport. The hut was barely an opening with a corrugated roof over it. No vehicle was in the carport. McCall moved forward with more purpose now, his ankle bringing a new flare-up of pain. He came to a small well with a pipe two inches in diameter sticking up with a hand pump to draw water to an animal trough. He was certain that Insurgents and the FSA Rebel forces used the well, but not at this time of night. McCall sloshed through a ditch, half full of water, right into a goat herd at the side of the road. They scattered, but formed up again. McCall looked down at the GPS tracker and the coordinates on the dial of the chronometer.

They were perfectly triangulated.

McCall noticed something that stopped him. A flare that was part of the silvery landscape. McCall looked closer through the night goggles. On the gray-green scope were what looked like small blotches of color. McCall knelt down when he reached the carport. There was no mistaking it. The blood trail was fresh. McCall straightened. He took out the Makarov pistol and approached the small hut from the carport.

He stepped inside.

McCall used the night goggles to get accustomed to the gloom, then took them off. More brilliant moonlight shone through the window at the back wall. Between it and the entrance two-by-fours were piled up, an old bicycle with two wheels missing, some rusting farm implements, piles of goat turds, and more blood.

McCall saw a shadow move.

He whirled and trained the Makarov pistol at the rumpled figure that was barely able to stand. He was holding a Colt .45 M1911 handgun pointed directly at McCall.

In one swift move, McCall took the Colt away from him.

The figure staggered back and slumped down against the wall. He could only see McCall in the moonlight that flared across his dark figure.

McCall put away the Makarov pistol.

"My name is Robert McCall," he said gently to Captain Josh Coleman. "I've come to get you out of here."

CHAPTER 22

McCall took out the med kit from his backpack. He took out his canteen and gave it to Josh. The American Army officer held it in his hands, splashing some of the water as he tried to drink it.

"Take it easy," McCall said. "We'll fill the canteens up from the well when we leave."

Josh handed back the canteen. Pain obviously raked his body and his voice was weak. "I've been listening to vehicles coming and leaving by the well, snatched conversations, most of it in Arabic, Kurdish, and Azeri. I needed my younger brother to translate them. But the accents are different to the ones used by the Free Syrian Army. You're not with them?"

"No." McCall opened Josh's multipatterned camouflage uniform, revealing the makeshift bandage he'd stuffed over his shoulder wound.

"If you were with the Insurgents, I'd be dead now. Or dragged out of here to be paraded around for the cameras before they beheaded me. You're not Army. Special Forces?"

"No."

"A mercenary." Josh nodded, as if trying to assimilate the information. "The Lions of Rojava, run by the Kurdish YPG movement, asked for mercenaries on their Facebook page to send the terrorists to hell and save humanity."

"Try not to talk." McCall realized Josh was delirious, wavering into and out of lucidity.

"You're a predator. Preying on the weak. You don't leave a dying animal beside the road if you can put it out of its misery."

"Look up the Anti-Pinkerton Act of 1893 that forbade the US government using Pinkerton Detective Agency employees or similar police companies. I'm not a mercenary. I work alone."

"But you came here. You were looking for me."

"You radioed these coordinates to your mother, who gave them to me."

"Why would she contact you?"

"I told her I would try to find her son if he was still alive."

"Who the hell are you?" Josh started to rise up, but he was seized with a coughing fit and slumped down again.

"I didn't expect to find you here. It was a very long shot. Help me with this."

Josh got his uniform jacket off with McCall's help. "But you're not here alone?"

"Parachuted in. It's an unauthorized mission. Let me look at this wound."

McCall lifted Josh up, examining his right shoulder. "The bullet went right through. The muscles, ligaments, and cartilages were damaged, but the brachial plexus wasn't touched. I'm going to clean the wound up and bind it. I'm going to give you a shot of morphine." McCall set Josh back onto the filthy floor and dragged over a bunch of tires to prop him up. He took out the small morphine bottle. "Do you suffer from asthma?"

"No."

"The bullet didn't rupture the stomach or the intestines. This will ease the pain and slow your breathing." McCall readied the syringe. "It'll take effect in under a minute. It'll bind the opioid receptors on the surface to the nerve cells and make them sluggish so you won't fire so many impulses."

McCall pushed the syringe into a muscle in Josh's shoulder. Josh didn't react. McCall put the syringe and the bottle back into the med kit.

"I'll give you another shot of it in about an hour. Tell me what happened."

Josh's voice had more volume to it, just a little above a fevered whisper. "We were dropping supplies from Doctors Without Borders to al-Sukhnah. It's been raided by the Insurgents in the past few weeks. The Homs Governorate has been driven out of the town. Only small pockets are still resisting, mainly bedouin tribes. The villages have been shelled relentlessly, but we needed to get medical supplies to the predominately Sunni Muslims there."

Josh started coughing again and McCall waited until it passed.

"Go ahead."

"Our convoy was made up of one Humvee jeep and a BTR-152 armored personal carrier as a backup. We had been hit by an Insurgent patrol in Al Tabqah and we fought them off, but they weren't expecting us to go to al-Sukhnah, which was mostly decimated."

Josh winced, clenching his teeth against the pain as McCall put the needle and thread through the edges of his shoulder wound.

"The morphine will be kicking in about now. Try to relax into it. You got separated in the firefight?"

"Yeah. I had a meeting in one of the village huts. We'd unloaded the last of the supplies. I came outside and there were bullets flying. I got hit right away. I got a couple more nicks, one in the left arm and one that ripped up my right leg. I couldn't walk. My commanding officer saw me take fire, but he couldn't get to me. There were too many Insurgents and the UN peacekeeping force retreated back into their Humvee. The BTR-152 carrier took a direct RPG hit and exploded."

"Your mother called your commanding officer by a nickname."

"Yeah, Colonel Michael G. Ralston, they call him Gunner. Three NCOs were wounded and the two Doctors Without Borders workers were dead. Gunner saw me on the ground, but I was covered with blood. They would never have got out of there if they hadn't taken the Humvee."

"Leave no one behind."

"Gunner came back for me. He took another Humvee with two more officers and came back to al-Sukhnah, but the Insurgents had gone. He looked for my body, but didn't find it. He talked to the tribal chieftains, but they were evacuating the village and weren't looking for a fallen American soldier. One of them had a report I had been seen in al-Asharak, to the east, and Gunner drove his Humvee like a madman there, but didn't find me. He made it back to the team house in Ar Raqqah and had to report me as KIA."

McCall had stitched up the shoulder wound now. He pressed an emergency trauma dressing in the front and secured it with surgical tape. He had to be careful as he hoisted Josh up and put the second ETD on his shoulder where the bullet had exited and secured it with surgical tape also.

"How long have you been at this location?"

"I wanted to get away from al-Sukhnah, but I lost my way. I was trying to reach Highway Six, but I was looking for Insurgent patrols and couldn't risk it. I don't know how long it was until I came upon the goat herd milling around the water trough. I wasn't sure the little pipe was still operational, never mind the hand pump, but it was, so I filled the trough and took some water. The goat herd was thirsty. There were no herders around. The carport had a 1994 Mazda T3500 in it and I tried to start it, but it wasn't moving. I fell into the hut. I made a shelter of the tires and the planking in case anyone came inside."

"What happened then?"

"I passed out. When I came to, it was night. I managed to get to the doorway. The Mazda was gone. Someone had returned for it and driven it away. I figured it was the goatherder. If he came into the hut, he didn't see my hiding place. He got out of here as fast as he could." Josh shook his head, as if woozy. "But there might never have been a Mazda. My memory of the carport is hazy. I lost track of time. All I could hear were the goats bleating. I went back to the water trough and filled up my canteen and gave the goats water, but I was losing consciousness and I had to get back into the hut before I passed out. At some point I heard activity outside. I don't know if that was the Insurgents filling their canteens and their vehicles. I heard some movement toward the goatherder's hut, but it was cut short when they discovered the carport was empty. They climbed into their vehicles and drove away. I lost consciousness. The next sound I heard was you moving up to the hut."

McCall buttoned Josh's Army tunic and eased Josh back to the ground, propped up by the tires. McCall fished out an oatmeal-raisin PowerBar from his backpack and tore off the wrapper. Josh took a couple of bites.

"Does your radio work?" McCall asked.

"It was smashed in the firefight."

"But you're wearing a chronometer on your wrist."

"Gunner gave each of his team one when we landed in Syria. It was fractured when I got hit, but after I'd crawled in here, I managed to send out the coordinates of my position to my mother at the UN. Then the chronometer stopped working."

"Why didn't you send the coordinates to your commanding officer in the field?"

Josh was bleary. The morphine had kicked in, and the Army captain was fighting it. "I had no idea if the coordinates were accurate, or if Helen would get them. I didn't know if she would even know what they were."

"But your commanding officer knew what they were. He would have had a field map out at your HQ in Ar Raqqah, and it wouldn't have taken him long to triangulate the coordinates. But he didn't do that. Or he would have led another rescue attempt right here."

"Too risky," Josh said, his manner suddenly evasive. "They believed I was KIA. The intel had been sent to the Pentagon. They couldn't have been sure where I had strayed off the road. There have been sandstorms wiping out the tracks down through the gullies. Even Highway Six has been almost impassable. If you were looking for this goatherder's station, you would miss it."

McCall knew Josh was lying to him. Josh had carefully laid out the coordinates to his mother, of all people, a high-ranking UN executive, in a Hail Mary pass before his chronometer had stopped. No one had come to rescue him. No one had prepped him to be ready to reach an evacuation point. His own CO had not given up on him, but the news was bleak. They'd left one of their own behind, and he was expected to die in this godforsaken place.

McCall wasn't buying it.

But this wasn't the time to press Josh to tell him the truth.

"Wait here."

McCall got to his feet. Not until the howl of the wind registered and he ran outside did he realize the severity of the sandstorm whipping around the dilapidated hut and carport. The sand sheeted across the road leading back to Highway 6.

McCall staggered through the blinding maelstrom up to the animal trough and filled his canteen and Josh's. He moved back inside the goatherd's hut and helped Josh to his feet.

"Can you walk?"

"I can walk. What if the Insurgents come back?"

"They've been looking for you, moving down Highway Six, but they won't find you in this sandstorm. When I saw them, they were heading away from the highway out onto one of the side roads, probably Highway Seven, to Ak Kut and Shakrak. They won't come back to this location now, and if they do, we'll be gone. Have you got an extraction point?"

"I had the coordinates, but the rendezvous point was changed at the last minute because of the stepped-up Insurgent patrols in the area."

"I'm getting you to a new extraction point. We can make it to the railway tracks on the other side of Highway Six. We can make the night train if we can move out of the sandstorm. I've got these night goggles for you." McCall pulled a second pair of night-vision goggles out of his backpack and handed them to Josh, who put them around his eyes. "Ready to move out?"

Josh looked at McCall, focusing through the pain, and nodded. "I'm good."

"Let's go."

McCall and Josh moved out of the goatherder's hut and into the sandstorm.

CHAPTER 23

McCall supported Josh as the biting wind whipped into their faces. They walked from the hut and the vacant carport and almost tripped right over the goats, who were bleating in the elements. They struck out in a northwesterly direction, which McCall reckoned would take them away from Highway 6. McCall needed to find them more shelter. One of the Insurgent patrols might come back for water, search the goatherder's hut, and find Josh's blood on the floor. They would set out to find him again, paralleling Highway 6. Josh was limping on his right leg where the bullet had grazed him. McCall's own twisted ankle was throbbing badly. He would need to rebind it if he was going to travel any distance in this terrain.

The first of the buildings appeared out of the murk like a trick of the light.

McCall brought them both to a halt. The moon was capriciously going into and out of the cloud cover. The buildings looked like an eerie mirage glowing in the desert. McCall took the Makarov pistol out of his jacket and held it in his right hand. The gusting sand uncovered another building, then another, then submerged them in shadow again. McCall strained for a sound, but there was nothing but wailing of the wind.

McCall motioned to Josh, and they staggered to the first village hut. It was nothing more than a packed-earth edifice without a door or windows. Beyond it were other huts, most of them destroyed, pocked with mortar fire.

"There are other villages like this one, straight down Highway Six, patrolled by the Insurgents." Josh had to shout as the wind whipped around the white-faced buildings. "Foua and Kfary, adjacent Shiite villages, had been besieged by antigovernment militants for more than a year. The Jihadists blasted them apart."

"And the people in the villages?"

"Massacred. It was too late by the time our US observation unit got here from the neighboring village of Alhora. But we were only observing from the road, and we had to get out of here before the Insurgents came back."

Both of them were being assaulted by the blinding storm. McCall signaled to conserve their voices. They made their way to the first village hut. There was a wraparound wooden porch with broken slats. One cane chair with mother-of-pearl inlay was unraveling beside the doorway.

"Sit here," McCall said. "Stay off your leg."

He helped Josh down into the cane chair, then stepped into the first hut. There was nothing to find; some discarded bags of rice and scattered cooking utensils were on the floor. McCall stepped off the porch, motioned for Josh to stay where he was, and walked through the ghost town. The next building had a sloping roof, blown sand almost halfway to the top. It was deserted. McCall gripped the Makarov pistol tighter and checked four more abandoned huts, all of them reeking of death.

Josh limped over from the porch of the first building. "There'll be a massive gravesite near this last hut. Where the bodies would have been tossed into like so much garbage."

"We don't have time to find it."

In the sixth hut were more cooking utensils, earthen bowls, signs of a family living there. Josh sat down in a Moroccan chair made of walnut wood and lemon-tree wood. McCall looked around what had been a living room. He saw a small bright figure shaped by the moon before it fled again.

He knelt and picked it up.

The Barbie doll had flaxen hair, some of it pulled out by the roots. One of Barbie's arms was missing. The doll was dressed in a canary-yellow

Fashion Pack Firefighting Uniform with black boots and a round pink hat. Some child had hugged that doll and dragged it around the village, and maybe it had been her constant companion until she had been killed. McCall had come here for one American soldier. But the personal tragedies that surrounded him were ghosts he recognized. He wondered bitterly if the Equalizer had any chance of lifting even one human being out of despair.

But it was all he could cling to in the new life he had chosen.

He stuffed the Barbie doll into his backpack. Josh got up from the Moroccan chair, hobbled to the doorway, and looked out into the sandstorm.

"The Insurgents won't come back to this village unless they're looking for you," McCall said. "If they do, then they're looking for some intel you've got. Do you want to tell me what that is?"

"It's classified."

"Only two of us here, Josh. Maybe I can help."

"Through your mercenary contacts? So you can sell the intel to the highest bidder?" Josh staggered in the doorway.

McCall steadied him. "I came here to pick you up. That's still the plan." McCall looked out onto the wooden porch. "The storm's abating a little. Let's go."

McCall put his arm around Josh's shoulders. They moved out of the dwelling with its ghosts wailing for the dead.

If McCall's instincts hadn't immediately kicked in, he would not have seen the apparition coming at him out of the sandstorm. The Insurgent fighter had just stepped onto the crumbling porch. McCall let go of Josh and wrenched a weapon right out of the Jihadist's hands. He had been carrying a Norinco CQ 5 NATO assault rifle commandeered from the People's Republic of China. McCall smashed the barrel against the man's face, bringing him to his knees. The Jihadist reached for the Totarev TT-33 semiautomatic pistol in his holster. McCall kicked it out of his hands and swung the butt of the assault rifle hard across his head, taking off most of the back of it.

In the swirl of sand McCall saw the second Jihadist fighter swing up his own assault rifle, a Zastava M70 Yugoslavian M43. The slim throwing knife was in McCall's hand a split second later, embedded in the man's throat. A third Insurgent was running for the dwelling. Josh had drawn his Colt .45 and fired four rounds. All of them hit the fighter in the chest. He collapsed onto the sand.

Josh steadied himself. McCall ran to where the second Jihadist had fallen. He examined the Zastava M43 in the sand and saw that the weapon had seen better days. He didn't want it exploding in his hands. He tossed it aside, but did help himself to the Browning semiautomatic pistol in the Insurgent's holster. Josh was off the porch now, limping toward where the third soldier lay. He was similarly armed with an AK-47 assault rifle and a Makarov PM pistol.

McCall listened to the mournful whimper of the wind, but didn't hear any vehicles. This patrol had been on its own, having come back to the abandoned village for some reason. Their vehicle was parked right outside the first village dwelling. The confiscated US Army Humvee M988 two-man cargo 1985 model had been modified, with the back of it ripped out.

Josh limped up to McCall. He was carrying the Jihadist's AK-47 with the Makarov pistol.

"Good shooting," McCall said. "We'll keep the Norinco NATO assault rifle and I'll add the Tokarev TT-33 pistol and the Browning."

He put his arm around Josh's shoulders, but Josh wanted to get to the Humvee on his own. McCall let him. The swirling sand was letting up around them, showing swathes of the terrain and, beyond the ghost village, what looked like Highway 6. McCall slid off his backpack and heaved it up into the back of the Humvee. He helped Josh take off his backpack, threw it into the back, and helped Josh into the right side of the vehicle. McCall covered their gear with an old, oil-spattered tarpaulin. He climbed into the driver's side of the Humvee and pulled away from the sepulchral village, with its memories of slaughter and grief, and headed out into the abating sandstorm.

Josh lay back against the right-hand seat, eyes closed. McCall debated giving him another shot of morphine, but decided to get them farther from the abandoned village. He consulted his chronometer, which now gave him his position in feet and inches. They were heading away from Highway 6 toward the northeast. McCall kept a lookout for Jihadist patrols.

He needed to get to the railway tracks.

Josh opened his eyes.

"I can give you another shot of the morphine in twenty minutes," McCall said. "Right now I need to access the maps in my backpack."

Josh grabbed McCall's backpack and rummaged in it. He brought out a sheaf of maps. He unfolded the one McCall indicated to him, with red-shaded areas that slanted across Syria.

"Find the railway lines," McCall said.

It took all Josh's concentration to focus on the map. "We're northwest of them, maybe twenty miles. There's no train running across this terrain at night. The extraction point was further south, at the Turkish border, at Latakia."

"You were given the wrong intel. Latakia is too close to the coast. You'd have crossed at the Akçakale checkpoint in Turkey and Tel Adyad, in Syria, and that's a bottleneck. We need to head north to avoid Kahramanmaras and Urfa. We'll head to Afrin on the Aleppo Road. It's marked there by the bridge into Aleppo."

"I got it. There was one train on the extraction route I was instructed to take."

"Same wrong intel. We could get the Ic Anadola Maui Trento Adana, then the Mersin-Haler train from Aleppo and change at Damascus, but that train has been canceled at the Turkish border."

"Gunner's XO, a chief warrant officer, had an alternate route picked out for me."

"Probably to pick up the Toros Ekspersi, the Taurus Express, from Istanbul, but that's a long shot. Might or might not be running. We can take the train from Aleppo that goes via Deir-ez-Zor and Al-Qamishli."

Josh sat back. He looked out at the road that twisted and turned back onto itself, flooded with moonlight now. The sandstorm had died considerably with only mild gusting across the lonely terrain.

"So all of the intel I received on the extraction points has been compromised."

"I'd say so," McCall said.

"That's not possible, unless . . ." The words died in Josh's throat.

"Unless the intel you've been given has been deliberately false."

Josh had no response.

McCall weighed the realization of the betrayal that was going on inside the young Army captain's head.

"Get some rest. We're eighty kilometers away from Aleppo, where we'll pick up the train."

Josh closed his eyes. The pain was starting to overtake him. McCall kept to the twisting road for another twenty miles, then pulled over at the side of the highway. He took out the med kit, loaded up the syringe, and gave Josh another shot of morphine.

He had a new concern.

The gas gauge on the Humvee had read just above half when he'd driven away from the Syrian village. Now it had dropped below a quarter of a tank. McCall crawled under the vehicle and inspected the tank. It had been punctured on one side, a small hole, but enough to do damage. He rooted in the back of the Humvee, found a switchblade, and cut a piece of the seat canvas. He stuffed it into the bullet hole to slow the flow of the gas leak. He climbed back into the Humvee and pulled off the road, heading through the desert toward the small town of Afrin. He glanced at the chronometer on his wrist.

They would be cutting it very fine.

McCall followed the map as a guide, using the GPS to transverse their most direct route. The sandstorm had fully abated. Stars gleamed in the desert sky so close McCall felt he could reach out for them. Josh had slipped back into unconsciousness. McCall knew he had to get the Army captain to an ER facility across the Turkish border, maybe in Suruç, but that had been heavily bombed and might even have been evacuated by now. There was a hospital in the Kurdish area southeast of Diyarbakir that McCall knew was run by the Joint Commission International, but that was 190 kilometers away from the border with Syria.

McCall drove for over an hour while the mountains rose up around him. In the distance he caught a glimpse of the Haradara steel-truss railway bridge that spanned the valley. Moonlight cradled it as it gleamed like a frozen jewel outlining the two steel supports that descended into the river gorge below. McCall had noted the small bridge on the Aleppo road they'd passed ten minutes ago. He looked at the Humvee's fuel gauge. It quivered at empty. McCall roused Josh and pointed to the Haradara Bridge, spanning the gorge.

"The CFS trains running on the Damascus al-Hizjaz Railway are all diesel-electric traction, but none of them can go higher than fifty kilometers an hour. The bridges of the Kurd-Dagh are seriously in need of repair, and the locomotive engineers slow down across some of them. This is the longest one. I'm going to try to delay them even more."

Josh looked over at the fuel gauge. "You know we're out of gas?"

"The Insurgents had their tank ruptured and didn't bother to repair it. We just need to squeeze a few more miles out this vehicle before the bridge."

McCall drove fast from the old Aleppo road, turning around a hairpin bend. The engine was catching now, sputtering badly. McCall coasted down the rest of the way to where the Haradara Bridge spanned the gorge and pulled over to the edge just as the Humvee died.

The train whistle blasted six chimes through the night. McCall noted a white building on the edge of the bridge, but it looked like it had been looted and abandoned some time ago. He strapped on his backpack and helped Josh get out the other side. McCall hopped into the back of the Humvee to do an asset inventory. He threw some old tarpaulins to one side and dug out some black parkas buried in the debris. One of them would fit Josh. He also found an old overcoat. McCall jumped back down and handed the parka and overcoat to Josh.

"I don't want anyone on that train recognizing you as an US Army officer."

Josh pulled the parka over his head. McCall wrapped the old overcoat around Josh's shoulders.

"What about the assault rifles?" Josh asked.

"We're not going to shoot up the train. Put your Colt .45 into your backpack. Also the Makarov pistol."

McCall had already put the Totarev TT-33 and the Browning semi pistol confiscated from the Insurgents in his backpack. If they searched him, McCall would take them out, firing. He still had his own Makarov pistol in the pocket of his coat.

One more blast of the six chimes and the train was traveling to the bridge span.

McCall and Josh slid down the steep slope to the bridge. The train started over the bridge. Its speed was much slower, but even so, it was already at the first steel span. McCall took out one of the packs of four signal flares from his backpack. He hit the first one on the ground to strike the explosive percussion cap, emitting orange smoke. McCall threw the flare as far as he could. It landed on the rails, sending plumes of smoke drifting across it. If the locomotive engineer knew his track geometry, he'd have already applied the brakes. McCall threw the rest of the flares across the tracks, all of them exploding with orange and red smoke.

McCall and Josh ran out onto the railway bridge above the dizzying gorge.

The train emerged from the billowing red and orange smoke, a gray metallic color with a red stripe running down the railway cars. The smoke was dissipating slowly. The brake was still being applied hydraulically as the locomotive engineer put pressure against the reservoir at each train car.

McCall figured that they had maybe twenty seconds until the train came to a full stop.

But the train wasn't coming to a full stop.

It was picking up speed again.

McCall and Josh ran along the edge of the bridge span as the train reached them.

McCall lifted Josh up at the second carriage and he fell onto the moving platform. McCall joined him and opened the door to the train car.

They moved inside.

CHAPTER 24

The railway car had two blue cloth seats on either side of the aisle with white cloths draped at their tops. It was not as packed as McCall had feared. There was a cross section of Syrian civilians, mainly older people, the women wearing various scarves and head coverings, the men dressed casually in jackets, some children wearing jeans and T-shirts and hoodies. People looked at them warily, avoiding their eyes, looking out the windows at the glinting steel bridge span. McCall recognized their uneasiness. He and Josh were white foreigners who had boarded the train while it had come almost to a stop. They shouldn't be here. Their very presence brought a sense of foreboding to a populace sick of war.

McCall found them two seats almost at the back of the railway car. He dropped his backpack onto the floor and stuffed Josh's backpack behind the rear seat. Josh collapsed into the window seat. His breathing was shallow. He nodded in answer to McCall's unspoken question, but McCall felt like he was losing him. He leaned close to Josh, speaking softly as the train accelerated across the bridge.

"If there's a ticket collector, I'll take care of him. Don't talk to anyone. I'm going to check out the rest of the train cars. That last shot of morphine should buy you another hour or more. You okay?"

Josh nodded again and closed his eyes. McCall left him there and made his way to the connecting door and out onto the short platform to the next car. This one was crowded. McCall moved down the car, not making eye contact. The passengers would have reacted to the shudder of the train as it had decelerated. Some of them on the right-hand-side windows would have seen the smoke billowing its tendrils of orange and red streamers.

McCall walked through the connecting door to the next carriage. Same curious stares. He reached the last train carriage. A door at the end of it led to an enclosed baggage compartment. If there were Insurgents in it, McCall would have to take them out. He couldn't have anyone radioing ahead, even though he knew there would be limited communications this far out.

Nothing was in the enclosed baggage compartment except piles of luggage.

McCall moved back through the other railway cars, rocking with the sway of the train as it thundered toward Aleppo. The train would stop there and people would get off.

First point of vulnerability.

When McCall entered the second-to-last train car, he saw a young woman seated beside Josh. She was in her midtwenties, black hair caught up in a red scarf. As McCall got closer he saw bright green eyes, a high fore-head, prominent cheekbones. She was very attractive. A child was asleep at the window seat opposite, dressed in jeans, a black Syrian-flag T-shirt, and a blue jacket.

The young woman looked up at McCall without the requisite suspicion in her eyes and said, *"Masaa el kheer."* Good evening.

McCall addressed her in Arabic. *"Hal beemkani mos'adatt."* Can I help you?

"Ana bekhair, shukran." I'm fine, thanks!

McCall noted a strong French accent coming through the Arabic. *"Tu parle français?"* You speak French?

Now she lapsed into rapid-fire French.

McCall nodded. "You speak it well," he said, also in French.

She told him she had attended the Lycée Français Charles de Gaulle in London, but she had returned to Syria and her French was a little rusty. *"Je suis un peu rouillé."*

McCall told her her French was fine and knelt down beside her. She told him she and her daughter, Aleena, lived in Aleppo. Her name was Brielle. Both her Syrian parents were working in the city and were living in fear. She was a student and wanted to return to the United Kingdom, but now she had a two-year-old daughter to look after. She kept up her guileless appraisal of McCall's face. She told him he had a kind face. He assured her that it wasn't, but she insisted he had seen much tragedy. He didn't argue.

Brielle looked around the train carriage. Everyone in the passenger car had known tragedy. It was part of their lives now. She told him that she knew his friend was hurt. She could see some bleeding under the overcoat he wore across his shoulders. She could help McCall re-dress his wound, if he wanted her to. No one in the train car would have to know.

McCall told her to go ahead.

Brielle helped Josh out of the overcoat and the parka, revealing the US Army uniform beneath. If she was stunned to see it, she did not let on. The girl unbuttoned his Army tunic and took it off. McCall shielded them as he pulled the trauma kit out of his backpack and took out another emergency trauma dressing and a roll of surgical tape. They removed Josh's bloody bandage. Brielle used hydrogen peroxide to clean the wounds with antiseptic swabs. McCall gave her some QuikClot clotting gauze, which she put across the wound. He found another pouch in the trauma kit with a triangle bandage, which they wrapped around the wound, and bound it tight. It would have to do until McCall could get Josh across the Turkish border. His makeshift nurse watched as McCall fitted the syringe into the small morphine bottle. It would be empty soon. He found a vein and pushed the needle into Josh's arm. Josh relaxed, but his breathing remained shallow. McCall put the trauma kit back in the backpack while Brielle buttoned Josh's Army shirt and pulled the parka over his head. She pulled the old overcoat around his shoulders.

Josh nodded his thanks. His pale face was glistening with perspiration. McCall got up and let Brielle out from the seat. The train was losing speed as it rolled through the streets of Aleppo. People around them were up on their feet, pulling backpacks and small items out of the overhead racks. Brielle sat down across from her daughter and gently awakened her. She was sleepy and didn't want to move. Brielle told her in Arabic they had to get off the train. Time to go home.

The train pulled into the station platform opposite a low-hanging veranda and came to a shuddering halt. Their train compartment was parked opposite a station entrance, where a bright window overlooked a squat marble fountain surrounded by polished floors. An ornate sign said THE HALL. Even though it was in the middle of the night, whole families were getting off the train. No passengers were boarding the train. This would be the place where armed Insurgents would attack the train if they'd found their quarry.

Brielle had fastened her daughter's jacket around her and put a balaclava on her head, which the child was trying to take off. Brielle moved out of her seat with the child in her arms and looked at McCall and Josh.

"*Bettawfeeq.*" Good luck!

"*Shukran jazeelan.*" Thank you very much.

McCall added, in English, "Your name, Brielle, means 'God is my strength' in Arabic. It's a beautiful name. Keep yourself and your daughter safe."

None of the Syrians took any notice of the hasty English words. Brielle nodded and looked at McCall and Captain Josh Coleman as if her heart would break for both of them. Then she moved quickly to the train door, where a heavyset railway official helped her and her child onto the platform. The train started up again. McCall watched as Brielle and Aleena walked into the station and were swallowed up in the midst of the other passengers. Aleppo station slipped away as the train picked up speed. They were heading toward Myslimiya–Ar Ra'y–Çöbanbey before crossing the Turkish border to the city of Mersin. In five minutes they would be back into the countryside.

"Will Brielle and her daughter make it?" Josh said.

It was a rhetorical question, but McCall answered it anyway.

"They're vulnerable. But these people are resilient. They will resist. They'll survive."

"Maybe I was wrong about the mercenary instincts in you."

McCall ignored that. "We're going to get off the train just before the Turkish border. That last shot of morphine should you get that far."

The Army captain looked out the train window.

McCall waited.

"There's a secret list," Josh said, keeping his voice low.

McCall noted the passengers who were left in the railway car had moved down some rows to be farther away from them. "What kind of a list?" McCall asked softly.

"Names of men fighting with the Insurgents in Syria. They have been radicalized. They have an elitist status and are fully committed to the Insurgent doctrine. Colonel Michael Ralston and I have been compiling the list through intelligence sources while on this UN peacekeeping mission. It's grown exponentially. A few of them are deserters, Insurgent sympathizers, and mercenaries. But not all of them."

Pain racked the Army captain's body and he sat back, fighting off the wave of nausea. McCall gave him an antinausea shot of Phenergan. He didn't want him passing out. Josh looked at the Syrian landscape flashing past, bathed in moonlight, high cirrus clouds streaked with blurred edges making a patchwork of sailing ships.

When he found his voice again it was stronger. "They are all American citizens."

McCall looked at him. "They're Americans?"

"That's right. If just one of them made their way out of Syria or Iraq, had his hair cut short, cleaned up, and returned with a valid passport, they'd go right through US Customs, no questions asked. They would be assimilated right back into our society with no one realizing what kind of a threat they posed to our national security. Their crimes are treason against the United States."

"Where is that list?"

"The photographs, barely recognizable as Americans, were up on a bulletin board at the team HQ at Ar Raqqah with as much intel as we've been able to compile. I had a duplicate copy of the list. We were going to submit the intel to the Pentagon, but we were still working on the identities of the fighters."

"How many American names had you compiled?"

"Nine."

"How many in your UN contingent had access to this list?"

"Just myself and Colonel Ralston. We were compiling the photographs and sightings, some of them from Kurdish tribal leaders, but we weren't making any headway with them. There are talks to include Syria in an UN-backed plan that was agreed to by top diplomats in Vienna, of which my mother, Helen, was one of the principal architects, followed by the creation of a transitional government, a new constitution, and elections within eighteen months. But there were no invitations sent to the Democratic Union Party about this first stage of the Syrian talks. According to Gunner, the concern at the Pentagon is the possibility, however temporary, of an accord being reached between Syria's Arab tribes and militant Salafist groups such as the al-Qaeda–affiliated Jabhat al-Nusra, the Victory Front. A tribal sheikh told us that, with no international support, Syrian tribes would do what they had to do to protect their assets, including aligning with military Salafist groups, even Iran, to maintain their autonomy with both the Syrian state and armed opposition. They're not interested in helping the US Army hunt down traitors to the American way of life, which is viewed as corrupt and against the will of Allah."

Josh fought off another bout of pain and let it subside. "There was a contact I was liaising with in Syria who had deserted from the Insurgents. He was hiding out in the village of al-Sukhnah. The villagers took me to meet with him. I briefed Colonel Ralston about it. He was going to arrange to get him airlifted out of Syria. This deserter was going to give us more American names. And there was something else." McCall waited. "He said there were mercenaries who were *protecting* these traitors. Hired by *our own government*."

McCall was stunned. "Did he have any proof of that?"

"He said he'd overheard conversations. Then there was firing in the village. The man bolted and the Insurgents shot him. That was when I got hit in the firefight. I managed to get out of the village before the Insurgents could find me."

McCall was looking out the window at the countryside flashing past. Then he looked out the far window, which reflected only darkness.

"What is it?" Josh asked.

"We're slowing down."

McCall slid across the aisle to where the two seats had been vacated by Brielle and her daughter and looked out. Ahead he saw an abandoned railway station that looked like some forgotten relic from US pioneer days. The two-story structure had yellow sidings and red roofs, one of which had partially caved in. Next to one of the station entrances was a hole you could have driven a truck through. The annex beside the main station and a water tower beyond it also looked derelict. The station had nothing surrounding it. The train tracks were overgrown with tall weeds that grew eight feet high. The train whistle gave its two-chime warning, the brakes were applied grudgingly, slowing the train further. McCall could see a white sign above a low roof under the main station entrance.

YOUDEHI.

There was no movement inside the abandoned station.

No train has pulled up here for a very long time, McCall thought.

The passengers in the railway car had their faces pressed to the glass. Whispers of *Daesh* came back to him.

"Company," McCall said.

He grabbed his backpack and hauled it up on his back. He pulled Josh out of his seat, swinging his backpack up to him. "They'll search the train. We need to get to the back of the last car."

The train came to a shuddering halt outside Youdehi station. McCall could hear faint shouting now. He and Josh moved through the connecting door. Passengers were in the next railway car. Heads turned as McCall supported Josh through it. The train started to sway. It had been boarded. More shouted voices, in Arabic. Questioning, demanding. No shooting yet.

The last car was filled with passengers. McCall and Josh moved through the enclosed baggage area to the last door and out onto the platform. A blast of night air engulfed them. Now the shouted voices of the Insurgents were loud and strident. McCall looked down the train. Two vehicles had pulled up near the station. One was a UAZ-469 Russian military all-terrain vehicle, filled to capacity. McCall recognized the other vehicle as a US Army light strike vehicle, small and mobile, a version of the desert patrol vehicle that must've been stolen by the Jihadists in a raid. It should have carried a two-man contingent, but it was so loaded with manpower it looked as if it might just topple over.

McCall helped Josh down to the tracks. Both of them were swallowed up in the eight-foot weeds as they ran into the abandoned railway station. The interior was littered with debris, and one of the walls had partially collapsed, spewing bricks across the station floor. A staircase led up to the second floor, but most of the stairs were smashed. McCall and Josh ran to a back entrance—none of the entrances had doors—and McCall pulled up short. He had been expecting to see a wide expanse of scrub terrain ahead of them. Instead, an abandoned train with tank wagons sat rusting on the tracks. McCall scrambled under the first wagon. Josh crawled after him, then both of them were on the other side.

"The Insurgents will have to search every one of these tank wagons in case you're hiding in one of them," McCall said tersely. "They don't have any idea we were on that train. They would be looking for you to be traveling alone if they had found that goatherder's hut outside the water trough."

More shouting reached them. McCall heard the throaty roar of the light strike vehicle as it raced along the rails outside the abandoned station. He and Josh came to a steep gradient that towered twelve feet. They skidded down the incline, both remaining upright until they reached the lower bank.

McCall looked up.

The towering tank wagons blocked out the sky. McCall heard more shouting in Arabic. The Insurgents were searching the abandoned station. He heard the LSV crisscrossing back and forth, between the train and the station.

They don't know we're even here, McCall thought.

At that moment the moon plunged back under its cloud cover, throwing the indigo-violet terrain into darkness.

McCall and Josh were swallowed in the shadows.

They stayed in the cloud cover, for which McCall was grateful. After twenty minutes he called a halt in the fields that crisscrossed the landscape. They could still hear the train idling on the tracks. It hadn't continued its journey toward the Turkish border. The Insurgents had found nothing on the train or the abandoned station and had starting searching the stationary tank wagons. McCall pulled a bunch of maps out of his backpack and checked their GPS coordinates on the chronometer on his wrist.

"We can't reach the Turkish border," Josh said.

The wind had come up again and swirled around them, but it brought no sand eddying with it.

McCall unfolded one of the maps. "We could reach Rmeilan Airfield in Hasakah."

"I know it. Colonel Ralston said that Rmeilan has been handed back to the Kurdish People's Protection Units. But the airfield was also to be given back to the SDF with a deal to provide weapons and US planes."

"I don't know if the Pentagon followed up on that deal," McCall said, "but I know the US military has been expanding the airfield. It's too far to reach, but there's an abandoned Syrian airfield fifteen miles from these coordinates. My pilot said it was being used for MiGs to refuel, but that intel is sketchy. It's probably got some hangars and an admin building. It may be completely abandoned, but I don't have a better idea. If there are planes there, I can fly one of them."

In the distance was the sound of the Daesh vehicles revving. The passenger train started up again, moving down the rails toward the Turkish border.

McCall refolded the maps, put them into the backpack, and recalculated their position on the GPS. "As long as the moonlight doesn't come back out, we've got a chance. But we've got to move as fast as we can."

"I'm good."

McCall nodded. "Let's go."

CHAPTER 25

They headed due northwest for four miles, then crossed two fields and came to a rural road. McCall consulted the GPS on the chronometer, correcting their course, until out of the murk he saw the silhouettes of the buildings rear up out of the night sky.

Then the moon came back out from the cloud cover.

McCall could make out a fence. He took out the pair of Steiner binoculars from his backpack, adjusted the laser range finder, and looked through them. The gray-green sheen made the cluster of buildings look surrealistic, like crouched insects. The six hangars had seen better days. The administration building looked completely deserted. No lights were burning; there was no movement at all. McCall swept the glasses down the field. There was an AN-Coke Soviet Union twin-engine military transport, turboprop-powered with twin engines on high monoplane wings with a single rudder fin fit to the empennage. It didn't look to McCall as if it had ever left the airfield, much less got airborne. There was a Dassault Falcon 20C, equipped with low-pressure tires for gravel runways, with a reinforced belly, larger wheels, and no main gear doors. McCall remembered that a Falcon 20 was the first civil jet to fly on 100 percent biofuel. No good to him. A half dozen Cessnas were around the hangars, including a Cessna 182 RC, a Cessna 210, a Cessna 205, and a 207, which was an eight-seat model turbo Skywagon. McCall recalled the aircraft's tail had been moved relative to the main wheel, which made landing without striking the tail skid on the runway a challenge.

McCall lowered the glasses. Beside him, Josh was feverish. McCall didn't like the look of his eyes. His skin was the color of wax paper. McCall listened for the sounds of pursuit behind them, but there was nothing now but the mournful wind stirring the tall grass.

When they reached the chain fence, McCall took out a small multitool from his backpack and cut through the wire. He pulled back a section just wide enough for them to gain access with their backpacks. It took them another minute to reach the first hangar. The doors were wide open, probably housing one of the Cessnas. Another hangar was beside it, with a sixteen-meter span, five-meter-high doors, and two more set back beside the administration building with coarse grass rising ten feet. The hangars were all empty. McCall found a metal folding chair that he dragged out of the first hangar for Josh.

McCall said, "I'm going to check out the Cessnas, see if they have any fuel on board. If not, I'll check the hangars. Don't move from this spot." McCall rummaged through his backpack and came up with a 12-gauge flare-gun pistol with four 12-gauge aerial flares. He loaded one of them into the pistol and handed it to Josh. "That flare will burn for seven seconds and reach a height of five hundred feet. Don't fire it if you don't have to."

Josh lay back against the gray metal hangar door where it retracted and waited. McCall ran to where the Cessna airplanes were strung out in front of the hangars. He climbed into the 182 RC, but there were no keys to turn it on. He climbed into the Cessna 210 and rummaged through a side pocket and found a set of spare keys. He slid into the cockpit and turned the key on the front panel.

The lighted gas gauge hovered at empty.

McCall nodded. All of the aircraft would have been drained of fuel. An abandoned airfield like this been had left derelict for a reason. The YPG, the People's Protection Units of the Kurdish militia, had made sure the planes were not operational. It was another ghost town, this one made up of expensive airplane carcasses.

McCall climbed into the Cessna 207, the eight-seat Skywagon, still hoping for a miracle. He found a spare set of keys in the side pocket and turned the aircraft on. Same story. No fuel. McCall cursed softly. He had to get Captain Josh Coleman to a hospital over the Turkish border before it was too late. He looked through the Cessna window at the long shadows that played in and out of the grounded airplanes. There was no sign of the MiGs that were purported to be stationed at the airfield. McCall suspected they were at Rmeilan Airfield.

He heard the whine of the pistol and then the burst of the flare overhead. It bathed the Cessna in rainbows as illuminated starbursts soared down to the ground. McCall swung out of the Cessna Skywagon and ran to the first hangar building. Josh was back inside in the shadows. McCall looked out across the chain fence. Shapes were rolling toward them: the bulky UAZ-469 Russian military vehicle, packed with Insurgents, and the small US Army LSV desert patrol vehicle.

McCall and Josh had been *off* the radar, swallowed up in the terrain. Two silhouetted figures on the run, with no GPS tracking them, reaching an abandoned airfield with no personnel, no security, no armed patrols.

So how had the Insurgents found them?

Josh moved out of the hangar to McCall and handed him the empty flare pistol. He had drawn his Colt .45.

"No fuel?"

"No."

Josh nodded. There was nowhere else to run.

This was where they would make their final stand.

McCall drew the Makarov pistol from his belt and backed into the deeper shadows in the hangar beside the Army captain.

And then all hell broke loose.

A steady thrumming had insinuated itself into the night. McCall stepped into the moonlight and saw a helicopter angling over the small airfield. The Soviet Mi-24 gunship, a low-capacity transport, had room for eight passengers. It was a dull gunmetal and was camouflaged with flat glass that surrounded the cockpit that McCall recalled Soviet pilots called drinking glass. A rapid-fire machine gun in the chin turret of the chopper erupted at the oncoming Insurgents. Then the pilot fired a 9K114 Shturm antitank missile. It exploded just behind the UAZ-469 military vehicle, upending it, sending the Jihadists out into the desert. The desert patrol vehicle swerved around the blast, still heading for the airfield.

McCall knew who was at the controls of the helicopter.

He ran back to the open hangar to Josh.

"What's happening?"

"The cavalry's arrived," McCall said. "Let's go!"

They sprinted out into the phosphorescence refracted across the Cessnas. The chopper dropped down toward the tarmac. That's when McCall saw a *third* vehicle, a 2007 Hummer H2 from the US Army. It was crammed to capacity with Jihadists. It crashed right through a section of the fence. Behind it came the light strike vehicle, its two-man crew firing from their iron shell.

The Mi-24 helicopter came in for a landing, its downdraft heavy.

McCall took aim with the Makarov pistol at the LSV and shot one of the Insurgents, who was leaning so far out that if he hadn't been shot, he would have fallen out. The second Jihadist fighter overcorrected the light vehicle's trajectory. McCall fired, sending the Makarov bullets through his head. The light strike vehicle spun around and crashed over onto its steel rib cage. McCall ran past the Cessnas 210 and 205, angling past the Cessna Skywagon to where the Mi-24 chopper had settled on the tarmac. McCall could hear Josh's breathing as he ran. The Army captain was pushing for the helicopter with every fiber of his being. McCall saw Hayden Vallance firing a borrowed AMD-65 assault rifle.

They were so close.

The Hummer served around the parked Cessnas.

More machine-gun fire.

Bullets slammed into Josh's body.

A cry exploded from McCall's very being. He practically lifted Josh off the ground as they reached the Mi-24. Vallance emptied the rest of the AMD-65 into the oncoming Hummer. The vehicle spun and slammed into the parked Cessna Skywagon.

It exploded into a fireball.

Vallance pulled Josh inside the helicopter. McCall climbed up after him. Vallance was already at the controls, lifting off. McCall turned in the open door of the chopper, firing at the Hummer, from which more Insurgents had scrambled. He picked off six more of the enemy. The Cessna was blazing brightly, throwing a red glow across the other aircraft. One of the Jihadists ran limping toward the rising helicopter, firing at it, the bullets ricocheting as it peeled off.

McCall's Makarov was empty.

He fell back at a forty-five-degree angle, grabbed the 12-gauge flare-gun pistol that Josh had stuffed into his belt, loaded another flare into it, and fired. The flare slammed right into the Jihadist fighter, blowing him back into the conflagration of the Cessna Skywagon.

By that time the helicopter was angled over the fence surrounding the small airfield. Josh lay back with his head against one of the chopper's rear seats, his eyes closed. McCall moved beside him and tore off the overcoat and the parka and examined the bullet wounds. There were three. All of them had entered Josh's body at the side and had not exited. McCall took off his backpack, took out the med kit, and filled a syringe with morphine. It was the last dose he had. He pulled the Army tunic off Josh's shoulder and plunged the syringe into his arm.

"We're taking you to the Suruç Hospital in Turkey."

Josh opened his eyes and looked up at McCall with remarkably clear vision. "Need to show you something," Josh managed through the pain.

"It'll wait. Lie still. I'll find out how far we are from the Turkish border."

McCall pulled Josh's tunic back on his shoulder and climbed into the copilot's chair. The helicopter was across the terrain with the stars to light its way. Vallance kept close to the ground. McCall understood. Vallance didn't want to be shot at again by Insurgents carrying antiaircraft weapons.

"Where are we headed?"

"We can't reach Suruç Devlet Hastanesi Hospital," Vallance said. "It has been bombed into the ground. The Özel Pirsus Tip Merkezi Hospital off the Curhuriyet, near Marut Sokah, is our next bet. I'll be flying right off the radar. They will scramble Turkish fighters to pick us up, but they have to catch us first."

"How long?"

"Maybe under an hour."

"Where you pick up the Crocodile?"

"At Aleppo. I had to ditch the Vista. They left the chopper sitting right on one of the far runways."

"How did you find us?"

"I had your GPS tracking intel from your wrist chronometer. I flew over the coordinates you'd shown me, but there was no sign of anyone except a herd of goats. I lost you for a time at the railway, then I picked up the train from Aleppo. I thought you were on your way, but right before I peeled off, the train stopped. I tracked your GPS coordinates to this airfield. I had no idea if you were alone or if you'd found your Army captain. I should have known better."

"You came back for me."

"I changed my mind. How bad is he?"

"He's on me."

McCall clambered back into the interior of the chopper and sat beside Josh. "Almost home," he said softly.

The Army captain had taken a sheet of folded paper out of his tunic pocket. His voice was barely above a whisper, almost lost entirely in the racket the helicopter was making. He sounded delirious.

"Nine American names on the list that I made up with Colonel Ralston. But there's a tenth man. Not on the list. I saw him in Al Tabqah. Standing beside a stolen US Humvee. He'd torn off his balaclava and face covering. I *saw* him!"

"*Who* did you see?"

Josh gripped McCall's arm tighter. The delirium was thicker. "The mercenaries are protecting all three of them. Not a part of the Pentagon. They're being run from a spy organization. One man knew what was happening.

Couldn't stop it. A conspiracy against our country. National security threatened."

Josh started coughing, spitting up blood. McCall caught him as he pitched forward, but he was just holding a shell. Josh pressed the piece of folded paper into McCall's hands. He put his lips up to McCall's ear and whispered. The words were so faint, but . . .

McCall didn't *believe* what he had just heard.

He pushed Josh away and held him rigid. "What was that name?"

"Tell Helen I'm sorry," Josh said, rallying. "You came for me. No one else could have done that. We almost made it. Tell her I love her. That I'm sorry about . . ."

He faltered again.

"What was that name you whispered to me?" McCall said, almost shaking him.

But Josh had slumped back, his eyes finding something in McCall's face that made him sad. Then he shook his head and closed his eyes and was gone.

McCall settled him back onto the helicopter seat and, as an afterthought, fastened the seat belt to keep him in place. He unfolded the piece of paper Josh had given him.

It was the list of American-extremist names.

McCall looked out at the Syrian landscape. Did he tell Helen Coleman that her son had lived long enough to tell him dangerous secrets? That Helen's Equalizer had rescued a good man and then let him die in his arms?

McCall raised his voice. "Can you pick up another jet in Turkey?"

Vallance said, "I'll have to explain why I was flying a Soviet attack helicopter, but I'll do what you would do and improvise. I'll make for Sabiha Gökçen International Airport in Turkey. I can pick up a Challenger 350 in Malta. You can owe me. Do I bring the captain home?"

"Yes, to Washington, DC, but before that you have to land in London. I need to meet someone there."

"He whispered something to you. Something important?"

"Why should you care, Vallance? As far as Captain Josh Coleman was concerned, we're mercenaries, predators preying on the weak. Motivated to take part in whatever hostilities we are confronted with for our own personal gain."

"That works for me," Vallance said quietly. "I don't think that works for you. We're close to the Turkish border. Keep your eyes open."

Vallance turned his attention back to bringing the attack helicopter under the Turkish radar and out of Syrian airspace. He'd said all he was going to say. More than he should have.

McCall sat beside the body of Captain Josh Coleman and thought about his last words. It was the name of someone Josh could not have known.

It was the name of a man who no longer existed.

Captain Josh Coleman had leaned close to Robert McCall and whispered urgently to him Control's *real* name.

CHAPTER 26

It had been a grueling class. Only six students were in the dojo, most of them his age, although one kid stood out, he had to be ten years old, whom the sensi called Young Tiger. The Equalizer had worked on his kata, his *Kizami-zuki,* Thrust Punch; *Age-uke,* Upper Forearm Block; *Migazuki-geri,* his Crescent Kick. He had hoped to work on transforming himself into a Snake. He would bend backward, raising his head to strike, stretching out his palm to prepare to push and hack. But his sensi had told him he wasn't ready for that yet. The sensi called out encouragement to the class: "Tight fist, elbows in, head down, bend your knee." When the class had finally broken, his sensi had told him he had to work on his discipline. Then he was dismissed. He did not take it personally. He needed to master these martial arts moves for his work.

The Equalizer picked up the 1 subway at Eighteenth Street and took it to Sixty-Sixth Street and Lincoln Center. From there he walked to the Liberty Belle Hotel. He didn't have to wait long for Sam Kinney to exit the hotel. The Equalizer followed him back to Lincoln Center. The old man took the 1 subway to Fourteenth Street, walked down until he was at Sixth Avenue, changed to the L train, and got out farther along Fourteenth Street. He turned down Avenue A until he was at Tompkins Square Park, then turned east on Tenth Street until he reached a four-story redbrick apartment building on the corner of Avenue C. Sam ran up the limestone steps, put a key into the apartment door, and entered.

The Equalizer moved on down to the East Village Tavern on Tenth Street and ordered a coffee. He waited for Sam Kinney to come out again.

·   ·   ·

The two college types manhandled Melody into the cavernous ware-house room. Moonlight shafted in, but the windows were high and little of it filtered down to the floor. It was thick with shadows. Melody could make out gleaming steel cages. There were ten of them, fifteen feet by six feet, bolted to the floor. In eight of them were the silhouetted forms of young women, two to a cage, their clothes disheveled, faces pale, blondes and bru-nettes. They barely moved in their low prisons, most of them lying on the cage floors, a couple with fingers clenched around the bars. In the ninth cage there was only one woman, who sat up against the back bars, her face in shadow. The tenth cage was empty.

Melody had given up struggling. The young woman in the ninth cage didn't move as they reached it. College Boy #1 unlocked the padlock on the cage door and thrust Melody inside. She stumbled to the floor. College Boy #2 closed the cage door, snapped the padlock home. Their footfalls echoed to silence.

Melody shivered violently. Mr. McCall had told her this would be dan-gerous. But Blake had been *such* a gentleman during the few days she had been dating him. He had escorted her to her apartment building after an-other of their expensive lunches. Melody had said she was suffering from a migraine and didn't know if she would go to Dolls that night. Blake had told her she should lie down in a darkened room and try to feel better. He gave her another Rock Hudson kiss on the lips and hailed a cab. Melody had gone up to her apartment wondering if Mr. McCall had been wrong about this guy. She had gone to bed with two Excedrin migraine tablets with the curtains closed at her bedroom window.

Six hours later they had come for her. She'd heard a muffled sound, sat up in bed, grabbed her cell phone, but couldn't remember Mr. McCall's cell number. She had Tara Langley's number on speed dial. She'd pressed TEXT, typed in *I,* as in *I think someone is in my apartment,* and they'd grabbed her. Her silk teddy was pulled over her head. When she struggled, College Boy #1, a big guy, backhanded her. Her nose started to bleed. College Boy #2 slipped the blue dress over her head. College Boy #1 forced shoes onto her feet. They injected her with some kind of sedative that sent her right out. She had regained consciousness just as they were dragging her into the warehouse room.

Melody looked out at the other defeated, terrified young women locked in their cages. It was barbaric. There were too many for them to have been kidnapped for ransom or to satisfy Blake Cunningham's sexual fantasies.

This was business. Mr. McCall hadn't mentioned the words, but perhaps he didn't know yet.

White slavery.

Her cage partner crawled forward. She was a little younger than Melody, her short black dress ripped until it was basically tatters exposing most of her breasts and legs. Melody instinctively flinched. The girl put her arms around Melody and held her close. Melody laid her head against the girl's chest.

"It'll be okay," Emily Masden whispered. "Someone is coming for us."

Norman Rosemont had found a key to apartment 4B in the pants pocket of his Hugo Boss suit that he had missed before. In the morning, he marched across the corridor and pounded on the door of apartment 4A. Sam Kinney opened it with his usual flourish. He wasn't wearing his Liberty Belle Hotel uniform, but a brown cardigan over a maroon silk shirt that looked as if he'd borrowed it from Mick Jagger and flip-flops. Sam's face lit up.

"Hey, new neighbor! All moved in now?"

"I haven't got any hot water!" Rosemont accused Sam, as if it were *his* fault.

"Furnace is out again, huh?" Sam shook his head, still grinning. "Come on in, you're just in time for breakfast!"

Sam ushered Rosemont to an alcove where he could see a dining table set for two. Sam had a stack of pancakes on a platter, a pitcher of OJ, some cold cuts, and English muffins. "I'm just cooking a Colorado omelet and I got coffee brewing."

"You eat like this every morning?" Rosemont was flustered that his moral indignation had been put on hold.

"Oh, I never know which one of my neighbors is going to come gate-crashing! Sit! Sit!"

Sam hustled through a doorway where Rosemont could see a kitchen with a counter cluttered with enough gadgets to open a restaurant. Rosemount sat down at the dining table. "I looked for the super, but I couldn't find him anywhere."

Sam came back out into the dining room with a Presto stainless-steel coffeemaker. "When anything bad happens in the building you'll find the super at the Meadowlands racetrack, the fat fuck." Sam poured them coffee. "City Roast Colombia Supremo."

"Get the landlord who owns the building out here," Rosemont said, then realized what he'd just suggested.

"That'll be the day."

Sam hurried back into the kitchen. Rosemont took a swallow of his coffee. It was *really* good. Sam came back with two big plates heaped with Colorado omelets, bacon, and hash browns. "The tenants in this building have more to deal with than a furnace that could blow up any minute. You see the size of the rats down in the basement? We used to take 'em for walks with leashes in Tompkins Square Park until the pit bulls and Dobermans started retreating."

Sam sat at the dining table. Rosemont took a bite of his Colorado omelet and shrugged.

"That's pretty good."

"*Pretty good!* Gordon Ramsay has been chasing my recipes for years!"

The doorbell rang. Sam shot up from the dining table and returned with an attractive older woman, well dressed, her hair looking like she had spent two hours at the beauty salon. Rosemont thought she was probably in her late seventies, but didn't look it.

"Sam! I'm so sorry to barge in when you're having breakfast, but—" She pulled up short. "Oh, I'm sorry, I didn't know you had a guest."

"Four B, across the hall," Sam said affably. "Just moved in. I can whip up another omelet for you, Connie, throw in some jalapeños, I know you like them real hot."

"It has been said," Connie murmured, and almost got a smile from Rosemont. "No, no, I left Donald in our apartment looking for reruns of *Game of Thrones*. It's Mr. Toast, Sam! He went missing this morning!"

"I'll check for him." Sam said to Rosemont, "Connie was a Rockette, you know!"

Sam dashed out through the kitchen, down a short corridor into a bedroom.

Connie smiled. "My Rockette days are long gone now, but I do get the chance to kick my legs at Christmastime when we watch the show on TV. Much to my husband's horror when we have guests over!"

"How long were you a Rockette?" Rosemont asked in spite of himself.

"I joined the troupe in 1955. Was a part of it for thirty-six years. Had to give it up when I was pushing sixty up a hill." She took a small photo from her jacket pocket and showed it to Rosemont. "Here's a picture of me with the Rockettes, circa 1962. Our hearts were all aflutter because we were posing with Cary Grant. God, what a hunk. That's me in the first row, second from the left. Oh, my, look at that gorgeous red hair, comes out of a Clairol bottle of Born Red Nice'n Easy now. Mr. Grant was *so* gallant and charming." Connie's face suddenly lit up. "Oh, Mr. Toast!"

Sam had entered the alcove with a large short-haired Egyptian Mau cat with a mottled body with leopard's spots. He was squirming in Sam's arms and hissed at Rosemont, who almost leapt off his chair. Connie grabbed the cat from Sam and snuggled him against her copious chest.

"Where did you find the rapscallion?"

"He was under my bed."

"Well, there are worse places I could find myself!" Sam actually blushed. "This is a red-letter day! What's the lyric, Sam? You know the Broadway show I'm thinking of? 'I'm in the mood to get high with, love until I'm totally blind! Going to find me a guy with, the same kind of future in mind!' 'Red Letter Day!' *Rumple,* 1957, Broadway!"

Sam grinned as he sat back down to his breakfast. "Connie is a encyclopedia for Broadway shows. Forget *Wicked* or *Book of Mormon* or *The Lion King.* Sing one more for me, Connie! Just to make an old spy happy!"

"Oh, you never were a spy, Sam! You can't fool an old hoofer, but okay." If she'd been projecting, Rosemont thought she could have been heard out on the street. "'The little things you do together . . . that make perfect relationships, The concerts you enjoy together, Neighbors you annoy together, Children you destroy together, That keep marriage intact.' Can't go wrong with lyrics from Sondheim. Thanks for rescuing Mr. Toast. Nice to meet you, Mr. . . . ?"

"Just call him Mr. Apartment Four-B," Sam said.

Connie nodded and let herself out. Sam grinned and took another bite of his omelet. "She's something our Connie, isn't she?"

"Are all of the tenants in this building so gregarious?"

"I haven't met all of them, but some real nice folks."

Then there was another pounding on Sam's apartment door.

"It's like Grand Central in here this morning." Sam jumped up. "Have some more coffee."

Sam disappeared. Rosemont heard raised voices, then Sam returned with Linda Hathaway and her daughter, Gemma. Rosemont stiffened immediately. He recognized the little girl who had been bitten by rats in his building. Gemma was in shy mode today, hugging her mom.

Linda was apologetic. "I didn't mean to interrupt your breakfast, Sam."

"No problem. Say hi to my new neighbor, Four B. What can I do for ya?"

"My daughter has ripped up her jeans! It's the only pair she's got that isn't in the wash, she's got a school play today with all of her friends looking nice with their parents attending. I can't sew on a button!"

"Sit down right here, Gemma," Sam said. "Scoot out of those jeans! Be right back!"

He disappeared. Linda sat Gemma down on one of the dining-table chairs and pulled off her jeans. Rosemont couldn't help but notice the myriad bites on the child's legs. Sam came back with a sewing kit and sat down. "What did you *do* to these jeans, Gemma?"

"I was playing monsters in the playground."

Linda noted that Rosemont had noticed the telltale marks on Gemma's legs. "Rat bites. The building is infested with them."

"So do something about it!" Rosemont snapped, the guilt getting to him. "The building super can have the basement fumigated and the rats cleaned out in two days. No child should suffer like that."

"I've told Gemma *not* to go down into that basement! The hot water is off again, Sam, did you know that? So what's the verdict?"

"Almost finished. It's just a patch job. Done!"

Sam handed the jeans to Gemma, who squirmed back into them.

Linda kissed Sam on the cheek. "You're a lifesaver! We can't be late for the school bus." She scooted Gemma toward Sam's front door, acknowledging Rosemont. "Nice to meet you!"

Linda flew out into Sam's living room, and in another moment the front door slammed. Sam put away his sewing kit.

"Nice young gal. Warm up that coffee for ya?"

"No, I need to be on my way, too." Rosemont hastily got to his feet. "I'll have that furnace working by tonight." He glanced down at his Rolex Daytona watch. "And I'm late for a shareholders meeting. Another fiasco waiting to happen."

"If you want to drop in for breakfast tomorrow morning, I'll be whipping up a spinach-and-mushroom omelet with fresh vegetables." Sam's cell rang on the kitchen counter. "I'm telling ya, Grand Central Station. Let yourself out, okay?"

Sam ran into the kitchen to answer his cell, and Rosemont left the apartment.

"Hello?" Sam said. "Yeah, he's gone. You did great, Connie. I could listen to your Broadway repertoire all morning. Right after you left, Linda Hathaway came by with Gemma, who needed some repair work on her jeans.

Spontaneous visit. Linda didn't recognize Rosemont, but he recognized her daughter. He's kind of an in-your-face cold bastard, but I think those rat bites resonated with him. Thanks for helping out."

Sam hung up and looked around the small, shabby apartment he'd rented the day before yesterday. In that time he had made it a point to meet and greet as many of the tenants as he could, all of whom had grievances against Norman Rosemont and his real estate company. Sam didn't know if McCall's scheme would work. He thought McCall should do what he was good at and leave Norman Rosemont beaten up in an alleyway somewhere. But McCall's sense of justice wouldn't allow for that. Too bad. Sam wanted to see the billionaire taken down a few notches.

Down in front of the apartment building, Norman Rosemont almost collided with a young black student who ran down the apartment steps and leaped over the rancid garbage bags. He gestured to Rosemont he was sorry and ran on. Rosemont climbed into his silver Mercedes-Maybach S600 that he'd had delivered the night before. He pulled away from the curb, then recognized Linda Hathaway and Gemma running for the school bus parked at the corner. The bus doors closed and the vehicle drove off. Rosemont pulled over and purred the Mercedes passenger window down.

"I can give you and your daughter a lift to her school."

"Thanks, but we'll take the L at Fourteenth Street and First Avenue," Linda said, out of breath. "Thanks, anyway."

Linda grabbed Gemma's hand and they ran down the street. Rosemont was pissed off that she hadn't taken him up on his offer. But he couldn't get those rat bites on Gemma's arms and legs out of his mind. Behind him, Sam Kinney came running down the steps of the apartment building, but Rosemont had already pulled back out into the traffic.

The young man seated in the East Village Tavern on the corner of Tenth Street and Avenue C had left about 2:00 a.m. in the morning when he had realized that Sam Kinney was *staying* in this apartment building. Obviously he was spending the night. He was kind of an old fart to be visiting some woman's apartment, but to each his own. The Equalizer had returned to his table outside the East Village Tavern at six the next morning, where he ordered coffee and an apple bran muffin. Finally Sam Kinney came out of the apartment building and headed toward Avenue B and the L subway.

The Equalizer took a last swallow of coffee, devoured the apple bran muffin, and followed him.

CHAPTER 27

McCall waited for Control's executive assistant at the bar of the Duke of Argyll pub in London's Soho. It was packed with the after-theater crowd that had also spilled outside onto Brewer Street. The atmosphere in the pub was boisterous. McCall liked it. In an olde-worlde pub such as the Duke of Argyll, you met your friends, found out the scores of the soccer matches, what was on the telly, and who was screwing who while you nursed a pint for two hours. There was no TV, no music, no games. He'd last met Control in a pub like this. Control had brought him the dossier on Vladimir Gredenko, a Russian interrogator known in intelligence circles as Arbon, the "devil," whom Control had wanted McCall to impersonate. The life of a Company agent named Serena Johanssen was on the line. Six months later Serena Johanssen was dead and McCall had killed her assassin.

It would be the last assignment he ever took from Control.

McCall saw Emma Marshall enter the pub. It was a balmy night in London, which meant her skirt was just a little shorter than one a *Star Trek* yeoman would wear. She had on a man's white shirt showing a lot of cleavage and low pumps. She spotted McCall and slid onto the barstool beside him. She picked up his drink.

"Organic wheat beer?"

"When in Rome . . ."

One of the bartenders came over. Emma said, "Hey, Jeff, the place is jumping tonight. Give me a large gin and tonic with a slice of lemon, easy on the ice."

Jeff moved away. Emma looked around at the boisterous crowd. "I just came from the Apollo Theatre, *Nell Gwynn*, pretty racy for 1660. It was either that or seeing *No Man's Land* at the Wyndham's with Sir Ian McKellen and Sir Patrick Stewart, two old farts, one gay, the other straight, being obtuse and brilliant, but I wasn't in the mood for Pinter and complex ambiguities." She looked back at him. "I know you didn't come all the way to London to see me."

"Control. What happened?"

"I was summoned to his office and sent packing. A nice golden handshake and don't let the door hit your ass on your way out."

"Control fired you personally?"

"Not his style. He used one of the other Controls. There was a shake-up at The Company. I was just squeezed out."

"Control wouldn't have tolerated that. You were close to him."

"You never got too close to Control." Emma broke off as the bartender dropped her gin and tonic on the bar and moved back into the fray. "There was always a barrier up."

"No cups of coffee late at night when there was no one else there but the two of you?"

"He was my boss and I loved him. He looked down my shirt occasionally, particularly on days when I'd left my bra in the washing machine, and there was one night when he opened a bottle of Rémy Martin XO Excellence cognac and we got a little tipsy."

"Tell me about that night."

"He wanted to talk. About a lot of memories that had nothing to do with the spy business. Places he'd traveled to. In Singapore he liked going to the PasarBella in Bukit Timah, a marketplace like the one here in Covent Garden, with shops that sold steamer trunks and colonial dressers from a bygone era. He liked taking walks around the sacred sites in Lhasa in Tibet— I think he said they were *koras*—which one circumambulates, whatever the hell that is, where he'd go to the Potala Palace to see the lifeless halls where His Holiness used to live. The Tibetan Buddhists walk in a clockwise direction, did you know that? Did you ever see Control when he was pacing? Always did it in a clockwise direction. He spent time in Venice at the Scala Contarini del Bovolo in the San Marco area, which has a spectacular open spiral staircase called the snail shell, where you could climb up to the top of the palace and look out on the domes of Saint Mark. He liked Wharariki Beach on the tip of New Zealand, which has towering stone archways and windswept dunes where he could wrestle with the atrocities that were on his conscience."

McCall had noticed a young man enter the pub and look around. He was in his midtwenties with a gaunt face and close-cropped hair that was almost white-blond. His gray silk suit was expertly tailored with a coral twill paisley tie and diamond cuff links that caught the light. McCall saw his gaze fix on Emma. He moved toward her with the liquid grace of a caged jaguar. McCall noted a silver ring on his right hand of a demon-claws skull and, beside it, a second silver ring. As the man got closer, McCall saw that the engraving on the slim silver ring said REMEMBER THAT YOU MUST DIE.

"Memento mori," McCall said.

Emma paused in her reminiscences. "What's that?"

"It's a warning to prompt human beings to remember the inevitability of death and their own mortality. Philippe de Champaigne's painting *Still-life with a Skull* in the 1600s took the three basic elements: life, death, and the inexorable march of time."

"How charming." Emma motioned to the bartender for another round. "I'm broke, out of work, and my mother would drive any healthy, heterosexual daughter into an early grave. Where was I?"

"Telling me about your late-night session with Control."

"There were other exotic places Control said I should go to on my bucket list, but he didn't offer to take me to any of them."

"Did he talk about any enemies in The Company?"

"He had a lot of enemies, but he *had* been acting strangely the last time I saw him. Something was going on. He said it had to do with national security and people were talking conspiracy theories, but he had his *own* theories."

"Did he tell you anything about any of the other Controls?"

"I know Jason Mazer. He still has a hard-on about you, but you're kind of yesterday's news."

"What about Matthew Goddard?"

"I don't know him."

"He has an assistant named Samantha Gregson, who was sitting at your desk."

"She must've moved in when I moved out."

"What aren't you telling me?"

Emma glanced around. The decibel level in the pub was like being at an Iron Maiden rock concert. "It was no big deal."

Silver Skull had moved to the bar and ordered a drink, a B-52, one-third shot of Kahlúa, one-third shot of almond, and one-third shot of Baileys Irish Cream.

Emma sighed. "We'd polished off the bottle of Rémy Martin between us. The lights in the office were mostly out. Control was sitting on the edge of his desk. I remember his face was shiny and he was breathing a little heavy. He leaned down and kissed me. I kissed him back. He moved his hand down inside my shirt. I took his other hand and brought it up under my skirt. He pulled off my black panties, but then it was like he suddenly came up for air. He took his hand from my breast and his other hand from under my skirt and retreated to the window. I put my panties back on and left a couple buttons open on my shirt, just for appearances. I remember rain was streaking the window with crushed jewels. He never said a word about what had just happened. Forty hours later the bastard fired me."

"He's disappeared."

The bartender dropped Emma's second gin and tonic off to her. She squeezed fresh lemon into it, staring at McCall. "You mean he dropped off the grid the way you did? Control would never leave The Company. It's what he lives for."

"That late-night session between the two of you never happened."

"I don't remove my panties for just anyone. Well, that's not true. There was this bloke I met two nights ago who had broken down in Hampstead and I gave him a lift to the garage, and things got a little hot and heavy back at my place while the mechanic fixed his motor. I told him I'd call him, but I scribbled his number on a box of Dim T Chinese and it went into the rubbish."

"Control hasn't disappeared. He's been deleted."

"What the hell is that supposed to mean?"

"He was never in intelligence. He never lived in Virginia. He's not married to his wife, and there were never any children. He never existed."

Emma stared at him. "That's not possible."

"Someone at The Company has gone to great lengths to make it possible. And the only human being who actually knew Control's name—his *real* name—died in my arms sixteen hours ago. So if there's any more you can tell me about your erotic late session with the old man, I'd appreciate it."

"Bloody hell." Emma took a swallow of her drink.

McCall had watched the white-blond man make his way through the patrons three-deep at the bar. He had an Irish American accent that was melodious. "Excuse me."

He leaned right over Emma, smiled at her, grabbed a bar coaster, ignored McCall, and moved to one of the small tables. He sat at a cloth-covered stool and looked into the pub with his back to them.

"There was one other memory he shared that night," Emma said suddenly.

McCall looked back at her. "What was it?"

"A place he liked to go. No one else knew about it."

"A safe house?"

"No, it was off-the-books. It was somewhere he'd visited as a boy. He said he wasn't very old, maybe four or five. It was in the countryside, a big old house surrounded by forest. There was some workroom where his father made scale models, ships I think, where you fitted them into bottles. Control had liked looking at the models when his father was asleep, but he said he had to be careful not to be caught. I think he had his own key to the workroom. He loved wandering through the woods having grand adventures. There was another place he wasn't allowed to go where there were swings and old rotting buildings, high-up towers and dangerous curves, but I couldn't make out what he was talking about. He liked to sneak in there."

"This wasn't far from his house?"

"I don't think so. He also said he had found a special place in the woods. He had his own staircase."

"His *own staircase*?"

"It wasn't high up, not many steps. He said it didn't lead anywhere."

"It must've led somewhere."

"No, he said it had no beginning and no end."

"Where was this house?"

"Somewhere in Virginia? He said something about 'leopards.' That they were coming for him, but he had a pal with him in the woods, some RAF flying ace from World War Two who took him on adventures and kept the leopards from attacking them. He was a kid then, you know? Kids make shit up."

Emma finished her second gin and tonic and pushed it away from her. She looked a little woozy. "I think Jeff must've poured me a triple. I'm going to the loo."

She jumped off the barstool and dashed for a corridor to the restrooms. McCall noted that Silver Skull had finished his B-52 cocktail and was making his way to the doorway out onto Brewer Street. So maybe he didn't have anything to do with Emma Marshall.

McCall's cell rang. He moved out of the pub onto Brewer Street, pausing below the sign of what was presumably the Duke of Argyll. Through the pub windows he watched for Emma's return as he answered his cell.

"This is Robert McCall."

Helen Coleman said, "I knew when you didn't call me that I had lost my son."

McCall had been dreading the call. He had set out to find Josh Coleman. It didn't matter that he had rescued his client's son only to have him die in his arms. He had failed her.

"I heard from Colonel Ralston. Your pilot landed in Berlin and got in touch with the Pentagon. He told them he had the body of Captain Josh Coleman in a helicopter. He was waiting to get a small commercial jet to bring him back to the States. Your pilot didn't tell Gunner much, except that Josh was dead. He said you did all you could for him."

"It wasn't enough."

McCall heard Helen's voice tighten with suppressed emotion. "You told me that finding Josh in Syria was a very long shot, Mr. McCall. I kept hoping against hope. But I guess the odds were too great. I want to talk to you about what happened to Josh. Maybe after the funeral."

"I'll be there."

He was still looking through the bright pub windows. There was no sign of Emma. She might have been throwing up in the ladies' room, but something was sending alarm signals through his head.

"I will see you in New York, Helen."

McCall disconnected. He pushed through the throng of people back into the pub. Emma's spot at the barstool was still vacant. The bartender was looking after her bag where she'd left it. McCall made his way to the restrooms. He pushed past two gorgeous models who only had eyes for each other and knocked loudly on the ladies'-room door.

"Emma?" he shouted. "Are you okay?"

There was no response. One of the models said, "Some of us have to pee, too, you know."

McCall put weight against the old door and the hook, and the eye gave way. He burst inside. The ladies' room had two stalls. A young woman in jeans, a black turtleneck, and lots of jewelery was coming out of the first stall. She looked mildly surprised as she looped back up her belt.

"You shouldn't be in here, but your friend was a little green around the gills when she came in."

McCall threw open the door to the second stall.

It was empty.

The window was open, mainly because of the warm night.

McCall pushed out of the ladies' room and found a rear exit from the pub.

The narrow cobbled alleyway outside was deserted. McCall ran the length of it to a cross street. Two shadowy figures were manhandling Emma Marshall between them. She was doubled over, but suddenly she pulled out of their grasp and hit the first man across the face. She kicked the second man in the balls and staggered back down the street, but she didn't get far. She fell to her hands and knees and was sick in the gutter. It gave the thugs time to reach her.

McCall reached them first.

They were in their twenties, six-foot-three, and they were twins. Both of them had the same cropped white-blond hair and were mirror images of each other. They wore black. They were half turned around to McCall, so they formed a half circle. McCall recognized their moves immediately. Krav Maga.

Twin #1 threw a fist, which McCall sidestepped, smashing an elbow into his face. It shattered his cheekbone. At the same time, Twin #2 hit Mc-Call with the heel of his palm. It rocked him back. Twin #2 leaned down and wrapped his hands around McCall's throat. Instead of trying to clutch at the choke hold, McCall used his hands in a hooked shape to tear the assailant away. He locked his elbows around the back of Twin #2's neck. The grip was unbreakable. McCall dropped to a midcrouch, sending the thug to the cobblestones, knocking him unconscious.

Twin #1 was turning back. McCall kicked Twin #1's knee that was facing the wrong way. It cracked sickeningly. McCall followed with a palm strike just above Twin #1's ear. He staggered and pulled out a wicked paring knife from his pocket. He slashed at McCall's throat. McCall spun the knife away and swept Twin #1's legs out from under him. He crashed beside his brother, his head hitting the sidewalk. He didn't move.

McCall straightened.

The fight had lasted for two and a half seconds.

McCall picked Emma up. She held on to him, gasping for breath.

"They were waiting for me in the ladies' room. One of the Bobbsey Twins was the creep I gave a lift to when he had his car towed. That'll teach me not to give blow jobs to strangers who look like aliens."

"Come on." McCall moved her back down the street.

"What happened to me?"

"Your drink was spiked."

"You mean like a roofie? I didn't see either of them in the pub."

"It was someone else."

They moved down the cross street into the alleyway. Laughter wafted over from outside the pub. A pair of headlights suddenly blinded McCall. A Honda Civic jumped the sidewalk. McCall pushed Emma down to the cobblestones. He got out the way before the car could pin him against the building. He staggered and his right foot hit against an open cellar door. The figure was out of the Honda now, keeping the engine running. He kicked out languidly.

McCall was propelled into empty air.

He twisted so that he wouldn't break his back. He tumbled down the flight of wooden stairs and landed heavily. He looked to his left and recognized he was in the cellar of the Duke of Argyll pub. He scrambled back, but pain shot through his left ankle, which he'd twisted in the parachute jump in Syria. Above him, a figure climbed carefully down into the cramped space. McCall saw the close-cropped white-blond hair and the gray of his lightweight suit.

The silver skull gleamed on the man's right hand in the semidarkness. Memento mori.

McCall pulled himself up, clutching one of the fifteen-gallon steel kegs. Silver Skull jumped down the last two stairs. He attacked, throwing hammerfist strikes at McCall's head. McCall parried them with fast reflexes, but the assassin followed with knifehand strikes aimed at the mastoid muscles at McCall's neck, jugular, and collarbones. McCall fought them off and executed a kick to the man's left knee. It did only minimal damage, but gave McCall the chance to hobble on his injured ankle farther into the darkness of the beer cellar.

The two fighters struck with lightning ferocity at each other, probing for weaknesses, until McCall literally climbed up Silver Skull's body and ramped up over it, sending them both crashing down to the cellar floor. The assassin kicked at McCall's throat, just missing his jugular. McCall tried to get the man's head in a leg lock, but Silver Skull was stronger and scrambled out of it. Both of them leapt to their feet. Silver Skull came at McCall with a raw fury now, lashing out with punches and hammerfists, going for the nerve endings. McCall parried the blows, then dropped to his knees as if his ankle had given out on him. At the same time he pulled the paring knife from his pocket. Silver Skull caught hold of McCall's hair, savagely throwing his head back, but he didn't see the blade in McCall's hand. McCall cut through the silk material of Silver Skull's trousers and cut the tendons in his left leg to the bone. Silver Skull looked down, not knowing for a moment where the pain was coming from. He let go of McCall's hair. McCall, still on his knees, ripped through Silver Skull's right pant leg and sliced through to the tendons there as if they were made of tissue paper. With the tendons severed to both the assassin's legs, Silver Skull toppled backward toward the floor of the cellar. McCall rammed the paring knife up through his throat. Blood gushed out of the assassin's mouth, nose, and ears. McCall knew he was dead before his head slammed into the cement.

CHAPTER 28

McCall sat back onto the bottom of the stairs and wiped off the serrated blade of the paring knife. He went through Silver Skull's pockets and found nothing in them, no wallet ID, *no* passport, just some English pounds and euros. He climbed up the wooden steps and emerged into the night air. The blue Honda was still on the sidewalk, its engine running. McCall leaned in and pulled out the key. Emma had pulled herself into a standing position by this time.

"He came out of nowhere!" she gasped.

"He was in the pub watching you."

"Did you kill him?"

"Had no choice."

Emma focused on the paring knife with the serrated edge in his hand. "Bloody hell! That's my paring knife! I've got a matched pair in my kitchen! Where the hell did you get that?"

"I took it off one of the twins who attacked you."

"Cheeky bugger. He must've stolen it from my flat."

McCall put the paring knife in the pocket of his leather jacket. He closed the iron cellar doors and latched them with the padlock. The publican would find Silver Skull's body, but maybe not yet.

"Stand right here," McCall instructed her. He ran to the top of the street and turned the corner. The two assailants who'd been lying in the gutter had disappeared. He ran back to Emma. "The other two are gone."

McCall opened the Honda door and went through the glove compartment. It was a Hertz rental, and he only found the rental agreement and an A-Z of London. McCall slammed the car door and put his arm around Emma's shoulders. They walked back into the pub, and Emma retrieved her bag. McCall surreptitiously slid the paring knife into it before she closed it up.

One of the other bartenders came over. "Another round, love?"

"Bad tummy," Emma said. "Might have been the Indian meal I had earlier."

McCall hustled her outside. A black London cab had just disgorged two couples right in front of the pub. McCall took Emma to Charing Cross Hospital, where they pumped her stomach. She walked out of the ER a little weak, but she was steadier. McCall hailed another cab and took Emma to her flat on Templewood Avenue just below Hampstead Heath. He kept the cab waiting. When she came down five minutes later, she had a small overnight bag with her. McCall gave the cabbie instructions and they pulled away from the curb.

Emma asked, "Where are you taking me?"

"To stay with your mother."

"Just kill me now."

"How isolated is she?"

"She lives in Camberley in a little cottage about three miles from the Frimley Road. She walks to the shops, avoids the neighbors like the plague, and has a mean bulldog named Churchill who'd tear your throat out as soon as look at you. But looks can be deceiving. He walks with a limp, has a wonky eye, and spends all of his time out in the garden destroying my mother's rosebushes."

"If you see anyone at your mother's house or in the High Street who doesn't look like they should be there, call me. I'll let you know when it's safe for you to return home."

McCall dropped Emma at the H10 London Waterloo hotel. It was too late for her to go anywhere else tonight. He told her he'd pick her up in the morning. If she saw anything suspicious, if she thought anyone was following her, she would call his cell. She knew the number. Emma reminded McCall that she had been Control's executive assistant for how many bloody years and she knew the warning signs for trouble. Then she admitted those instincts hadn't helped her in the Duke of Argyll pub when memento-mori man had spiked her drink. She promised to be careful, and he left her in the lobby of the hotel.

McCall spent one night at the Strand Palace Hotel, then in the morning he picked Emma Marshall up and they walked down Waterloo Road to Waterloo Station. He took her to the platform to catch the 7:30 a.m. train to Ascot, where she would change trains to Camberley. Emma had color back in her face, but her ebullient cheerfulness had abandoned her. Her voice was quiet, her manner subdued.

"Thanks for saving my life. I've never seen you in action before. Rambo and the Transporter all rolled up into one. Will you find Control?"

"I'll find him."

Emma kissed him on the lips because that was the way she kissed anyone who was not a complete stranger and merged with the passengers on the platform. McCall saw her climb onto the train. He waited until the train pulled out of the station.

McCall sat down outside the Caffè Nero in Waterloo Station. He swept the concourse, but didn't see the white-blond twins among the crowd. He took something from the pocket of his leather jacket. It caught the light: the silver demon-claws skull that he had taken from the ring finger of the assassin's hand in the pub cellar.

McCall had also slipped off the assassin's silver ring that said REMEMBER THAT YOU MUST DIE. He turned the silver skull ring over. On the back were seven etched symbols that McCall had never before seen. They resembled Egyptian hieroglyphics.

But would they lead him to Control?

The sun beat down, heating up the new day. The carpet shop was hidden away in the bazaar in one of its myriad streets, which he accessed at the Nuruosmaniye Gate. At the back of the shop, where no tourist went, he wheeled his bicycle down a rickety staircase to a workshop.

Where he'd taken the bicycle apart.

It was like dismantling an old friend.

He took off the pedals first, reminding himself that the right crank on the side chain was threaded normally, and that the left side was threaded backward. Using a pedal wrench, he unscrewed the pedal at the edge of the crank arms. He removed the wheels by loosening the nuts attaching their hub bolts to the frame and the fork rear and front brackets. He unscrewed the brake lever from the handlebars, disposed of the brake pads, slipped off the stem, removed the seat, then deflated the two tires. Once he got the tire lever under the cinch part of the tires, between the rubber tire tube and the metal rim, and worked the tire so that a part of it was over the rim, the rest was easy.

He spread the bicycle parts on a table and pulled apart the double metal frame, which was hollowed out, as were the handlebars. He slit the tires. Then he packed the metal frame, the handlebars, and the tires with C-4 explosives, tightly molded like modeling clay. He had been trained in its use, but recited the components to himself as he worked: 91 percent RDX, 5.3 percent DOS as the plasticizer, 2.1 percent polyisobutylene as a binder, and 1.6 percent of a mineral oil called the process oil. Once packed, the C-4 would not explode when set on fire or even in microwave radiation. It used a detonator. The tests that he had carried out had shown the gases expanded at an explosive velocity of 8,092 meters per second. After the explosion, gases rushed back to the center of ignition, causing a second explosion. There were more sophisticated explosives, but this could be molded to fit into the spaces he needed.

He welded the metal frames back together and the handlebars. Then he packed up the bicycle parts into a black Tourmaster nylon traveler backpack with heavy-duty 840-denier with a built-in helmet house that could accommodate most helmets. In case the backpack was opened, the helmet would be a nice touch. He packed the backpack into a blue-and-black Nike Team duffel bag. He had no worries. He was clean shaven with an American passport. He would be returning home. He found his contact who would deliver the bag to him. At the airport it would be checked in with his other luggage.

He left the workshop, climbed back into the carpet store, and found his way out into the labyrinthe tunnels that erupted into the bazaar. It took him almost an hour and a half to walk back through the teeming streets.

He was in a state of euphoric peace.

Not even the death in the family could touch him.

Dr. Patrick Cross stepped out of the Atlanta Checker cab looking exhausted. Beth's Jeep Wagoneer was parked in the driveway of the Maple Park suburban house. David's bike was discarded on one of the swathes of manicured lawn. Cross didn't get far up the flagstone path before the front door flew open and his kids came tearing out of the house. David leapt up into Cross's arms. Lisa held back to be cool, but then she succumbed to the homecoming and wrapped her arms around her father's legs. Beth came out last, dropping her children's backpacks into the back of the Wagoneer. Dr. Cross let go of his son and daughter and moved to Beth. He was immediately struck by how great she always looked. She had long curly blond hair that tumbled over her shoulders like Farrah Fawcett's, had flawless skin, and stood almost five-eleven. Around her piercing blue eyes were little crow's-feet, which she thought marred her beauty, but he had always loved them. She moved into her husband's arms. They kissed, a promise to the kiss, of clothes discarded as their mouths explored each other, the shroud of Beth's hair enveloping him as she went down on him. But right now she was the perfect wife, cool and practical. They were already late for school. Dr. Cross said he was going to shower and change clothes and then head in to the Centers for Disease Control on Clifton Road. He also had an office at Emory University nearby, but first he'd need to file his report for the CDC about the Ebola outbreak in Monrovia.

Once Beth and the kids were away from the house, he would store his precious vials in the massive freezer and refrigerator in the garage. His family knew never to go near it. He could have taken the vials straight to the CDC's biosafety Level 4 laboratories, but the risk was too high. He wouldn't be staying long in Atlanta, no matter what lies he told Beth about taking another tour of duty for Doctors Without Borders. Before then he wanted to take his son to one of the Braves' AAA games at the Gwinnett Braves' stadium.

Beth herded Lisa and David into the Jeep Wagoneer and slid into the driver's seat. The kids had on their earpods, engrossed in their music. Two exquisite diamond tennis bracelets on Beth's slim wrist caught the light. Cross had promised her a new princess diamond bracelet for her birthday. He already had it in the desk of his office at Emory University. He would bring it home and gift wrap it and leave it for her on the vanity table in their bedroom.

He remembered Ann Crosby, naked in bed with him in a tangle of sheets, asking him, "Will you tell your wife about us?" She had regretted it instantly, he was sure.

He thought of her now lying in the shallow grave in the sweltering tropical rain forest.

Beth backed out, gave her husband a wave, and drove off down the street.

Dr. Patrick Cross picked up his suitcase and backpack.

Tom Renquist sat in his rented Volvo S80 parked across the street. He wore dark sunglasses and a cashmere sweater over black jeans. His face was rugged and chiseled, the eyes gray. He carried a Glock 26 subcompact pistol in a snug holster in the small of his back. He watched Dr. Patrick Cross walk into his house and close the front door. Renquist picked up his cell and dialed. He was thinking about The Company. A great many shadow executives had been killed in the past few years. Mickey Kostmayer had been captured in that North Korean prison fiasco and been left there to rot.

Granny had been killed. Renquist had been sorry to hear about that. Granny had been the only other agent in The Company Renquist had ever liked. There were only three Controls now. And, of course, *Control* himself.

And he was no longer functioning.

But the shadow executive who had quit The Company had been the closest to him. He was still out there. Renquist had read the intel that had come in to Virginia last night. It had been a hasty and ill-conceived mission in London. The twins had escaped, but the publican at the Duke of Argyll had found the third man in the cellar of his pub when he had opened up in the morning. The tendons in both of his legs had been severed. He had been stabbed through the throat. Renquist had never liked the bastard, but he had been an ally. Not just anyone could have taken him out.

Renquist waited for his call to be rerouted. He idly fingered the silver demon-claws skull on his right hand. Beside it was a silver ring that had etched on it REMEMBER THAT YOU MUST DIE. Neither of the rings had been mentioned in the intel. The killer had taken them off the assassin's right hand. Renquist vowed he would retrieve them when he avenged him.

The call was picked up.

Renquist said, "Dr. Cross is back in the country."

Matthew Goddard said, "You're positive of the ID?"

"He just kissed his wife and hugged his kids."

"What are the ages of the kids?"

"I'd say the boy, David, is six, the girl, Lisa, is nine or ten."

"How about Cross's wife?"

"In her forties. Cool and detached, but a babe. You want me to stay in Atlanta?"

"Until he leaves. Keep me updated."

The connection was broken. Renquist thought about checking in with the house in the country. Just to make sure they hadn't had any visitors. It was unlikely, but he'd make the call. Renquist hadn't been told the name of this onetime Company agent—*need to know*—but he was going to find him.

Then he would cut off his head and send it back to his Jihadist comrades in a box.

Tara sat in the Starbucks on Broadway at West Forty-Seventh Street, just down from the Hotel Edison, where she was staying, sipping a Caffè Mocha. She was worried about Melody. She hadn't answered her cell all day yesterday. Tara had gone down to Dolls nightclub. The owner was Samuel

Clemens, a good ole boy who looked like he should be selling used Caddys in Fort Worth—which McCall had told Tara he *had* been doing until he relocated to New York City. Clemens had greeted Tara as if she'd just told him Davy Crockett was a distant relative. Tara had told him Melody Fairbrother was an old friend and she wanted to look her up. What time did she come to work? Clemens had told her that Melody had not come into Dolls that night or the previous night. But then, she often skipped nights at the club. He cut her some slack because she was his *favorite* of all the dancers there. Clemens was sure she would be back at Dolls tomorrow night. He would let Melody know an old friend had stopped by to see her. Tara had thanked him and left.

Tara knew that Melody had been out for lunch with Blake Cunningham two days ago. After their cosy rendezvous at Gaby in the Sofitel Hotel, Blake had escorted Melody home to her apartment. He had wanted to come up for a drink, but Melody had been complaining of a migraine and wanted to lie down. Blake had, as usual, been the consummate gentleman. He got his Rock Hudson kiss, which Tara had upgraded to a Ryan Seacrest kiss, and taken off in a cab. Tara had watched it all from Mike Gammon's Prius. Nothing new or remarkable. Melody had gone into her apartment building. Tara wasn't worried about her when she was at Dolls. She had friends there, and the pro-wrestling bouncer at the doors was careful about whom he let in or kept out of the club.

Except Melody had *not* gone into Dolls nightclub that night. Or the next night.

Tara remembered Melody's migraine headache. She knew how bad they could be. It could have lasted for a couple of days. Still . . .

The detective took another swallow of her Caffè Mocha and checked the messages on her cell phone one more time.

She had missed one.

It was a text from Melody's phone from two nights ago. Tara had thought it had been a glitch because she'd noted there *was* no message. But *one letter* was in the text: *I*. That was it.

An icy chill went through her. What had Melody been trying to say that night? *I need to talk to Mr. McCall? I think someone is in my apartment?*

CHAPTER 29

Tara finished off her Caffè Mocha and hailed a yellow cab. She told the cabbie to take her to the corner of Jane Street and Eighth Avenue. When the cab pulled up in front of Melody's apartment building, Tara paid the driver and ran up the four steps to the front door. She rang the silver button outside for apartment 3B. No response. She tried the front door and saw it hadn't completely closed. She walked down the dim hallway to apartment 1A, which had SUPERINTENDENT lettered on it. She knocked loudly. After a pause three bolts were thrown back. *As long as the super is safe,* Tara thought. He opened the door. Tara thought he should be teaching a calculus class at Columbia. He was in his fifties, dressed in a tweed suit. Glasses hung around his neck on a cord. A frozen dinner was on a table beside a big easy chair. The TV was on. The super was watching a rerun of *NCIS*. Tara liked that show. She especially liked Ducky Mallard, the coroner. She gave the super her highest-wattage smile, which had been known to floor lesser men.

"Hi! I'm Melody Fairbrother's sister, Diana. I'm staying with her for a few days and I'm supposed to meet her for lunch. We're going to the matinee of *Aladdin,* I hear it's great, and I just realized I left my wallet and my emerald earrings in her apartment, and I don't have a set of keys. Could you let me in? Apartment 3B."

"I know Ms. Fairbrother's apartment number." The super's tone suggested he didn't believe a word Tara had said. "How do I know you're her sister?"

"We come from Geneva, *not* the city in Switzerland, but the town in Wisconsin. Look, here's a selfie we took together at a party last night."

Tara dug out her cell phone, scrolled down, and showed him a selfie they *had* taken together at the rave party some nights ago. The super sighed, closed his apartment door, and they trudged up the stairs to the third floor. He opened apartment 3B from a big ring of keys.

"Thanks so much!" Tara gushed. "I think I know where I left the earrings, but I might have to hunt around a little for the wallet."

"I'll be waiting right here."

Great, she thought. "Okay, no prob. Be right back!"

Tara moved into an apartment she had never before entered. The living room was small and cozy. She ran into a bedroom. A Tiffany lamp was on one bedside table shedding a soft glow through the room. The sheets on the bed were rumpled and thrown to one side, as if Melody had got up in a hurry. A short silk teddy was lying in a heap on the floor. Tara didn't think young girls even *wore* those anymore. She opened the closet. Dresses were on hangers, and sweaters and underwear were on shelves. Lots of shoes, but no sign of the blue dress that Melody would certainly have hung up. Maybe she had decided to go out nightclubbing, but she didn't seem like much of a nightclub girl to Tara, especially since Melody worked in one. Tara turned back into the room.

That's when she saw the blood.

It was splattered in a thin line across the top sheet. A series of subliminal images flashed through Tara's mind:

Melody being slapped and the blood spitting out of her mouth across the sheet . . .

The short nightdress being pulled up over her head . . .

The blue dress being dropped over her naked body . . .

Shoes being thrust onto her bare feet . . .

Tara didn't need to look for clues. She knew who'd taken her. She moved fast out of the bedroom into the living room, taking something small wrapped in tissue paper out of her Giorgio Armani shoulder bag. She unwrapped a pair of emerald earrings. She grabbed her wallet from the bag and ran out into the corridor. She showed the earrings and the wallet to the super with a look of triumph.

"Here they are! The earrings were on the bedside table, and the wallet was scrunched down between the back of the couch and one of the cushions!"

The super nodded, locked the door to apartment 3B, and escorted Tara down the stairs to the front door of the building. "Let me know how your sister liked *Aladdin*. I'm supposed to take my grandson to it for his birthday."

"Sure will," Tara said breezily, and was out the door.

She walked to the corner of Eighth Avenue and pulled out the small receiver from her bag. The tracking device on Blake no longer emitted a signal. Tara dialed her cell phone. McCall didn't pick up. She cursed and caught a cab uptown to the Morgan Stanley building on Broadway. Tara tried to talk her way into Blake Cunningham's offices, but was told by the officious receptionist he was in a series of meetings. If Tara left her name and number, Blake's assistant would get back to her. Tara left the building.

For the hell of it she walked over to Rockefeller Center and looked for Melody at the Rock Café, where she'd be watching the skaters on the ice. She wasn't there. By then it was afternoon.

Tara tried calling Robert McCall again.

McCall was in the back of an old-fashioned black London taxi that looked like it had first been driven right after the Blitz. His cell phone vibrated in his jacket pocket. He took it out, looked at the caller ID, and said, "This is McCall, Tara."

"Where are you?"

"In London. What's happened?"

"Melody's been grabbed. She didn't go into Dolls nightclub for two nights. I just accessed a text from her. There was one letter in it—*I*. I managed to get into her apartment with the super waiting outside in the corridor. I found a silk teddy on the floor of Melody's bedroom and bloodstains on her sheets. I should have known Blake would come for her sooner rather than later. I tried to see him at his Morgan Stanley offices today, but that was a lost cause."

"What would you have done if you *had* confronted him? He'd have told you that Melody was a girl he sometimes dated, but he didn't have any idea where she was."

"I know. I had to do *something*! I even went down to the skating rink in Rockefeller Center, but there was no sign of her."

"I'm catching an afternoon flight to JFK in a couple of hours. We'll regroup at the Liberty Belle Hotel."

"One more thing. The signal on the receiver you gave me to track Blake is dead. Either he threw his sunglasses away or he found the tracking device. This is my fault, McCall."

"No, it's not. We'll find her."

"Like we found Emily Masden?" Tara said bitterly.

"Just sit tight. I'll call you as soon as I get into New York." McCall disconnected. *No,* he thought, *this wasn't Tara's fault.*

It was his.

Bo watched the Feds winding up the driveway to the main two-story ranch house in a tight procession. He was sitting on the big flagstone porch drinking coffee. A one-story flagstone building was beside it with a redwood roof. It had been built as a bunkhouse for the cowboys when the property had been developed, but it was used now by the families who lived on the compound. Three more ranch-style buildings in the enclosure also housed his Texas Minutemen Militia. Some raucous kids were running around, shooting hoops, throwing horseshoes at stakes in the ground, tossing a football around. Most of them were in school; the young'uns kept close to the compound. Bo had strict rules for the families of his Minutemen Militia. The wives and girlfriends were allowed to go into town for supplies and did laundry and sundry chores and serviced their men when they were told to.

Some of Bo's militia were on patrol on the grounds, all of them carrying M4 rifles, all with holstered Smith & Wesson Shield 9mm pistols. They watched the federal procession reach the main ranch house, but none of them took any action. They were too well trained for that. The pickup games at the hoops and the horseshoe tossing ceased. Within two minutes Bo noted with satisfaction that all of the kids were inside the structures and the women had closed the doors.

Four Crown Victoria sedans and three Dodge Durango SUVs came to a stop in the driveway. Federal officers poured out of them, some of them carrying their own M4 rifles. Bo wasn't in a hurry to finish his coffee. It was Texas Coffee Traders, produced in Austin.

FBI special agent Todd Blakemore climbed the flagstone stairs onto the wraparound porch. Bo caught the eye of one of his minutemen, his cousin Kyle. He was barely twenty-one, green, intense, anxious to please. Bo made one of the minutemen signals he had developed, nothing overt, just a gesture as he raised his coffee to his lips. Kyle understood and stepped down.

Bo finished his coffee and stood up. Special Agent Todd Blakemore was flanked by four federal officers, all looking edgy and a little excited. Blakemore showed his badge and FBI credentials to Bo.

"FBI special agent Todd Blakemore, Mr. Ellsworth. We've met before." He dropped a document on the rough-hewn table. "I have a federal warrant to search this property. I'd like to ask you to read it, sir."

Bo cursorily glanced at the warrant and dropped it back onto the table. "All of the firearms at the Minutemen Ranch are protected by the Texas legislature. All of the permits for the handguns are here in the main ranch house."

"And the permits to carry M4 assault rifles?"

"Inside in my den."

Bo made another secret signal. His cousin came trotting along the porch, his M4 over his shoulder. "Kyle, show these officers into the main ranch house. Do not impede their progress. They have federal business here."

Kyle stepped up to the ornate wooden door with the other federal officers. Bo turned back to Blakemore.

"I'm going to get a beer. Y'all have yourselves a pleasant day now," Bo said, echoing the words Special Agent Blakemore had said to him a few days ago.

Bo jumped down from the porch and walked to where his 2014 black Ford Explorer XLT was parked. He powered it up and swung away from the compound. In his rearview mirror he saw federal officers moving through the door of the main ranch house into the interior. More officers were moving to the second ranch house. A couple of them jogged to the smaller buildings. They were shadowed by Bo's minutemen, but at a discreet distance. The Feds wouldn't find anything in the ranch buildings.

It was the violation of Bo's rights that put the burr under his saddle.

He hated these sons of bitches.

Bo drove down State Highway 46, past Kronkosky State Natural Area into Boerne. He drove past the Alley on Main Street, past the El Chaparral Mexican restaurant, turned left on Frederick, and right into the driveway at the Alamo Plaza Bar and Grill. The asphalt was jammed with SUVs and pickup trucks. Music pounded faintly from the bar. Bo parked his Ford Explorer and walked to the main door with its Live Oak Brewing Company flowering-oak motif and pushed it open.

A wall of noise hit him. The bar was packed. Some good ole boys and some hard-bitten cowboys were at their usual spots. Bo spotted Randy Wyatt and Jeremiah Buchanan in earnest conversation in one of the booths. He acknowledged Big Teddy Danfield at the bar, who was already getting the gal who served there—*Damn, she was looking spectacular today*—to pull him a beer on draft.

Bo's cell phone chirped. It played "The Yellow Rose of Texas," but you couldn't hear it over the jukebox playing fifties oldies. Bo answered it as he made his way to the bar, acknowledging two other minutemen off duty, nursing beers. If Bo had wanted to, he would only have had to whisper to them that the compound and been overrun by federal officers and they would have come running, guns blazing. But Bo didn't do that. They had to keep a low profile. Business as usual.

Until it wasn't.

The man's voice on the phone said two words: "I'm home."

Bo hung up and reached the bar, where Big Teddy Danfield handed him a brew.

It had *started*.

CHAPTER 30

College Boy #1 came for Emily about seven o'clock. She thought he had a pretty hefty beer belly for a twentysomething. Droopy eyes and sallow skin. *Exactly* the one she had been praying would come for her. She'd been flirting with him for days. She got to her feet and put on her black high-heeled shoes. College Boy #1 unlocked the padlock and opened the cage door. His sports coat was unbuttoned to show her the Colt Anaconda .44 Magnum in his belt. As if he'd need to use it. Emily didn't look as if she had the strength to strangle a mouse. He gripped her shoulder.

"Blake wants to see you."

Melody stirred from a restless sleep beside Emily and rose up on one elbow.

"He'll get to you when he's ready," College Boy #1 told her.

"Where is Blake?" Emily asked.

"Right now at his office in Rockefeller Center. But he'll be here soon." He half dragged Emily out of the cage, slammed the door, and snapped the padlock.

"You're Calvin, right?"

"Yep. Named after Coolidge. Not much of a role model." He started to wrap a thin leather thong around Emily's wrists.

"How much do you weigh, Cal?"

He seemed surprised by the question. "Maybe two-forty."

"I'm probably down to one hundred and ten pounds right out of the shower. You really think you need to tie my wrists? You don't think you could grab me if I tried to make a run for it? Let me keep my hands free, okay?"

He considered, then unwrapped the cord from her wrists. He dragged her into one of the deeper shadows, as if mindful of her privacy. He lifted her dress and ran his hands up her inner thighs looking for a concealed weapon. There wasn't one. His knuckles brushed across the crotch of her black panties, then he ran his hands over the cheeks of her ass. He dropped the hem of the dress, turned her around, unzipped the back of her dress, and let it fall to her waist. He groped her bare breasts, ran his hands over her shoulders, reached up into her hair, found nothing. He zipped the dress back up and motioned to some wooden stairs leading up to a second floor. More of the prisoners stirred in their cages. A couple of them shouted out obscenities. A few pleaded to be let out. They just wanted to go home. "Please, let us go home."

Calvin ignored them and shoved Emily toward the stairs.

It had taken her almost four weeks to rip a small, jagged piece of metal from the bottom of her cage. She had hidden it under her dress. Before Calvin had let her out of the cage, she had pulled down her panties and slid the piece of steel up into her rectum. It was cold and uncomfortable, but she didn't believe Calvin would have been ordered to do a cavity search. Theoretically, no weapons were available to any of the victims.

She needed her hands to be free. That was the crucial part of her plan. And her plea had worked. Now she had to initiate the other part of her plan. One of Blake's college chums—Emily thought his name was, swear to God, Chip—usually sat in a chair at the bottom of the stairs, but he was on a bathroom break.

She had to get to Cal before they reached those stairs.

"Let me go," Emily whispered. "I know you want to fuck me. Afterwards you can say I kicked you in the nuts and scrambled away. You went after me, but I just vanished. This is a big place." He said nothing, but she thought his asthmatic breathing was a little more labored. "I'll do anything you want. Why should Blake get all the pussy? No one will ever know."

Calvin grabbed hold of her shoulders suddenly, steering her away from the stairs. Emily had never been in the other part of the warehouse room that stretched out in deep shadow. Now she saw it was honeycombed with small abandoned offices. Calvin dragged her into one of them and threw her against the desk.

"You'll let me go? After I fuck you?"

"Sure. We're in this together."

He kissed her hard. He smelled of wine and sweat. She pulled out of his grasp and ran to the office door. He caught up with her in two strides and grabbed her.

"I was just going to lock the door!" she gasped.

Calvin smirked. "To give us some privacy? Good call."

He shoved her back into the shadowed office. She stumbled. He gripped her shoulders to steady her and stepped in front of her. She pulled up her dress from behind, slid her hand down her panties, grabbed the tip of the piece of steel, and pulled it out of her rectum, without his seeing a thing. He turned back to her.

She stabbed the piece of steel up into Calvin's throat. A geyser of blood spurted as if a faucet had been turned on. She rammed the skeletal splinter up higher and he fell to his knees. She wanted to grab his .44 Magnum, but he fell onto his side, right *onto* the gun. She abandoned that idea, threw open the office door, and looked back. Calvin's body was shuddering, but he wasn't getting up.

Emily plunged back the way they'd come.

A door on the other side of the cages was never used. Behind her she heard the cages rattling. It was as if the other girls were urging her on.

If the door was padlocked on the other side, she was done for.

It wasn't.

Emily pushed open the door. Fresh night air swept over her.

She ran down the narrow alleyway between two huge warehouse buildings. She had no idea where it led. There was no sound of pursuit behind her. She fell over some broken crates, sprawled onto the cobblestones, scrambled back to her feet, and ran on. She could hear muted traffic now. She made three more turns into identical narrow alleyways, then she burst out onto Broad Street. There was a lot of pedestrian traffic and she caught a few disapproving glances. She looked like a hooker. She could go into a store, ask to use a phone, and dial 911—but she had no idea of the location of the warehouse. So she just started walking north. She didn't know long it would be before one of the Blake's cronies saw that she was missing from her cage. It would take them longer to find Calvin's body. Would they rush out after her? Probably not. But she wanted to put as much distance between herself and that warehouse prison as possible. She walked fast, not once looking over her shoulder. She had to get away.

But *to where?*

McCall walked through JFK International Airport and paused by one of the Hudson News stands. The *New York Post* headline read, "Vigilante Foils Madison Ave Robbery." McCall bought the paper and took a yellow cab into Manhattan. There had been a jewel robbery on Madison Avenue, in broad daylight. The Equalizer had come out of nowhere, taken down the thieves, and killed them both. A salesgirl had been shot in the stomach. She was in critical condition at Mount Sinai Hospital, undergoing surgery. McCall read that Detective Steve Lansing from the Seventh Precinct was helping the Nineteenth Precinct homicide cops in their investigation. A grainy black-and-white picture of the Equalizer had been taken by one of the salesgirls in the store on her cell phone. It had already gone viral, but the man's face was too blurred to be recognizable. The vigilante had escaped in the chaos, already making him an urban legend. The cops had an APB on him and several BOLOs in other states.

McCall's cabdriver was a native New Yorker with an accent so thick you could spread it on the sandwiches at Artie's Delicatessen on Eighty-Second Street.

"How about this Equalizer guy, huh? He's bringing the crime rate in the city down single-handed!"

"He shot and killed two men."

"Lowlifes, right? Better they should be off the streets. You gotta love this guy!"

"The cops want to catch him."

"Yeah, 'cause he's making them look bad, right? This Equalizer takes the odds against ordinary citizens and makes them better. He'd be a sensation in Vegas. He knows how to beat the house."

"He's an amateur," McCall said. "That's why innocent people are getting killed."

"And what if my man the Equalizer *hadn't* been in that jewelery store? The cops would have been haulin' body bags out onto Madison Avenue. My man takes care of business and gets out before anyone can discover his secret identity. He's already got a hundred thousand followers on Twitter. Guy's a folk hero. Here we are!" The cabbie pulled up outside the Liberty Belle Hotel. "Enjoy your time in the city. If you get into any bad neighborhoods, the Equalizer's got your back."

McCall stepped out of the cab and pushed through the glass doors into the lobby.

It was a madhouse. Chloe, Lisa, and two new front-of-house girls were busy with guests, while uniformed bellmen pushed the brass luggage carts back and forth to the elevators. Sam Kinney had changed from his apartment clothes into his gray slacks, a crisp white shirt, and his LIBERTY BELLE HOTEL blazer with the lettering stitched on the breast pocket. He detached himself from the reception counter and made his way to McCall. Sam had a folded copy of the *New York Post* under his arm.

"Glad you're back. Here's the scoop on your real estate mogul Norman Rosemont. He doesn't much like his new apartment, but his neighbors are starting to grow on him. How long did you give him to live with the rats and the overflowing garbage bags?"

"Two weeks."

"He should come to appreciate my breakfasts by then. Did you see this headline in the *Post*?"

"I saw it when I came through JFK."

"I just heard on CNN that that gal in the jewelery-store robbery is out of surgery. She's going to make it. You know about this Equalizer wannabe?"

"I know about him."

"You know who he is?"

"Not yet."

"Better find out. You had a call at reception right before you walked into the lobby. A woman's voice. Maybe that hottie who was waiting for you in your hotel suite a few nights ago? Classy dame." Sam motioned to the Irish bellman who was passing by with an empty luggage cart. "Hey, Vinnie, take Mr. McCall's backpack up to the seventeenth floor, will you?"

"Sure thing."

Vinnie grabbed McCall's backpack and dropped it onto the cart. Sam beat McCall to the reception counter and handed him the cell phone there.

"This is Robert McCall." McCall listened. "Stay right where you are. I'll come to you."

McCall hung up and walked fast through the lobby.

"She sounded like she needed the Equalizer's help?" Sam called out after him, somewhat hopefully, but McCall was already out the lobby door. He took out his cell and dialed a number.

"Sure, don't include me in your life," Sam muttered.

McCall didn't notice the young man in blue denims with a hoodie pushed back sitting in the lobby on one of the plush couches. He was looking through the lobby doors where McCall had just hailed a cab. It pulled away from the curb. The young man nodded. He would bide his time. No one was looking for him. The staff in the jewelery robbery had all given conflicting descriptions. You could always depend on eyewitnesses to get their stories all mixed up.

The young man watched Sam Kinney move over to help Chloe behind the reception counter. This hotel manager was a good friend of McCall's. The young man had watched them on a number of occasions chatting together. McCall trusted this man.

The Equalizer had decided that the best way to lure Robert McCall into a trap would be to kill someone he was close to.

CHAPTER 31

Emily was waiting for him at a table at the back of a Starbucks on Fulton Street. McCall walked past the usual line of folks desperate for a caffeine rush and sat opposite her. He noted she was wearing the same dress he'd last seen her in, a little more ripped up and disheveled. She immediately reached for his hand and gripped it tightly. She was trembling.

"I'm glad you remembered my phone number," McCall said gently.

"Told you I would."

"Where have you been for the last month?"

"In a cage. And I mean, really, in a fucking cage."

"Tell me what happened."

She kept her voice soft. She told him how she'd been grabbed by one of Blake Cunningham's asshole cronies in the old Mercury Theater. Calvin, a big guy. He'd jabbed a needle into her arm and she had lost consciousness. When she'd awakened, she'd found herself curled up in a steel cage bolted to the floor in some big abandoned warehouse. She hadn't been alone. *Other* young women were in other cages, all of them prisoners. Emily had had some company in her cage over the five weeks, two different girls who'd been brought in, bewildered and terrified. But over time they'd been taken out again and never came back. There'd been a new victim, a blonde in a blue dress who'd been thrown in with her a couple of nights ago.

"Did she tell you her name?"

"Yeah, Melanie or Melody, something like that."

"How did you get out of there?"

Her voice dropped so low McCall could barely hear her. "I killed one of them."

"How?"

She told him about convincing Calvin to take her into an empty office for sex and then stabbing him with the piece of jagged metal.

"You can't be sure you killed him."

"I'm sure," she whispered.

"How did you escape from the warehouse?"

"There was a side door that was unlocked."

"Where is this warehouse?"

"I don't know. I ran down these narrow little alleyways, and then I was out onto a street and I just starting walking away as fast as I could. I couldn't take you to that warehouse if my life depended on it."

"Nothing you heard while you were incarcerated?"

"No foghorns, no train whistles, none of the things the plucky heroine hears in movies so she can figure out where she is. There was just silence." Her voice was softer again. "Except for the girls sobbing and pleading in their cages."

At that moment Tara Langley walked into the Starbucks and made her way to the back.

Emily stiffened. A look of panic leaped into her eyes. "I told you, that's *not* my mother!" she said tersely.

"She's a private detective. Impersonating your mother was her cover."

Tara reached the table, touching McCall's arm. "I was so happy to get your call." She sat down and smiled at Emily. "My name is Tara Langley, Emily. I can't tell you what it means to me that you're alive."

"Yeah, well, it feels pretty fucking good to me, too. My mother really hired a PI to come and find me? That's so cool. My mother can't make a decision on which breakfast cereal to buy in the supermarket without agonizing over it."

"I didn't do a very good job. If it wasn't for Robert McCall . . ."

Emily looked at McCall. "So that's your name? Yeah, my tarnished white knight."

"What's Blake into?" Tara asked.

McCall said, "Women in cages in an abandoned warehouse somewhere near the docks. Being sold into slavery."

"Yeah," Emily said. "And we're not talking about some grubby Middle Eastern rug merchants or Russian mobsters or foreign terrorists, these are *college* guys. They've all got nine-to-five jobs on Wall Street somewhere. But this is how they make their real money. Blake is the point man. He finds some vulnerable babe barely into her twenties who's just arrived in the Big Apple from Bumfuck, Kansas, like me, wines and dines and seduces them, and then they find themselves in a little cage begging for a scrap of bread or to go to the bathroom. It's so disgusting."

"Blake will have moved all of the girls out of that warehouse location," McCall said.

"I was running away in a blind panic. I don't think he'll pack up shop just because I ran out into the night. But I heard them talking. They *are* going to move the girls to a new location. And pretty soon. Maybe tonight."

"Then we're too late," Tara said.

"Not if I can take you there," Emily said.

"You said you have no idea where the warehouse is," McCall reminded her.

"I don't. I'll get Blake to tell me. Put a wire on me, isn't that what they do if you're trying to trap some creep and the FBI are with you?"

"Blake would make sure you weren't wearing a wire," Tara said. "He'd strip you naked to be sure."

"That's the idea."

McCall was looking at Emily. "What's your plan?"

"Go to Blake's office. He's there right now. Calvin told me that. I'll come on to him. Let him know that I escaped, if he doesn't know it already, but that I wanted to be with him. He doesn't want to sell me into slavery like the other girls. He wants me for himself. I'll ask him where the warehouse is, and you guys can be listening. Have the cops with you. Once he's said the location, you can swoop in and grab him."

"Too great a risk," Tara said. "He might not give up the location."

"Those girls are going to be *sold*, okay?" Emily said with more passion in her voice. "I killed a man tonight. If Blake moves the girls out of that warehouse, I killed Calvin for nothing."

"Even if you seduce Blake, he'll take you back to that warehouse," Tara insisted.

"That's what we want him to do." McCall looked back at Emily. "Can you make Blake believe you want to be with him no matter what business he's in?"

"I can do it. I can make this work."

"We'll have to make a pit stop first," McCall said.

No lights were on at Manhattan Electronics when McCall, Tara, and Emily got out of their cab, but Mary unlocked the door and let them in. Tara led

Emily over to the main counter. McCall followed Mary through the darkened store toward Brahms's office at the back.

"How did it go with Norman Rosemont?" McCall asked her.

"Piece of cake. He did manage to get his hand down my cleavage and cop a good feel. Mind you, so did I. He's a big boy."

"Probably more information than I needed," McCall murmured. "He's in place?"

"Jimmy let me out at Sloan Kettering that night. I don't know where he took Rosemont after that." They were almost to the back, where light spilled from Brahms's office. Mary stopped McCall with a squeeze on his arm. There was no more lightness to her voice. "I don't know who you really are, or what kind of work you're doing now. I don't care who that girl is or what's happening to her. I only care about my boss, and this is not a good night to drag him away from the hospital to cook up some nifty little gadget for you."

"There are lives at stake. And I'm out of time."

"So his feelings aren't that important to you." Mary nodded. "You're really a ruthless person, aren't you, Mr. McCall?"

He didn't answer that.

"Just remember he's sick with worry." Mary moved over to where Tara and Emily were waiting.

McCall walked into Brahms's office.

Brahms was sitting at his cluttered desk working on a tiny electronic tracking device. "Just checking the circuit. You going to nail this bad guy tonight?"

"That's the plan."

Brahms slipped the back onto the small circular device, clicked it into place, and handed it to McCall. "I don't have time to make up another one for you. Go, go! I have to get back to the hospital, but first I need to talk to God."

McCall left him sitting at his desk, murmuring words he wanted only God to hear. McCall walked over to where Mary was standing with Emily and Tara. "I need a bra, and Emily isn't wearing one."

"I guess that leaves me," Tara said.

She shrugged off her leather jacket, pulled off her shirt, took off her bra without a hint of embarrassment, and handed it to McCall. Then she put her shirt back on.

"You two must've got cozy," Emily muttered.

McCall turned to Mary with the bra in one hand and the silver tracking device in the other. "How good at sewing are you?"

"You're lucky I keep a sewing set here at the store. The boss manages to get holes in all of his sweaters. Give me five minutes."

Mary disappeared behind the main counter. McCall took out his cell phone and handed it to Emily. "Call Blake in his office and let him know you're about to take a cab over there to see him. The caller ID won't come up. Make sure he doesn't leave until you get there."

"But call your mother first," Tara said quietly. "Let her hear your voice. Let her know her daughter is still alive."

Emily nodded and took the phone.

A uniformed security officer escorted Emily up in the elevator at 1290 Avenue of the Americas to the thirteenth floor. He said, "Mr. Cunningham is expecting you," his tone indicating he knew she was a hooker, and the elevator door closed. She walked past empty glass offices to the corner office, from which light spilled. When she walked in, she was greeted with a magnificent panorama of the skyline of Manhattan through two huge windows. There was a leather couch, an armchair, and two client chairs. Blake was sitting behind a modern desk working on his laptop computer. He was wearing gray flannel trousers, a classic white oxford cotton shirt and a gray Bucharest paisley tie and a twill blue blazer.

He stood up. His gaze was like laser beams going right through her. "Close the door."

She closed it.

Blake did an odd thing. He turned his laptop computer around so that the screen faced *into* the office. He came around the desk. Every instinct screamed at Emily to get out of there, but she stood her ground.

He looked at her for a long moment. "You killed a friend of mine tonight."

"He tried to rape me."

"Where did you get the shiv?"

"I found it on the warehouse floor."

"Why didn't you keep running? Why aren't you on the first Greyhound bus back home to good old New Brighton, Minnesota?"

"Because I want to be with you."

He took a step toward her. Fear shot through her body in a tremor, but she controlled it.

"You look like shit."

"You wouldn't look so good yourself if you'd spent a month caged up like an animal," she retorted.

"And you're not afraid that I'll take you right back to that cage?"

"Is that what you really want? To sell me to the highest bidder with the others? I thought you wanted me all to yourself."

She wondered if she'd hurled the challenge at him too fast, but he slowly nodded and smiled—the smile of a cobra.

"I never had any intention of handing you over to some sleazy Arab who jerks off at the sight of an American girl's tits. But I had to teach you a lesson. How do I know you haven't brought the cops with you? That you're not wired for sound?"

"I'm not," she said simply.

"Strip for me."

She stepped out of her black high heels and turned around for him to unzip the back of her dress. He did, and the dress fell to the floor. She picked it up, dropped it onto the leather easy chair, turned back to face him, unclasped Tara's bra, and dropped it onto the black dress. She stepped out of her black panties and tossed them onto the easy chair.

"Turn around."

She turned once in a full circle. "No wire."

He took two swift strides to her and grabbed her by the throat, almost lifting her off her feet. She gasped. His face was close to hers.

"I'd known Calvin since high school," he hissed. Then he let her go and smiled again. "But we were never close. You didn't run. You came here. That's all I needed to know."

He kissed her and pushed her down to her knees. She unzipped his slacks and pulled his boxers down. After she performed the oral sex he wanted, he threw her onto the couch, took off the rest of his clothes, and climbed on top of her. She closed her eyes as he kneaded her breasts and massaged her shoulders and then moved inside her. It was the most vile fifteen minutes of her life. But she was still alive. Once he'd climaxed, Blake rolled off the couch and got dressed. Emily picked up her panties from the chair and slid them on. She picked up the bra.

"Keep it off. I like you better without a bra."

"I'd feel weird not wearing one."

"I said *leave it*!"

She shrugged like it was no big deal and dropped the bra back onto the armchair. She picked up her dress and stepped into it. Blake zipped her up.

"That dress is a disgrace. You need a new wardrobe. We'll go shopping tomorrow. I have to go to the warehouse. There's a shipment going out tonight. Then we're moving our location. You cool with that?"

"None of those girls mean anything to me. I told you, I want to be with you."

"You'll come with me to the warehouse. Then we'll go to a late dinner."

She stepped back into her black high-heeled shoes. Blake opened the office door for her. She glanced down at the bra lying on the easy chair with its concealed tracking device. "Shouldn't I at least take it with me? You don't want the cleaning guys finding it."

Blake grinned. "They've found them before. Let's go."

She walked through the doorway and Blake closed the door behind her.

Now she was trapped.

CHAPTER 32

McCall sat in the passenger seat of Mike Gammon's Prius, parked on West Fifty-Second Street just above the side entrance to 1290 Avenue of the Americas. Gammon was behind the wheel, Tara in the back. McCall had no way of knowing which exit Blake and Emily would take from 1290. Two parking facilities were close by, one in the CBS building at West Fifty-Second Street, another one at 354 West Fifty-Second Street. McCall had to rely on the tracking device that Emily was wearing. He checked the small receiver in his hand. The little red light in the bottom right-hand corner remained static

"She's not moving."

"Maybe Blake's going to stay in his office with her," Tara said. "Drink champagne, ball her all night."

"With news that one of his guys is dead and the warehouse may be compromised?" McCall shook his head. "He'd get her out of there as soon as the sex was over."

"So why hasn't he?" Gammon asked.

McCall shook his head. He could feel the frustration coiling into a ball in his gut. He hadn't wanted to send Emily into the lion's den alone. But if they had burst in with cops, Blake would have denied all of the charges, a high-priced attorney would have had him out on bail in two seconds, and the warehouse—*if* they ever discovered its location—would have been completely abandoned. Emily's gutsy plan had been the only one that had made sense. Blake would take her with him to the warehouse. They would follow.

But the light on the receiver remained static.

Emily still wasn't moving.

Or she left the bra behind, McCall suddenly realized.

They had exited the Morgan Stanley building from a back entrance and walked a couple of blocks to a parking facility where Blake had picked up his BMW. He'd made a phone call and then pulled out into the traffic. Emily noted that he had a pair of Italian Persol sunglasses hanging from the top button of his shirt.

"What happened to your Fendi 411s?"

"I dropped them in my apartment last night and then managed to step on them. Had to toss 'em out."

After that he didn't say another word to her.

She knew it was over.

He had seen right through her charade, but he had wanted to have that sex with her before he returned her to her fate. Her nipples chafed against her dress as if a reminder that she should not have left the bra behind.

After twenty minutes, Blake turned down a street that looked vaguely familiar to Emily. She recognized the partially constructed building on the right where she'd met Blake and Robert McCall at the rave party. She glanced past Blake and saw the old Mercury Theater with its scaffolding gleaming in the streetlights. Four blocks later Blake turned left onto a narrow street between two huge warehouse buildings, and then right into a cul-de-sac that led up to another warehouse. Two black Ford SUVs were parked outside it. She knew *this* was the warehouse where she'd been imprisoned.

"I need to call my mom," Emily said suddenly, "let her know I'm okay. Can I do that? Just so she hears my voice?"

Blake shrugged and handed her his iPhone 6. "Make it quick. I'll be listening."

Emily took the iPhone, turned slightly away, and tapped out a number. After a pause, she said, "Hi, Mom, it's me. I know it's been weeks since I've called you. I'm so sorry."

At the other end of the call, in Mike Gammon's Prius, McCall motioned for Gammon to drive out into the traffic. Tara leaned forward from the back.

"Where are you, Emily?" McCall asked softly.

In Blake's BMW, Emily sounded exasperated on the cell phone. "Of course it's really me, Mom! Don't you recognize my voice? I'll prove it to you. The last play we saw together in Minneapolis, at the Mercury Theater, was a thriller called *Catspaw* by Robert McCullough. Really creepy. You remember how hard it was snowing that night? We had to walk four blocks in a blizzard from the parking lot, remember that?"

"Wrap it up," Blake said.

"I gotta go, Mom. I'll call you soon. Lova ya." She disconnected and handed Blake his iPhone, praying he wouldn't look at the last number she'd dialed. "Thanks."

Blake slipped the phone into his blazer jacket and pulled up to the warehouse building.

Emily prayed to God that Robert McCall had understood her message.

Melody looked out from her cage at the sudden flurry of activity in the warehouse room. One of Blake's college thugs had opened the cage nearest to her and was dragging out the two young women in it. He handcuffed both of them together, then clamped them with a second handcuff around the cage-door bars. Other men were pulling the other girls out of their cages. The realization of what was happening sent a shiver through Melody.

They were moving them.

Emily had never come back. Melody feared she might be dead. Melody thought that was what happened to the girls who didn't cooperate. Her cage door was unlocked and a man she'd never before seen—he looked like he should be coaching a Little League team—dragged Melody to her feet and thrust her out of the cell. He was holding on to the arm of another blond girl, in sweats with her hair pulled back in a ponytail. Little League Man cuffed them together, then snapped them with a second pair of handcuffs over the bars of Melody's cage door.

The other blonde pleaded, "Let me go home! I won't say a word about this! I swear it!"

Little League Man didn't bother to answer or even acknowledge her. He moved away to help with the handcuffing of the other prisoners.

"My name's Amy," the blonde whispered. "What are they going to do with us?"

"Sell us," Melody said softly.

There was a commotion at the big front doors of the warehouse. Melody looked over and saw the last person she'd ever hoped to see back here—Emily. At least she was alive. And she didn't look as if she was a prisoner. Blake Cunningham was with her, an arm around her shoulders. Another of their captors, Melody had heard him called Chip, lunged forward and grabbed hold of Emily.

"Don't harm her!" Blake warned.

"She murdered Cal!"

"You heard me!" Blake said sharply. "I was on Skype when she came to my office. I made sure the buyer saw me fucking her. He's going to pay double for her."

Chip motioned to one of Blake's other men, who thrust a brunette over to him. Chip handcuffed the brunette to Emily, then snapped another handcuff over Emily's other wrist that, in turn, snapped over a railing near the warehouse doors.

Melody's stomach churned.

There'd be no rescue now.

Mike Gammon's Prius passed the old Mercury Theater. McCall counted four blocks. A narrow alleyway was on the left.

"Turn here!" McCall said.

Gammon made the turn, traveling between two large warehouse buildings. After fifty feet there was a right-hand turn into a cul-de-sac. The narrow alleyway continued on. Gammon braked to a halt. They could see two of Blake's men manhandling two bleary young women, handcuffed together, into the open back of one of two black SUVs. McCall reached into his pocket and handed Tara a card.

"Call the Seventh Precinct. Ask for Detective Lansing."

"Shouldn't we call the Feds?"

"Detective Lansing is hoping to hear from me," McCall said, the irony lost on her. "Tell him to bring a SWAT team with him. Stay in the car until the cops get here. Back up into the alleyway so you're facing south. If one of the SUVs drives away, follow it."

McCall and Gammon got out and disappeared down the alleyway. Tara slid into the driver's seat, reversed back down the alleyway, turned around in the street, and reversed back until she was just above the cul-de-sac. She picked up her cell to call the cops.

McCall and Mike Gammon reached the side of the warehouse, where an old pickup truck was parked. A couple of the cages had been collapsed and were lying in the open truck bed. This warehouse wall had no doors. Blake's men were bringing the cages around from the front. One of them disappeared around the corner. His partner readjusted the second cage on top of the first. McCall recognized him as one of the two from the first rave party who'd been standing at the second-floor balcony with a Heckler & Koch 9mm in his belt.

McCall moved silently to the back of the pickup. The man half turned. McCall grabbed him and broke his neck in one fluid movement. Gammon signaled he was going around to the back of the warehouse and disappeared into the shadows. McCall rolled the dead man under the pickup. A boarded-up window was at ground level in the warehouse. McCall climbed onto the cab of the truck and jumped onto the brick wall. His fingers dug into the crumbling mortar. He hung there for a moment, then climbed higher.

He slipped.

He fell two feet before his scrabbling fingers caught hold of another line of disintegrating mortar. He held on as his toes found another edge. He stayed still, calming his breathing. Then he climbed back up until he reached a small ledge right under a second-story window. It was black with grime. He heaved up on the windowpane.

It didn't move.

He tried again.

This time the window raised a couple of groaning inches.

McCall put all of his weight under it and raised the window just high enough for him to crawl through. He dropped down into a dark corridor. In front of him was one long room with half-glass partitions. The only light source there spilled down a set of wooden stairs at the far right end of the corridor. McCall looked to the left. He could make out a similar set of stairs going down to the warehouse main room.

One of Blake's college buddies exited the big long room—the second man from the railing at the first rave party. He was carrying a sheaf of manila folders. McCall ran silently forward, but the man's sixth sense kicked in. He whirled, pulling his Heckler & Koch 9mm pistol from his belt. McCall kicked it out of his hand and slammed him back through the open doorway into the long room. They fell together onto the floor. The white slaver tried to stab his thumbs into McCall's eyes. McCall blocked his hand, twisted it, and broke his wrist. He clamped a hand over the man's mouth, pressing a forearm against his throat. McCall had all of his weight on top of him. He tried to punch at McCall with his left hand, but it was like hitting a bar of steel. His writhing diminished until his body slackened. McCall, still on his knees, went through the dead man's coat pockets. He came up with a silver flash drive and pocketed it. He dragged the corpse into a corner and moved through the open doorway to the top of the stairs. Below he could hear the sound of movement, intermingled voices. Some of the prisoners were demanding to be set free. Others were crying.

McCall took out his Glock 19 and started down the stairs.

Detective Steve Lansing was in the lead car that sped down the narrow alleyway. The red light on top was flashing. Two more cop cars were behind him and the SWAT truck behind them. Lansing noted a deserted Prius parked farther up the alleyway. He turned right into a cul-de-sac. Six men, all of them college types, were herding young women handcuffed together toward the backs of two parked SUVs. The cop cars came to a screeching halt. Lansing and three other detectives jumped out, drawing their weapons. The college boys immediately opened fire. Lansing took cover behind his Nissan. Uniformed police officers piled out of the two other cars, firing on the white slavers. One of them shoved two blond girls away and fired at Lansing. One of the blondes, in a blue dress, stuck out her foot and tripped him. His bullets went wide, exploding the glass in the Sentra's driver's door. Lansing shot him four times. He keeled over. The handcuffed girls threw themselves down to the ground. SWAT officers poured out of the back of their vehicle with M4 carbine assault rifles.

Mike Gammon entered the warehouse through the small door that Emily had used to escape. He had a Glock 37 in his right hand. More of the young women were in here, all of them handcuffed together. He could hear firing from outside. Cops and the SWAT team had arrived. There was chaos, Blake's men running through the oblique shadows. One of them pulled out a .44 Magnum from his belt. Gammon shot him through the head. Gammon went through the white slaver's pockets and came up with a key ring, two sizes of keys on it, one large and one small. The smaller keys were for the handcuffs, the bigger ones for the cages. Gammon heard a scuff of sound behind him. He whirled.

Chip was standing twenty feet away with a gun pointed at Gammon's head.

Gammon was a dead man.

Two bullets exploded through Chip's back and he pitched forward. Tara came out of the shadows, holding a Glock 27 Gen4 in her hand.

Gammon raised a hand in acknowledgment.

The SWAT team broke into the warehouse. There was no more shooting. The rest of Blake's crew threw up their hands, tossing their guns onto the warehouse floor. Gammon caught sight of Emily, no longer shackled to one of the other victims, being shoved by Blake toward the other end of the warehouse. Deep shadows swallowed them up. For some reason Gammon glanced up and saw a shadow turning the corner of the wooden staircase above him.

Blake dragged Emily along with him, his hand on her shoulder. He had a Smith & Wesson .357 Sig pistol in one hand. He knew there was another exit from the warehouse at this end that they didn't use. In the confusion he could escape, but he'd taken his insurance with him. He glanced once behind them. No one was following them.

Blake turned back, looking ahead.

One of one shadows coalesced into the shape of a man, standing motionless, almost serene, blocking Blake's path. He had a gun in his right hand, but it was pointed down at the ground.

Blake jerked Emily to a halt. She was like a rag doll in his grasp, looking as if she would collapse at any moment. He pushed the barrel of the pistol hard into her temple.

"So your dad is back, eh, Emily? Except he's not *really* your dad." Blake looked at Robert McCall. "Move out of my way or I'll put a bullet through her brain."

"I'll give you one chance. Throw down the gun."

Blake just smiled.

Emily ground her right heel into Blake's instep. McCall threw up the Glock 19 and fired at Blake's head. The bullet drilled a hole through his frontal lobe, carrying into his cerebrum, and burrowing right into the thalamus, which is the relay center for the cortex and handles incoming and outgoing signals.

The message to fire the gun never reached Blake's trigger finger.

He fell back. McCall grabbed the .357 pistol out of Blake's hand before he hit the ground. Emily collapsed into McCall's arms, sobbing.

"I'd given up hope," she whispered.

"Never do that," he said softly.

Twenty minutes later McCall was standing outside the open warehouse doors. The survivors of Blake's white-slavery ring were being herded into a police van that was now parked in the cul-de-sac. McCall noted Detective Steve Lansing had taken charge. The Feds had also arrived. The SWAT team were packing up. Two ambulances were in the cul-de-sac. EMTs were checking on the young women, all of them out of their handcuffs now. A couple of them were put onto gurneys. The media had also arrived. Emily was talking to an attractive female reporter with a news crew behind her filming the interview. Tara was nearby.

Melody detached herself from a group of her fellow prisoners, ran over to McCall, and embraced him.

"I'm so sorry," he said to her.

She broke the embrace. "I was pretty scared, but Emily said someone was coming for us. I knew who she meant. So we did it, right? We brought the cobra and his creepy band of snakes down."

McCall smiled at the imagery he'd put in her mind. "We did."

"I have to make a statement to the police and then talk with some federal agents. Will you come and see me at Dolls sometime soon?"

"I will."

Melody ran back to one of the other victims she'd been talking to. McCall headed across the cul-de-sac to where Mike Gammon was impatiently waiting at the wheel of his Prius. Emily's interview was over. The news crew were moving to other victims.

Tara jogged over and fell into step beside McCall.

"I thought I told you to stay in the car."

"I don't take orders very well. Personality flaw. Besides, I thought you guys could use some backup."

"I'm sure Mike Gammon's happy for your personality flaw. What did Emily tell the media?"

"She didn't mention your name. I'll go with her to the Seventh Precinct. When they're done there, I'm going to help her pack her things, leave a note for the landlord breaking her lease, then she'll come back with me to my hotel. We're catching a plane to Minneapolis in the morning. I'm going to hand-deliver Emily to her mother."

"That sounds good to me."

Tara stopped walking, so McCall paused. He thought he might get a new embrace and a kiss, especially after what had happened—or *nearly* happened—between them, but Tara said, "I'd better get back to her."

"I'll pick you both up at your hotel tomorrow and take you to the airport."

Tara nodded and ran back to where Emily was now talking to a couple of federal officers.

McCall almost made it to the Prius, but Detective Lansing motioned him over. McCall thought Mike Gammon was going to have a fit.

Lansing looked at the aftermath of the firefight and shook his head. "White slavery with college guys. Just another facet of the American dream. What did you have to do with it?"

"I was trying to help two of the victims."

"The Feds are pretty pissed that you called me before they were called in. They're going to want to talk to you."

"Tell them I was your man undercover. You can't reveal my identity." McCall took the flash drive he'd taken from one of Blake's college pals and handed it to Lansing. "Give them this. I'd say it has all of Blake Cunningham's buyers on it."

Then McCall walked away.

"Stay in touch with me about our Equalizer problem," Lansing called after him.

McCall said nothing and slid into the passenger seat of the Prius.

"You took your sweet time," Gammon said. "I got in trouble in the warehouse. One of Blake's guys had a gun pointed at my head. Your PI friend shot him in the back."

"I'm sure she would have shot him in the front if he'd been facing her."

"God bless her," Gammon murmured. "Let's get out of here. Manhattan cops might not appreciate help from a retired Brooklyn detective."

Gammon drove down the alleyway. McCall looked up in the rearview mirror. He caught a fleeting glimpse of Detective Lansing watching the car pull away, then they were out into the street and heading back toward the Liberty Belle Hotel.

CHAPTER 33

McCall picked up Tara and Emily in a cab outside the Hotel Edison and accompanied them to LaGuardia. The women had a 9:05 a.m. flight to Minneapolis, changing planes in Chicago. Emily didn't say a word on the cab ride. Once they were in the airport, McCall showed a pass he carried to security that allowed him to go to the gate areas. All shadow-executive agents carried them. Emily didn't say a word until they were at her gate. Then she turned to McCall and said softly, "I was so scared."

"Not so scared you didn't let me know *exactly* where you were. You saved a lot of lives last night."

"You did that."

"Not alone."

"No one does anything worthwhile alone," Tara said, more for McCall's benefit.

"So I go home," Emily said. "To everything I ran away from. My mom doesn't *get* me. She doesn't listen."

"She will now."

Emily slowly nodded. "Yeah, maybe. Maybe you're right." Suddenly her mood lifted. "I'm going to grab a few magazines."

She ran over to the Hudson newsstand and picked up *People, Us, Entertainment Weekly,* and *Rolling Stone.*

"I'm scared to go home too, but I hide it better," Tara said wryly. "Someone tried to kill you in your hotel suite. You know who it is yet?"

"I'm one step closer."

"I'll take that as a no."

Emily ran back to them, stuffing the magazines into her backpack. The passengers were starting to board. Emily grabbed McCall's hand. "I liked being in that Mercury Theater with you," she whispered. "I mean, before you killed a bunch of guys and I got kidnapped. I felt close to you."

She kissed him on the cheek and moved into the boarding line.

Tara looked at McCall with that insouciant glint in her beautiful eyes. "Take care of yourself, big guy. Don't make me come back here to protect you. I'll send you a cape for Christmas."

She kissed him gently on the lips and joined Emily in line.

McCall was out of the terminal building heading for the taxi stand when he got the call from Mary. He only had to hear the quaver in her voice to know what had happened. Even though he had been expecting it, the weight of the remorse weighed heavily on him. He should have made more time for the people he cared for.

There weren't many of them left.

McCall found Brahms at a model-railway store on Third Avenue at East Seventy-Second Street near the Blumka Gallery. The three-story building looked like it been there since the Central Pacific and the Union Pacific had joined up at Promontory Summit in Utah in 1869. It was full of collectors and train enthusiasts. McCall descended a rickety flight of stairs. The basement room had several railway displays on vast tables with entire towns, scenic mountains, and tunnels with intricate multilevel routes. McCall located Brahms at a post–World War II train layout through the Chicago stockyards. McCall knew that Brahms had dedicated a room in his apartment to his train sets. Hilda had once told McCall you could hear the various train whistles and faint thrumming from every room.

Brahms walked over to another table with a Christmas train layout, bathed in moonlight, two separate trains thundering past the houses and the Christmas trees. McCall joined him.

"Hilda liked to visit the Polar Express with me." Brahms's voice was a little hoarse. "You got the steam locomotive and tender, a passenger coach, observation car, twenty-four curved and eight straight tracks, authentic train sounds, bell, a whistle, and a working headlight. Look at the craftsmanship. You can see the silhouettes of the passengers through the passenger-coach windows. You can even make it snow by using a light effect. Hilda always wanted to buy me a Polar Express, but I wanted a New York Yankees LionChief subway train. You got three Yankees players on the cars, a batter, a pitcher, and a player sliding into base, maybe Mickey Mantle, he stole twenty-one bases in 1959. But Hilda said the Polar Express was special, and when Yogi Berra died, so did the Yankees. She liked his Yogism 'When you come to a fork in the road, take it.'"

McCall didn't say anything. Brahms looked at him as the Polar Express sped through the snowy countryside toward the North Pole. "I don't know which fork to take now," Brahms said softly.

The old spy suddenly collapsed against McCall's shoulder, wracked by soundless sobs. McCall held him tightly. No one came near them. Brahms finally straightened up. "It happened at a little before four p.m. In her sleep."

McCall nodded. Didn't speak.

"You need a favor."

"I do."

"It couldn't wait?"

"It's about Control."

"You've got tonight. I am sitting shivah tomorrow after the funeral."

It had taken six days to get the furnace working at the apartment building. Norman Rosemont had paid for it, careful not let the super of the building—who *was* a fat fuck, as Sam Kinney had described—know who had authorized the repair work. Rosemont didn't know if bringing heat back to the apartment building violated his *deal* with whoever this maniac was who was keeping him a prisoner in his own building. Rosemont had climbed the stairs to the third floor and felt the radiator. It was lukewarm. Better than nothing. The door to apartment 3B had opened and Mavis and Elliott Weinberger had invited Rosemont in for tea with a little something added to warm them up. Rosemont had met them on his second night in the apartment building. Mavis Weinberger was a frail sparrow of a woman who had lived sixty years in the same apartment. She had retired from Macy's department store, where she had worked she since was sixteen. She spent her days watching the news shows and was an outspoken critic of anyone who wasn't a Republican. Her husband, Elliott, was a bull of a man who looked like he could crush Mavis if he gave her one good hug. He'd been a foreman at the Eastern Steel Corporation in Brooklyn who had retired in 2008. He was soft-spoken and read voraciously from beautiful leatherbound books with spines of twenty-two-karat gold that filled his bookcases from the floor to the ceiling. Right now he was reading *The Decline and Fall of the Roman Empire* in two volumes. Rosemont only read *The Wall Street Journal*. The Weinbergers had welcomed him into their home the same way that Sam Kinney had greeted him, with hospitality and warmth. It was as if Rosemont had been visiting the Weinbergers for a lifetime. Both of them were suffering from emphysema. Right now Mavis was debating politics with one of the CNN anchors, even though the conversation was one-sided and Elliott was saying how Rome had succumbed to barbarian invaders due to the gradual loss of civic virtue. Mavis had rolled her eyes and said the tea needed more sugar and more Johnnie Walker Black. Rosemont offered to get it.

Rosemont noted two big garbage bags were in the Weinberger kitchen to be taken down for recycling. He looked in the cabinets for a sugar bowl and spilled sugar all over the floor. Rosemont cursed, knelt down with a dustpan and broom to sweep it up, and saw that the cabinet beneath the sink was ajar. He took out his Apple iPhone 5S and lit up the interior. Black mold was around the sink so thick Rosemont could scrape it off with a knife. He was sure it was probably the same in the bathroom. He brought the Weinbergers more tea, properly sweetened, with splashes of Johnnie Walker Black and mentioned the mold. Mavis said it had always been black under the sink, and Elliott said they didn't have the money to fix the leaks. That most of the apartments in the building were the same.

Rosemont finished his tea and offered to take the garbage bags down the stairs to the back of the building. Elliott said he'd take them down later, but Rosemont assured the older couple it was no trouble and hauled the bags out of the kitchen. He left Mavis chiding Wolf Blitzer about his critique on foreign policy, and Elliott commented how the Praetorian Guard had been the primary catalyst of the Roman Empire's eventual collapse.

On the second floor Rosemont turned the corner, dragging the garbage bags behind him, and almost ran into Linda Hathaway. Gemma was in the doorway of the apartment waving to her mother.

"Close the door, honey!" Linda Hathaway said. "Eat your dinner and you can watch television until seven thirty."

The babysitter closed the door and Linda jogged ahead of Rosemont.

"Hi there, sorry to be rude, I'm late for work."

"Your daughter's bites seem to be fading."

"Yeah, until she gets bitten by another rat."

"I'm going to bring in fumigators for the whole apartment building."

"I've been trying to get the super to bring them in for months. I won't hold my breath. Thanks for the offer of the lift the other day. Gotta go!"

She was down the stairs to the first floor, and Rosemont heard the front door slam. He *hadn't* called the fumigators yet, but he was going to talk to the fat-fuck super about it. Rosemont hauled the garbage bags to the back door to the apartment building. Outside he ran into the young black student, who was dropping his garbage bags beside the overflowing bins.

"From the Weinbergers' apartment," Rosemont said, as if embarrassed about his good deed.

"Sure, I know them. A real nice couple."

"You a college student?"

"NYU."

"You don't live on campus?"

"This is my aunt's apartment."

"The Weinbergers have got a lot of mold in their kitchen. No wonder they're suffering from emphysema."

"Yeah, it's all through my apartment, too. I'm Jesse Driscoll, by the way."

Rosemont didn't want any of the tenants to know his real name, so he just said, "Norman," and shook hands. "How do you like living here?"

"It's a shithole, but I can't afford anywhere else. You want to help me take the rest of these garbage bags out to the front?"

"Sure, why not?"

It took Rosemont and Jesse about ten minutes, but they finally got all of the black garbage bags lined up at the curb in front of the apartment building. The physical exercise made Rosemont feel good. Like he'd accomplished something.

"I'm going to make sure the Sanitation Department is going to clear this block," Rosemont said. "I've got a call in to the city."

Jesse nodded. Whatever. "I'm meeting some friends at the Blind Barber, it's a little speakeasy in Tompkins Square Park, a cool spot. You're welcome to join us."

Norman Rosemont couldn't remember when such a casual and friendly offer had been made to him, but he couldn't accept it. He was in the apartment building under false pretenses.

"Not tonight. But thank you."

"Sure, no problem. Say hi to the Weinbergers for me."

Jesse jogged down Tenth Street. Rosemont entered the apartment building and climbed the stairs to the third floor. The door to the Weinbergers' apartment was closed. Rosemont debated whether he should knock, but what did he have in common with some old couple who watched the news and read books?

Except memories that they were prepared to share.

He could give them nothing.

Rosemont climbed to the fourth floor and was surprised to see a young man coming out of Sam Kinney's apartment. He almost barreled right into Rosemont. He was dressed in jeans, wearing a Windbreaker with a hoodie and Adidas.

"Hey, man, sorry!"

"Is Sam home?"

"No, he's at work. He manages a hotel up on the West Side. I'm his son, by the way."

Rosemont noted the young man didn't give him a name. "I didn't know Sam had a son."

"Oh, yeah, the bad penny turns up when he needs money! You a friend of his?"

"No, I'm his neighbor: Four-B."

"Nice to meet ya. I'll tell my dad you came over."

The young man closed the door to Sam Kinney's apartment and walked briskly to the staircase. Something about his attitude bothered Rosemont. But it was none of his business. None of his new neighbors were any of his business. He would soon be gone, and he'd never see any of them again.

Then why was he going to miss old Sam and the Weinbergers and that NYU student?

Rosemont opened the door to apartment 4B.

On the stairs, the Equalizer thought he had had a close call there. He didn't want to run into any more of Sam Kinney's neighbors who might remember him. But that was okay.

Sam would be dead within forty-eight hours.

CHAPTER 34

McCall stood in Brahms's cluttered office while the old spymaster brought up various images of Virginia on his computer screen. He also had the states of West Virginia, North Carolina, Maryland, and Pennsylvania in boxes around the perimeter. Mary arrived after twenty minutes. Her eyes were red rimmed from crying, but she was keeping a tight rein on her emotions. She had brought them plastic Starbucks containers, one filled with Eastern D.R. Congo Lake Kivu for her boss, the other containing Sulawesi whole-bean roast for McCall. She put a Mr. Coffee eight-cup black-and-chrome carafe on the counter to start brewing in the darkened store. She moved back into the office to where McCall was watching the computer screen but staying out of Brahms's peripheral vision.

"I can't believe you asked him to come here," Mary said tersely.

"He needs to find someone for me. Better he's here than sitting in his apartment with all of Hilda's memories around him."

"Is that how you justify it to yourself? He needs to do one more job for you and then you'll allow him to grieve? You don't have much of a con-science, do you, Mr. McCall?"

McCall didn't answer.

Control's story to Emma Marshall could have just been a fond remi-niscence of a childhood outing one summer. Or he could have made it up on the spot. Control was good at fabricating scenarios. Captain Josh Cole-man had *known Control's real name:* James Thurgood Cameron. He had been taken out of *existence* because he had stumbled upon a sinister plot that had been unfolding at The Company. One that had dire consequences that McCall was not privy to. All he knew was that the stakes were high.

"Brahms is talking about closing the store," Mary said. "What is he going to do then?"

"What will *you* do then?"

"I'll have to look for a new job. I've *loved* being here with him, just the two of us against the world. My dad left my mother four weeks after I was born. I could have found him. Hell, I'm working for a onetime spy, *he* could have found him, but I never wanted to do that. I have three younger sisters that I raised with my mom, and I love them all to pieces, but they live out in the countryside in Connecticut, and I don't think my mom has ever even walked down Broadway. This was our little piece of the city, and now with Hilda gone, I don't think it means anything to Brahms anymore."

"He's more resilient than you think."

Mary looked at her boss, shrouded by shadows, his full attention on his computer screen. "I've always worried that someone from your world will find him one night in his lonely apartment with his trains running and put a bullet in his head."

"I wouldn't allow that to happen."

"He has no one else to turn to."

"He has you," McCall said quietly. "You're the daughter he and Hilda had always wanted. He won't abandon you. You'll see him through this."

"If you're going to comfort me," Brahms said without looking up from his laptop, "I'll take a hug and another cup of coffee."

"One hug and another cup of coffee coming up." Mary kissed her boss on the top of his balding head and moved into the store to where the Mr. Coffee percolator was ready. McCall leaned over Brahms's laptop. Brahms was putting images onto the computer screen in rapid succession.

"I don't have much here for you, McCall. I found some old mining towns in Virginia and Pennsylvania buried in forests that might have been attractive to a young child. Here's one, Curtain Village, Pennsylvania, no residents, about three miles from Milesburg. An old mill, a 1830 plantation house, a couple of old houses. Then there's Portuguese Road in Virginia. The US Army were worried that the Germans would bomb the airport, so they built a fake town just east of the Richmond International Airport, then called Byrd Airport. Roads, sidewalks, driveways leading nowhere, mailboxes, streets signs, even the occasional park bench. A boy of Control's age might soon have grown tired of it, even if it did look like something out of the *Twilight Zone*. I found this abandoned Bethlehem steel mill, Pennsylvania, lots of connecting walkways and big rooms and rusting iron ladders, a great spooky place for a kid to play, but there's no forests around it."

Mary came back with a cup of Maxwell House, which she set beside Brahms's laptop. "I grew up with forests all around our little house in the middle of nowhere."

"Where'd you sneak off to play?" McCall asked.

"There was an abandoned trolley graveyard were my sisters and I used to go."

"Like this?" Brahms moved to another panel, which depicted rusting and dilapidated trolley cars on tracks surrounded by forest. "There must be a dozen pictures, but this is in West Virginia."

"Emma Marshall thought Control had talked about this location being in Virginia, but she couldn't say for certain," McCall said. "She said it had 'old rotting buildings and high-up towers and dangerous curves.'"

"Maybe an abandoned fairground?" Mary suggested.

Brahms's fingers flew around the keyboard, producing multiple images of old abandoned fairgrounds. "Here's one in Virginia. The Renaissance Fair in Fredericksburg. Forests bordering it, laid out on a lake, abandoned buildings, pointed turrets, gingerbread cottages, high towers, all decaying, lots of NO TRESPASSING signs. You might have snuck in there when you were a kid forty years ago, but now you'd get caught."

"But maybe you're on the right track," McCall said. "Maybe some smaller fairgrounds in Virginia, long forgotten, hemmed in by forests."

"I'll have to search it by Google Earth quadrants."

"You also have to look for a set of stairs," McCall said. "Maybe cut in the rock face around some caves. Or boat stairs leading down to a dock by a lake. Control said the stairs didn't lead anywhere, but that might have been an exaggeration."

"We're clutching at straws," Brahms said. "*All* of it might have just been in Control's head."

Two hours later McCall was pouring himself the last Maxwell House cup of coffee and Brahms had taken a break to rest his eyes. Mary was sitting at Brahms's computer searching the next quadrant of forest when she said, "I might have found something."

Brahms immediately took her place at his desk chair. McCall came back from the darkened store. Mary pointed to what looked like vague shapes through the trees. Brahms scrolled and magnified the images until he came to what looked like an abandoned fairground buried in the forest. There was a wooden fence to keep people out, but it was in bad need of repair with several pieces of it rotting away. A set of rusting swings was in tall grass with a jungle gym. A tall, skeletal structure had at one time held some kind of ride that went in a circle, but all of the seats had been removed, so what was left were just the struts and hanging steel lines. Several wooden structures in a maze pattern, most of them collapsed, had been arcade stalls. Brahms descended the view and rotated the forest to show more of the fairground. McCall noted a wooden enclosure with bright bumper cars painted on it, but only one car was left. There were the remains of a Kamikaze pendulum ride and a partially demolished structure that had two rainbow-colored cars on two levels.

"What would that have been?" Mary wondered.

"A Tilt-A-Whirl," McCall said. "Seven freely spinning cars that held four riders, all attached at fixed points on a rotating platform. As the platform revolves, parts of the platform are raised and lowered, and the resulting centrifugal and gravitational forces on the cars cause them to spin in different directions and at variable speeds. When the fairground was dismantled, most of the rides were taken away."

"The Ferris wheel is still standing," Brahms said. "You can see it from this angle through the trees. All of the passenger cars are still attached, but I doubt there'd be any electricity to power it."

Mary looked at McCall. "Is this what you're looking for?"

"It could be."

"There may be more destroyed fairgrounds or playgrounds or fenced-off recreational areas all through these Virginia woods," Brahms said. "You can't check all of them, McCall. It was forty years ago."

"I have to start somewhere. Can you print out the GPS coordinates for this abandoned fairground?"

"Coming right up."

Brahms moved over to an old HP printer and jabbed at a button.

"And after that, your search is over," Mary said, softer. "You're going to leave my boss alone to mourn Hilda the way he should have been doing tonight."

Brahms came back over and put a gentle hand on Mary's shoulder. "Hilda would have said, 'So, Chaim'—she *never* called me Brahms—'are you happy now that you've done one last favor for your old friend Robert McCall?'"

"How long does the debt to Mr. McCall have to be paid off?" Mary asked.

"Not after tonight," McCall said.

Brahms handed the two printed pages to McCall.

"Tell Hilda I say good-bye, Brahms."

Brahms nodded. He followed McCall out into the darkened store. Behind them, from inside Brahms's office, they both heard Mary sobbing.

Brahms touched McCall's arm, turning him around. "You've got no backup. Mickey Kostmayer is gone and he's not coming back. Sam's intel is that Granny was killed in that raid on the North Korean prison camp. No one from The Company would come anywhere near you." As if ironic: "So who you gonna call?"

"There's one person I might be able to reach out to."

McCall opened the front door to Manhattan Electronics. They could still hear Mary softly crying.

"She loves you very much," McCall said. "She'll be there for you."

"Will you be?"

"Always."

McCall walked out of the store, and Brahms closed the door gently behind him.

McCall drove a rental Venetian-red Hyundai into Petersburg, Virginia, past the old train station, the Siege Museum, the courthouse on East Tabb, through Old Towne with its historic buildings, to the Destiny Inn Bed and Breakfast building, circa 1894. He met her on the colonial front porch overlooking High Street. She was dressed in a Tahari pin-striped pantsuit with a Ralph Lauren silk kimono shirt and Andiamo Latosha birdcage sandals. She rose to her feet.

Cassie said, "You know there's a statewide manhunt out for you."

"Not for me."

"Have you found this wannabe vigilante yet?"

"Not yet."

"Why did you want to meet me on the veranda of this very charming colonial inn?"

"You've heard me mention a man named Control. He's disappeared off the face of the earth as far as anyone at The Company is concerned."

"But you've got an idea where he is?"

"Maybe in an old house somewhere in the forests here around Petersburg. It may be two miles from this veranda, or it may be several miles, or it may not be here at all."

There was a pause while Cassie looked out at the picturesque streets around the Destiny Inn. "You still have friends within The Company, but for some reason you couldn't contact them. That would only leave your enemies there. So you reached out to your ex-wife, who also happens to be an ADA in New York City, which is a long way from Petersburg with no jurisdiction. Did you really believe I would help you in some covert mission?"

"I'm counting on it."

Cassie looked up at McCall, shading out the glare that fell across the veranda. "How dangerous is this on a scale of one to ten?"

"If I find Control, *if* he's alive, it will depend on how many men are guarding him and what kind of advantage I'll have. You would be a diversionary measure. You wouldn't look like a threat. You're elegant, sophisticated, visiting friends in Petersburg, but you got lost in the forest. You won't have to be outside this house long, maybe three or four minutes."

"So while I keep these guards busy, you sneak into this house and rescue your friend. I make that an eight or a nine on the danger scale." McCall waited. There was no irony in his ex-wife's voice. "How are my chances of equalizing the odds you've stacked up against me?"

"I won't know until I find the house. You can turn me down."

Cassie sighed. "And give up a chance to help *you* out for once?" She moved closed to him. "Do you have a map of Petersburg in your car?"

McCall handed her a folded map. "For the time being, stay right here."

"How long should I wait?"

"I'll call you before two hours."

"Unless you can't."

"That's right. Then you drive back to New York."

Cassie looked up into McCall's face, and her voice took on a husky quality. "I hated you for leaving me and our son all those years ago. That doesn't mean I don't care. I remember this man—what did you call him again? *Control?* He meant a lot to you once. But the odds won't always be the way you want them to be."

"I'll call you with the GPS coordinates if I find the house."

McCall stepped down from the veranda, fired up the rental car, and pulled away.

Cassie looked after him with sad eyes.

CHAPTER 35

McCall drove down South Sycamore Street, over the I-85 freeway, turned right onto Belmeade Street, drove right to the end, where it petered it out into dense forest. He parked the Hyundai off a rutted track. He checked the Glock 19 in his jacket pocket and the chronometer on his wrist that contained the coordinates Brahms had plugged in. Then he got out and headed north-northwest, following the GPS signal. It was just a blip in the green gray on the dial with no distinguishing features except for paths that cut randomly through the trees. There were no signposts. After a mile and a half he passed a road completely obliterated with tangled vegetation; a sign said OLD HILLCREST ROAD, but that didn't lead anywhere. The density of the forest had given way now to sparser trees and foliage. In another five hundred yards McCall saw a wooden fence ahead. He came out into a clearing.

The fairground lay before him rotting in the Virginia sunlight.

The fencing had barbed wire intertwined across the top, but there were gaps in the wooden slats. He saw the top of the Ferris wheel and, beyond it, the skeletal spike that had once held rides that whirled around in a full circle. It still held the struts with hanging chains dangling. McCall ran to a stretch of fence and found a gap he could squeeze through.

He wandered into the old abandoned fairground.

The remnants of the vendors' booths were weathered and rotting. McCall noted there were shooting galleries, hook-a-duck, Tin Can Alley, a sign proclaiming ALL PRIZES CAN BE WON. All of the arcades were empty. There was the wreckage of the Tilt-A-Whirl with two cars left, their colors indistinguishable. Both cars had been dismantled and left in pieces. The Kamikaze pendulum had also been ravaged, with only one ride remaining intact. Litter was everywhere, Diet Coke cans and McDonald's wrappers and chicken boxes around the arcades. Some teenagers had snuck into the abandoned fairground recently, but he doubted there was anything much to hold their attention now. One lone red-and-green bumper car was intact on a circular flooring. At intervals throughout the fairground were swings, some set in concrete, some swinging over tall grass.

That left the Ferris wheel.

It stood imposing against the sky. McCall found a mechanism and pulled on a lever. As he thought, there was no electricity to power the ride. But it was high enough and the steel rims were intact, although a healthy coating of rust was on them. McCall climbed up the structure to its center point. He went hand over hand along one of the spokes until he reached a car that creaked in the wind. McCall reached up and unlatched it. He climbed into the Ferris-wheel car and swung the door closed.

The car swung crazily with his weight.

He waited for it to stabilize. Then he looked down at the forest hemming in the abandoned fairground from four sides. He was at the highest point he could get to unless he flew a chopper across the woods. He took out the Steiner LRF binoculars from his jacket pocket and swept the trees. There was nothing to see, just acres of forest. Intermittent shafts of brilliance were among the sentinels, but no houses. McCall thought of Emma's description of Control being in the woods stalked by leopards with his imaginary RAF hero, someone from the pages of a book. All made up. McCall realized the fairground must have been closed since probably the late eighties. The boy would have moved away with his parents long before then.

The Ferris-wheel car swung again.

A flash of light blinded McCall's eyes, just for a moment.

He raised the binoculars. The sunlight was *reflecting* off something. McCall adjusted the focus and found it.

An ornate, marble stairway.

It had thick marble balustrades on either side, the stairs sweeping up as if it had been lifted from the ballroom of the *Titanic* and transported to the middle of a Virginia forest. There were sixteen or seventeen wide steps, and then it just ended. McCall could see there was no back to the stairs.

He had his own staircase, Emma had said. *He said it wasn't high up and didn't lead anywhere.*

McCall climbed out of the Ferris-wheel car and slid hand over hand down to the center spoke. Then he climbed down the rest of the skeletal structure to the ground. He ran over to where the fence had partially caved in and kicked in one of the boards. He went under it and plunged back into the forest. Five minutes later he came out of the dense shrubbery into a small clearing where the marble staircase stood. It was surreal, sunlight shafting across it in places. McCall ran to the staircase and up the steps, the way Control must have done when he was a boy.

It led nowhere.

The marble stairs just stopped. It was a good eight feet to the ground. McCall descended the stairs and immediately found a path through the trees. It was trampled down, but passable. He ran down the path until it petered out.

McCall saw the shape of a house through the trees.

He ran closer and saw a distant wraparound porch in gray paint. He came out of the trees at the end of a sweeping gravel driveway. A road curved through the trees in both directions.

The house was a two-story, cedar-sided log cabin, probably a thousand square feet, with a back porch where wood was stacked.

Three men were seated on the front porch in wooden chairs, drinking coffee.

McCall knelt down in the shrubbery and dialed Cassie. Softly he told her the GPS coordinates. She said she would be there in twenty minutes. She didn't ask how he had found the house. McCall put the iPhone into his jacket pocket.

It took him about fifteen minutes to find the two motion detectors hidden in the trees. They had been painted dark brown to blend in, with a field of view of sixty yards. He deactivated both of them and ran around to the deserted back porch. He climbed up to one of the two eaves. The window there was unlocked.

McCall climbed into one of the bedrooms.

There was a stone fireplace and rustic furniture, all of it in cedar, on wood floors. He checked out the other bedrooms on the second floor, both of them in use. There was no sound or movement. He was halfway down the wooden staircase when he heard a car driving up the winding road to the front of the house. He heard gravel spitting from under the wheels as the vehicle halted. A car door slammed. McCall reached the ground floor, an open plan with a kitchen, living room, and dining room. A heavy oak door led to the rear of the house.

McCall heard one of the guards jumping down from the porch. Cassie's voice reached McCall through an open window in the kitchen.

"Hey, there! Boy, am I glad I found you guys!"

The man who responded had a slight accent, maybe Croatian, his voice pleasant. Nothing in Cassie's body language would be threatening, but they were in the middle of nowhere and visitors would be scarce.

"Can we help you?"

Cassie kept her voice raised, mostly for McCall's benefit. "I am seriously lost! I've been driving around these woods for the last forty-five minutes! My GPS is on the fritz and the directions I was given sounded like they were written out when Davy Crockett had a homestead here! Except we're in Virginia, not Tennessee, but really, I was going to call in the National Guard to come and find me!"

"Where are you from?" the Croatian asked, his voice still friendly.

"New York City. I'm visiting some friends of my daughter who live somewhere out here, but God knows where!"

The man laughed. Through the kitchen window McCall saw the other two men relax and sit back down to finish their coffee.

"I'll show you my directions." Cassie's voice still echoed through the open window. "It's a bluegrass log cabin like this, but much smaller."

There was a rustle of paper. The Croatian said, "You're way off course."

"I know! Can you point me in the right direction?"

"Of course. It will be my pleasure."

The way the Croatian said it gave McCall pause. In this lonely, secluded area, the three men were bored, babysitting some old spymaster, if indeed they *were* incarcerating him, and the arrival of a beautiful women in her forties might provide some welcome diversion. McCall could walk out onto the porch and shoot all three of them, but that would be the end of any stealth, he thought wryly. He needed to get Control away from here before any of his captors had even realized he had gone.

"Thank you so much," Cassie said, laughing. "I feel like a Manhattan native who can only find her way around Broadway and Brooklyn."

"I'm familiar with Broadway, but not Brooklyn," the Croatian said. "You have a map of this area?"

"I do!"

"Let me see it."

McCall moved through the oak door into a spacious study.

It had another stone fireplace and bookshelves on three of the walls, all of them crowded with popular paperbacks. A lower shelf had hardback books, all of them mysteries or boys' adventure fiction. Not books McCall would have expected to see in anyone's library. The mysteries had titles like *The Clue of the Coiled Cobra, The Mystery of the Grinning Tiger, The Mystery of the Plumed Serpent,* with a section of colorful jackets with a jagged-lightning insignia on them with titles like *The Caves of Fear, The Wailing Octopus, The Whispering Box Mystery.* On the next shelf there were hardback books from England featuring a hero named Biggles, whom McCall had never heard of, *Biggles Defies the Swastika, Biggles in the Orient, Biggles at the World's End.* Beside the bookcase was a passageway, also finished in cedar, that led to another room. McCall thought it might have been built as an add-on. No padlock was on the door, but no key was in the lock. McCall listened at the door and heard nothing. He tried the doorknob, but it didn't move. Control could be in the room beyond, or it could be some locked storage room.

McCall walked back into the study. There was no way he could break down the door into the small room. It was solid oak. He would have to get the key from one of the guards, and at that time all bets would be off.

He turned away from the lower shelves with the boys' adventure books, then suddenly swung back. Control had said something to Emma about being able to sneak into his father's workshop.

There was some workroom where his father made scale models, ships I think, where you fitted them into bottles, but Control wasn't allowed to go in there. He had liked looking at the models his father was working on when his mother and father were asleep, but he said he had to be careful not be caught. I think he had his own key.

McCall scanned the boys' adventure books. He knelt down and checked out the titles. More Biggles adventures. The author had compiled an impressive number of books written during the 1930s, 1940s, and 1950s. *Biggles and the Pirate Treasure, Biggles in Borneo, Biggles Buries a Hatchet,* then McCall found one where the title leapt out at him: *Biggles and the Leopards of Zinn.* Hadn't Control talked about his RAF hero pal protecting him from *leopards*? McCall flipped through the book and came to a page near the end.

An old-fashioned iron key was taped to it.

McCall untaped it. He slid the book back with the others and stood silently in the study. More conversation was coming faintly from the front of the house. McCall couldn't hear what was being said, but it sounded as if Cassie was ready to leave.

He moved quickly to the door at the end of the small passageway.

He fitted the key into the lock on the door.

It turned.

McCall opened the door and moved inside the room.

It was no longer a workshop. The only furniture in it were a single bed and an end table. Boxes holding paintings were stacked on the wall.

Control lay on the bed, with a quilt lying half on the floor. He was dressed in sweats, no shoes. His breathing was ragged and shallow. When McCall moved to him, he didn't stir. McCall had no doubt that Control had been drugged, and probably for a long time. His skin was the same color as the porches. McCall pulled him to his feet. He staggered, but his eyes didn't open. McCall hauled him up onto his shoulder. He closed the door to the prison room, turned the key in the lock, and walked back into the study. He set Control down in an antique rocking chair. He returned the old key to the pages of *Biggles and the Leopards of Zinn,* returned the book to the lower bookshelf, then picked Control up and carried him to the sliding glass door that led onto the back porch. It was still deserted. He carried Control onto the porch and jumped down onto the ground.

Now McCall heard more clearly the voices drifting from the front porch.

He didn't like the sound of it.

The Croatian gunman was poring over the Virginia map Cassie had handed him. His two pals on the front porch were still drinking coffee, although one of them had got up from the table and found a spot on the porch steps. He was thin and angular with a shock of unruly strawberry-blond hair and stared at Cassie as if he'd never before seen a young woman this close. When he smiled at her, his teeth were crooked and so stained with tobacco they were yellow. He followed her every move.

Why do I have the feeling he's seeing me naked? she thought.

His partner on the porch just looked bored. Cassie had noticed a silver skull ring on the heavyset Croatian's right hand. In fact, *all* of them were wearing identical silver skull rings.

How creepy was that?

The heavyset Croatian looked up at her from the map. "Follow this road for two miles to a fork, make a right, go straight for about six miles, and you'll come to a cathedral set of high trees, make a left, and you'll be back on East Boulevard. That turns into West Tuckahoe Street, and you're back on track."

She took the map from the Croatian and folded it. "Thank you so much."

"All these woods look the same, especially at night. Stay for a while. I'll make a fresh pot of coffee."

"I'd better get back on the road."

"If you get lost again, come back."

"I won't be coming back."

The smile on the Croatian's face never wavered. "Our loss."

Cassie was trembling just a little as she opened the car door. It caught on the seat belt.

"Let me help you," the Croatian said.

He held the car door open for her. Cassie looked at the porch, where neither man had moved. The smaller one was stoic with eyes as cold as ice. The thin one on the porch steps was smiling at her and picking something out of his teeth.

"Get this kid a banjo," Cassie murmured, and slid into the driver's seat.

After the barest pause, the Croatian slammed the Mercedes door.

Cassie drove away from the house. She had never been more grateful to have got out of anywhere in her life.

CHAPTER 36

McCall carried Control through the forest, past the marble staircase that led nowhere, until they came out of the trees and he saw the top of the Ferris wheel. He kicked out another slat from the fence and carried Control into the deserted fairground. He was conscious. McCall set him down. Control staggered a little, bleary and disoriented.

"I've got you," McCall said.

Control nodded, but McCall didn't think he knew who McCall was. He helped Control past the arcade stalls, what was left of the Tilt-A-Whirl and the dodge-'em car, past the Ferris wheel with its cars swinging in the strong breeze. McCall found the gap at the back of the abandoned fence. It took ten minutes to reach the parked Hyundai. By that time Control had lost consciousness again. McCall set him down gently on the backseat. McCall turned the vehicle around and headed out of the woods. In another ten minutes he was back in Petersburg. He saw Cassie waiting beside her Mercedes on Market Street near the city hall and St. Paul's Episcopal Church. He locked up the Hyundai and walked to Cassie. Her hands were still trembling.

"I'm glad you found your friend. Is he all right?"

"He's been drugged."

"Why did those men incarcerate him?"

"It's a matter of national security."

"Will they come for him?"

"I'm taking him somewhere they won't find him. Thanks for having my back."

"The life you lead is suicidal. I don't want any part of it. If you have run out of backups, I'm withdrawing my name to be thrown into the hat."

"Fair enough."

"Be careful."

Cassie kissed him on the cheek, got into her Mercedes, and drove off. McCall bought a blanket and a pillow in the Walgreens in the square. He transferred Control to the trunk of the Hyundai, put the blanket around him and the pillow beneath his head, and closed the trunk.

McCall drove back to New York City and met Mike Gammon at the Hertz place at Morton Street. Gammon transferred Control to the trunk of his Prius. He was still unconscious. McCall came out of the Hertz office and slid into the passenger seat. Gammon drove north and parked on West Seventieth Street between Columbus Avenue and Broadway. McCall opened the trunk and picked Control up, still wrapped in the blanket, and heaved him up onto his shoulder.

Gammon put a BROOKLYN SOUTH HOMICIDE SCENE placard in the driver's window. "Comes in handy when you're trying to get through traffic." Gammon didn't know who the unconscious man was or why McCall had rescued him. "Where are we taking him?"

"Right here." McCall set Control down so that he was lying flat on a bench. "Help me with the manhole cover."

McCall and Gammon moved the manhole cover, which might have weighed two hundred pounds, but it was not secured tightly. McCall remembered where this location was from the times he had walked the subway tunnels with Jackson T. Foozelman, when McCall had first discovered the subterranean dwellers beneath the Manhattan streets. It took McCall and Gammon's combined efforts, but they moved the manhole cover far enough to one side. McCall climbed down the rusting metal ladder. Gammon picked up Control and handed him down to McCall. The New Yorkers around them were only mildly interested.

Brooklyn Homicide business.

"Good luck," Gammon said. "You get any word on Granny, you can find me in Central Park at the chess tables."

McCall nodded. He carried Control to the bottom of the iron ladder, stepping into dank ankle-deep water. Work lights provided wan radiance in the tunnel. McCall hoped he remembered which way to go. It took him twenty minutes to find the subway tunnel beneath the streets that housed Fooz's homage to Sherlock Holmes. The old black man was up on his feet as soon as McCall carried Control in. He laid him down gently onto Fooz's Lucinda sleigh bed.

"Is Dr. Bennett still working in the subway tunnels?"

"Sure thing. Been down here for almost twenty years."

"Get him."

Fooz disappeared into the shadows. McCall got a compress of water and wiped it over Control's forehead. He was sweating and feverish. In another twenty minutes Fooz was back with Dr. Bennett, who still wore the same rumpled gray suit and carried his old-fashioned doctor's bag.

Without a word Dr. Bennett took Control's pulse and listened to his chest with his stethoscope. "This man's breathing is shallow and there are dark bruises and lacerations on his arms. You didn't do this to him, did you, Mr. McCall?"

"No. This is how I found him."

"Your friend has been given sedatives, benzodiazepines. Probably clonazepam, too. It's a wonder his heart hasn't given up on him. My son works at the ER at the New York–Presbyterian in Washington Heights. I can take you there."

"I have to leave him here."

"You do what you have to do," Dr. Bennett snapped. "If his fever spikes to 104 to 107 Fahrenheit, or what we call hyperpyrexia, call me. Otherwise, don't bother."

Dr. Bennett, who reminded McCall of the crotchety Doc Adams character in that western series *Gunsmoke*, left a bottle of Tylenol, nodded brusquely to Fooz, and strode out.

"He ain't much for a bedside manner," Fooz murmured.

"Can you get to a phone when you have to?"

"Oh, sure, that gal Alicia from Braker's Territory, foxy and tough? She lets me use an unlisted number she's got in case of emergencies."

"If he awakens, call me."

"You know I got your back, Mr. McCall."

McCall walked out. He knew a postmortem would be going on at the house in the Virginia woods. Matthew Goddard would be searching all of the known Company safe houses in Washington, DC, Philadelphia, Boston, and New York.

But McCall didn't think anyone would be looking for Control in a Sherlock Holmesian subway-tunnel home beneath the Manhattan streets.

Norman Rosemont walked into his corporate offices to find sixty messages waiting for him, all marked urgent. His assistant, Mark, was trying to prioritize them, remarking to his coworkers that his boss's attitude to their current dilemma seemed to be ambivalent. Rosemont had more important matters to attend to. He had met two city health inspectors at the apartment building at 4:00 p.m., and right away he knew it was a waste of time. First he took them down to the basement. The furnace had only been patched up and was in need of a complete overhaul. The super for the building finally made an appearance and didn't know anything about any health hazards. Rosemont took the inspectors to Mavis and Elliott Weinberger's apartment and showed them the black mold under the sink in the kitchen and bathroom. He took the inspectors to Linda Hathaway's apartment, where she brought Gemma out into the corridor and showed them the rat bites on her arms and legs. Rosemont took them up to his *own* apartment in 4B to show them the black mold there and told them there was more of it in 4A. The inspectors made notes and said they would be in touch with the owner of the building, which was Rosemont, but no one knew that. Then they left.

Rosemont was seething. He was sure they'd been bought off. So he decided to generate a petition signed by all of the tenants in the building. He didn't bother with the super's signature, but started on the ground floor at the other apartment there, which was occupied by Jesse Driscoll. The NYU student was happy to sign a petition that delineated all of the health concerns in the building, but he didn't think it would do any good. Rosemont hustled up the stairs to the second floor and got Linda Hathaway to sign the petition. He wanted to write her a check to ease his own conscience about her daughter's rat bites, but how would he even broach the subject? Across the hall Rosemont knocked on apartment 2A, where he met Connie's husband, Donald, who was holding Mr. Toast as if he wanted to strangle him. Connie signed the petition and sang Rosemont a chorus from *Promises, Promises* before he could escape. On the third floor, Mavis and Elliott Weinberger welcomed him in for tea. They both signed the petition, and as he left, Mavis said that Anderson Cooper was sharp as a tack, but wasn't he gay? Apartment 3A was vacant. Rosemont climbed up to the fourth floor and knocked on Sam Kinney's apartment. There was no answer. On an impulse, Rosemont climbed the stairs to the roof, which he noted were wood. He pushed through the fire door and found Sam sitting on the roof on a folding canvas chair, smoking a cigar. Rosemont found another canvas chair and sat down beside him.

"Mind if I join you?"

"Sure. I try to come up here when it's just after twilight, smoke a good cigar, just by myself. There's no smoking in the building, except I think Donald Hewitt in 2A is a secret smoker, but in this building the air itself will asphyxiate you. What have you got there?"

Rosemont showed him the petition. "I got all of the tenants to sign this. You're the last signature, except for that fat fuck of a super."

"He's not such a bad guy. Our Broadway chorus girl, Connie, says Miguel sends every cent he makes home to his family in Chile. They escaped that big quake a couple of years ago in Iquique. Maybe we should cut him a little slack."

"Why should we? He doesn't care that old Mrs. Weinberger's lungs are as black as coal dust or that Linda Hathaway's daughter was gnawed by rats. I'm going to deliver this petition to the New York health department tomorrow, and I'm not leaving until I get these health concerns dealt with. I've got clout there."

Sam didn't doubt it. "I'm glad you've had the chance to get to know your neighbors. They're nice folks." Sam signed the petition, put out the cigar in an astray on the folding table, and stood. "I'm going to turn in. I got to be at work at six in the morning."

"I met your son yesterday. He was coming out of your apartment."

"Oh, sure, he comes by now and then," Sam said, not missing a beat.

"He seemed like a nice guy."

They disappeared down the stairs to the fourth floor of the building.

The Equalizer stepped out of the shadows on the roof. He wasn't too worried about being called Sam Kinney's son. The old fart that Sam was talking to didn't know the Equalizer wasn't. He now knew Sam Kinney's routine. Tomorrow night he would put his plan into motion.

And Robert McCall would lose his only friend in the world.

Mickey Kostmayer had been expecting the prisoners' rebellion. They'd been whispering about it for weeks. None of the prisoners or guards had any idea that Kostmayer spoke Korean. The roads they were assigned to clearing had large rocks and massive tree limbs blocking them. It had been so bad that the North Korean guards had unshackled the prisoners so they could clear one stretch of impassable road. The guards carried Type 63 SKS rifles and were vigilant, but tedium and boredom had set in. The murmur among the prisoners had reached a fever pitch, and a moment later they charged their guards. The guards opened fire but were unprepared for the onslaught. Half of the rebelling prisoners were cut down, but the other half tore into their captors. The fighting was fierce and vicious. Too many atrocities had to be answered.

Kostmayer escaped into the dense forest bordering the road. He stumbled down a steep ravine until he came to a fast-flowing stream. Bullets erupted into the water, and Kostmayer went under. More bullets zipped inches from his face as he swam deeper. He didn't know how many of the North Korean guards had come after him. Probably only one or two. They had their hands full quelling the rebellion.

Kostmayer came up for air about a quarter mile downstream. He turned and saw one of the North Korean guards running along the stream toward him. Kostmayer submerged again. The soldier reached the edge of the stream, firing down randomly.

He was looking the wrong way.

Kostmayer came out of the water and grabbed the guard's foot, upending him into the stream. His SKS rifle skittered down the bank. Kostmayer grabbed the guard's lapels. He hit him using the ancient art of Arakan, striking with the bottom of a clenched fist, resembling swinging a hammer. The guard was stunned. Then Kostmayer put his arms around the guard's throat and held him underwater. A few seconds later the guard went limp. Kostmayer dragged him onto the mossy bank. The woods were thick and shielded them from surveillance. Kostmayer changed clothes with the guard, loaded his pockets with rocks, then dropped him back into the stream and saw him disappear from sight.

The North Korean's uniform hung loosely on Kostmayer, but it was better than the gray jumpsuits he'd been wearing for weeks. He followed the stream until it emerged from the dense woods at the Yalu River. He was at the Chinese border. He could see Dandong across the Sino-Korean Friendship Bridge. He could try to cross on the bridge, but the border crossing would be tricky. Instead he slipped into the river and swam to one of the many islands between the two waterfronts. He made it to a no-man's-land where there was nothing but a ten-foot fence. Granny had said that the border on either side of the Yula River was porous at best. He thought about Granny. Two of Kostmayer's fellow prisoners had talked about a mass grave dug in the swamp about two miles from the prison camp. Their description of a white man with butter-colored hair had been chilling. Kostmayer had other evidence that Granny had been killed, little snippets of information he had gleaned from some of the guards' conversations. Granny would have told him to keep focused on getting out.

Kostmayer swam from the island to the waterfront. From there he made it to a road. A truck stopped for him. The driver made no mention that he was dripping wet. Kostmayer explained in Cantonese that he had a special pass to visit his grandmother in Beijing. When he was dropped off in Dandong, he made his way to Zhenba Street and got on a train to Shenyang, from where he would go on to Beijing. He'd stolen a wallet in the train station so he would have some money. Once in Beijing, he would ditch the North Korean uniform, get some clothes, and contact the local Company man there, an American expatriate named Jensen. He would get Kostmayer a passport and onto a Cathay Pacific flight to New York City.

Kostmayer waited for the Beijing train. He and the other mercenaries had liberated over a hundred souls from the prison camp, but in his mind, Kostmayer had failed in his mission.

He had left Granny behind.

CHAPTER 37

Their lovemaking was more erotic than he remembered it ever being. As usual, Beth was the aggressor, raking her fingernails down his back until they drew blood. She wanted him to slap her. Then she was on him like a lioness until he turned her onto her stomach to enter her from behind. But she had a surprise for him. She reached under her pillow and pulled out a

silken noose. Cross pressed his knee into the small of her back and slipped
the noose around her throat. He applied pressure, choking her. She clutched
at the noose, crying out, the sexual energy flowing through her. He brought
her to a climax twice; each time after totally restricting her airways, bringing her to the moment of asphyxiation, he then loosened the noose. Cross
knew when the carotid arteries were compressed, the sudden loss of oxygen
to the brain and the accumulation of carbon dioxide produced feelings of
giddiness and intense sexual arousal, which heightened the masturbatory
sensations. It sent Beth into a semihallucinogenic state called hypoxia. Cross
didn't encourage this dangerous sexual practice. Beth urged him to do it one
more time, but he had had enough. He threw the silken noose onto the floor
and entered her. She took handfuls of his hair and curled them into her
fingers until she almost pulled them out. Both of them climaxed. Beth
screamed so loudly that Cross worried it might've awakened Lisa and David.
He listened, but he didn't hear running footfalls to the bedroom door. Beth
whispered the sexual release had been exquisite.

Cross got up from the bed. It had been different when he'd strangled
Ann Crosby. That had been cold-blooded and premeditated. With Beth
he had to be careful that her sexual fantasies didn't go too far. He went into
the bathroom and showered. When he reemerged into the darkened bedroom, Beth was sobbing uncontrollably. He didn't go to her. He just closed
the door behind him.

Cross padded down the staircase. His suitcase was already waiting in
the hallway. He poured himself a cup of coffee, buttered some toast and
added honey, then walked into the living room. He picked up a framed
photograph of the family at the Georgia Aquarium. Beth had been fasci-
nated by the gentle whale sharks, only four of them in captivity in North
America. Lisa had fallen in love with the dolphins, and David had been
obsessed with the albino alligators.

He stared at the picture and knew that he had no feelings for his
family.

He despised them.

He had seen too much suffering since his time with Doctors Without
Borders. Innocents who could not be cured. Old people without a tooth in
their head and children with all kinds of diseases. He had realized as a
young doctor that he couldn't save them all. By the time he had reached his
late thirties, he knew they were beyond saving. So was the human race. He
knew that was the ultimate nihilistic response. But unlike his Jihadist

brothers, who worshipped, as far as he was concerned, a vengeful God, Cross believed existence had no point at all. Love or caring had no objective meaning; no comprehensible truth was to be found in human contact. Human beings were worthless entities.

Life had no truth to search for.

The Jihadists called the United States the Far Enemy, but there *were* no enemies. There was only apathy and indifference to pain and suffering. Americans were shallow, hypocritical, and petty, and Cross had no problem sacrificing as many of them as possible. His fellow terrorists—it occurred to him that he would soon *also* be called a terrorist—thought of themselves as having a divine purpose. They didn't.

Cross would kill a great many innocent people.

And it would all be meaningless.

He finished the toast and coffee and went into the garage. He retrieved his Medicool vial cooler and protection case from the refrigerator and transferred them into the trunk of his BMW. They had Doctors Without Borders FRAGILE stickers on them, and he carried paperwork from the CDC authorizing him to carry the vials. It would take him over fifteen hours to make the journey from Atlanta to Boerne, Texas. He had vacation time from Emory University. His superiors knew he was working on a vaccine to combat Ebola, and they were excited about the "breakthrough" he was close to. Cross had flirted with the idea of taking a plane from Atlanta to San Antonio, but that would have meant checking his luggage at the airport, and luggage could be lost. His vials were too important to leave to some baggage handler to screw up.

Cross raised the garage door, backed out into the driveway, and got out of the car. He looked up at the second floor. Beth was standing in their bedroom window stark naked, looking down at him.

Giving the neighbors an early-morning thrill, he thought ironically.

She waved down to him, then retreated from the window as if suddenly realizing she made a pretty provocative figure. Cross looked up at the sky. Dawn was spreading orange fingers across the suburban houses. He got back into his BMW, turned around, and headed for Texas.

He knew he'd never see his wife or his children again.

McCall told the security officer at the gates of Arlington National Cemetery his name, which was on a list, and parked outside the beautiful administration building. He noted the flags were all flown at half-staff, beginning half an hour from the first service. The funeral for Josh Coleman wasn't until 11:00 a.m., but McCall took some time to walk through the rows of the white grave markers, many of them adorned with wreaths and fresh flowers. In Section 1 he found the grave of Captain Edward P. Doherty, who had captured President Lincoln's assassin. In Section 2 he found the grave of Major Lieutenant George Crook, who had captured Geronimo. In Section 3 he found the grave of Lieutenant Colonel F. Benteen, who was Custer's subordinate at Little Bighorn. Nearby were the markers of Lieutenant Commander Robert B. Chaffee and Lieutenant Colonel Virgil I. Grissom, the Apollo astronauts who'd been killed in the flash fire in the Saturn IB rocket at Cape Kennedy on January 27, 1967. McCall visited the grave of Lieutenant John F. Kennedy, PT boat commander during World War II, where the eternal flame had been ignited by Jacqueline Bouvier Kennedy at the center of a five-foot-circular flat granite stone. McCall recalled President Kennedy's speech on Armistice Day, November 11, 1961, twelve days before his assassination, when he had said, "Man's capacity to devise new ways of killing his fellow men have far outstripped his capacity to live in peace with his fellow men."

[handwritten margin note: Nov 23 1963]

McCall walked over to the Tomb of the Unknowns, which was up on a hill. He knew the tomb had been perpetually guarded since July 1937 by the Third US Infantry Regiment. McCall watched as the guard on duty took twenty-one steps down the black mat behind the tomb. He turned and faced east for twenty-one seconds, then turned and faced north for twenty-one seconds. Then he took twenty-one steps down the mat. He executed a sharp "shoulder-arms" movement to place his rifle on the shoulder closer to visitors to signify that he was standing between the tomb and any possible threat.

Somehow it was a stirring sight.

McCall made his way through the stark white markers to some trees near the site for Captain Josh Coleman's grave. Mourners were already waiting for the funeral procession to arrive. There were also about thirty Army-band members, a firing squad comprising of a senior NCO officer and seven shooters, two buglers, a bunch of dignitaries, and a chaplain. McCall spotted a two-star general among the mourners. He also noted a good-looking gray-haired officer who he thought might be Colonel Michael G. Ralston, known to all as Gunner.

A man brushed past McCall. He looked up and said politely, "Pardon me." He was a little taller than McCall, probably in his late thirties with brown hair with an athlete's grace and power. He walked through the white markers to where the mourners were waiting.

His name was Renquist, but McCall didn't know that.

He just knew the man was an assassin.

The funeral possession arrived at the graveside. Eight honor guards carried the coffin, draped in an American flag. Helen Coleman, dressed in black, sat in the front row of fold-up seats beside her younger son, Tom, who was wearing a dark suit and a tie, resolutely holding on to his mother's hand. He was eighteen, lanky, and somehow fragile. On the other side was Helen's daughter, Rebecca, probably twenty-five, with expressive eyes in a face that more than resembled Josh Coleman's. Her hair was black and reached right down her back. She gripped her mother's other hand. Colonel Michael G. Ralston sat down behind Helen and put a gentle hand on her shoulder. There was something *courtly* in his attitude that McCall liked.

The chaplain gave a eulogy that McCall couldn't hear. The service took twenty-five minutes. Seven members of the firing squad raised their rifles in the air and fired three volleys. McCall knew the tradition dated back to the Civil War to alert the other side that the funeral of the dead was complete. The senior NCO of the honor guard folded the flag from the coffin. He passed it to the two-star general, who presented it to Helen Coleman. McCall could hear the general's voice ringing above the sighing of the wind:

"On behalf of a grateful nation."

Helen took the flag and nodded her acceptance. McCall had failed her. He had promised to find her son and bring him back. Yet the message that Josh had tried to bring back home now had a greater purpose.

A conspiracy, he had said. *National security was at stake.*

The funeral slowly broke up. McCall waited another half hour before he showed up at the Army and Navy Club on Farragut Square in Washington, DC. The reception was packed. The mood was somber. McCall saw Helen Coleman standing with her children. He caught her eye to let her know he was there. At that same moment Gunner detached himself from the three-star general he was talking to and moved over to McCall and offered his hand.

"Colonel Michael G. Ralston. They call me Gunner."

McCall shook hands. "Helen Coleman has mentioned you. You were Captain Josh Coleman's CO in Syria."

"Yes, I was. She hasn't told me much about you, Mr. McCall, except that she said you used to work in intelligence." McCall waited. "She told me you were responsible for bringing Captain Coleman home."

"She's mistaken."

"You didn't fly to Syria to rescue him?"

"I'm here to pay my respects to him."

"Our intel says you flew to Syria in a Bombardier Global 6000 VistaJet. You were parachuted into Syria south of Ar Raqqah and east of Aleppo, near Highway Six. The Insurgents fired at your plane with antiaircraft guns."

"What else did your intel tell you?"

"Not much after that. Captain Coleman had been wounded in a firefight in the Syrian village of al-Sukhnah. That's where we lost contact with him. You couldn't have gone there. The village was evacuated right before I came Stateside."

"Helen Coleman wasn't given that information. She was only told her son had been killed in action in Syria."

Gunner was tight-lipped. "The Army had to find out if Captain Coleman was still alive. We had no intelligence that could pinpoint his location. Helen Coleman was told that he'd been killed in al-Sukhnah."

"But it wasn't the truth. At least, it wasn't at the time."

"We were still looking for him. You must have found him. How did you do that?"

After a moment, McCall said, "Captain Coleman sent his coordinates to his mother. The intel he got from an Insurgent deserter in al-Sukhnah said there were forces working closely with the Jihadists. He didn't know who in the military he could trust."

"That's very disturbing to hear." McCall waited. "Your pilot is a mercenary named Hayden Vallance. He arrived in Berlin where he contacted us. How he got there from Syria is another gap in our information."

"I'd say you pieced together your intel meticulously."

"Whatever Captain Coleman told you in Syria is highly classified. The Pentagon wants to talk to you."

"I haven't got anything to say to the Army."

"We're also going to talk to Hayden Vallance."

"If you can find him."

Gunner nodded, glancing around at the mourners and the Army officers in the room. "You're a civilian, Mr. McCall. I am familiar with the intelligence unit you used to work for, but their records are also highly classified and not for my eyes. You went into Syria and rescued an Army captain who was very dear to me. We don't leave any soldier behind. I don't know how you did it, but you almost got him out. I'm speaking on behalf of Helen Coleman and the US Army when I tell you that you have our gratitude and thanks."

"But you want to know what Captain Coleman told me."

Gunner looked back at McCall. "There was a list that Captain Coleman had in his possession. Names of *American* fighters who had been radicalized by our enemy."

"Don't you have that same list?"

"I'd need to see Captain Coleman's list for comparison."

McCall took out the folded piece of paper that Josh had given him in the helicopter in Syria and handed it Colonel Ralston. "I never gave that to you. I never came into contact with Captain Coleman."

Gunner put the list into the pocket of his dress uniform. "Thank you. The Jihadist deserter from ISIS whom Captain Coleman had been liaising with had told him about some kind of a conspiracy."

"I don't know anything about it."

"Helen told me you were someone who helped people. But we're talking about national security and a very real threat to the lives of ordinary Americans. That's why the Pentagon needs to debrief you." Gunner lowered his voice a little. "My superiors are talking to Homeland Security. If they think they have enough evidence to issue a warrant for your arrest, you could be having this briefing at the Pentagon within twenty-four hours."

"They would have to prove I was in Syria and I was in contact with Captain Coleman. Which they can't. Whatever intel Captain Coleman had at the time of his death died with him."

Gunner met McCall's steady gaze. "But *you're* going to act on it?"

McCall's eyes were expressionless, but Gunner just nodded. At that moment Helen Coleman joined them with her children. Tom Coleman had wild hair that had been combed for the occasion. His eyes were red from crying. Rebecca Coleman was beautiful and had her mother's eyes. She was tense, but it struck McCall that there was something more to her grief. Helen just put her arms around McCall.

"Thank you for coming," she said simply. She reached into her coat pocket and brought out three brass casings. "The senior NCO of the honor guard explained to me these casings are from the three volleys the firing squad fired. I found them tucked into the folds of the flag."

"It's a tradition of respect from the soldiers," Gunner said.

"Mr. McCall, this is my son Tom."

He shook McCall's hand. "Pleased to meet you, sir."

"And my daughter, Rebecca."

Rebecca didn't shake hands. "Mom said you were someone who looked for the truth." It was an odd thing for her to say.

Before McCall had a chance to reply, the three-star general whom Gunner had been talking to earlier motioned for Helen to join him and his entourage.

She took McCall's hand and said, "Call me when you have time."

She moved with her son Tom in tow. The general had included Gunner in his invitation, so he escorted Helen across the room. Rebecca Coleman looked at McCall as if making a decision. She took something out of her coat pocket and pressed it into his hand. Then she walked across the room to be with her mother and her brother.

McCall had paid his respects and needed to leave the reception before any more Army officers tried to confront him. When he got outside to Farragut Square, he walked down Seventeenth Street NW until he was at the White House before he looked at what Rebecca Coleman had given him. It was a small envelope.

He tore it open.

A safe-deposit key fell into the palm of his hand.

CHAPTER 38

Bo drove down the I-10 toward San Antonio nursing a bad hangover after a fight at the Shadywood Cantina, where he'd had to teach some unruly yahoos some manners. He was already late for his meeting with his Texas Minutemen Militia. But his mind was somewhere else.

It was the anniversary of his niece's death.

Crystal had been in a car crash in Pennsylvania, where she was going to college. Bo had arrived at the hospital, and the triage nurse had told him that his niece was still in the OR. He had called his sister and had told her to be strong.

Crystal had died just after 2:00 p.m.

She'd been on her way to a restaurant in Philadelphia. Crystal's boyfriend, Diego, had been driving erratically. He'd survived because he hadn't been thrown through the windshield. Crystal hadn't been wearing her seat belt. They'd been hit by another car being driven by a male student and his three pals, who'd been drinking. All four of the undergrads had survived.

All of them were Muslims.

Ultimately the four students had been cleared of reckless driving. Their alcohol content and been just below the legal limit. Bo had harassed the police department to issue warrants to the students for vehicular manslaughter, but that never happened. So Bo had painstakingly collected information on the murderers of his sister. He knew what courses they were taking at U of Penn, who their friends were, where they hung out. He spent a lot of time in Smokey Joe's tavern on South Street and in McGillin's Old Ale House on Drury Street. He'd waited until Aaban, his pals called him Abe, had come staggering out of Smokey Joe's one night shit-faced. Bo had dragged him to an alleyway behind the bar and beat him until he was a bloody pulp. He had dialed 911 himself, said he'd witnessed a fight but didn't want to become involved, gave the 911 operator the name of the bar, and hung up. The cops had found Aaban's body and had mounted a full-scale investigation, but it never led anywhere.

Bo gave himself another two months before he got the second Muslim. His name was Kahil, which meant "lover and friend," or so the internet said. He had been coming out of McGillin's Old Ale House in Philly with a group of friends. He'd said his good-byes and crossed the street when Bo had roared out of a side street and hit him. He had been flung over Bo's Explorer and his head had split open like a ripe melon. None of his friends saw the make or model of the SUV. Bo had taken off the license plates for the night. He had waited another month to find the third student, whose name was Deen, *not* Dean, whom he drowned in White Clay Creek, a tributary of the Christina River in southern Pennsylvania. Deen had been going home to his folks and had got out of his car to look at the beautiful river. Bo had weighted him down with rocks and had watched as he submerged.

As far as Bo knew, the police had never connected the dots to the three students.

The fourth student, Shayaan, had dropped out of U of Penn halfway through his senior year. Bo didn't know if Shayaan had been frightened by what had happened to his friends, but he had disappeared, and Bo couldn't find him. It didn't matter. He was out there somewhere and Bo had photos of him. He would find and kill him. By the time Bo was in San Antonio sitting at one of the small tables on River Walk, he had cleared his head of these vengeful thoughts.

There were *new* Muslim targets to be dealt with.

The riverfront was crowded with tourists strolling leisurely or sitting at the tables shrouded by their colorful umbrellas. Bo nursed an Alamo Golden beer and watched the flat-bottom boats drift by with their guides pointing out places of interest. He looked up at one of the magnificent hotels that fringed River Walk. It had been called the Valencia Hotel, but now it had a new name, Riverwalk Hotel. The renovations had taken almost a year. It was open again, bigger and better, bustling with activity.

Bo's cousins Steve and Kyle arrived first. Both had forsaken their Texas Minutemen Militia uniforms and were casually dressed in polo shirts and Salvage Mayhem straight jeans. Randy Wyatt rounded out the trio, bringing his laptop with him. Randy was a good ole boy who had his own unique fashion statement. He dressed like Wild Bill Hickok in a long frock coat, a vest with a folding pocket watch and chain, a silk bow tie, corded pants, and big black calf boots. The tourists loved it. Particularly the young women. Big Teddy Danfield was the last to arrive.

Bo was a patriot. He knew his most trusted companions were equally loyal to his cause. The zealots who had taken over the Riverwalk Hotel weren't Americans. They were Muslims, who did not belong in their city. Bo remembered seeing on the internet that when the mayor of London had been sworn in, there had been a great swelling of British pride. What the American public had *not* seen were the protesting and near riots that had taken place in the London streets. Muslims marched and chanted, carrying banners that said EUROPE YOUR 9/11 IS ON ITS WAY—BUTCHER THOSE WHO MOCK ISLAM—ISLAM WILL DOMINATE THE WORLD. Bo and his minutemen had not been radicalized in the way some Europeans had been and, yes, even some Americans had been. No member of the Jihadists would ever have recruited Bo or his men. But they would be labeled as terrorists just the same.

Except the Jihadists would take the blame and the responsibility.

Randy tossed his broad-brimmed cowboy hat on the table and opened his laptop. He brought up some schematics of the hotel and swung the laptop around to face Bo. He had done his homework.

Bo smiled. "Like taking candy from a baby."

McCall took a train out of Penn Station to Red Bank, New Jersey. The OceanFirst Bank was at 175 Monmouth Street in the picturesque little town.

Along with the safe-deposit key in the small envelope had been a folded letter, signed by Rebecca Coleman, authorizing McCall to open the box and
remove the contents. The manager of the branch, whose brass plaque on his
lapel said LEON OUDABASHIAN, was heavset with a ready smile who looked
like Tony Soprano. He had not heard the sad news about Captain Josh Coleman. He asked McCall to convey his condolences to the family. He took
McCall into the locked vault, took out the safe-deposit box, and led McCall
to a small room, where he was left alone.

McCall opened the box.

Personal letters were in it, a duplicate copy of Josh's birth certificate,
letters from the Army, and various *Star Wars* action figures, keepsakes from
Josh's childhood. Under the letters McCall found three small photographs.
One of the photographs was of Josh Coleman when he was fourteen or
fifteen. The other two were also of teenage boys. McCall set the three
photographs side by side on the table.

There was no doubt in McCall's mind that the teenagers were related.

McCall had arranged to meet Helen Coleman at the Gallow rooftop bar in
the McKittrick Hotel in Chelsea just after 7:00 p.m. Trellises of flowers were
interspersed with towering trees sparkling with tiny white Christmas lights
above a floor of pebbles and slate. From where McCall sat at the weathered
wooden table, West Side buildings were stark against the Hudson. The entire
bar had the feeling of an old colonial house that had gradually gone to seed.
The setting was charming until you remembered that the bar, Gallow
Green, was named for a Scottish field where six witches had been hanged
and burned. The waiters and waitresses were dressed in white, with, for the
most part, faux-British accents. There would be more of them after the im-
provised show *Sleep No More* was over and the actors mingled with the
theater crowd.

Helen made her way through the tables and sat down opposite McCall.
One of the waitresses appeared as if she'd come through a trapdoor set in a
stage. Helen ordered a Sleep Bowmore, a single-malt Scotch with Madeira
wine and orange shrub sweetened with demerara sugar poured tableside
out of a pitcher over ice in a copper bowl. McCall nursed an eighteen-year-
old Glenfiddich single malt. Helen looked out at the cloud-streaked sky that
was darkening above the rooftop.

"I was grateful that you came to Josh's funeral. I didn't know if you
would be there. Your job was done."

"But Josh's job wasn't. He was compiling a list, supervised by his CO, of Jihadist fighters. *All* of them are Americans. There were nine men on the list. There's a rogue shadow unit within one of the branches of our intelligence departments who is protecting these traitors."

"So this is a matter of national security?" Helen asked, concerned.

"Yes. There is a *tenth* Jihadist fighter on Josh's list. I want you to look at three photographs." McCall put the three faded photographs onto the table.

Helen picked up the first one immediately. "That's Josh when he was fifteen! Where was this taken? I don't recognize the setting at all."

"It wasn't for your eyes. Tell me about the young men in these other two photographs."

Helen picked up the first photograph. It was Patrick Cross, taken at the same age, maybe a year or so younger. Helen stared at the teenager, without commenting, then picked up the photo of Beauregard "Bo" Ellsworth. He was a strapping youth, a couple of years younger than the others, grinning for the camera. Helen put the three photographs side by side.

"They're all brothers," she said, nonplussed. "Obviously *Josh's* brothers. The resemblances are striking. But I don't know them. I'm certainly *not* the mother of the other two."

"Do you know who their father was?"

"Yes, of course, Richard Coleman. I divorced him over thirty years ago, right after I gave birth to Josh. But I haven't seen him or heard from him for over thirty years."

"But Josh heard from his brothers. They corresponded for years. All of the letters were in a safe-deposit box that belonged to Josh that I managed to get hold of. The letters are fairly innocuous, but you'd have to read between the lines to get a clearer meaning in them."

"I never knew about these letters," Helen said, clearly distraught.

"Josh didn't want to share them, and he had his reasons. His brothers may have known those reasons. Josh was a threat to them."

"What kind of a threat?"

McCall ignored her question. "I put the other brothers' IDs into the system. Patrick Cross is twenty-eight years old, a doctor. He's been working for Doctors Without Borders for four years. He just came back from a tour in Monrovia. He's living in Atlanta with a wife and two kids, six and nine. Beauregard "Bo" Ellsworth, twenty-four, runs a pseudo-paramilitary unit called the Texas Minutemen Militia. They're on the radar at the NSA, but not much is known about them. Bo is a loner who works as a manager at a plant in his hometown of Boerne, Texas. He's been treated for severe depression on and off since his eighteenth birthday and is being treated now for schizophrenia. He's been taking Vraylar for the past year."

"But if Josh had two brothers, whom he kept in touch with through occasional letters, what does that matter now?" Helen exclaimed. "Josh is gone. One of his brothers is a doctor in Atlanta, the other is a foreman at a factory in Texas. So what?"

"I believe Josh was investigating links that his two brothers may have had with the Jihadist forces in Iraq and Syria. There is *another* person of interest he was investigating. One who may have been in contact with his brothers."

"Who?"

"You have another son, Tom."

All of the color drained out of Helen Coleman's face. "My God, what are you saying? Tom's just celebrated his eighteenth birthday. He's studying Arabic at the School of Islamic Studies at Istanbul's Sehir University. He's devastated by the loss of his older brother. I don't want you questioning him." Helen stood up abruptly. "I'm grateful to you, Mr. McCall, for trying to save Josh. Send me an invoice for your services and I'll send you a check."

"Helen—"

"Stay away from my son Tom. Stay away from my family. You and I have nothing more to say to one another."

Helen strode through the tables and the trees with their trellises and twinkling white lights and disappeared. McCall got up, put money on the table for their drinks, and moved to the bar.

Rebecca Coleman scooted her barstool over to make room for him.

"I told you that's the way my mother would react. She's very protective of Tom."

"She wouldn't be happy to know that you were waiting at the bar for me."

"My mother and I haven't got along since I was a teenager. She's very driven. I've lived in Manhattan since I moved out of the house when I was twenty."

"How did you know about Josh's safe-deposit box?"

"He told me about it once. It was our secret. But then I got a letter from Josh. He sent me the key to the box. He wanted me to check that it still had the letters and photographs in it. I never had the time to go to Red Bank. Josh was killed three days later, or so we believed."

McCall set the three photographs of Josh, Dr. Patrick Cross, and Bo Ellsworth on the bar for her.

She shrugged. "I've never seen his brothers before."

"Tell me about your other brother."

Rebecca took a sip of her Touch of Evil cocktail, which was made with Dorothy Parker gin, El Buho mezcal, sparkling mineral water, raspberry ale, and nutmeg.

"Tom has been very high-strung since he was a child. Tantrums, then big tears, then mea culpa, sorry, Mom. But he always got exactly what he wanted. Tom starting reading about Islam when he was twelve."

"Nothing wrong with that. Millions of Americans study Islam and believe in its teachings."

"Tom was fixated on the Quran, and it became the cornerstone of his life. I don't want to use the wrong word here . . . there is an *intensity* to Tom that borders on the fanatical."

"Was Tom ever in contact with the Jihadist forces in Syria? Would he ever have fought with the Insurgents?"

Rebecca looked at him, shocked. "Tom is an *American*!"

"Your brother Josh was compiling a list of Americans fighting with the Jihadists. He started to tell me about a marketplace in the village of Al Tabqah. There was chaos, Insurgents slaughtering the populace. Josh and his peacekeeping force were pinned down. He had a clear view of one of the Jihadist fighters standing beside a stolen US Army Humvee."

"Did he say it was Tom?"

"No. I tried to get more from him, but he was dying."

Rebecca took another swallow of her drink, and her hands were shaking. "People were being killed. Who knows what Josh may or may not have seen."

"Where does Tom stay when he's home in New York?"

"He didn't want to live on campus at NYU. He's got a small apartment on Eighteenth Street near the Flatiron Building."

"Do you have a key to it?"

Rebecca looked away. "I have a key."

"I need to get into Tom's apartment tonight."

Rebecca finished the last of her cocktail and stood. "I'll go with you."

CHAPTER 39

He knew someone was in his apartment as soon as he entered it. Dishes were piled in the sink and several small glass bowls were on the kitchen counter filled with candy. The door to the bedroom was ajar. Kostmayer went into the kitchenette, took down a large sugar canister, took off the top, and pulled out an S&W 9mm pistol. He moved to the bedroom. Moonlight flooded through an open window. A figure got up from the bed in the shadows. Kostmayer gestured with the pistol.

"Keep coming."

Candy Annie walked forward and stood in the breeze from the window. She seemed oblivious to the fact that she was naked and that the intruder was pointing a gun at her.

"I'm a friend of Mr. McCall's," she said, as if that would explain everything in any given circumstance.

"What are you doing here?" Kostmayer demanded.

"Mr. McCall said I could stay for a few weeks. He said you were away on a trip. You're Mr. Kostmayer, right? I recognized you from the picture on the mantelpiece. I guess you were startled by seeing a naked girl in your bed."

"It's been known to happen from time to time," Kostmayer murmured, and lowered the S&W. "Sorry about the gun, I wasn't expecting company. You might put on some clothes."

Candy Annie pulled a T-shirt off the rocking chair and put it on. It didn't cover much of her voluptuous figure. It came down to just below her hips.

"I borrowed it from one of the Subs," she said, embarrassed. "She's a preteen who's living in the tunnels beneath Columbus Avenue. I guess I should get a bigger size."

"You're not living under the streets any longer?"

"Mr. McCall got me a job in a restaurant here in the Upworld."

Kostmayer moved back into the living room and sank onto the couch. Candy Annie moved into the kitchenette and heated up a coffeemaker.

"You look as if you could use some coffee. I'm—"

"Candy Annie. I recognized you from McCall's description. What's your full name?"

She looked at him as if surprised. "It's Anne Levine. It's so long since I ever heard anyone use it."

"Where is McCall? I went to his old apartment in SoHo, but he'd moved out."

"He's living at a hotel on the Upper West Side. Liberty something."

"Liberty Belle. That make sense. Sam is the manager there."

"Who's Sam?"

"Someone who used to be in the same business with myself and McCall. I'll go over there."

"Please! Stay for a little while. You look very tired."

"My last accommodations weren't too comfortable."

"This is *your* apartment. I am just a guest. Let me at least give you some coffee and listen to your story. I'm a very good listener."

Candy Annie came around the kitchenette with a silver tray with two cups, a silver creamer, and a sugar bowl. She poured them coffee. Kostmayer took it black with sugar. Candy Annie curled up in one of the leather chairs with her long legs tucked behind her.

"Your friend Mr. McCall is a good man."

"As I've said to him before, the jury is probably still out on that."

"He saved my life. He's my only friend here in the Upworld. But sometimes, when he leaves, I have this terrible feeling that I will never see him again."

"There is always that chance," Kostmayer agreed quietly.

Tom Coleman's one-room apartment in Chelsea was the size of a postage stamp. Clearly it gave Rebecca pause to search it with McCall. This was a violation of her brother's privacy. She looked in the closet and went through a small kitchenette with virtually no food. An end table was beside a single bed with rows of paperbacks on a shelf. At one end was a leatherbound English version of the Quran. Rebecca sat on the narrow bed and flipped through the pages, "The Opening," "The Ascension," "The Holy Prophet," "The Believers," "The Spider." McCall knelt at a chest of drawers and was going through them methodically.

"Maybe you're not going to find anything."

But McCall had found what he was looking for. It was in the bottom drawer under some jeans and folded T-shirts. He lifted it out without unfolding it and set it on the foot of the bed. Rebecca stared at it in shock.

"It's an ISIS flag."

"I know what it is," Rebecca said softly. "I watch the news. It doesn't prove anything."

"Your brother is entitled to read as many books on Islam as he wants. Concealing an ISIS flag in his apartment is something else."

Something caught McCall's eye on the shelf of books. He took out a couple of paperback thrillers, reached to the back, and took something wrapped in tissue paper. He carefully unfolded it. Inside the tissue paper was a silver demon-claws skull and a second silver ring. Rebecca picked up the second ring and read the engraving.

"Memento mori," McCall said. "'Remember that you must die.'"

He placed the silver demon-claws skull and the silver ring back in the tissue paper, returned them to behind the paperbacks, and restored the order of the books. He knelt back beside the open drawer.

"This doesn't feel right." McCall pulled the drawer out and turned it over. A small book was taped to it. McCall gingerly untaped it and flipped through it.

"What have you found?"

"A journal. Hardly any entries in it, most of them in Arabic."

McCall took out his cell phone and photographed the pages. Then he retaped the journal to the bottom of the drawer and slid the drawer back into the chest. He moved over to Rebecca. "Your life could be in danger. Your mother's also."

"I don't believe that." But the shock and worry were etched in Rebecca's eyes. "I can't believe it."

McCall looked around the small apartment. Everything was the same as when he and Rebecca had found it. Outside the building, McCall found her a cruising yellow cab.

She gripped his hands. "Find out the truth," she pleaded.

Then she climbed into the cab and it pulled away.

McCall knew he was being followed.

His tail had picked him up at the Gallow rooftop bar and followed him and Rebecca to Tom's apartment. McCall recognized him from Arlington National Cemetery, where the man had brushed past him. He was from The Company. Matthew Goddard had wanted McCall followed because he could lead them to Control.

McCall walked ten blocks to Bentley's. The restaurant was packed.

Andrew Ladd was alone at the bar serving drinks and loading up the trays the servers brought. He smiled when he saw McCall. "Hey, there! Take a seat, if you can find one. I'm a little swamped right now."

"I need an apron."

Laddie reacted, surprised. "Are you back?"

"Just for a few minutes."

Laddie reached down beneath the bar, came up with a folded Bentley's apron, and tossed it to him. "I could do with a hand."

McCall put on the apron and went under the bar. Gina and Amanda came up. Gina was in her usual hurry. Amanda's hair today was *blue*.

"Are you back with us?" Gina asked. "I need a Yellow Rose of Texas, a Hunting Party—make sure it's gold tequila—a White Russian, and a Tom Collins. Thanks, Bobby!"

Gina rushed off. McCall starting mixing her drinks.

Amanda looked at him with dreamy eyes. "We miss you here. I need a gin sour, a Blue Hawaii, and an apple martini."

McCall started mixing those drinks, too. "I like your hair color."

"It's my Supergirl look."

He looked past Amanda to the front door. McCall's shadower entered, looking around. He moved to one of the small tables.

"You see the guy who just walked in?"

Amanda followed his gaze. "Yeah."

"I want you to go over and ask him if he needs a drink. I want you to look at what rings he is wearing on his right hand."

"That's easy."

Amanda grabbed the tray, loaded now with drinks, and made her way back into the fray. McCall reached into the refrigerator like he was looking for something.

"Going to get more bottles of chardonnay."

Laddie nodded. McCall ducked under the bar. He saw that Amanda had delivered her drinks to her booth and had paused beside the shadower's table. He gave her a no-thanks gesture, although he was momentarily taken by her blue hair. He nodded at the bar and asked her something. She nodded and smiled.

McCall moved into the kitchen. It was the usual madhouse. He took off the black Bentley's apron. A moment later Amanda entered after him, picking up a tray of food that was waiting for her.

"Dude's wearing a silver skull on his right hand. Kind of creepy, but I liked it."

"Did he ask you if I still worked here?"

"Yeah, I told him you were our best bartender, no offense to Laddie. Don't be a stranger." She kissed him, then went out the swinging door.

McCall went out the back door. He ran down the alleyway behind Bentley's to the corner of West Broadway, where he could see both the front of Bentley's and the side exit. His shadower did not come out of either one. McCall hailed a cab. He found Brahms just leaving the B'nai Jeshurun synagogue on the Upper West Side. They walked together down Eighty-Eighth toward Broadway.

"I'm sorry to interrupt your prayers. Will there be a service for Hilda?"

"You won't be invited. You'd have to be Jewish. Whatever it is you want, McCall, it's the last time."

McCall took out the silver ring with the demon-claws skull that he had taken from the assassin's hand in London. Brahms examined it. McCall told him what he needed. Brahms hailed a cab that took them to Lexington and Fifty-Second Street. Brahms unlocked the door to his Manhattan Electronics store and walked to his back office. He left the rest of the store in darkness. McCall made himself some Maxwell House Original Roast while he waited. When the old spy was finished, he dropped the silver demon-claws skull back into McCall's hand.

"I'm closing the store. Mary will need to find another job, God bless her. I'm going to make a pilgrimage to Jerusalem. I want to go to the Western Wall and take the cable car to see the site of Masada and the palaces of King Herod. I want to pray at the Tomb of Rachel the Matriarch in Bethlehem. Hilda wanted me to do these things."

"Will you come back?"

Brahms smiled sadly. "I don't know. When God talks to me, Hilda used to say, I am listening to Brahms. Take care of yourself, Robert."

McCall couldn't remember a time when Brahms had ever called him by his first name. When he got out onto Lexington, he got a text message. He hailed a cab and got out at Union Square. The chess players were hustling tourists for five bucks for a five-minute game, using their timers. It was especially crowded in the Greenmarket. McCall didn't think he was being followed again, but he wasn't taking any chances. He saw Jackson T. Foozelman standing in the crowd. McCall walked toward him and shook his head imperceptibly. Fooz sat down on a bench, took off his Mets baseball cap, and turned it around, begging for change. McCall paused to drop a dollar into the cap, then walked on down Broadway. He unfolded the piece of paper that had been in Fooz's cap. The address on it was on West Fiftieth Street between Ninth and Tenth Avenues.

McCall hailed another cab to take him there.

When he'd settled back, his cell phone rang.

McCall looked at the caller ID.

It was a call that he had never expected to get.

CHAPTER 40

He had no problem getting into Sam Kinney's apartment. Working the lock on Sam's door was child's play. He paused for a moment in Sam's living room and listened. He heard someone snoring in the bedroom. The Equalizer set down his backpack, took out the small can of kerosene, and doused the furniture and the drapes at the windows. He crept through the darkened alcove and kitchen to the open door to Sam's bedroom.

The old man was awake.

He must have heard a small noise that had aroused him. Sam was getting out of bed when the Equalizer grabbed him. He rabbit-punched the old man down to his knees. His breath was wheezing and coming in gasps. The Equalizer hit him in the gut, threw him back on the bed, and hit him in the face until the old man lost consciousness. The Equalizer could have dragged him into the living room, but there was no need. The flames and black smoke would reach him and he wasn't going anywhere. He was out cold.

The Equalizer checked that the old man didn't have a pistol stashed in the bedside table drawer. Then he retraced his steps back into the living room. He lit a match from an old book of matches and threw it carelessly onto the kerosene. It whooshed up with a roar. It wouldn't be long before the couch and the drapes were alight. He had checked the fire escapes on the windows facing the street. The windows there were all stuck tight.

The Equalizer packed the kerosene can into his backpack. He closed Sam's apartment door, but he couldn't get it to latch properly. It was an old building and the wooden door was warped. No matter. The fire would be blazing in the living room within a few minutes.

He ran down the stairs to the third-floor corridor. He knew that apartment 3A was vacant. He had already jimmied that door and seen the lack of furniture, but drapes were at the windows. He doused them, struck a match, tossed it, and the drapes went up in a roar of flames. He carefully put the kerosene can back into his backpack and closed the apartment door. He wasn't concerned with the old couple who lived in 3B. In fact, he wasn't concerned with *any* of the other tenants who lived in the apartment building. They got out or they didn't.

The Equalizer ran down the next flight of stairs, but something told him to check the second-floor corridor. He threw open the stairway door and saw a young blonde there. She was probably in her midthirties, five-eight, reasonably attractive, with dynamite breasts and her hair tied back in a ponytail. The door to apartment 2B was open. The blonde turned back.

"Gemma, *come now!*"

But the apartment door had closed. The blonde sighed and moved back toward it.

The Equalizer grabbed her. She struggled in his grasp and kneed him in the groin. It sent a wave of nausea through him. She tried to get past him, but he caught her shoulders, dragged her to the stairwell door, and pushed her. She tumbled heavily down the stairs, slamming her head on the last stair tread. He waited to see if the couple from 2A, up there in years, came charging out of their apartment. They didn't. He climbed down and knelt beside the blonde.

She had been knocked unconscious. Her forehead was bleeding profusely. He noticed two buttons on her shirt were undone. He entertained the idea of unbuttoning the rest of them, but he was working here and there wasn't time. He caressed her breasts through her shirt, feeling the nipples harden under his fingers, then left her where she had fallen.

He was on the first floor. He listened at the doors to apartments 1A and 1B, but heard nothing. Then he went down the basement stairs.

He didn't have much time left.

The Equalizer had earlier doused with kerosene some stacked cartons beside the old furnace. He set them alight and threw a lighted match onto more debris in a corner, which erupted. He scrambled away from the exploding aerosol cans that came at him like projectiles. He tossed the kerosene can and ran to the back door to the basement. A cement ramp led up to the street where the trash cans were. He stopped in the sudden biting wind and caught his breath. Setting the fire had been trickier than he had anticipated, but it was exciting.

He looked up.

There were flames in the windows of apartments 3A and 4A.

He jogged around to the front of the building and ran down Tenth

Street to Seventh Street before he turned. The apartment building looked deceptively quiet. No sign of fire. No sirens of approaching NYFD trucks yet.

The Equalizer sat down on the bottom step of an apartment building on Seventh Street. He smoked a cigarette from a crushed package of Marlboros and waited.

The Weinbergers had invited Norman Rosemont in for dinner. He had just finished a roast with Yorkshire pudding and mashed potatoes that was as good as the best pub fare in Manhattan. Elliott was the cook in the family. He and Mavis had told him something that had startled him, that Sam Kinney was a newcomer.

"A very nice man," Mavis Weinberger said, "except he says Nixon was framed about Watergate."

Her husband waved a deprecating hand. "Do we have any brandy for our guest?"

"Cabinet below the bookshelves." Mavis was transfixed by a CNN report about Cubans finding food, clothing, and shelter in El Paso, Texas.

"So Sam hasn't been in the building long?" Rosemont said, surprised.

"No, no," Mavis said. "Maybe a week and a half."

Elliott opened the cabinet and brought out a brandy bottle and three glasses.

Rosemont thought he could smell smoke. He walked to the front door of Apartment 3B and opened it. "Are there people living in 3A?"

Elliott set the brandy glasses down on the table. "No, that's been vacant for a few months."

Rosemont walked to apartment 3A and felt the door handle. It was warm. He didn't know any better, so he pulled the door open. Fire roared out of the apartment. Rosemont jumped back. Already the corridor was filling with black smoke. He ran back to the Weinbergers' apartment.

"There's a fire! You need to get out!"

Mavis was hard-pressed to turn away from her CNN report. Elliott ran over to one of the bookshelves, grabbing his *Decline and Fall of the Roman Empire* tomes.

"Just leave everything!" Rosemont shouted. "You can come back for your things!"

Rosemont helped Mavis out of her chair. She picked up some scrapbooks from a side table. Elliott caught up with them. Fire had crawled up the walls of the third-floor corridor. All three of them were coughing in the smoke. They descended the stairs to the second floor.

"You go on down!" Rosemont shouted.

Mavis and Elliott Weinberger continued to descend. Rosemont ran into the second-floor corridor and knocked on the door to apartment 2A. It was immediately opened by Connie Hewitt. Rosemont saw her husband, Donald, looking up from a couch where a TV played.

"There's a fire. Leave everything in your apartment and go down the stairs. Right now!"

Connie immediately ran back into the apartment to find Mr. Toast. Rosemont ran across the hall and pounded on the door to apartment 2B. There was no answer. He knocked louder. Behind him, Connie and Donald Hewitt came out of their apartment bringing nothing except Mr. Toast, who squirmed in Donald's arms, trying to scratch his face. If it had been up to Rosemont, he would have advocated leaving the cat behind in the apartment.

"Did you see Linda Hathaway leave her apartment?" Rosemont asked.

Connie shook her head. "She keeps to herself."

"Go, go!"

Connie and Donald plunged down the stairs to the first floor and suddenly stopped. Connie cried out. Mavis and Elliott were at the bottom of the stairwell. Rosemont climbed down and saw Linda Hathaway sprawled at the bottom. She was conscious, but disoriented. A dark bruise was on her forehead and it was bleeding.

Rosemont helped her to her feet. "Did you fall?"

Linda shook her head and staggered, unable to speak. Rosemont helped her out into the first-floor corridor. Smoke was seeping up the stairs from the basement.

"Take her outside!" Rosemont urged, and handed her to Donald Hewitt, who handed Mr. Toast to Connie. Elliott Weinberger still supported Mavis. They all moved to the front door of the building. Rosemont knocked loudly at the door to apartment 1A.

"Jesse, open the door! There's a fire!"

There was no response. The student was out most evenings, Rosemont recalled. He pounded on the door to 1B, the super's apartment. There was no response. Thick black smoke was now cloaking the first-floor corridor. Rosemont ran to the front door and headed down the ten limestone steps into the street.

A crowd was forming on the sidewalk in front of the building. Elliott

Weinberger sat Mavis on the bottom step of the apartment building next door. Connie Hewitt was perched on the hood of a parked car, trying to keep Mr. Toast from running away.

Rosemont noted Jesse Driscoll pushing through the crowd. "What's happened?"

"Fire," Rosemont said. "It may have started in that vacant apartment on the third floor. Are there fire sprinklers in the building?"

"Not that I've ever seen," Jesse said. "Is everyone out?"

"I think so," Rosemont said.

Linda Hathaway pushed through the crowd and grabbed Rosemont's arm. The blood had congealed on her face. Her eyes were wild.

"Gemma! She was right behind me!"

"She wasn't with you when we found you," Rosemont said. "I pounded on your apartment door, but there was no response."

"Someone grabbed me! He threw me down the stairs! Gemma may still be in the apartment! She's not out here!"

"We'll get her!" Rosemont climbed up the apartment-building stairs.

A woman in the crowd said, "I called 911. Fire department's on their way!"

Jesse bounded up the front steps after Rosemont.

Smoke had now completely enveloped the first-floor corridor. Jesse starting coughing, looking for Rosemont, but didn't see him. He threw open the stairwell door and heard Rosemont reaching the second floor. The student pounded up the stairs and came out onto the second-floor corridor. Black smoke drifted down it. Rosemont was at the door of apartment 2B, trying to wrench it open. Jesse disappeared into the smoke, and Rosemont heard glass breaking. Jesse came back hefting an ax that he had smashed from a glass case on the far corridor wall. Rosemont had never noticed any firefighting gear anywhere in the building. Rosemont stood back from the door to 2B. Jesse swung the ax, splintering the wood. He hefted it again, wood chips spitting out. Jesse dropped the ax. Rosemont reached in, unlocked the door, and swung it open. Both of them ran inside. The apartment was filled with smoke. Fire was blazing in the living room.

"Gemma!" Rosemont called out. "Gemma, where are you?" There was no response. "Get to the kitchen or Linda's bedroom. I'll see if there's a child's room."

Jesse veered off to the kitchen. Rosemont looked through the thick smoke, seeing if the little girl was under a table or behind the couch.

"Gemma! Gemma!"

He thought he heard a whimper from somewhere. Rosemont ran into the smoke and saw a door leading to a child's bedroom. He ran inside.

It was ablaze.

"Gemma!"

The whimper was coming from under the child's bed. Rosemont looked under the bed. He saw Gemma's face, her eyes wide with fear.

"I've got you, Gemma! Crawl out from under there!"

Gemma crawled out from under her bed. She was holding a purple plush Courage the Cowardly Dog by his ear. Rosemont picked her up.

"Turn in to my shoulder and close your eyes."

"Where's Mom?"

"She's already outside." Rosemont ran out of Gemma's bedroom through the living room to the front door.

Jesse came out of the smoke, coughing, his eyes streaming. "You got her?"

"Yeah. Anyone else back there?"

"All clear. Can we get out through the window onto the balcony with the fire escape?"

"That way is blocked."

They went through the smashed front door. Immediately Rosemont handed Gemma to Jesse and picked up the fallen ax.

"I'm going to see if my friend Sam is out of his apartment. You get Gemma downstairs to her mother."

"Don't be an idiot!"

"Just get her out of here!"

Rosemont threw open the stairwell door. He heard Jesse climbing down to the first floor carrying Gemma. When Rosemont got to the fourth floor and came through the stairwell door, the corridor was blazing. The door to *his* apartment, 4B, showed no signs of fire yet. Rosemont ran to Apartment 4A. The door was unlocked and buckled. Rosemont didn't need the ax. He dropped it and kicked in the door.

The living room was totally ablaze. Smoke was everywhere.

"Sam! Sam!"

No response. Rosemont ran through the dining-room alcove and the kitchen, both burning, to Sam's bedroom. The ceiling in the bedroom was on fire and chunks of it were coming down. Rosemont gagged in the dense smoke. He saw the shape of a man's figure in the bed. He moved to it, thinking that Sam had been overcome from smoke inhalation.

He hadn't.

He had been beaten.

Sam's face was swollen and blood had congealed under his nose. He was conscious, but barely. Rosemont hauled him out of bed and was surprised how light he was. For all of Sam's robust camaraderie, he was like a husk in Rosemont's arms.

Something caught Rosemont's eye on the bedroom floor. It seemed out of place. A piece of jewelry. Rosemont scooped it up into his pocket and carried Sam out of the bedroom. The old man slid, so Rosemont hauled him up over his shoulder in a fireman's lift. He staggered with him to the living room and was greeted by a wall of flames.

Norman Rosemont was terrified.

He put his head down and ran through the flames, his hair singeing, his face burning. He got out of the apartment with Sam still over his shoulder. He didn't hear a murmur from the old man. He couldn't tell if Sam was alive or dead.

When he turned with his burden, Rosemont was greeted by another wall of flames. He couldn't get through it, the heat was too intense. He stumbled to the wooden stairs leading up to the roof. Fire was raging up them, but no other course was open to him. He climbed the stairs through the flames and reached the top just before they gave way behind him. He leapt for the roof door, still holding on to Sam, and looked down.

The stairs leading up to the roof had collapsed.

Rosemont ran out onto the roof. He laid Sam gently down on one of the folding chairs and ran to the edge. One fire truck was already outside the apartment building, and another was pulling up. Firefighters were everywhere. Rosemont searched the crowd below and saw Linda Hathaway. Jesse was handing Gemma to her mother. Linda hugged her child, sobbing and shaking. Jesse looked up at the roof and gave Rosemont a thumbs-up.

One of the ladders on the first fire truck was almost at the roof. Rosemont ran across to Sam, who was conscious, barely seeing through his left eye.

"My right eye ain't so good now," he mumbled. "That's what happens when you know Robert McCall."

The old man wasn't making sense, but Rosemont didn't care. Sam was alive. Rosemont picked Sam up and supported him to the edge of the roof. He got there just as the firefighter climbed onto the roof.

"I got him!" the firefighter said. "I'll take him down. Any way back into the building?"

"No, the stairs to the roof have collapsed."

"Okay. Stay right here. Another firefighter will come back up to get you."

"Got it."

"Nice job."

The firefighter put Sam onto his shoulder and started climbing down the ladder with him.

Rosemont took a deep breath, trying to force the night air into his parched lungs. He couldn't stop shaking. At that moment he realized he had not taken his inhaler with him from his apartment. Maybe he didn't need it anymore. When the second firefighter got to the top of the ladder, Rosemont was determined not to be carried down over the firefighter's shoulder.

"I can climb down!"

Rosemont climbed onto the ladder. It took him a full minute to get to the bottom, where two other firefighters set him down on the sidewalk.

Miguel, the fat super, had pushed through the crowd and was staring up at the burning building. He turned when he saw Rosemont. "Hey there, Miguel Vásquez. You're the new tenant, right? I was in the tavern on the corner. Did everyone get out okay?"

"Yes. Everyone has been accounted for."

"Jesus, hell of thing to happen! Course, I've been telling the management firm that we needed new sprinklers, but they could give a fuck."

A much bigger crowd was now being held back by yellow tape. Two cop cars had pulled up, and the officers were moving people away. The tenants of the apartment building were still together on the sidewalk. They mobbed Rosemont when he joined them. Jesse shook his hand. Elliott Weinberger squeezed his shoulder. Connie Hewitt was singing softly, some Broadway tune only meant to be heard by her.

Linda Hathaway handed Gemma to Jesse and threw her arms around Rosemont. "Thank you," she whispered. "You saved my little girl."

"Jesse carried her down the stairs and out of the building," Rosemont stammered, embarrassed. "He's the one you need to thank."

Linda broke from him, tears brimming in her eyes. "That's not the way I heard it."

She kissed him, then winced in pain. Rosemont, grateful for the escape, looked at her forehead where she'd hit the stairs. Dried blood was down one side of her face.

"You need to get that seen to."

"They'll get to me. How are you?"

His face was blackened with smoke, but he nodded. They all looked up. Fire had erupted from every window in the front of the building. The firefighters were fighting the blaze. Some of them had entered the building. Another fire truck was on its way, siren wailing. A firefighter started moving the tenants back beyond the yellow tape.

Mavis Weinberger shook her head, clutching her scrapbooks. Tears escaped from her eyes and spilled down her old, tired face. "This has been our home for sixty years."

Rosemont took her hand. "We'll get you and Elliott a new home," he promised her softly.

Several streets behind the fire trucks, the Equalizer stood with his hands deep in his pockets, seething. He watched Sam Kinney being wheeled on a gurney to one of the ambulances. If he made it out of the hospital, the Equalizer would have to try again. This time he wouldn't use such an elaborate scheme, even though it should have worked just fine.

This time he would just put a bullet in the old man's head.

One of the tenants had moved away from the others. The Equalizer didn't think the old dude was looking at him, but he slid back into the shadows. It was time for him to disappear. He had streets to clean up and innocent lives to save.

Norman Rosemont stared down into Tenth Street. He reached into his pocket and took out the piece of jewelry he'd found on Sam Kinney's bedroom rug.

He looked down at it and wondered.

CHAPTER 41

McCall worked a skeleton key into the lock on the brick building on Fiftieth Street just down from the Jadite Galleries. He moved into a darkened hallway in front of an elevator, a redwood staircase ascending to his left. He waited in the stillness.

Mickey Kostmayer stepped out of the shadows. McCall's gaze hard-ened at the sight of him.

Kostmayer smiled ruefully. "This is where you tell me I've lost a lot of weight and look like crap."

"What happened?"

"We carried out the raid on the North Korean prison camp. Eight mer-cenaries, including Granny. We got over a hundred people out, but we were supposed to be picked up by four Chinese AVIC AC391 helicopters, and only three of them made it. My guys were all killed except for the two of us. I escaped during a prisoner rebellion in the woods right outside the prison. I made it to the Yalu River at the Sino-Korean Friendship Bridge. I swam across to an island in no-man's-land, got into the port at Dandong, and picked up a truck going into the city. I was dressed in a stolen North Korean guard's uniform. A local Company contact named Jensen got me to Beijing."

"Did he contact The Company?"

"No, he was afraid of repercussions because the NK mission was un-sanctioned."

"A lot has happened at The Company since you were away. How did you get home?"

"I took a Cathay Pacific flight to JFK, got in tonight. I went to your old apartment, found out you had moved out, and went to my place."

"Did you meet your new roommate?"

"Oh, yeah. Very sweet, if you're into Lolita. You might invest in some clothes for her. The T-shirt she was wearing to bed didn't even cover her legs."

"You'll get used it. Do you want me to move her?"

"She's fine there."

The silence gathered around them again.

"What happened to Granny?"

"He didn't make it."

McCall nodded, but the pain was evident in his eyes. "I know you wouldn't have left him there if there had been any chance of getting him out."

"There wasn't. Is this a safe house?"

"Only Control knows about it. It's not on The Company's books."

"What's he doing here?"

"We'll let him tell us."

They took the elevator to the fourth floor and stopped outside a door with no number on it. McCall used another skeleton key to get inside. A short hall led into a main study. It was decorated with dark wood shelving, wood slats on the two windows overlooking Fiftieth Street, mahogany walls with a cathedral ceiling, a wet bar, a leather couch, and a desk. A laptop computer was on the desk. The only light came from a Tiffany lamp.

Two people were in the room.

Control looked exhausted. His hands had a slight tremor. Beside him, Dr. Bennett had just given him an injection and put away the syringe and snapped his doctor's bag. He directed his attention only to McCall.

"Your friend needs rest. I left him some diazepam, or Valium. He will have to get his own doctor to write him a prescription. He said there were bad people hunting for him, and perhaps for you as well, Mr. McCall, but I've done all I can. I have patients beneath the streets to attend to. I wish both of you well."

Dr. Bennett walked briskly to the door to the apartment and closed it behind him.

Control looked at Kostmayer. His voice was hoarse and faint. "I was told you were in a North Korean prison camp."

"I pissed them off. They let me go."

"Was Granny on the mission?"

"He didn't make it."

Control nodded, as if the weight of Granny's death weighed heavily on his shoulders. Kostmayer had never seen him like this before. McCall sat on the couch beside him. Kostmayer perched on the edge of the desk.

"I have been on the track of a mole in The Company," Control said. "He's been there for a very long time. He was the man responsible for hiring Jovan Durković to take out Serena Johanssen in Yaroslavl at the Spaso-Preobrazhensky Monastery. I didn't have all of the intel at the time you quit, Robert. I didn't get part of it until after you had killed Durković at the château outside Prague. But I was aware of some kind of a conspiracy at The Company that had far-reaching consequences. There was a Company executive who left some time ago. His name is Matthew Goddard. But there was a shake-up at The Company. I got a phone call to say Goddard was back."

Control paused, disoriented, looking around him as if he were surprised by his surroundings.

"Did anyone else call you?" McCall asked.

"Only my wife."

"Did you tell her the situation?"

"I told Jenny to pack some things and get out of the house."

"The one in Arlington?"

"Yes. She took Kerry and Megan with her. I gave her a number to call me in forty-eight hours."

"You should've given her my number," McCall said.

"You're no longer with The Company. They're not your concern. Nor am I. I had a lunch meeting at the Capital Grille. I stepped into a waiting Uber car on Pennsylvania Avenue, and they were waiting inside for me."

"Did you recognize them?"

"No. Mercenaries, *not* Company men, hired assassins. They knew each other. They injected me with some kind of a sedative. That's the last thing I remembered for a long time."

"How long?"

"It must have been weeks. They kept me drugged."

"How did you get to the house in the Virginia countryside?"

Control looked up. "How did you know where it was?"

"A chance remark that your secretary, Emma Marshall, made. You were reminiscing about a house you'd visited when you were five or six."

"My parents used it as a summer place. We never sold it. I would go there sometimes off the radar when I wanted to get away. It had special childhood memories for me."

"Why would the kidnappers take you there?"

"Because it was out of the way and isolated. No one knew about it. If Matthew Goddard was behind my kidnapping, he must have had some perverse satisfaction in taking me there. I lost track of all time. I heard nothing about The Company or what was going on in the world." Control reached out for McCall's wrist, holding him tightly. "No one else could have found me."

"Goddard made it tough. You weren't just kidnapped. All traces of your identity were erased."

Control let McCall go. "What are you talking about?"

"You were never at The Company offices in Virginia. You were never in the spy business. You never had a wife and children. Your friends were all gone. Matthew Goddard made sure that *you had never existed.*"

Control stared at McCall in disbelief. "That isn't possible." Control's voice was barely above a whisper.

"There are no records about you at all. Brahms went through all of the databases."

"Does *Brahms* remember me?"

"Sure, but he's been out of The Company for years. I'm sure if Goddard thought he was a threat to exposing your identity, he would have had him killed."

"But there's Jason Mazer . . . other Controls . . ."

"Jason Mazer is resourceful and smart. I don't know if they killed him or if he saw the writing on the wall and got out. No one at The Company knows you now. Matthew Goddard is in charge of the section."

"But what about Emma?" Control tried to assimilate this information. "She knows me about as well as anyone."

"They fired her and sent her home with a golden handshake. But they came for her in London. Probably the same rogue assassins. Just to make sure she didn't mention your name to any of her family or friends. I got her out of London to stay with her mother."

"That must have gone over well," Control murmured.

"It was better than her lying in a Soho street with her throat cut. Go back to before you were grabbed."

"I realized I had stumbled upon some kind of a plot. It wasn't just that Matthew Goddard was selling top-secret information to the Russians or the Chinese. It was a plot aimed at our country's security. But before I could find out anything vital, they grabbed me."

"Goddard *knew* you were onto him," McCall said. "Your name was mentioned by Jihadists in Syria fighting for ISIS."

"*My* name?"

"That's right. But this rogue cell in The Company made one mistake. There was someone else who knew you. At least, he knew your name."

"I've never known that myself," Kostmayer said. "You've always been *Control*."

"My name is James Thurgood Cameron," Control said softly.

"I went into Syria to try and rescue an American Army captain named Josh Coleman," McCall said. "He didn't make it, but he whispered your name before he died."

"I don't know him. What do I have to do with Captain Coleman?"

"He was working on a secret list of names associated with the Taliban and the Jihadist Insurgents in Syria and Iraq. This rogue unit within The Company has been protecting them. The Insurgents found Captain Coleman and myself in an abandoned airfield in Syria near the Turkish border. I believe Matthew Goddard had been liaising with them. That's how the Insurgents had tracked our position."

"Why would Matthew Goddard be sending our enemies intel? What would he gain from such an act of treason?"

"I'd say a great deal of money. Probably in the millions."

"This secret list of names that Captain Coleman had of Insurgent fighters. Have you turned their names over to the Pentagon?"

"They're *American* names," McCall said quietly. He let that sink in.

"Where is Goddard now?" Control asked. "Is he still heading The Company?"

"Brahms called one of his old contacts there. Matthew Goddard has disappeared. Some kind of a covert mission. I'd say he's gone to ground while this terror scenario is put into play."

"*What* terror scenario?"

McCall took out the eight-by-ten pictures from his pocket and laid them on the desk. "Three brothers, they were probably fourteen or fifteen when these photos were taken. Captain Josh Coleman was the oldest. The second brother is Dr. Patrick Cross; he's with Doctors Without Borders. The youngest brother is Bo Ellsworth, who works at a plant in Boerne, Texas." McCall set a fourth picture down beside the other three. "This is a picture of Tom Coleman, Captain Coleman's younger brother. I took it from his sister, Rebecca. Tom's eighteen, going to NYU, also studying Arabic at the School of Islamic Studies at the Istanbul Sehir University. He's a part of this conspiracy."

"What are you saying is going to happen?" asked Kostmayer.

"I believe there are going to be three separate terrorist attacks on American soil." McCall took out his iPhone and scrolled down. "I found a journal taped to the bottom dresser drawer in Tom Coleman's Chelsea apartment. I took photographs of the pages. Copy them down."

Kostmayer picked up a yellow pad from the desk. Control was looking at the pages on McCall's iPhone. "Most of it is in code."

"Weren't you once a cryptographer?" Kostmayer asked.

"It's from the Greek word *kryptos*, meaning 'hidden, secret,'" Control murmured. He sat at the desk and started writing down the coded pages from Tom Coleman's journal.

McCall picked up the picture of Tom Coleman and handed it to Kostmayer. "Tom's sister told me he usually hangs out in a bar in Greenwich

Village called the Peculier Pub. If he was going to drown his sorrows about his brother for appearance' sake, it would be there."

Kostmayer followed McCall to the short hallway. Control looked up. He saw McCall drop something into Kostmayer's hand. He pocketed the item and left.

McCall walked back to the desk. "Can you break the code in Tom Coleman's journal?"

"I don't know."

McCall shook him. "I need you to focus, James." It felt strange calling Control by his real name. "I don't know what these three brothers—Patrick Cross, Bo Ellsworth, and Tom Coleman—are going to do, but I know American lives are at stake."

"How much time do we have?"

Control's hands had stopped shaking. McCall let him go. "Probably not long."

CHAPTER 42

Norman Rosemont stood in the street in a fine drizzle waiting for Jesse Driscoll. When Rosemont didn't see him, he walked back into the Liberty Belle Hotel. Linda Hathaway was seated on a leather couch holding Mavis Weinberger's palsied hands. Elliott sat beside them. Gemma was running around behind the couch carrying her Courage the Cowardly Dog. Miguel was sitting a little distance from them. Donald Hewitt was standing with Connie at the reception counter going through his wallet.

Rosemont strode up. "Is there a problem here?" he snapped to Chloe, then caught himself. "I'm sorry, we've had a pretty rough night. Can I help?"

Donald Hewitt looked embarrassed. "I'm afraid my credit card is maxed."

"It's my fault," Connie said. "I just got us tickets to see *Wicked* for the third time, and it took us over the top. I can cancel them."

Rosemont handed his Platinum Card to Chloe. "Put their reservation on my card." He gestured to the Weinbergers, Linda Hathaway, Gemma, and Miguel Vásquez. "Put all of these folks on my card."

"Certainly, sir." Chloe ran Rosemont's AmEx card and handed it back to him. He moved over to the couch. "You can go up and register for your-self and Mavis, Elliott."

Elliott moved to the reception counter. Linda Hathaway shook her head. "I can't stay in a hotel like this for even one night."

"It's on me."

"That's very generous, but where do we go tomorrow?"

Without even thinking about it, Rosemont squeezed her shoulder. "You and Gemma can stay here for as long as you need to. All of you."

"That's so kind," Mavis said fondly. "Have you met our friend Mr. Rosemont, Linda? He's probably a Democrat, but we don't hold that against him."

Sam entered the lobby from the side entrance. A small bandage was on his nose and another on his forehead.

Chloe immediately came around the reception counter. "What hap-pened to you?" she demanded.

"Got in a fight," Sam said shortly.

"At your age? You should be ashamed of yourself!"

"I'm medicated up to the eyeballs. Give me a break!"

Sam saw the apartment tenants in the lobby and strode away from Chloe, who sighed, "You're going to give us all heart attacks!" But she went back behind the reception counter.

Sam noted that Jesse Driscoll was moving through the lobby now. He spoke softly to Miguel Vásquez and propelled him over to the others.

Elliott Weinberger came back from the reception counter at the same Sam arrived. "We're all checked in."

"Sam, are you okay?" Rosemont asked.

"I'm good. What's the story at the building?"

"All of the apartments have sustained severe smoke and water dam-age," Jesse said. "But they're all still standing. The fire department is going to contact me when we can go back to find what's left of our stuff."

"You should register, Miguel," Rosemont said gently.

Jesse took Miguel over to the reception counter. Chloe greeted them with a smile.

At the leather couches, Sam looked at the other tenants. "That fire wasn't an accident. The apartment building was deliberately torched."

"That's terrible," Mavis Weinberger whispered.

"Someone tried to kill me. He was in my apartment. I didn't get a good look at him, but he was young, I know that."

"I was also attacked." Linda Hathaway glanced around, but Gemma was racing around the lobby. "Better Gemma doesn't hear this anyway. The intruder grabbed me as I was leaving my apartment and pushed me down the stairs."

"We found her at the bottom," Connie Hewitt told Sam.

"Must be the same guy. The police will want to question all of us. If it hadn't been for Norman, I wouldn't have got out of that fire trap. He carried me up to the roof."

"He's a hero," Linda said.

Rosemont colored, trying to hide his embarrassment. "But why would someone try to kill you, Sam?"

"I have enemies."

"From the hotel business?" Connie asked, suddenly intrigued.

"I worked for an intelligence agency a long time ago."

"I knew it!" Connie exclaimed. "I knew you were a spy!"

She sang a chorus from a Broadway show. 'Hey, kid, failed your test? Dream girl unimpressed? Show her you're the best. If you can shoot a president.' Opening number, 'Everybody's Got the Right,' in *Assassins*."

Jesse returned from the reception counter with Miguel. "Miguel is all set. I can stay at my aunt's place in Brooklyn."

"I know what you all thought of me," Miguel murmured. "You'll be well rid of me."

"The building still needs a super," Rosemont said. "No one has fired you."

"As soon as the management company knows what has happened, I'll be out on my ass. I know I let you all down. I'm sorry."

"I'll make some calls," Rosemont offered.

Sam was watching him carefully. The real estate tycoon met Sam's gaze.

"How can you do anything for us?" Linda asked him.

"Because I owned the building. I was your landlord."

The statement was met with stunned silence.

"I will see to it that rebuilding starts right away," Rosemont assured them. "I've already phoned a construction outfit, who are going to meet me down on Tenth Street at eight a.m. tomorrow. You can all stay here at the Liberty Belle Hotel for as long as you want." Rosemont looked at Sam. "If that's okay?"

"Fine by me."

Rosemont turned to Linda Hathaway, a little tentatively. "May I escort you to the reception counter to register, Linda?"

"We'll look after Gemma," Connie Hewitt offered.

Linda shook her head, as if she didn't quite believe it. Then she got up and kissed Norman Rosemont on the cheek. They walked to the reception counter.

Mavis looked at Sam accusingly. "Did you know Mr. Rosemont was our landlord?"

"Of course he knew," Connie said. "He's been playing a trick on the man."

"What kind of a trick?"

"In the circumstances, a pretty mean one," Sam said quietly.

Kostmayer found the Peculier Pub on Bleecker Street just off Washington Square Park. It was packed with students sitting at long wooden tables and crowding around the bar. He immediately spotted Tom Coleman at one of the back booths sitting with a willowy blonde. Tom scooted out to bring them some more beer. Kostmayer moved to the bar and nudged Tom as he passed.

"Sorry," Kostmayer murmured. "Crowded tonight."

"Every night." Tom signaled the bartender for two more Coronas. Kostmayer thought Tom's eyes were glassy. He'd already had a lot to drink.

Kostmayer glanced down at Tom Coleman's hands.

He was wearing the demon-claws silver skull on the ring finger of his right hand.

Tom was served immediately. He was a regular. He grabbed the beers and made his way back to the booth. He handed the blonde her beer and kissed her.

So much for grieving for your older brother, Kostmayer thought.

Kostmayer walked outside to use his cell phone. It rang twice and McCall answered. "Tom Coleman is wearing a silver skull ring. He must've gone back to his apartment and slipped it on. He's getting pretty hammered. He's with a blonde who looks like she'd like to crawl into his lap."

McCall told him to stay close to Tom Coleman. Kostmayer said he would and disconnected. He walked back into the pub and found an empty seat at the bar. He ordered a Stella Artois and watched the NYU student and his date getting cozier and drunker.

·   ·   ·

Sam Kinney met Rosemont as he stepped out of the elevator of the hotel.

"Everyone checked in?"

"They're all set," Rosemont said. "They're meeting me in the dining room for dinner. Not that they want to celebrate. They've all lost their homes."

"But not their lives," Sam said simply.

Norman Rosemont looked at him for a moment. "Who are you?"

Sam was expecting that. But all he said was "I'm your friend."

"About ten days ago a rather elegant black man walked into my offices on Fifth Avenue with an ultimatum. He said he represented a client who wanted me to live in one of my apartment buildings—a *slum* building, he called it—for two weeks. All of the computers that I need to run my business have gone dark. My business empire came crashing down. I agreed to this maniac's terms and moved into the building on Tenth Street, apartment 4B." Rosemont took a breath, then he just smiled. "It was the greatest thing that has ever happened to me."

"Why was that?"

"Because it forced me to look at myself in a way I never had before. I made new friends in the building. I started to *care* about these people and the miserable conditions they were living under. Before I could make it right, the building was torched. Now I *can* do something about their lives. There will be a new building and it's going to be spectacular. But that won't matter to you, Sam. I don't think you really live there."

"No, I live in an apartment building a few blocks up on Amsterdam and Seventieth," Sam admitted. "But I *did* stay in that apartment for a few nights."

"And you know this mysterious 'client' that Mr. Foozelman is representing?"

"I do."

"Why did he single me out?"

"I wouldn't know."

"Because he thought I needed to learn a few life lessons?"

"Maybe."

"Well, he would have been right. Do you still make great breakfasts here at the hotel?"

Sam smiled. "I've been known to whip up a Colorado omelet once in a while to piss off the chef."

Linda Hathaway moved to one side of Rosemont and Connie Hewitt to the other.

"I just put Gemma down to sleep," Linda said. "She's over the moon about her new room! It's a *suite* of rooms!"

Connie took Rosemont's arm. "We're all in the dining room. *We're* going to buy *you* dinner, Mr. Rosemont!"

"Oh, I almost forgot this." Rosemont reached into his coat pocket and took out a piece of jewelry. It was a man's silver bracelet, tarnished with age. "I found this on the floor of your bedroom in the apartment, Sam. Is it yours?"

"Never seen it before."

"You should give it to the police."

Rosemont dropped the bracelet into Sam's hand. Linda and Connie hustled their new friend through the lobby. Connie was singing a Broadway song from *Hamilton,* but she stopped abruptly. "I haven't quite got the rhythm of hip-hop yet."

Rosemont laughed outright. They disappeared into the dining room. Sam looked down at the bracelet in his hand.

He wouldn't be giving it to the police.

But he *would* give it to Robert McCall.

Kostmayer watched Tom Coleman stagger out of the Peculier Pub with the blonde whose name, Kostmayer had discovered, was Brittney. She was an NYU student majoring in political science. She and Tom climbed into a cab, and Kostmayer followed in another. The first cab pulled up to Tom's apartment building on Eighteenth. Kostmayer stopped his cab at Union Square, paid the driver, and hustled onto Eighteenth in time to see Tom and Brittney entering the apartment building. A minute later a light went on in a third-floor window.

Five minutes later the light went out. Kostmayer waited another forty-five minutes before he let himself into the building with the duplicate key that McCall had given him. He climbed the stairs to the third floor and listened at Tom Coleman's apartment door. There was no sound. He turned a second key in the lock and entered silently.

Tom Coleman was lying naked on his bed, passed out. Unfortunately Brittney was lying naked on top of him, also passed out. Kostmayer walked to Tom's side of the bed, and Brittney's figure stirred. She half turned with her left breast nestled over Tom's right hand.

Kostmayer took out the silver demons-claws skull from his jacket pocket. It matched exactly the ring that Tom was wearing—except that

Brahms had removed a small piece of the back of it and had inserted a tiny tracking device. He had soldered the piece back so that it was seamless.

Kostmayer just had to make the switch.

He knelt down and moved Brittney's breast from the top of Tom's hand. She stirred but didn't awaken. Carefully Kostmayer clutched Tom's hand and tried to slide the silver skull off his ring finger.

It wouldn't budge.

Kostmayer was sweating in the hot little room. He moved the silver skull back and forth on Tom's finger, each time tugging at it a little more. It took him a full three minutes, but finally the ring came off. Kostmayer pocketed it and slid the duplicate ring onto Tom's finger. It was a little less tight. Kostmayer slid the silver skull up and over the knuckle.

Tom moved.

He turned over, turning Brittney over, putting his hands onto her breasts. They were both still asleep.

Kostmayer let out his breath slowly. He crept around the bed and exited. He listened for another five minutes, but no sound came from the apartment. He climbed down the stairs and out on Eighteenth Street. He took out of his pocket the small receiver that Brahms had given McCall and which he had given to Kostmayer. It glowed red. The tracking device was activated. Kostmayer could go home and sleep on his couch while Candy Annie slept in his bedroom. He would keep track of Tom's Coleman's movements and report them.

What happened next would be up to McCall.

CHAPTER 43

McCall brought Control up to speed on everything that had happened in Syria with Captain Josh Coleman and everything McCall knew about Josh's three brothers. It was a lot of intel for the spymaster to assimilate in his present physical condition. But he listened to it all and made notes. Then he went to work on the laptop computer. McCall left him alone for almost two hours and brewed coffee in the small modern kitchen in the apartment. Finally Control motioned to McCall to join him at the desk, where he could see the laptop screen. On one side were the pages Control had copied off McCall's cell phone from Tom Coleman's journal. On the other side were notes scrawled over dozens of sheets of yellow foolscap paper. They consisted of various phrases written out by Control, all of them crossed out except for three lines of recognizable text. It didn't look promising, but McCall didn't offer a comment.

"Not all of the scribbled notes in Tom Coleman's journal were in code," Control said. "The ones that were, I started out using monoalphabetic ciphers, which use the same substitution letter for the entire message. That's where *A* is, let's say, *D,* using the cryptanalysis technique of the frequency that letters occurred in the encrypted text. The most common letter in Tom Coleman's journal code is *E*, and that doesn't work in the Caesar cipher I was using. I tried using the Atbash cipher, where the letters of the alphabet are reversed—the *As* are *Zs*, the *Bs* are *Ys*, you get the idea. When you've got the phrases, reversing the alphabet twice will get you the same algorithm in a substitution cipher, so you can decipher the message. That didn't work. So I moved on to a polyalphabetic cipher. I used the Vigenére cipher, which is a Caesar cipher. Each letter of the alphabet is shifted along a few places. I got up to shift three, where *A* would be *D*, *B* would be *E*. The Vigenère cipher consists of using several Caesar ciphers in sequence with different values.

"I made a columns graph of the alphabet horizontally and vertically. The tabula recta can be used, or a Vigenère square. It consists of the alphabet written out twenty-six times in different rows, each alphabet letter shifted cyclically to the twenty-six possible Caesar ciphers. At different points in the encryption process, the cipher uses a different alphabet from one of the rows. The alphabet at each point depends on a repeating keyword. I tried several, none of them any good.

"Then I started reading some of Tom Coleman's passages in his journal that weren't encrypted. They were all from various books." Control scrolled down them. McCall leaned forward. "'The man of knowledge must be able not only to love his enemies, but also hate his friends.' Friedrich Nietzsche. 'I hate rarely, though when I hate, I hate murderously.' Anaïs Nin. 'In time we hate that which we often fear.' William Shakespeare, *Antony and Cleopatra.*

"There are more on the next page." Control scrolled to it. "'I'm enjoying my hatred so much more than I ever enjoyed love.' Janet Fitch, *White Oleander.* 'Hatred is clear, metallic, one-handed, unmoving; unlike love.' Margaret Atwood, *Cat's Eye.*"

McCall read, "'There is no shark like hatred.' Buddha."

"There are a lot of these quotes, some rambling, some taken out of context, but they all have one word that recurs over and over: *hatred*. So I wrote the word *hatred* in twelve letters—*HATREDHATRED*—and I was able to decipher the first encrypted entry in the journal."

McCall picked up the yellow pad. Control had written in block letters: *NEW YORK CITY—BOERNE—SAN ANTONIO.*

"Tom Coleman is in New York City," McCall said. "Dr. Patrick Cross lives in Atlanta. Boerne, Texas, is where Bo Ellsworth lives. I don't see where San Antonio fits in."

"Except it's only about thirty miles southwest of Boerne."

McCall had already programmed the profiles for Tom Coleman, Dr. Patrick Cross, and Bo Ellsworth onto Control's laptop. McCall brought up Cross's file. "Dr. Cross works for Emory University Hospital and also has an office at the CDC. We need to know if he's at home, or if he's going to his offices at the hospital or the CDC. His wife is named Beth—there's her picture—and there are two kids, Lisa, nine, and David, six. It lists Beth's phone number. You keep working."

"It's taken me two hours to come up with one breakthrough, six words," Control said wearily.

"You've got the keyword now for the cipher. I'll call Beth Cross."

McCall dialed his iPhone.

A sleepy Beth Cross answered, "Yes?"

McCall told her he was an old friend of her husband's and asked to speak to him.

McCall could see Beth Cross in his mind's eye, sitting up in bed, wide awake now. "Has something happened to Patrick?"

McCall told her nothing was wrong and her husband was fine.

"It's midnight," Beth said, irritated. "Who is this?"

McCall told her it was a personal matter.

"Patrick's not home," Beth said shortly. "He left yesterday morning to drive to Texas. If you know him personally, then you've got his cell number. If you don't, he probably doesn't want to hear from you."

She hung up.

McCall thought he heard anxiety in her voice. He walked back to Control, who was working on the next passage of coded text.

"Beth Cross said her husband is driving to Texas, whether to Boerne or San Antonio I don't know."

"If he didn't drive directly to Texas and stayed somewhere for the night, he'll be back on the road tomorrow morning," Control said. "He'll have a

GPS unit. You can track it using a Live Trak vehicle-tracking device. I can link you up."

Control found the link, then went back to his deciphering. McCall located the signal from Dr. Cross's GPS unit and looked at the surveillance footage along the route. Dr. Cross had stopped his BMW at a McDonald's off I-65 in Montgomery, Alabama. McCall picked him up again at Love's Travel Stop #264 service station off the I-10 in Mobile, Alabama, where he'd stopped for gas. Then Cross had stopped at the Hyatt Place on Bluebonnet Boulevard just off the I-10 in Baton Rouge. McCall accessed Cross's Master-Card when he paid for his room. On one of the hotel's surveillance cameras, McCall found Cross's BMW still parked in the parking lot.

So Dr. Cross was in Baton Rouge until morning.

Control balled up another piece of yellow paper and tossed it into the wastepaper basket. His hands clenched into fists.

McCall moved back to the desk.

"Tom changed ciphers. The Vigenère cipher now makes no sense. It's like he wanted to mix it up, make sure he couldn't be decoded."

"Is there another cipher you can try?"

"There's the rail cipher. The plain text is written on a succession of 'rails' of an imaginary fence, starting with a new column when the bottom is reached. The message is then read off in rows. I may have to use some random letters as placeholders. The message is then condensed and regrouped. I need to figure out how many rails Tom is using. I'll start with three, then go to four if I can't make sense of it. Then I have to stack the groups on top of each other and read the message vertically. If it's gibberish, there may be a couple of random letters that should be deleted. The messages are short, but he's put a lot of work into them."

McCall poured Control a shot of Rémy Martin XO cognac. He sipped it as he started scribbling more notes and calculations. McCall moved to the window and looked out at the traffic moving east down Fiftieth Street. He saw no sign of the rogue cell who was looking for Control right now.

At 3:00 a.m. Control sat back. "Almost got it."

McCall crossed to the desk. Control had various windows on the computer screen open and a new sheet of yellow foolscap beside him. Only a few lines were written on it in Control's block writing.

"There are two words that I still have to decipher. I need to go back to one of the other ciphers. What we've got here is significant, but it's all based on conjecture. We have no proof of any terrorist acts that are going to be carried out on our soil, no matter how provocative this journal reads. Give me another hour."

McCall made some phone calls.

At 4:00 a.m. three more men were crowded around the computer on the desk in the safe house. Mickey Kostmayer had been the first to arrive. The ordeal he had suffered in the North Korean prison camp had taken its toll on him. Candy Annie had heard him crying out in the night and had run into the living room to find him sitting up on the couch, bathed in sweat. She had folded her arms around him and held him close. It had been such an innocent gesture that he had accepted it without question.

McCall had found Hayden Vallance in a jazz club called Cleopatra's Needle uptown on Broadway and Ninety-Second Street. Vallance didn't work well with authority figures such as Control, but he knew that McCall wouldn't have called him without a good reason.

Colonel Michael G. Ralston had been in New York City to be close to Helen Coleman. McCall had told him that his call was a matter of national security. Ralston could tell no one at the Pentagon about this meeting. This briefing would be classified top secret.

McCall introduced Control under his real name of James Thurgood Cameron, but told them to use his Company name of *Control*. McCall told them about the Jihadist flag that he'd found in the bottom drawer in the chest at Tom Coleman's apartment and about the notebook.

"We're dealing with three brothers," Control said, "all of whom have been in contact with each other, even if they haven't seen each other in a long time. Tom Coleman is a student at NYU, Dr. Patrick Cross works with Doctors Without Borders, and 'Bo' Ellsworth is a factory foreman. We believe they are planning to carry out three separate terrorist attacks on American soil. All of them are United States citizens. None of them have profiles with Homeland Security, although the third brother, Bo Ellsworth, has been questioned by the FBI, and the compound where he lives in Boerne, Texas, has been searched at least once. The Feds were looking for armaments, of which Bo has plenty, but all of them were legally purchased."

"Will you get in touch with the FBI?" Gunner asked.

"When I get to Texas. There's a clock on this, gentlemen. But I'll get to that at the end. Let's take it one line at a time."

Control brought up the first line of Tom Coleman's deciphered text: *NEW YORK CITY—BOERNE—SAN ANTONIO.*

"Tom Coleman is New York. Dr. Cross is on the road from Atlanta, and we're pretty sure he's heading to Texas to meet up with Bo Ellsworth. I don't know yet what the reference to San Antonio means."

Control put up the next deciphered sentence of plain text: *ALAMO RENDEZVOUS—MINUTEMEN—VALENCIA.*

"We don't know what 'Alamo rendezvous' means. Dr. Cross and Bo Ellsworth could be planning an attack on the Alamo Mission, which would be a Jihadist target, but it's heavily guarded. And Bo Ellsworth's profile doesn't match. He considers himself a patriot and would never condone an attack on a Texas shrine. He commands a local military force, the Texas Minutemen Militia, dedicated to preserving the rights of American citizens. This 'Alamo rendezvous' may just be a place with the name Alamo in it."

"What's the significance of Valencia?" Kostmayer asked.

"We don't know," Control said. He brought up the next line of plain text: *BULL AND HORSE—BRUTALITY AND DARKNESS.*

"This makes no sense," Control said. "No correlation that I can find between 'bull and horse' and 'brutality and darkness.' But here's a dark passage from the Quran that I deciphered from Tom Coleman's quotes."

THOSE OF DISBELIEVE FROM THE PEOPLE OF THE BOOK AND AMONG THE POLYTHEISTS WILL BE IN HELL-FIRE, TO DWELL THEREIN (FOR AYE). THEY ARE THE WORST OF CREATURES. (96.6)

"In Tom's eyes the disbelievers are the 'worst of creatures.' Even though the Quran teaches universal love, it also preaches supremacy, hatred, and hostility."

"Show them the last entry," McCall said.

"I used the Gronsfèld cipher, where there are only ten rows and the keyword is a number instead of a letter. It took another hour, but I came up with it."

Control brought up the last line: *JUNE 17TH.*

"Here's the deciphered text from Tom Coleman's journal."

NEW YORK CITY—BOERNE—SAN ANTONIO
ALAMO RENDEZVOUS—MINUTEMEN—VALENCIA
BULL AND HORSE—BRUTALITY AND DARKNESS
THOSE OF DISBELIEVE FROM THE PEOPLE OF THE BOOK

*AND AMONG THE POLYTHEISTS WILL BE IN HELL-FIRE, TO
DWELL THEREIN (FOR AYE). THEY ARE THE WORST OF
CREATURES. (96.6)*
JUNE 17TH

Control sat back, totally exhausted, looking at the men in the room.
"*If* these deadly attacks happen, they will be perpetrated on June seventeenth."

"Which is tomorrow," McCall said.

Silence followed as the import of the date sank in.

"We believe all three brothers are being protected by what McCall
calls a 'rogue assassin' unit," Control said, "operating from within an intelligence entity called The Company. I used to be the head of that unit. No
one there will have any idea that these assassins are operating on a covert
basis. They're dedicated to bringing down the American government and
sacrificing thousands of lives. *All* of their members wear these rings. If you
see one of them, you're looking at an assassin."

Control took out the silver demon-claws skull that Kostmayer had
lifted from Tom Coleman's right hand, before switching the duplicate for it,
and dropped it onto the desk.

Hayden Vallance turned it over. "What do the hieroglyphs signify?"

"I haven't been able to decipher them."

"Tom came back for his brother's funeral at Arlington National Cemetery," McCall said. "He's wearing one of these rings with a tiny tracker in it.
Mickey Kostmayer will be able to follow him wherever he goes."

"I'm having lunch with Helen Coleman tomorrow," Gunner said. "She's
a friend. I may be able to find out her son's schedule."

"I'm going to catch an early United flight from LaGuardia and get
into San Antonio at noon," McCall said. "I'll pick up a rental car and drive
to Boerne. Hopefully I can beat Dr. Cross there."

"I'm also catching a flight out of LaGuardia that gets into San Antonio
at 2:09 p.m.," Control said. "I'm going to meet with local FBI agents."

"What do you need from me?" Vallance asked.

"Can you put together a mercenary team and fly to Texas?"

Vallance nodded. "I can arrange it."

"Remember, we have no proof that *American* terrorists are going to
carry out these attacks. This mission has no sanction from any of the
intelligence agencies. These Company mercenaries kidnapped me

because I might have found out about the plot. My real name was known to Captain Josh Coleman. He whispered it to McCall before he died. If he hadn't, we would have had no idea that this covert unit of rogue assassins even existed."

"So these assassins are conspiring to attack their own country?" Kostmayer asked.

"And probably will be paid handsomely to protect our three terrorists. We have one chance to stop these terrorist attacks from being perpetrated on American soil. Good luck, gentlemen."

Control lay down on the couch and closed his eyes. Gunner had a room at the Park Lane Hotel, where he always stayed when he was in New York. He agreed to meet Kostmayer for breakfast there tomorrow morning. They left the apartment together. McCall stood with Hayden Vallance, who looked down at Control on the couch. His breathing was shallow.

"I don't want to leave him alone," McCall said softly. "The assassins within The Company will be searching for both of us."

"Are you buying into this conspiracy theory?"

McCall looked at Vallance. "You're not?"

Vallance shrugged. "A college student is writing a hate-filled journal and is studying Islam in Istanbul. Your Doctor Without Borders physician may be visiting friends in Texas. The Minutemen Militia dude may be just a good old boy who likes to get together with his pals to down a few beers and rail against the government. Rogue Company assassins may have nothing to do with it. Getting rid of your onetime boss was just a coup. None of it means anything."

"You want to risk that?"

"I don't take risks. I'll see this through."

"I'm going to get Control some clean clothes," McCall said.

"I'll stay with him until you get back. When you go to LaGuardia, I'll round up a couple of good old boys of my own and fly to Texas."

McCall nodded. "Good enough."

The lobby of the Liberty Belle Hotel was like a tomb at this time of the night. McCall went up to his suite, put together some clothes and toiletries for Control, and packed a small suitcase for himself. He took the second six-inch Black Tiger throwing knife from his backpack. He thought of bringing it with him, but he left it on the coffee table. He didn't know what he was facing in Texas, and a weapon such as the throwing knife might not be viable. He'd take the Glock 19 with him in checked luggage.

Sam Kinney was waiting for McCall in the lobby. The old spy told him that the apartment building on Tenth Street had been torched.

"You're all right?"

"Yeah, thanks to our real-estate mogul. He pulled me out of my apartment. Saved that little girl, too, the one who suffered all of those rat bites? He was quite a hero. Might be time to cut him a little slack."

McCall nodded. "Call Brahms. He'd like to hear from you. He's leaving for the Holy Land tomorrow. Ask him to put Norman Rosemont's computers back online tonight." McCall could sense Sam's tension. "What else?"

"The arsonist tried to kill me."

"Why would he do that?"

"We've all got our demons who come out of the woodwork. Rosemont picked this up from the floor of my onetime bedroom, before it went up in smoke." Sam dropped the tarnished bracelet into McCall's hand. "You seen it before?"

"I may have," McCall said softly. He dropped the bracelet back into the old spy's hand. "Keep it for me until I get back."

"Where you goin'?"

McCall didn't respond. Sam would tell Norman Rosemont the good news in the morning that his company was back in business.

McCall walked out of the Liberty Belle Hotel and flagged a cab.

He felt a sense of dread.

The terrorists' countdown had begun.

CHAPTER 44

6:00 A.M. EDT

McCall arrived in San Antonio at 11:53 a.m. He picked up a 2015 Buick LaCrosse sedan at Hertz at the airport. At the counter were several hotel brochures. One of them caught his eye. It had the name Valencia on it. The girl behind the counter told him it was one of the best hotels in San Antonio. It *had* been called the Valencia, but it had been taken over a year ago and extensive remodeling had been done. It was now called the Riverwalk Hotel.

McCall got into the Buick and pulled up twenty minutes later outside the hotel. A young Mexican American youth wearing a uniform with a name tag that said JESUS jumped forward to get the keys.

"Checking in, sir?"

"I'm meeting someone. I understand the hotel is under new management?"

"Yes, sir. It was bought by a Saudi sheikh about a year ago. But we're up and running again, better than ever."

"New front-of-house staff?"

"Yes, sir, very strict Muslims, but they're supernice guys. Park your car for you, sir?"

"Keep it out here at the front."

McCall slipped him a twenty and walked into the lobby. A big staircase of Mexican Talavera hand-painted ceramic tiles curved up gracefully to the first floor. A large modern fireplace was beside it. Waterfalls cascaded at several places amid plush couches and easy chairs. The front desk was pale sandalwood, and McCall could see two or three lounges leading to a bar area. He climbed up the staircase and noted a terrace with wood tables and blue-striped umbrellas and stairs that led down through gardens to the San Antonio River. He got a glimpse of River Walk with its multicolored umbrellas at the tables. One of the flat-bottomed boats drifted past, its guide working the tourists.

McCall walked back down the staircase and out of the hotel.

He recognized one of the parking valets who was just taking the keys from a young couple.

He was one of Bo Ellsworth's Texas Minutemen Militia.

McCall couldn't remember his name, but Control had written it down under Bo Ellsworth's profile. Jesus brought McCall's Buick LaCrosse right over to him.

McCall nodded at the young minutemen who whisked the couple's Taurus away. "How's the new guy working out?"

"He's getting the hang of parking cars without denting them." Jesus grinned. "He's only been here a week."

McCall slid into the Buick and drove away. He was carrying his iPhone and also a burner cell. From the burner he called Control, who answered at once.

"Where are you, Robert?"

"In San Antonio. You're on your way from New York?"

"I'm in Houston, just about to get onto the San Antonio flight. Hayden Vallance is with me. He's meeting a couple of his guys in San Antonio."

"There's a beautiful downtown hotel that used to be called the Valencia. It's been closed for a year for renovation and just reopened. Now it's called the Riverwalk Hotel. The front-of-staff employees are all Muslims."

Control lowered his voice. "But it's Americans that are being targeted."

"Maybe not in this case. One of Bo Ellsworth's Minutemen Militia is on the valet staff parking cars. The hotel could be one of the targets."

"I'll let Vallance know. "

McCall disconnected and headed on the I-10 toward Boerne, Texas.

11:05 A.M. EDT

Kostmayer waited outside Tom Coleman's apartment on Eighteenth Street. He had seen Brittney, his nubile blond date, exit the building just after 9:00 a.m. She had caught a cab going uptown. Not until almost twelve did the tracking receiver in Kostmayer's hands come alive. Tom Coleman came out of his apartment building and headed west. He was walking. Kostmayer got out of the Chrysler Delta he had rented and followed. The NYU student turned south on Eighth Avenue to the Fourteenth Street subway, which was accessed on Sixteenth Street. Kostmayer followed him down the subway stairs and went through onto the platform just as an A train came thundering in. Tom boarded. So did Kostmayer. Tom rode the subway past Fulton Street, Broadway Junction, heading toward Rockaway Boulevard. He got out at Grant Avenue. Kostmayer gave Tom time to get up to the street before he climbed up after him. The tracking signal had feathered in and out in the subway car, but once Kostmayer was back up on the sidewalk, it was back to full strength.

Tom walked along Sutter Avenue, turned down Forbell Street, then turned on Dumont Avenue, heading east. Kostmayer kept a good distance back. He found himself in what amounted to a slum. The underbrush in the vacant lots was so thick it looked as if it hadn't been cleared since Prohibition. Kostmayer saw murky pools of stagnant water everywhere because there was no sewer drainage. He remembered this section of Brooklyn was known as the Hole. There were no corner grocery stores, no 7-Elevens, no McDonald's restaurants, and few single residences. You didn't venture into this neighborhood unless you were driving, and if you broke down, you were dead.

Tom Coleman turned up Seventy-Sixth Street. Fenced-off lots and brick buildings were ahead. To Tom's left were some three-story warehouses. In the last one was a warped door half off its hinges. Tom looked around, but no one was in the rank street. He entered the building.

Kostmayer took a chance, ran over to the warehouse, and pushed inside. A short corridor was in front of him. He came to a door and listened. He could hear faint voices raised. The door opened into some glass-fronted offices. In the last one Kostmayer could see Tom Coleman talking to two Middle Eastern men in their thirties, maybe Syrian or Iraqi. One was short and chunky, the other one was taller, wearing thick glasses with wire frames. They were both casually dressed.

Kostmayer took out his cell phone and zoomed in on the faces of the men. He took photos before a small noise betrayed him.

Tom Coleman looked through the grimy glass from the other office. Kostmayer had knelt and kept still. One of the men asked Tom in Arabic what was the matter, and Tom said he'd heard something. They hadn't heard anything. Finally they started speaking again. Kostmayer put the cell phone away and exited the office. He knelt down in the tall brush in the vacant lot opposite, looking at the tracking receiver. Tom Coleman was moving again. He came out of the warehouse carrying a square package. It had some weight to it, but it didn't look heavy.

Tom walked back to Dumont Avenue. Kostmayer gave him a full two minutes before following. Kostmayer backtracked until he was at Grant Avenue station again and climbed down the stairs. A subway train was in the station, doors open. The NYU student was sitting in one of the cars. Only a handful of other passengers were with him.

Too risky.

The doors closed and the subway train headed into the tunnel. Kostmayer waited to catch the next train. He was taking a chance, but it couldn't be helped. He couldn't let Tom see him with this few people around. Kostmayer rode the next subway car back to Manhattan and walked to Eighteenth Street. There was no sign of Tom, but the tracking signal was blinking and put him back in his apartment.

Kostmayer slid into his Chrysler Delta. He could call Homeland Security and have them raid Tom Coleman's apartment right now. But Kostmayer had no idea what was in the package that Tom had picked up. And two other components had to come together. Doing anything to tip off Dr. Patrick Cross or Bo Ellsworth would be the worst thing Kostmayer could do.

But he *could* run the faces of the two men he'd photographed in Brooklyn through a facial-recognition program.

1:24 P.M. CDT

McCall drove down Main Street in Boerne, Texas. Storefronts were on either side with colorful roofs above the boardwalks. He turned left on Rosewood Avenue, followed it to where it petered out, turned around until he was back on Main Street. He passed the El Chaparral restaurant, a local landmark. When he came to Frederick Street, he turned left and saw the Alamo Plaza Bar and Grill about halfway down the street on the right-hand side.

Not the Alamo.

Tom Coleman's journal pages and specified *Alamo rendezvous.*

The Alamo Plaza Bar and Grill was built like a cantina, set back from the street with its own parking lot. McCall pulled into it, his Buick LaCrosse looking out of place among the SUVs and pickup trucks. He took out his iPhone and found Bo Ellsworth's license. He noted Bo's black Ford Explorer XLT was parked in one of the slots.

Now McCall had to wait for Dr. Patrick Cross to arrive—if he was, indeed, heading for Texas.

2:30 P.M. EDT

Colonel Michael G. Ralston slid into the passenger seat of Kostmayer's Chrysler and glanced at the receiver in the panel between the seats. The tracking red beacon was still blinking.

"He hasn't moved from his apartment?"

"Not since coming back from Brooklyn."

Gunner took out some folded pages and passed them over to Kostmayer. "I sent the facial-recognition intel you texted me to my Army CO in Virginia, and his guys came up with two hits. Nedim al-Attar works as a mechanic for Brooklyn Auto Repair on Union Street, and Khalid al-Fakhri has his own Laundromat on Avenue K, also in Brooklyn. Both of them are Iraqis who grew up in the United States and are US citizens. Both of them are on the no-fly lists. Did you get a good look at the package Tom was picking up?"

"Rectangular, maybe six inches in height, a little heavy for him to carry. What happened with Helen Coleman?"

"Over lunch we talked about Josh and how much he meant to both of us. She didn't talk about her son Tom at all. When Captain Coleman and

I came under fire from Jihadists in a Syrian village, Josh seemed to recognize one of the fighters. When we got back to the team house in Ar Raqqah, he showed me the man's photograph on our bulletin board. But there was something about his attitude that didn't ring true. I asked him if the Insurgent was one of our targets and he said he was."

"But now you don't think so?"

"I think Captain Coleman *did* recognize the Jihadist fighter, but he couldn't share that intel with me."

"Because it was his younger brother Tom."

Gunner nodded. "It was the look in Josh's eyes. It was as if he were haunted by the sight he had just witnessed."

"You didn't talk to him about it later?"

"I didn't get the chance. We were separated when we came under enemy fire in a village called al-Sukhnah. I found out later that Robert McCall had picked him up and tried to get him out of Syria."

"How did you leave things with Helen?"

"She is going to a meeting at the UN tonight about the worldwide refugee crisis. It deals with an amendment to Resolution 2139 that calls for easing of aid delivery to Syria and guarantees unhindered access for UN agencies and its partners, including to areas across conflict lines. I told her that I'd meet her there tonight."

"That's when you'll tell her about Tom?"

"Maybe I won't have to. Maybe we're being paranoid. What's your call on this?"

"I usually follow McCall's lead. If it was up to me, I'd storm Tom's apartment with a SWAT team and FBI agents. But that might blow the whole deal apart. So we'll wait for Tom Coleman to come out and follow him."

3:00 P.M. CDT

McCall was sitting in his Buick rental when Dr. Patrick Cross pulled into the parking lot of the Alamo Plaza Bar and Grill. It was just after 3:00 p.m. McCall recognized Cross's BMW and the license number. When Cross stepped out of his car, stretching his back, McCall recognized him from Control's profile. Cross spotted the SUV belonging to Bo Ellsworth and walked into the Alamo Plaza Bar and Grill. McCall got out quickly and ran to the front door. Inside he was greeted with a wall of sound: people talking and laughing, country-and-western music blaring from an old-fashioned jukebox.

McCall was in time to see Dr. Cross and his brother Bo Ellsworth embracing each other. They moved to a table and sat down, talking animatedly. Cross was the cooler one, but Bo was grinning and got in another hug for his brother. McCall made his way to the bar, found a seat, and ordered a local beer, a Blue Star. He watched Cross and Bo in the big mirror behind the bar. At one point they got up abruptly and exited. McCall left his beer and hustled to the front door. He was in time to see Cross lifting something in an Atlanta Greenbriar Mall shopping bag from the trunk of his BMW. He moved with Bo to a side door of the Alamo Plaza.

McCall went back to the bar. Two minutes later Cross and Bo came back. Cross had obviously left the shopping bag somewhere in the restaurant, perhaps in the kitchen. The two brothers resumed their seats, but now Cross was doing all the talking and Bo was listening.

McCall waited.

CHAPTER 45

3:12 P.M. CDT

Hayden Vallance walked into the lobby of what had been the Valencia, now called the Riverwalk Hotel, at 3:12 p.m. Two other mercenaries were waiting for him. Gabriel Paul Dubois was an Algerian in his midthirties who had been fighting Boko Haram in Nigeria since the beginning of 2016. He had no allegiance to any country and fought his battles for the highest bidder. He had rescued four of the Chibok children from the Sambisa Forest who had been taken prisoner by Boko Haram and was looking for the rest of the victims. He'd come back to visit his mother, who was at a hospice in New Jersey, when Vallance had reached out to him. Vallance hadn't given Dubois any details except the flight number. That was all that Gabriel had required. If Vallance had called for his services, he was there, no questions asked. He would negotiate his fee later.

Clive Ashley-Talbot was a Brit who came from a family who had had a seat in the House of Lords for three hundred years. He was in his late twenties, amoral and feral. He had been fighting in the conflict between separatist forces of the self-declared Donetsk and Luhansk People's Republics and pro-Russian forces in the Ukraine. Clive made a lot of money and owed no one anything, not his loyalty, not his respect, nor his allegiance.

But he owed his life to Hayden Vallance.

Vallance had pulled Clive out of a battle where pro-Russian insurgents had surrounded the Donetsk International Airport. Clive had been badly wounded. Vallance had airlifted both of them to a hospital in Gödöllo just outside Budapest.

Clive didn't like to be in debt to anyone.

The two mercenaries checked in first. Both of them had weapons stashed in their leather bags. They went up to their rooms. The reception girl, who was seriously cute with short-cropped blond hair, asked Vallance why he was in San Antonio. He told her he was there to visit the Alamo. The girl smiled and said he wouldn't be disappointed.

But he wasn't listening to her.

He'd seen one of the rogue mercenaries, as McCall had labeled them, sitting in a rattan chair. He was casually dressed in slacks and a black cashmere turtleneck and loafers with no socks. Vallance figured he was in his thirties. He was reading a paperback thriller.

There was no mistaking the silver demon-claws skull on his right hand.

Vallance walked to the elevator to go up to his room.

Tom Renquist barely glanced up from his book. He thought Vallance looked like a mercenary, but it didn't matter.

Renquist's target was Robert McCall.

3:22 P.M. CDT

Control sat at one of the tables along River Walk. It was crowded with tourists. One of the flat-bottomed boats floated by, the guide extolling the charms of the many restaurants and galleries. Looking up, Control could see the façade of the Riverwalk Hotel with its cascading gardens and steps leading down to the river. He knew that Hayden Vallance and his mercenaries had already checked into the hotel.

Maybe for no reason.

It wasn't hard to spot Todd Blakemore. He stood out from the crowd as if he had a sign around his neck that read FEDS. He was carrying a manila folder, his eyes hidden behind dark Ray•Ban aviator sunglasses. Control signaled to him, and Blakemore slid into the table opposite Control and set down the folder.

"FBI special agent Todd Blakemore." No preamble.

"James Thurgood Cameron."

"I ran your name through Bureau records. Not only was there no intel about a clandestine intelligence outfit called The Company, we couldn't find a single piece of evidence that you exist. Not a driver's license, a Social Security number, a residence, a high school or college you attended, no relatives, no family, zero."

"The Company is a black-ops operation that officially doesn't exist. My identity was carefully eradicated in a power struggle. None of that matters now. We have only hours before three separate terrorist attacks are going to be carried out."

"If your story has any validity. This is the file we've compiled on Bo Ellsworth and his Texas Minutemen Militia. They're a paramilitary unit who hold meetings, organize rallies for patriotic Americans, rail against the government and all kinds of ethnic groups, mostly Muslim. They've been disruptive at marches and have taken to guarding federal buildings in the name of homeland security. There are at least a dozen of these groups on our books. They rarely disturb the peace, and we've never found anything incriminating against any of them."

"But you keep an eye on them anyway." Control looked through the folder. "What is it about the Texas Minutemen Militia that doesn't sit right with you."

It wasn't a question. FBI agent Blakemore looked out at the boats on the river and the crowds of tourists surging along River Walk. The ambience was festive. No one was paying the least attention to their quiet oasis.

"There's something about Bo Ellsworth that sticks in my craw," Blakemore said. "I can't put it into words. Just a gut feeling."

"Would you describe him as an urban terrorist?"

"Bo Ellsworth and his militia are dangerous because of their misguided loyalties and hate rhetoric."

"Do you believe they would ever carry out a terrorist attack like the ones in Paris or Brussels?"

"No way in the world. Bo Ellsworth stands for American values, John Wayne, the Ku Klux Klan, and is one step away from white supremacy."

"So he would have nothing do with the Insurgent fighters in Syria?"

"Only what he reads in the newspapers or sees on Fox News."

Control closed the folder. "Do you have any closer shots of Bo Ellsworth's compound?"

Blakemore took out his Android cell phone, scrolled down, then handed it to Control. "This is footage from a drone we sent over the compound two days ago."

Control looked at the footage, noted the main ranch house and the smaller buildings, the SUVs parked in the compound, kids on the property, horses in a corral.

"I understand you searched the compound."

"From top to bottom. Bo Ellsworth has a lot of firepower, 9mm pistols, M4 assault rifles, all legally obtained with the necessary permits."

The drone footage ended, and Control handed the Android phone back to Blakemore.

The FBI agent took off his Ray•Ban sunglasses and regarded Control frankly. "I can't confirm your credentials. You say there's going to be a terrorist attack. Maybe here in San Antonio. But you've got no corroborating evidence to back this up. Why shouldn't I believe you're just another crackpot with conspiracy theories? I've got a bunch of them in my office that I make paper planes with."

Control took a breath, then told Blakemore everything he knew about the plot against the United States by three American citizens. He left out only the part about the rogue mercenaries from The Company who were guarding the American terrorists. When he'd finished, Agent Blakemore stared at him for a long time.

Then he put his Ray•Ban sunglasses back on. "What do you need?"

"I'd like to see Bo Ellsworth's compound."

"I'll have to talk to my boss."

Control nodded, got up, and walked away. Blakemore dialed his cell phone. Control called McCall on his burner. McCall told him that he was in the Alamo Plaza Bar and Grill and that Dr. Patrick Cross and Bo Ellsworth were there having some beers together.

"All it tells us is that they're brothers and they're reuniting," McCall said. "Nothing suspicious or threatening. What about you?"

Control said he was enlisting the help of the FBI to take a look at Bo Ellsworth's compound. "But I don't think they really believe me." Control gave McCall Todd Blakemore's cell phone number and said he'd urged the FBI agent to call in Homeland Security. "I'll call you if go to Boerne."

"What about Hayden Vallance?"

"He checked into the Riverwalk Hotel this afternoon with two mercenaries. Call me back if you can."

Control hung up as FBI agent Blakemore ended his call, got to his feet, walked over, and said, "Let's go to Boerne."

5:10 P.M. EDT

Tom Coleman came out of his apartment building and walked briskly down Eighteenth Street to a parking facility near Union Square. Kostmayer and Gunner followed him in the Chrysler and waited. Five minutes later the NYU student drove out of the garage in a classic red 1979 VW Beetle cabriolet. He headed west. Kostmayer gave him two minutes, while Gunner ascertained that the tracking device was working, then followed.

4:20 CDT

McCall sat in the Alamo Plaza Bar and Grill, nursing his Second Blue Star beer. In the mirror behind the bar he watched Cross and Bo's reunion become more intense. McCall was looking at Dr. Patrick Cross's eyes. They were cold and lifeless. The eyes of a dead man. But his body language had passion. He took out his iPhone and scrolled through some pictures. McCall got up and made his away past their table. He saw that Cross was scrolling through pictures of atrocities—Syrian and Iraqi civilians being massacred. Bo was staring at them, unmoving. Both men looked up as McCall murmured an apology as he passed by.

Neither of them had ever seen him before.

McCall went through the front door, gave it a few moments, then reentered the restaurant with his burner phone in one hand, as if he had forgotten it in his car. He went back to his barstool and picked up his Blue Star beer. In the mirror, Cross had put away his iPhone and was gripping Bo's hands. Bo nodded, like what Cross was saying made sense. Finally Cross let him go. Bo stared at his brother for a long time. Then he handed Cross a small .25 Colt semiautomatic pistol, which he put into his pocket. Bo slid out of the booth and headed to the corridor that led to the restrooms and the kitchen.

McCall slid off his barstool and followed him.

The corridor was deserted. McCall strode to a clear pane where you could look into the kitchen. Bo was moving to a large stainless-steel refrigerator.

The loop was thrown around McCall's throat and pulled tight.

McCall tucked in his chin and raised his right shoulder, trying to get his hips perpendicular to his assailant. At the same time he barreled back into him, sending both of them down the corridor, inside the men's room, smashing right back into one of the stalls. The severity of McCall's backward propulsion had taken his assailant completely by surprise. His head snapped back against the enamel. McCall smashed his elbow into the assailant's groin. When he doubled over, McCall gouged his right eye almost out of its socket. He savagely pulled the belt from around his throat, hauled the assailant in front of him, put his knee into his back and his arms around the man's neck, and twisted. The man's neck snapped and McCall caught his weight as he fell forward.

The entire attack and counterdefense had taken less than five seconds. McCall's adrenaline was pumping and he had to slow down his breathing. Clearly the man was not an assassin and had no real training. He had seen an opportunity and had slid his belt out of his jeans and looped it around McCall's neck, thinking the element of surprise and the sudden choking spasm would have done the trick. If it had been a cheese cutter looped around McCall's neck, he would have not survived.

He recognized the assailant as one of the men who had been guarding Control in the house in Virginia. A young guy with strawberry-colored hair and bad teeth. Cassie had described him as right out of *Deliverance*. McCall grabbed the fingers of the dead man's right hand and noted the silver demon-claws skull on his ring finger with the silver ring beside it. McCall put his arm around the dead man's shoulders, moving both of them out of the stall just as the men's-room door was pushed in by a cowboy who was in a real hurry to piss. Passing them, he shot McCall and his burden a look.

"Clay can't hold his liquor the way he used to," McCall explained, opening the men's-room door. "Come on, dude, let's get you back to your table."

The corridor outside the restrooms was deserted.

McCall pushed through the side entrance to the Alamo Plaza Bar and Grill. A blue Dumpster was in an alleyway. McCall opened it, revealing black polyethylene bags, and heaved the man inside. The Dumpster lid slammed down. McCall looked around, but no one was in the alleyway. He went back inside, moving to the kitchen door. A server carrying a tray piled with food almost barreled right into him.

"Sorry!" she said, and moved into the restaurant.

McCall looked through the clear plastic panel. Bo was gone, presumably having taken with him the shopping bag that he'd stashed in the refrigerator. McCall ran into the restaurant and saw that Dr. Patrick Cross had paid his check and left. McCall moved quickly outside.

In the parking lot Bo was just slamming down the trunk on his Ford Explorer. Cross sat in the passenger seat. McCall walked to his Buick and slid into it. By that time Bo Ellsworth was pulling out of the lot. McCall turned out of the Alamo Plaza Bar and Grill heading back to Main Street after the Explorer.

5:53 P.M. EDT

Kostmayer followed Tom Coleman through the Holland Tunnel into New Jersey. Tom kept going on through Five Corners, down Hoboken Avenue, and then down Summit Street. He turned onto Vroom Street, then onto Bergen Avenue, and parked beside the old Bergen church and cemetery in Jersey City. He climbed out of his vintage VW Beetle and entered the cemetery. Kostmayer made sure the tracking signal in Gunner's hands was still registering an intermittent red blip, then he climbed out of the Chrysler.

The Old Bergen Cemetery had an iron fence surrounding it. Parts of it were overgrown at the back where Tom Coleman's figure had disappeared. The cemetery had no other mourners or visitors right now. Kostmayer skirted around headstones in the gray afternoon light. He noted that the markers faced away from Bergen Avenue, the souls of the dead waiting for the coming of the Day of Judgment. Many of them were from Bergen's founding Dutch families, judging by the names: Brinkeroff, Van Reypen, Van Wagoner. Kostmayer spotted Tom Coleman kneeling beside a marker where he had just placed a single white rose. The headstone said *Cornelia Van Wagoner, b. 1859, d. May 1945,* age Eighty-Six years. *To have died in 1945,* Kostmayer thought, *she might be Tom's great-grandmother.*

Tom sat down beside the marker. He might have been praying or just meditating. Kostmayer moved to the wooded area that started just beyond the fence at the back. He watched Tom Coleman's profile and waited.

5:06 P.M. CDT

Control sat in the back of a cramped panel truck that was parked down a canyon road in the mesquite brush about a mile and a half off State Highway 46. Another road that branched off Highway 46 led directly to Bo Ellsworth's compound. Control had noted a sign that said MINUTEMAN RANCH. Two other FBI agents were sitting among some sophisticated electronic equipment and monitors. One of them was tall and lanky, looking like he'd been born in the saddle. He was in his late thirties, and if he had any facial expressions, they were fleeting. Blakemore had introduced him as FBI agent Hank Fulton. Beside him was a stocky agent named Willis Deevers Sutherland, whom his colleagues called Deaf because he had a discreet hearing aid in his left ear. He had just sent another drone soaring high above Bo's compound. Deaf told Control it was a DJI Inspire 1 Raw quadcopter with a Zenmuse X5R camera. The pictures the drone sent back were all benign: kids playing in the compound, some of the Texas minutemen, in uniform, patrolling the perimeter, wives and girlfriends watching the kids.

"Where's Bo?" Blakemore asked.

"In town," Hank Fulton said. "It's his day off today, so he's probably in the Alamo Plaza Bar and Grill."

"Are you keeping him under surveillance?" Control asked.

"He goes there virtually every day," Deaf said. "All the minutemen congregate in there. We can't track Bo Ellsworth twenty-four/seven."

"Deaf's right," Blakemore said. "These agents have been on duty for six days here, three eight-hour shifts. I'm pulling them at the end of this cycle."

"Give it a little more time," Control said.

The two other FBI agents glanced at each other, clearly irritated that an outsider was calling the shots here.

"Do you have a timeline for this terrorist attack, *if* it happens?" Blakemore asked.

"I don't. Except today's date. The seventeenth."

"I'll give it another two hours," Blakemore said. "Then I'm pulling the plug."

CHAPTER 46

5:08 P.M. CDT

Bo Ellsworth's Ford Explorer approached the West Texas Regional Water Treatment Plant just off the I-10. McCall pulled off the road, sheltered by some hickory trees. Five three-story buildings were protected by an eight-foot fence with coiled barbed wire at the top. An American flag and a Texas flag flew above a guard hut built into the sandstone wall that wound around the property. McCall was surprised to see a guard's hut on a local wastewater-treatment facility. Landscaped lawns were on either side of the buildings. The plant reached back probably a half mile, with massive circles laid out symmetrically behind the five main structures.

Bo stopped his Ford Explorer at the hut, and the uniformed guard stepped out. From the profile that McCall had compiled, he knew that Bo was a foreman at the plant. His manner was relaxed. After a little good-natured banter back and forth, Bo shrugged as if to say, *What can I do? My friend wanted to see the plant.* The guard raised the wooden barrier and waved Bo through.

McCall looked up and saw ominous storm clouds gathering. In half an hour it would be almost as if it were night.

McCall waited.

6:14 P.M. EDT

At 6:14 p.m. in New Jersey, Tom Coleman took out his cell phone from his Windbreaker. Kostmayer hadn't heard it ring. Tom didn't bother to look at the caller ID. He said something into the phone, listened for a moment, then added four more words and disconnected.

Kostmayer thought he had said, "Keep to the schedule," but he wasn't sure. Tom got to his feet, looking down at the marker for Cornelia Van Wagoner. From this angle Kostmayer could see that Tom had been crying. He strode through the cemetery toward the front gate. Kostmayer followed on a parallel course behind him. When Kostmayer got to the gate, Tom's VW Beetle was pulling away. Kostmayer jogged to the Chrysler, slid into the driver's side, and started it up. Gunner had the tracking device in his hand. The red light was flashing intermittently. Kostmayer pulled away from the Bergen cemetery.

Gunner said, "What was Tom doing for so long?"

"Visiting with his great-grandmother. He took a call on his cell. I couldn't make out what he first said as the wind had kicked up. I think his last words were 'Keep to the schedule.' If there are three brothers in this conspiracy, Tom is calling the shots."

"He would be the only one of them who has fought for the Insurgents. I can make one call and have Homeland Security pick him up when he reaches his next destination."

"We don't know where that will be. We've got to play this the way McCall wants us to. I've trusted him for a lot of years."

Gunner lapsed into a terse silence as Kostmayer turned off Bergen Avenue onto Vroom Street, then onto Summit Avenue heading north.

5:24 P.M. CDT

Hayden Vallance met up with Gabriel Paul Dubois and Clive Ashley-Talbot in the bar of the Riverwalk Hotel, which was jammed even at this early hour. One bartender was on duty, a pretty brunette with a ready smile who mixed the drinks with aplomb.

Vallance had no attack plan. Gabriel Dubois stationed himself on the first-floor terrace, with its blue-striped umbrellas at the square tables. He could see down the gardens to where the last steps led to the River Walk level. Clive Ashley-Talbot leaned against the brass railing on the staircase overlooking the lobby. He watched everyone who came in and went out.

Vallance had made periodic passes through the lounges and the lobby. The rogue Company agent he'd seen had gone. But there were at least two others. The first one was a big guy who moved like a ghost through the crowds. Vallance had heard him asking directions at the reception desk to River Walk with a heavy Croatian inflection. Vallance thought he might actually be from Bosnia-Herzegovina, probably from Sarajevo. Vallance prided himself on his accuracy in placing accents. The Croatian was wearing the silver demon-claws skull on his right hand. Beside it was a silver ring with the inscription for memento mori. Vallance was also sure the man was carrying a firearm in a shoulder holster.

On Vallance's next tour through the lounges he came upon the second rogue Company agent wearing the silver demon-claws skull. He was also from Croatia and small boned. His eyes were so dark they were almost black. His demeanor sent a chill through Vallance.

He knew that both of these men were stone-cold killers.

The two Croatians didn't acknowledge each other. The big man stayed in the bar area while the small-boned man wandered around a little more. Vallance had called Control on his iPhone, but he hadn't picked up. Vallance had tried to call McCall, but got the same result. Vallance now knew that whatever plan was unfolding, part of it was here at the Riverwalk Hotel.

He waited for the fireworks to start.

5:35 P.M. CDT

McCall stood outside the West Texas Regional Water Treatment Plant and looked up at the stormy sky. The rain hadn't come yet, but it was threatening. The smell of thunder was in the air. About five minutes later Bo drove his Ford Explorer through the front entrance of the plant. He had his tinted windows up. The guard was dealing with the flow of workers out of the plant, ticking names off a clipboard. Bo threw the guard a wave through the windshield and headed down the road to pick up the I-10.

From his vantage point in the trees, McCall saw that Bo was alone in the vehicle.

He had left his brother inside the plant.

McCall worked his way around to the side of the facility that was shrouded by trees. He ran to the fence and climbed up just as the first heavy raindrops exploded down. Thunder cracked like an echoing gunshot. McCall climbed to a place where the barbed wire was intermittently coiled around the top. He climbed past it and jumped down to the ground. He was facing one of the main buildings, where pipes led to one of the circles. He ran to the building, keeping in the shadows. Rain drummed down onto the buildings and lawns. He would wait until the last of the workforce had passed through the front gate.

Then he would find Dr. Patrick Cross.

Behind him, at the loading dock at the third building, a shadow moved closer to him.

5:45 P.M. CDT

FBI agent Todd Blakemore had called off the surveillance on the compound, and Deaf Sutherland was packing up his equipment when Hank Fulton said that Bo Ellsworth was returning home. They picked him up on State Highway 46 where he turned off to Minutemen Ranch. Deaf put the drone back into the air. By the time Bo had pulled his Ford Explorer into the compound, the drone was sending pictures from a high angle. Blakemore looked at several monitors that the drone was feeding. Texas minutemen congregated around Bo. He was obviously giving them orders.

"Can you record any sound?" Control asked.

"The drone is only used for visual reconnoitering," Blakemore said. "We've tried twice to bug Bo's compound, but the judge threw out our motions. Not enough evidence gathered against Bo and his minutemen. Hell, around here, they're heroes."

Control watched Bo climb the porch steps of the main ranch house and go inside. Some of his minutemen entered with him.

Control took a flash drive out of his pocket and handed it to Deaf Sutherland. "All right to call you Deaf?"

"Might as well. Everyone else does."

"Plug this flash drive into one of your laptops, Deaf."

He did so. A blueprint came up on the screen.

Hank Fulton leaned in close. "Damn, that's Bo's main ranch house. Where'd you get your hands on that?"

"I've still got connections in Homeland Security."

"It don't matter a damn," Blakemore said, pissed off. "I already told you we searched all of the ranch houses and didn't find a goddamn thing."

"But you didn't have any blueprints with you when you searched," Control said. "They'd be hard to come by. Bring it on to another monitor, Deaf, lay it out in sections."

Deaf brought up large sections of the blueprint.

"You searched the main ranch house," Control said, "but you didn't smash in any walls."

"Federal warrants don't cover demolishing a man's home," Blakemore said acidly. "And Texas judges damn well want to know what you are going after."

"Look at the blueprint," Control said, undaunted. "Look *there*."

Control nodded to Deaf Sutherland, who isolated a room in the house.

"We didn't find that room," Blakemore said grudgingly. "It simply wasn't there."

"I'd say it's a hidden armaments room," Control said. "See where it's located? It's really a closet that has been renovated and reinforced."

"Even if we'd found armaments in there, I guarantee you Bo has permits for every single M4 rifle and nine-millimeter pistol."

"Maybe not," Control said. "You don't go into a room like that unless you're going to war."

"We have no proof that Bo and his militia have a civilian target in mind," Blakemore insisted.

"No, we don't. But if he moves out with that kind of an arsenal, we'll follow him."

"We could just bottle him up on one of the arteries to the I-10," Hank said.

"Then we won't have any idea of the kind of civilian target he's going to hit," Control reasoned, exhaustion evident in his voice.

"He's right," Blakemore said, taking charge. "Let's see where Bo is going to and who he takes along with him."

7:02 P.M EDT

Tom Coleman parked outside his apartment building and disappeared inside. Kostmayer and Gunner pulled up across the street.

The red light flashing intermittently on Brahms's receiver went out.

"He's found the tracking device," Kostmayer said.

"Either that or he decided it was time to take off the silver rings."

In five minutes Tom was back out on the street. Kostmayer caught a quick glimpse of Tom's right hand as he zipped up his Windbreaker a little higher. The memento mori silver skull ring and the plain silver band were no longer on his right hand.

Probably left them on his bedside table, Kostmayer thought.

Which meant he wasn't going back for them.

"He changed jeans," Gunner said. "He also put on a pair of Nike Air Ultra running shoes. They look brand-new."

"He zipped up his jacket. He had it unzipped in the cemetery even though the wind was much stronger there."

Tom climbed back into his red classic VW and drove southeast on Eighteenth Street. Kostmayer pulled out into the heavy traffic to follow.

"He's heading for his final destination," Gunner said.

"And we still don't know where that is."

"There's some clue that your Control deciphered from Tom's pages. I just don't see it."

"You need to figure it out fast. It's just a little past seven. The day is waning."

"You're thinking zero hour is twenty hundred hours?" Gunner asked.

"That's what I'm thinking."

6:04 P.M. CDT

The rain swept across the circular water clarifiers and thickeners, driving the last of the workforce to their cars and pickup trucks. McCall ducked into the first building and crouched in the shadows. A hum of machinery that didn't change permeated the cavernous room. McCall listened for footfalls on the three levels of catwalks that gleamed dully throughout the room. He heard nothing. But Dr. Cross was forty minutes ahead of him.

McCall headed through the first building.

Behind him, his shadower moved from the entrance without a sound.

6:12 P.M. CDT

In the panel truck, FBI agent Todd Blakemore got the call at 6:12 p.m. He said, "Yes, sir," hung up his cell, and turned to Control. "I've got official authorization from Houston to raid Bo's minutemen compound. Four cars filled with FBI agents are en route from San Antonio along with a SWAT truck. Homeland Security has been alerted and is sending agents to this location. Rendezvous in twenty-four minutes."

"What happened to the plan to follow Bo?" Control demanded.

"My FBI director wants the Texas Minutemen Militia stopped right here."

"The clock is ticking down!"

"Do you have an ETA for when this attack on a civilian location is going to take place?"

"No, I don't!"

"No, sir, you don't. You're going to have stay out of this, Mr. Cameron."

Frustrated, Control said, "Is there a way I can get back to San Antonio?"

"I'll take him," Willis Sutherland offered. Deaf packed up his laptop, briefcase, and minitapes from the quadcopter drone. He nodded curtly to Control. "Let's go, sir."

7:15 P.M. EDT

Kostmayer followed Tom Coleman down Eighteenth Street all the way to First Avenue, where he turned north. He took First Avenue until he was past Forty-Second Street, where he turned onto United Nations Plaza.

"He's going to the UN," Kostmayer said.

"Guernica," Gunner said at once.

"What's that?"

"One of Picasso's most famous paintings. It depicts the Nazi bombing of the Basque town of Guernica during the Spanish Civil War. Picasso wanted to impart the tragedies of war and the suffering it inflicts upon individuals, particularly innocent civilians. It hangs right where you walk into the Security Council chamber."

"Why would that be important to Tom Coleman?"

"There's a wide-eyed bull standing over a woman with a child in her arms. The horse is dead, speared by a javelin, and under the horse is a dismembered soldier. For Picasso, the horse and bull represented *brutality and darkness*—part of Tom's code."

Ahead of them at the security gate, Tom Coleman powered his window down and handed the uniformed security guard a pass. Obviously Tom had been at the United Nations many times before, and the guard recognized him. He waved him through. Beyond the gate was the entrance to the underground parking facility.

Gunner dialed Helen Coleman's cell phone, but shook his head. "She's not answering."

The next car pulled up at the security gate. Kostmayer was three cars behind. "We're going to lose him."

6:20 P.M. CDT

The first water-processing building was a maze of high steel cylinders, electrical panels, and pumps. McCall climbed up the skeletal stairs to one of the steel catwalks, where he could see down into the shadows beneath. There was no sign of Dr. Patrick Cross. McCall was surrounded by more machinery that rose three stories from the floor of the building. He noted flow charts every few feet in primary colors that said FILTER BACKWASH PUMP—GRAVITY FILTERS—TRANSFER PUMPS—SLUDGE DRYING POND. McCall passed more silver and metallic cylinders and electrical circuitry with newer charts that read CHEMICAL COAGULANTS—PRE-CHLORINATION SEDIMENTA-TION BASIN—FLOCCULATION—SAND INFILTRATION POST-CHLORINATION—CLEAR WELL.

A shadow moved on the ground level below him. McCall reached into his leather coat and brought out the Glock 19.

The bullet exploded against McCall's left arm. It sent him down to the catwalk. The Glock flew out of his hand and plummeted down into the darkness.

6:30 P.M. CDT

Control sat beside Willis Deevers Sutherland in his Lincoln Town Car as they headed down I-10 toward San Antonio. Deaf picked up his radio when it squawked.

"This is Deaf." He listened. "Copy that." He hung up the radio. "FBI agent Blakemore is headed into Bo's minutemen compound." When Control didn't respond, Deaf glanced at him. "Bo wasn't expecting trouble. The agents are going to take that compound apart brick by brick. If there *is* a hidden armaments room, they'll find it."

"They may be too late."

"What do you mean by that?"

"I believe Bo Ellsworth and his Texas Minutemen Militia are long gone."

CHAPTER 47

Bo had been driving down the back roads heading toward San Antonio for a good half an hour. Twelve of them were in two black Durango SXTs, seven including Bo in the first one and another five in the second. Bo regretted having to discard their TMM uniforms, but it couldn't be helped. They all wore long coats, nondescript jeans, and sweatshirts with DuPont Kevlar ultralightweight bulletproof vests. They wore combat boots and black full-face ski masks. They carried their M4 assault rifles and Heckler & Koch .45-caliber semiautomatic pistols with twelve-round magazines. They also carried an RPG-7V2 reloadable launcher, a TGB-7V thermobaric rocket, and several OG-7V fragmentation grenades.

The Texas Minutemen Militia would be into and out of the hotel in under two minutes.

7:35 P.M. EDT

Kostmayer pulled up at the security gate. Gunner leaned across and handed a pass with his ID and photo to the security officer.

"Colonel Michael G. Ralston, US Army. Helen Coleman signed a pass for me and my associate to attend the Security Council meeting tonight."

The officer checked Gunner's ID and Helen's signature, consulted the computer in the hut, then passed the pass back.

"Drive down the ramp to the underground parking facility, Colonel. Park on level G."

"Appreciate it."

The barrier lifted and Kostmayer drove down the ramp. Gunner dialed Helen on his iPhone again, to no avail.

"We'll head down toward level G," Kostmayer said. "If we haven't spotted Tom's VW by then, we'll get out and split up."

Gunner nodded tersely.

6:40 P.M. CDT

Todd Blakemore's task force rolled into Bo Ellsworth's compound in full force. FBI agents swarmed out of their cars. There were no armed guards, just wives and children. Some Mexican laborers were working on the grounds. Homeland Security started questioning the women. The FBI agents searched the other ranch houses. Todd Blakemore's agents moved into the main ranch house and quickly ascertained it was deserted. Blakemore walked out onto the big porch and noted that several of the minutemen's SUVs were parked where he had last seen them, including Bo Ellsworth's Explorer. FBI agent Hank Fulton brought one of the Mexican groundskeepers up onto the porch with him. Blakemore asked him in Spanish where all of the men were. He shrugged.

"Any back roads out of this canyon?" Hank asked him.

"Many."

"How long have Mr. Ellsworth and his men been gone?"

Another shrug. The man had been working at his chores.

Blakemore and Hank Fulton moved into the main ranch house. The SWAT team was tearing down the walls in Bo's study with axes and sledge-hammers. Hank Fulton pinpointed the hidden room on the blueprint on his laptop. It took another six minutes, but they finally broke through. The room had rifle racks for M4s and AR-15s, tables for the Shield 9mm pistols, and another rack that looked like it might have held an RPG launcher.

The room was empty.

Blakemore felt the frustration rising within him. One of the Homeland Security agents, a soft-spoken man named Holtzman, walked over to him.

"I've questioned five or six of the Texas minutemen's wives. There're as closemouthed as the ranch workers. They know that the minutemen left in two vehicles, but they don't know what vehicles or where they were parked. One of the young women I questioned was scared. She didn't think her husband was coming back."

"Bo Ellsworth knows these back roads like the back of his hand," Hank Fulton said. "No good putting roadblocks up."

"Put two choppers in the air," Blakemore said.

7:40 P.M. EDT

Kostmayer drove down the UN parking facility to level G. He pulled over to one of the slots, and he and Gunner got out of the Chrysler.

"Tom wouldn't have driven down to the lowest level," Kostmayer said. "I didn't see his VW on our way down. He's got a spot all picked out. Not for visitors. For staff."

"You take the aisle on the left-hand side," Gunner said. "I'll take the one in the middle. Keep eye contact."

They started looking for Tom's distinctive red Beetle.

They had twenty minutes.

6:42 P.M. CDT

Renquist was certain he had hit his quarry. His Glock 26 had an Osprey 9 silencer, and even though he had been aiming from the floor level in semi-darkness, he did not miss a shot like that. He crept forward toward the cat-walk steps. Dr. Cross would be in the third building by now. Renquist didn't know how long it would take the doctor to disperse the poison in his vials and he didn't care. His mission was to keep Cross isolated and focused. Once it was 7:00 p.m., Renquist's mission would have been accomplished.

He ascended the steps. The catwalks spread steel fingers across the water-treatment building, branching off in three different directions. The rogue assassin moved silently to the place where he had shot McCall. It was streaked with shadows.

It was deserted.

6:46 P.M. CDT

When they got into San Antonio, Deaf got an update.

"You called it, Mr. Cameron. When the cars and the SWAT team rolled into Bo's compound, it was practically deserted. Bo and his militia are traveling, taking back roads, and there is no indication as to their destination. Agent Blakemore wants me to take you to our offices here in San Antonio."

"You know where the Valencia Hotel is?"

"Sure, it just reopened with a new management team. They're calling it the Riverwalk Hotel now."

"Can you drop me off there? I'm meeting some colleagues in the lobby. Can we enter from the back of the hotel?"

"Sure. Want to tell me what this is about?"

"I believe the hotel might be Bo Ellsworth's target in the city."

"What proof do you have of that?"

"The word *Valencia* in a journal that I deciphered belonging to an American student who may have been radicalized. It's a long shot."

"I'll have to call it in."

"Go ahead."

Deaf thought better of doing that. "I'll take you to the hotel."

7:47 P.M. EDT

Parking activity filtered down to Colonel Michael Ralston as he made his way up the center ramp to level F. He'd been traveling down the aisles of parked cars with a renewed sense of urgency. He hadn't seen Tom Coleman's distinctive red VW. He resolved that if he did not see it by the time he finished his search of level F, he wouldn't climb any higher. He'd take the stairs to the UN complex and contact one of the security guards. He would call Helen Coleman again when he got outside.

He'd hadn't expected the attack to come out of the semidarkness, and yet, in fact, he *had*. Since his graduation from The Citadel back in the day, he had always been aware of his surroundings, whether it was in a combat zone or just walking down a residential street. Gunner had a sixth sense of danger that was ingrained in him. So he turned in a split second toward the attacker.

He had five inches on Gunner, which made him six-foot-three with close-cropped blond hair that was almost white. He was wielding a bolas, weights on the ends of interconnected braided cords, used by gauchos in South America. Gunner knew they'd been known to bring down a two-hundred-pound guanaco, a llamalike mammal, with it. The assassin released the *boleadoras*, or *avestrucera*, one with two weighted balls, and it wrapped around Gunner's throat. Within a second it would have crushed his trachea, but the colonel was facing his assailant now, which had not been the man's plan. Gunner wrenched the strangling cord from his throat and brought the attacker to his knees with a vicious groin kick. Then Gunner threw the bolas. The weighted balls wrapped tightly around the assailant's throat, crushing *his* larynx. His body convulsed. Gunner pulled on the braided cords until the assassin's air was gone. Then he pulled the bolas from the dead man's throat.

Gunner was shaken. He lifted the assassin's right hand and saw the silver skull on his ring finger with the plain silver band beside it. Gunner couldn't remember what was etched on the silver band, something about you had to die. He pulled both rings off the assassin's hand and pocketed them. He dragged the dead man behind a parked Audi, tight up against one of the pillars, then straightened and moved forward.

He had to find Tom Coleman.

He was out of time.

6:48 P.M. CDT

McCall came up behind Renquist, slammed a punch into his kidney, grabbed the Glock 26, and wrenched it from his hand. But the man's reflexes were lightning fast. McCall had taken the bullet in his left arm, leaving it numb. Renquist pitched forward on the catwalk and pulled McCall over his body. McCall slammed onto the catwalk. Renquist kicked the gun from McCall's nerveless left grip. It skittered along the steel walkway. Renquist dived for it, but McCall slammed into him, sending him reeling. McCall gripped the catwalk railing and pulled himself up.

The two operatives circled each other, going into and out of intermittent shadow. Renquist aimed kicks at McCall's body and legs. McCall parried them, but he was hurt and the rogue assassin knew it.

Renquist kicked suddenly at McCall's left ankle. It was inflamed and the pain almost caused him to pass out. He countered with knifehand strikes aimed at the muscles in Renquist's neck and jugular. Renquist parried them with brutal ease.

"Thought you were favoring that ankle when I bumped into you at Arlington Cemetery," Renquist said, sizing up his adversary. "I figure you've got it taped up, but how long will that hold?"

Renquist came at McCall again, the silver skull on his right hand catching the light.

For a split second McCall had a sense memory of Granny when the two of them had been on a mission for Control in the civil war in South Sudan. Granny had showed McCall a move to incapacitate an attacker that Granny had learned when he was in his twenties. But he'd never attempted it in a real-life situation.

McCall struck with his rigid right-hand fingers in an upward move at certain groups of muscles around Renquist's chest so they contracted so violently they expelled air from his lungs. Granny had called it an "air dimmak point." At the same time, McCall grabbed Renquist's right wrist and gouged the pressure points there so that the assassin would think that his whole body had been hit. McCall followed it with a rigid palm strike at the "mind point" on the side of the chin where the jaw joins, just back a quarter of an inch. Granny had said it would cause serious internal damage. McCall used the fingers of his left hand to attack Renquist's colon points on the assassin's upper forearm. In conjunction with the other two moves, this would cause Renquist's body to suffer extreme low blood pressure, knocking him out.

According to Granny.

It took McCall about a second and a half to make the moves. Renquist's body collapsed as he pitched forward. McCall held him up, applied pressure to his throat, and pivoted his head back and forth, snapping his neck. Then McCall let the assassin down to the catwalk. McCall leaned against the railing, forcing air back into his own gasping lungs. Then he reached down, picked up Renquist's fallen Glock 26, and ran along the catwalk.

6:52 P.M. CDT

Control got out of Willis's Lincoln at the back entrance to what had formerly been the Valencia Hotel.

"I'll walk you in," Deaf said. "You can meet up with your colleagues, and I can call in our location to Agent Blakemore."

Control nodded and walked into the Riverwalk Hotel. He and Deaf parted company in the small lounge there. Deaf walked on toward the front of the hotel, and Control climbed up a back staircase. He ran down a hotel corridor and came out onto the big staircase to find Hayden Vallance leaning against the railing, looking down into the lobby. Below, Control saw Deaf enter, speaking into his cell phone.

Control hadn't made a sound emerging from the corridor, but Vallance turned to him. "No trouble yet, but we're in the right place. I've spotted three men that could pass as tourists, but they don't fit in. The tall guy below us with wavy black hair is from Croatia. He has a Makarov P-64 nine millimeter in a shoulder holster under his jacket."

"I know him. He was one of the rogue Company agents who kept me prisoner in the house in Virginia."

"There's another Croatian in the bar, taking walks out onto the terraces, looking at his watch. There's a third assassin with close-cropped blond hair, a giant, six-five, who's out on the first deck up here."

Control looked out through open French doors at the terrace. It was packed with people, waitresses and waiters moving back and forth with trays of food and drinks. Control spotted the blond assassin, leaning against the wooden railing, looking down at a side road that led up to the hotel.

"I don't recognize him."

"They're all wearing those silver skulls," Vallance said.

"Who's here with you?"

"Gabriel Paul Dubois, an Algerian mercenary I spent some time with fighting Boko Haram. He's right there on the deck. I pointed Blondie out to him. There's a Brit named Clive Ashley-Talbot I pulled out of the Donbass War in Ukraine. He's down in the lobby reading magazines. He's a little less stable than Dubois, but they both know why they're here."

Below, the small-boned Croatian strolled out of the bar into the lobby. Control walked onto the terrace, where'd he'd seen a flicker of movement from below. Two black Durango SUVs were driving down the winding road toward the side of the hotel. Control moved back to Hayden Vallance, who had also seen them. He took out a small walkie from his pocket and said softly into it, "We're on."

On the first-floor terrace, Gabriel Paul Dubois turned his attention to the grounds below.

In the lobby, Clive Ashley-Talbot moved back toward the reception desk.

"My guys are carrying nine-millimeter Lugers." Vallance took out a Glock 17 and handed it to Control. "Seventeen rounds, one in the chamber."

Vallance took out a Heckler & Koch VP9 9mm from his jacket.

It was 6:55 p.m. in Texas.

6:57 P.M. CDT

McCall moved through a doorway on the catwalk from the second water-treatment building into the third. Less machinery was humming now. McCall saw a shrouded figure at the far end of the catwalk in one of the concentric pools of light. He had his Greenbriar Mall shopping bag clutched in his hands.

McCall moved silently toward the figure, hampered by his injured ankle and the bullet that had grazed his left arm.

The figure didn't look up. He wasn't aware of McCall yet.

McCall stole a glance at the chronometer on his wrist: 6:58 p.m.

Why did he have the feeling that all of this waiting was going to culminate at 7:00 p.m. in Texas?

7:58 P.M. EDT

Kostmayer spotted Tom Coleman's VW Beetle at the back of the last row of level D. It was jammed into a small space, right beside one of the pillars. Kostmayer could see Tom's figure sitting in the driver's seat. He wasn't moving. Kostmayer made his way through the parked cars at an angle to the red VW, getting closer, not wanting to do anything that would spook Tom.

But he'd left it too late.

Tom stepped out of the VW. He slammed the car door and stood staring out into the parking structure. There was movement on level D, car doors opening and closing, people walking toward the elevators. Murmurs of indistinct conversations that didn't carry to Tom. He stood completely still, his eyes glassy, his head cocked to one side, as if listening to a sound that only he could hear.

Tom pulled down the zipper on his Windbreaker and left it unzipped.

Kostmayer saw that the student was wearing a suicide vest beneath it.

Still Tom Coleman didn't move.

Kostmayer walked to the last row of parked cars, diagonally over from the red VW, out of Tom's line of vision.

He was maybe six feet away from the suicide bomber.

Tom turned his head.

Kostmayer froze in the shadows created by one of the pillars. He didn't move so much as a muscle. After a few seconds, Tom turned back and remained completely still again.

Kostmayer glanced down at the watch on his wrist.

It said 8:00 p.m.

CHAPTER 48

7:00 P.M. CDT

From where he was standing on the terrace, Gabriel Paul Dubois watched the two black Durango SUVs pull right up to the side of the hotel. Bo Ellsworth climbed out with his Texas Minutemen Militia. They were wearing long black coats, ski masks, carrying M4 assault rifles and Heckler and Koch .45 semiautomatic pistols in their holsters. The last man out was carrying an RPG-7V2 reloadable launcher. They walked to the side entrance that would lead them into the main lobby.

Gabriel was watching the blond assassin turn back from the railing of the balcony. He brought out an HK submachine gun that he had been carrying slung down behind his dark overcoat. He opened fire at the tables, bullets smashing the glassware and dishes of food, blood spurting from people as they tried to scramble for cover. Gabriel upended one of the tables, ducking down from the torrent of destructive gunfire, pulling his Luger, and firing. The blond shooter had not been expecting return fire. Gabriel shot him twice in the head and once in the chest. The HK submachine gun fired in his hands as the assassin slid down the wooden railing. Gabriel ran forward and picked it up. He turned to the panicked people crouching down at the tables behind him.

"Down the stairs!" Gabriel shouted. "Go! Right now!" He herded them to the stairs leading down to the outdoor lounges below. "When you get to the bottom, go down the rest of the steps to River Walk."

The tourists pounded down the stairs. Gabriel ran to where bodies were littered beside the tables. Two women in their twenties were badly wounded, but breathing. A Texan in his forties lay on the ground with his ten-gallon Stetson lying beside him. He looked up at Gabriel with uncomprehending eyes before the life ran out of them. Gabriel knelt beside a blond woman, also in her forties, who was bleeding from a chest wound. Gabriel found a fallen linen napkin, ripped open her shirt, and put it into her hands.

"Press down tightly against the wound. Lie right here. An ambulance is on its way."

Gabriel didn't know if EMTs were on their way, but the woman nodded, still in shock. Gabriel straightened and ran for the French doors leading out to the main staircase.

Bo's Texas Minutemen Militia burst into the lobby firing their M4 assault rifles, strafing the reception desk. The Muslim front-of-house staff were riddled with bullets. The minuteman carrying the RPG-7V2 launcher fired at the door marked OFFICE and blew it and whoever was inside to pieces. More of the militia fired indiscriminately at the people milling in the lobby or sitting on the wicker chairs and low couches. Bodies went flying. Bo reminded himself that the Jihadists would be blamed for this atrocity.

Clive Ashley-Talbot, in the back of the lobby, drew his Luger. The minuteman wielding the RPG launcher reached into his long black coat for one of the fragmentation grenades there.

Clive shot him dead.

FBI agent Deaf Sutherland had already ducked down beside one of the plush couches, returning fire. Hayden Vallance was running down the sweeping Mexican staircase. Some of the Texas Minutemen Militia took aim on him. Vallance fired first, taking out Teddy Danfield and Randy Wyatt. Control came down the staircase behind Vallance, the Glock 17 in his hand. The small-boned Croatian looked up at the staircase, reacted to Control as if he were seeing a ghost, and fired at him.

Deaf took him out with one shot.

Gabriel ran down the staircase, firing the HK submachine gun at the urban terrorists. More of the minutemen were cut down. The Croatian assassin who had talked to Cassie outside the Virginia house drew his

Makarov 9mm pistol from his shoulder holster. He fired at Deaf, but Vallance reached the bottom of the staircase and fired again.

The assassin pitched over.

Bo Ellsworth fired at the staircase, sending Vallance to cover behind one of the easy chairs. Bo looked at the carnage around him, the innocent people broken and bleeding on the lobby tiles, collateral damage that couldn't be helped, but where had the firepower come from? Who was shooting at him and his minutemen?

What was *happening*?

7:01:20 P.M. CDT

McCall walked silently down the high catwalk past a long flow chart set at intervals amid the cylinders and panels that said PROTECTIVE BAR SCREEN—CHEMICAL COAGULANTS—PRE-CHLORINATION SEDIMENTA-TION BASIN FLOCCULATION. A little farther along, the flow chart contin-ued: COAGULATION SAND INFILTRATION POST-CHLORINATION—CLEAR WELL—PUMP WELL. Dr. Patrick Cross had sat down on the catwalk in front the sign that had stenciled on it CLEAR WELL. He had taken his Puma ProCat tote bag out of the Greenbriar Mall shopping bag and had removed the blue Medicool vial cooler and protection case. He had the Ebola virus in four vials in front of him. He had stacked the vials *right on the lip of the Clear Well.*

McCall's left ankle gave way suddenly and he had to grab the catwalk railing for support.

Dr. Cross turned to look at him.

McCall took another step in the shadows.

"What is in the vials?"

Cross's voice was barely above a whisper. *"Taï Forest ebolavirus."*

"But Ebola can only be contracted by close encounters with other Eb-ola victims."

"I changed the bacterial make-up so it can be transmitted through water. It is a virulent strain of the disease. It would be lethal in the city's water supply," Cross said, his voice softly hoarse.

McCall took another step forward.

"You'll infect millions of people with a deadly plague. Don't do this, Doctor."

McCall looked at the man's eyes.

They were totally dead.

8:02:42 P.M. EDT

Kostmayer took his S&W 9mm pistol from his belt and stepped out of the shadow of the parking pillar.

Tom Coleman turned at that moment and looked right at him. He opened his Windbreaker more fully, revealing more of the suicide vest.

Kostmayer froze again where he stood.

Tom's eyes were wild. "Those who reject our Signs, We shall soon cast out into the Fire!" Tom's voice was ranting, echoing through the parking spaces. "Those with diseased hearts are to be seized and slain with a fierce slaughter."

Tom's right hand was pressed against the trigger mechanism. If he let go, it would detonate.

Kostmayer saw a shadowy figure move behind Tom Coleman.

7:03:15 P.M. CDT

In the Riverwalk Hotel lobby, Bo Ellsworth ran through the smoke from the shattered offices. One of the staff grabbed the pretty blond girl who had talked to Hayden Vallance when he'd first registered. The Muslim man was using the girl as a human shield. *He* was the enemy here, Bo thought, not his Texas Minutemen Militia.

They were the *good guys*.

"Let her go!" Bo shouted.

The Muslim whirled and the blonde wrenched out of his grasp.

Bo fired a burst from his M4 rifle. The bullets exploded through the man. The girl stumbled to her knees, looking up at Bo with a mixture of gratitude and terror in her eyes.

Bo held out his hand, as if to help her up.

A bullet exploded into the side of Bo Ellsworth's head. He collapsed, dead before he even hit the tiles. Hayden Vallance turned and saw Control leaning against the railing on the stairs, the Glock 17 in his hand. Vallance was impressed. A pretty good shot for a civilian.

Gabriel Paul Dubois came down the rest of the sweeping stairs. Willis Deevers Sutherland came out from where he'd been kneeling beside one of the couches. Vallance holstered his Heckler & Koch pistol. The smoke from the smashed offices and decimated reception desk still hazed through the lobby. Cries and screams were coming from all sides. The survivors were picking themselves up from the carnage. The Riverwalk Hotel staff moved among the victims. Vallance found the body of Clive Ashley-Talbot near the reception desk, riddled with bullets.

Control walked into the shattered lobby. Bo's militiaman were scattered across the floor where they'd been unexpectedly struck down. Teddy Danfield, Randy Wyatt, Jeremiah Buchanan, Kyle Savage, and the rest of them were all dead. Control looked for more opposition, but there was none.

7:03:32 P.M. CDT

On the catwalk, Dr. Patrick Cross reached into his coat and brought out the .25 Colt semiautomatic pistol his brother Bo had given him. McCall shot him with Renquist's Glock 26. Cross collapsed beside the vials, his hand nudging them right to the edge of the Clear Well. McCall leapt past him, diving down onto the catwalk, grabbing the vials before they could smash their deadly plague into the city's water supply.

The last vial teetered on the brink.

McCall grabbed it. Slowly, agonizingly slowly, he slid the vials back onto the catwalk.

With trembling fingers he put the four vials filled with the altered Ebola virus into Cross's blue vial cooler and protection case.

8:03:51 P.M. EDT

Gunner reached Tom Coleman and grabbed his Windbreaker, yanking it down across his forearms, curtailing his ability to fully reach into his jacket. At the same time, Gunner clamped his right hand tightly around Tom's right hand, immobilizing it. Kostmayer slammed the butt of his S&W pistol against Tom's head. He slumped down, unconscious.

"He's got his finger pressed on the detonator of the device," Gunner said tersely. "If his finger moves from the button, it will detonate. Bring him gently down to the ground with me."

Together they brought Tom's inert body down to the concrete. Kostmayer turned him on his side with the suicide vest hugging his chest.

"I can't move my hand from this grip," Gunner said. "I want you to trace the wires from the detonator up the vest."

Kostmayer was sweating. He traced the wires up the vest to the place where they came together. "Right here?"

"Yes. Reach into my right jacket pocket. You'll find a small Leatherman. There's a penknife on it."

Kostmayer fished out the multitool from Gunner's pocket and flipped up the penknife blade.

"Now cut the wires." Gunner told him which of the wires to cut.

Kostmayer's hand was shaking. "In the movies it's always the red wire or the blue wire that gets cut."

"Just do it. Gently."

Kostmayer nodded.

He cut the wires.

Gunner released Tom's hand, which he had been holding in a death grip. Nothing happened.

Gunner said, "It's been deactivated."

Kostmayer sat down beside Tom's body.

"There may be a second mechanism as a backup," Gunner said. "There's a mercury switch on the vest. I am going to initiate the evacuation of the UN facility. You're going to have to stay here with Tom until the bomb squad arrives. If Tom wakes up, put a bullet into his brain, but don't move him or the vest."

Kostmayer nodded, his face awash with perspiration.

Gunner got to his feet and ran toward the banks of elevators.

Kostmayer settled himself, not moving, and tried to breathe.

McCall snapped shut Dr. Patrick Cross's vial cooler and protective case with the vials in their slots and put the cooler in the Greenbriar Mall shopping bag. He walked down the catwalk stairs to the ground level and through the shadows back to the first building. He located a workroom filled with tools, where he found a drawer with half a dozen open padlocks. There were no keys. He entered a deserted greenroom with a large refrigerator and placed the shopping bag with the cooler on a bottom shelf. He closed the refrigerator door and snapped the padlock over it. The authorities would have to use bolt cutters to open it.

McCall ran out of the building into the drenching rainstorm to the fence. He climbed it and jumped down into the churning mud. He ran to the Buick LaCrosse and slid into it. He turned the vehicle around, drove a quarter of a mile down the road, and pulled up under some Texas shade trees. He could see the facility through the curtain of rain. He dialed the cell number Control had given him for Todd Blakemore. The FBI agent answered. McCall asked him if he was still in Boerne. Blakemore said he was, and who was this? McCall ignored that and told Blakemore to get to the West Texas Regional Water Treatment Plant just out of town. McCall told him to bring a hazmat team to deal with a cooler with four vials of a contagious Ebola virus in a refrigerator in the first building. McCall advised him to alert the CDC in Atlanta. He told Blakemore he would find Dr. Patrick Cross, a physician with Doctors Without Borders, lying on a catwalk in the third building. Dr. Cross had attempted to poison the water supply. He was dead. McCall said they would also find an assassin who was part of a conspiracy plot. He was lying dead on the catwalk in the first facility building. McCall suggested Blakemore might consider bringing Homeland Security into this. Blakemore told him that Homeland Security agents were already with his task force and demanded to know if McCall was working with James Cameron. McCall said he'd never heard of him and disconnected. He smashed the chip, rendering the burner phone useless.

Then he waited.

Twenty minutes later four FBI cars and the SWAT truck converged on the West Texas Water Treatment Plant, along with half a dozen Boerne police cruisers and a couple of Homeland Security cars.

McCall nosed out of the trees and drove back into Boerne. He stopped at a McDonald's and tossed the useless phone burner into the trash. Then he cut across Highway 87 and picked up the I-10 going to San Antonio. He tried the first radio station he came to, which had breaking news that the UN buildings in New York City had been evacuated in response to a terror attack. A massive police presence was there with hundreds of NYPD officers. The evacuation of the UN workforce and visiting diplomats was ongoing. There were no reports of casualties, but details on the terror attack were sketchy. There was no word on the identity of the suicide bomber, except that he was thought to be an American living in Manhattan.

McCall thought about Mickey Kostmayer and wondered if he was still alive.

Kostmayer sat beside Tom Coleman's inert body for twenty minutes until the first bomb squad officers entered the UN level D parking facility. They moved with caution until six officers surrounded Kostmayer. They wore explosive-ordnance disposal protective suits. A senior NYPD Bomb Squad man was in charge, along with a sergeant. Kostmayer thought the bomb technicians were part of the NYPD Detective Bureau's Forensic Investigations Division.

The senior man knelt down beside Kostmayer and Tom Coleman. He noted the battery and the mercury switch on the vest, which hadn't been touched. The four rectangles of C-4 explosives were two inches by one and a half inches by eleven inches long, wrapped in olive Mylar-film containers with the detonator beside Tom's right index finger.

The bomb squad put sandbags around Tom's body.

"You can get up now," the senior man told Kostmayer.

He got up shakily.

It took the senior bomb squad officer twelve minutes to remove the mercury switch from the vest. He stood up. "The US Army colonel who was with you knew what he was doing. There *was* a second detonator rigged up, but the wiring was faulty and it didn't function."

The bomb squad sergeant pulled the vest off Tom Coleman's body. Two other officers took charge of him. He was still out cold.

Kostmayer was still shaking.

He rode up the elevator in police protective custody to the ground level. He emerged out into the bright lights, yellow police tape cordoning off the UN buildings. Word had already reached up top that the situation had been defused. Tom Coleman was taken to Bellevue Hospital Center on First Avenue. It took half an hour for Kostmayer to persuade the NYPD that he had not been a coconspirator with Tom Coleman. Kostmayer found Helen Coleman and Colonel Michael Ralston among the crowd surging around the UN facility.

Helen took Kostmayer's hands. "You could have killed him," she whispered.

"That wasn't what McCall would have done," Kostmayer said simply.

McCall walked into the chaos in the Riverwalk Hotel lobby. He'd been escorted inside by one of the San Antonio police officers. McCall saw Control talking to a senior FBI agent, who towered over him at six feet, four inches. He wore a dark suit and sported a well-groomed gray mustache. He carried a Glock 23 handgun in a holster on his hip.

Control spotted McCall and said, "He's with me."

The senior FBI agent, Calvin Locke, motioned to the San Antonio police officer that it was all right. Locke moved over to where Deaf was sitting talking quietly to a couple who were completely traumatized. Control moved over to McCall.

McCall spotted Hayden Vallance standing beside the body of Clive Ashley-Talbot. Gabriel Paul Dubois stood beside him. Vallance made eye contact with McCall, but that was all.

"Hayden Vallance brought two mercenaries with him," Control said. "One of them didn't make it." He noted McCall's left arm. "You're hurt."

"Bullet grazed it. What happened here?"

"Bo Ellsworth and his militia didn't realize they were walking into an ambush. It was all over in seconds."

"How many hostiles were killed?"

"All of them, including Bo. There was one man who was parking cars and would have joined his comrades, but when he saw the slaughter he took off. The senior FBI agent here in San Antonio, Calvin Locke, has a warrant out for his arrest. The Feds will be rounding up the rest of Bo's Texas Minutemen Militia, scattered around Texas. Without their leader, it won't take much disbanding. There's no evidence that any of them were directly involved with this bloodbath."

"What are the casualties?"

"Eight killed, twenty-two wounded, three of them critically. They've been taken to the San Antonio Metropolitan Methodist Hospital. Hayden Vallance did a hell of a job. That FBI agent talking to that couple on the couch? They call him Deaf. He saved my life."

"Todd Blakemore and his task force are out at the West Texas Regional Water Treatment Plant," McCall said. "They should have recovered four vials from a refrigerator that Dr. Patrick Cross was going to empty into a Clear Well at the facility. He's dead."

"What was in the vials?"

"A virus, *Taï Forest ebolavirus*. Modified to be contracted in water."

"My God. He was going to infect people's drinking water with a plague?"

"That was his intention."

"Any more than four vials?"

"Only the four."

"FBI agent Locke said there was a second man his agents found at the water plant facility."

"He tried to kill me. I had to deal with him."

"There were two of the Company rogue assassins here at the hotel, the ones who kept me prisoner in the house in Virginia. Both dead. There was a third one that Gabriel Dubois shot down on one of the terraces." Control looked over to where FBI agent Calvin Locke was talking to Deaf. "The FBI are going to want to talk to you."

"Does Calvin Locke know I have any involvement with these attacks?"

"Not yet."

"Then he doesn't need to talk to me. I heard the news reports on the radio about the UN being evacuated in New York."

"A lone suicide bomber. There were no casualties and Tom Coleman was taken into custody."

"How did Kostmayer disarm him?"

"It was a two-man effort. Colonel Michael Ralston brought him down, and Kostmayer knocked him out. Gunner has had some Army training with explosives. He knew what to do to disarm the bomb."

"So Helen Coleman didn't lose another son," McCall said quietly. He looked at Control. "What will you do now?"

"I don't know how many more of these memento mori conspirators are left at the Company. But I'm going to find out."

"So you're going home?"

Control smiled ruefully. "Let's see what kind of a reception I get when I walk into the building. If I can you get out of San Antonio before the Feds arrest you . . ."

"I have some unfinished business to take care of in New York City."

McCall squeezed his one-time boss's shoulder in a rare sign of affection and walked out of the decimated hotel.

CHAPTER 49

He'd been following two lowlifes, Delroy and Travis, for four days. Delroy was carrying an S&W .40 pistol, and his buddy was packing an S&W M&P 9mm. Neither of them had used them yet, but it was only a matter of time. The Equalizer knew they'd pulled off a series of convenience-store robberies in the neighborhood.

Tonight the pair were particularly agitated. They needed money. They had cased the twenty-four-hour Manhattan Deli on Allen Street near East Houston. They'd gone past it three times, so the Equalizer felt it was safe to stroll inside. He took a seat halfway along the counter, keeping his hoodie tight around him. He was wearing a backpack. He turned around on his barstool, facing out into the deli. In front of him were booths. A cash register was at the glass-fronted counter beside the front entrance, with more booths in the back.

An older Jewish woman in a booth was eating a three-decker pastrami on rye. She was chatting to a young man who might've been her son. He was well dressed and looked bored. The Equalizer sighed. Sons should respect their mothers. Although, to be fair, her voice jarred the fillings right out of the Equalizer's teeth.

Delroy and Travis finally entered the deli. They sauntered past the brunette at the cash register. Travis made his way toward the back. Delroy sat down on one of the empty stools at the counter. He turned to the Jewish mama, who was regaling her son with some story about the scandalous people in her building.

"Put your wallets and jewelery on the table!" Delroy shouted.

The old Jewish woman looked askance that she had been interrupted. Delroy took out the S&W pistol from his overcoat pocket and got up. Now she shrank back. Her son looked over at Delroy in astonishment.

"Your wallets! Out on the table!" Delroy shouted again. "*All* of you! And the jewelery! Come on, let's go!"

From the other deli room Travis took out his 9mm pistol and fired a shot in the air. That got everyone's attention. Travis motioned to the booths directly in front of him. "Wallets and jewelery out on the booths! And the cash from the register!"

The diners were slow to respond, so Travis fired another round into the ceiling. Now they started to comply. The Jewish woman took her wallet out of her bag. But she balked at taking off any of her jewelry.

Delroy waved his gun in her face. "Get those rings off, bitch!"

"Please," the old woman pleaded. "The wedding ring I've worn for fifty years. The signet ring belonged to my late husband. You can take my engagement ring and the others. But leave me my wedding ring."

"It's of great sentimental value to my mother," her son said, and Delroy pistol-whipped him in the face. He slumped in the booth.

The Jewish mama started to slide the rings off her fingers, but they were tight and she was having trouble. She started weeping. The Equalizer drew the Glock 34 that he had lifted from the thug in the grocery-store robbery and calmly shot Delroy. The lowlife collapsed on the floor, his gun falling from his hand. The Equalizer had shot him in the shoulder, but a wound like that could be more serious than it looked, so the Equalizer had to hurry this along. He knew the guys behind the deli counter were staring at him with admiration.

"This is justice!" the Equalizer said, his voice raised. "Equalizer justice!"

Robert McCall, sitting unnoticed at the end of the deli counter, stood up quickly. He grabbed the Equalizer's head, slammed it against the Formica counter, stunning him, and wrenched the Glock 34 out of his hand.

Travis ran forward, his 9mm raised. One of the New Yorkers sitting in a booth stuck out his foot. Travis sprawled to the floor. His pistol skittered out of his hand to the cash-register desk. The brunette leaned down and scooped it up. The two men slid out of their booth and sat down on Travis's back. They looked like they'd been linebackers for the New York Jets. There had to be 450 pounds on Travis's back.

McCall put the bogus Equalizer's fallen Glock 34 into his jacket pocket. He leaned down, still having one hand on the bogus Equalizer's collar, and felt for Delroy's pulse. "He's breathing." McCall looked over at the two burly New Yorkers who were sitting on Travis's back. "You got him?"

"You kiddin' us?" one of the men said. "Yeah, we got him!"

One of the guys at the deli counter said, "I just called the cops! They're on their way!"

McCall picked up Delroy's gun and tossed it onto the deli counter. He dragged the bogus Equalizer, who was wearing the same dark overcoat that McCall sometimes wore, to his feet. The Jewish woman's son sat down at the booth beside his mother, taking her hands. She hugged him, sobbing.

She had all of her rings on her fingers.

McCall dragged the bogus Equalizer toward the front of the deli. The brunette at the cash register, who didn't look fazed at all, said, "God bless you."

One of the guys behind the deli counter said, "Is that really the Equalizer?"

"No, it's not," McCall said, and dragged the young man out into the street.

McCall hauled the bogus Equalizer along Allen Street, onto Orchard Street, then dragged him into an alleyway, where he finally let him go. The young man fell to his knees. He kept his backpack on. His eyes were angry and fearful.

Isaac looked up at McCall, his attitude defiant. He tried to get to his feet, but McCall kicked him back down to his knees.

"I should've put it together sooner."

"I was *working* here tonight, man!" Isaac spit at McCall. "I was doing *your* job! I have to defend the people of New York! They *need* me!"

"They don't even know that you exist. But you wanted that to change. You weren't going to sleep in a corner of some alleyway like this one. You didn't want to be in *your spot. Isaac's spot!* You wanted respect. So you took the persona of the Equalizer because that appealed to you. A crime fighter who was shadowy and mysterious."

"I was *already* a crime fighter!" Isaac shouted. "I was inspired by your ad in the newspaper. 'Gotta problem? Odds against you? Call the Equalizer.' I phoned you. I called myself Demolition Man. You hung up on me. You wanted all the glory for yourself. But that wasn't going to fly, bro. 'Behold, all they that were incensed against thee shall be ashamed and confounded.' Isaiah forty-one:eleven."

"What happened to you, Isaac?"

"Shit is what happened to me. You want the whole sob story?"

"Sure."

"My mom died when she was in her forties. Throat cancer. My dad was a boozer. He liked to smack me around. I had two big brothers, Zachary and Caleb. I looked up to them. They took care of me."

"But your brothers didn't stop your dad from hitting you?"

"My brother Zach got taken out by the White Jaguars street gang in a drive-by shooting nine years ago. My brother Caleb took care of me the best he could, but he was attending law school and needed time to study. Didn't matter. He got wasted in a convenience-store robbery last year. My old man threw me out of the house. So what? I didn't need him. I wanted to be on my own. 'Folly is bound in the heart of a child, but the rod of discipline drives it far from him.' Proverbs twenty-two:fifteen."

"So you took to sleeping in the streets."

"But I had a plan, man. There was corruption everywhere. People were suffering. 'And they worshipped the beast, saying, 'Who is like the beast, and who can fight against it?' Revelation thirteen:four. *I* could fight that beast! I knew what I had to do for the people of this city. There was a new sheriff in town. A younger one. But you didn't like that, did you."

"So when did you decide to eliminate me from the picture? Right after I started questioning you? You found out I lived at the Liberty Belle Hotel. You took a shot at me in my hotel suite. When that didn't work out, you decided to hurt someone close to me. There was this one old guy, Sam Kinney, the manager of the hotel. *He* was a good friend. You'd observed that. You followed him. He was staying in an apartment down in the East Village. He'd only been there for just over a week."

"I don't know what you're talking about!" Isaac got back to his feet, expecting McCall to knock him down again, but McCall didn't.

"Old Sam was a target now. You'd kill him, but you'd make it look like an accident. Like he'd died in a devastating fire. Never mind there were *other* innocent tenants in the building who might have been hurt or killed."

"You can't prove that!"

"The police and the fire department have been all over that fire scene, collecting evidence. You dropped this on the floor of Sam's bedroom before it went up in flames." McCall took out the bracelet that Norman Rosemont had found and tossed it to Isaac. "You didn't realize this had dropped from your wrist. Your fingerprints and DNA are on it. It ties you into the arson scene."

Isaac's demeanor changed. His voice was pleading now. "You can have all the glory. Just let me help you! Let me protect people!"

"Like you protected them in that grocery-store robbery where the cashier was killed? Like at the Madison Avenue robbery where you shot two thieves dead? The salesgirl in that store was also shot, but she pulled through, by the way. So did the two gang members you beat half to death when Megan Forrester fled out of that alleyway on the Lower East Side. I found one of Megan's diamond earrings. I figure that you've got the other diamond earring in your backpack."

"So there is always going to be some collateral damage. Look, Mr. McCall, I'll work my neighborhood and you work yours. The Equalizer and Demolition Man! Between us we've got the streets of Manhattan covered, man!"

McCall looked at Isaac, his red-rimmed eyes crying and still pleading.

That's when he came for McCall.

Isaac took the switchblade that he'd lifted from one of the gangbangers he'd beaten up and slashed at McCall. McCall easily disarmed him, putting an arm around his throat. Isaac writhed, but McCall applied pressure, and the Equalizer wannabe slumped unconscious into McCall's arms.

Headlights washed the alleyway, and Jimmy's silver 2009 Lexus pulled up. Jimmy got out and helped McCall carry Isaac to the car.

"I didn't know how long you were going to be," Jimmy said. "There are cops all over that deli."

McCall lifted Isaac's wallet out of his back pocket and opened the back door of the Lexus. He threw an unconscious Isaac into it and got inside beside him. Jimmy got into the driver's seat and handed McCall a pair of handcuffs. McCall handcuffed Isaac's hands behind his back.

"Where to?" Jimmy asked.

"Delivery to the Seventh Precinct. It's on Broome Street."

"You sure you don't want to kill the bastard?"

"I would have if Sam Kinney had died in that fire."

Jimmy pulled out of the alleyway onto Orchard Street. Behind him more cop cars, lights flashing, were pulling up outside the Manhattan Deli.

Jimmy pulled up to the Seventh Precinct building. He jumped out, engine running, and hauled Isaac out of the back of the Lexus. He was coming to. McCall took charge of him.

"Let's not make a habit of this delivery service," Jimmy said. "Sarah still wants to cook dinner for you one night."

He slid back into the driver's seat and drove off. McCall marched a groggy Isaac right through the station house, up a flight of stairs, and into the bull pen. He dragged him up to Detective Steve Lansing's desk and dropped him into a chair. A couple of detectives jumped to their feet, but Lansing waved them off.

McCall pulled Isaac's backpack to the floor and dropped his wallet onto Lansing's desk. "Isaac Warnowski. Driver's license and not much else. Except *these*."

McCall turned Isaac's wallet upside down and a bunch of his Equalizer cards spilled out. The NYC skyline was prominent with a figure silhouetted with a gun in his hand and the words JUSTICE IS HERE written in raised letters.

"Hey, that belongs to me, man!" Isaac cried. "This dude attacked me! I want to bring charges against him! He violated my civil rights!"

Lansing nodded at the heavyset, craggy detective McCall had seen before. "Take him to Interview Room Three and lock him in the cage."

The detective hauled Isaac to his feet and propelled him out of the bull pen.

"This guy is a criminal!" Isaac shouted. "You should be locking *him* up, not me!"

The detective told Isaac to shut up and hustled him down the corridor. Lansing picked up one of Isaac's cards. "So this is the wannabe Equalizer?"

"Homeless, living on the streets." McCall reached into Isaac's backpack and found a diamond earring. "This belonged to Megan Forrester, the victim that Isaac 'saved' from those two gang thugs. Isaac pocketed it, maybe as a souvenir. I found the other earring in the alleyway. I'll return them to her." McCall dropped Isaac's gun onto Lansing's desk. "This is Isaac's Glock 34. You should get fingerprints and DNA from it that matches the shooter who foiled that Madison Avenue robbery. Two men dead, right?"

"That's right."

"Once Isaac had taken over the role of the Equalizer, he didn't want anyone else claiming the glory. He found out that I'm living at the Liberty Belle Hotel on the West Side and took a shot at me. When he missed, he decided the best way to make me pay was to murder one of my friends, Sam Kinney, the manager at the hotel. Isaac torched an apartment building on Tenth Street in the East Village where Sam was temporarily living. All of the tenants got out safely. One of them picked up this bracelet from the floor of Sam's bedroom." McCall dropped Isaac's bracelet onto Lansing's desk. "You'll find Isaac's prints and DNA on it, which puts him at the scene of the arson fire. Isaac may have left prints and DNA on a kerosene can. You'll have to talk to the Fire Department's arson squad. Isaac foiled an attempted robbery at the Manhattan Deli tonight on Allen, just off Houston. He shot one of the thieves, but it was a shoulder wound. The second thief had two guys who weighed about four hundred and fifty pounds between them sitting on his back. He might be in worse shape."

"I take it you were also at the diner?"

"I started following Isaac about four nights ago. I knew where his alleyway of preference was. He'd been tracking the thieves who hit the Manhattan Deli. I had to catch Isaac in the act of foiling one of these robberies."

"Any other witnesses beside yourself in the diner who could ID Isaac?"

"About twenty."

Lansing pulled a different card out of Isaac's wallet. It showed a figure on a construction site leaping toward camera with the initials DM on his shirt and the words DEMOLITION MAN beneath.

"Demolition Man?"

"Isaac's old persona."

"What made him do it?"

"Mother died early of cancer, father was an abusive alcoholic. Two older brothers who got killed, one by that White Jaguars street gang, the other in a convenience-store robbery. Isaac was looking for an escape. He wanted to be a hero."

"Like you?"

McCall ignored that.

Lansing sighed. "Sorry. Cheap shot."

"Isaac thought if he helped people, he would find his way back into a real life. He's psychotic and troubled. Keep him locked up."

Detective Lansing nodded. "The ADA is going to want to question you."

"Will it be Cassie Blake?"

"Probably."

"She knows where to find me."

McCall walked to the stairs.

Lansing followed him. "I may not condone your activities, but it's kind of nice to know the Equalizer really *is* out there." Lansing offered his hand, and McCall shook it. "Just don't give me a reason to come after you, all right?"

McCall smiled and walked down the stairs and out of the precinct house.

CHAPTER 50

McCall took a seat at the bar in Langan's Pub on West Forty-Seventh Street. It took five minutes for Candy Annie to come rushing up to him.

"Mr. McCall! I haven't seen you *forever*! Did you hear what happened at the UN? Oh, my God! It was awful!"

"It could have been."

"You know that your friend Mickey Kostmayer is back, right?"

"I heard."

"I don't know what kind of vacation he took, but he's very gaunt! You'd have thought *he* had been living down under the Manhattan streets! But I'm bringing him some steak and kidney pies and some bangers and mash from here."

"You haven't tried to seduce him, have you, Annie?"

"Mr. McCall!" Candy Annie was shocked. "Of course not! *You're* the only one I would do that with." Then she grinned. "But he *is* kind of cute."

"I brought you something." McCall reached into his jacket pocket and took out the firefighter Barbie doll and handed it to Candy Annie. "I found this in a deserted village in Syria. It used to belong to a little girl who lived there."

Candy Annie took the doll as if she'd just been given a special Christmas present. "I have no possessions. Just what I brought with me from the tunnels. I've never received a gift before."

"Barbie is a little the worse for wear, and she needs a new left arm, but I figured you could get that for her. I thought you might like to have the doll. I think the little girl would have liked that."

"She doesn't want the doll anymore?"

"She had to leave it behind."

"I'll treasure it." If anyone else had said that to him, McCall would have looked for the sarcasm. But not from Candy Annie. "Thank you."

She slipped the Barbie into the pocket of her apron and rushed off again.

Two minutes later Helen Coleman entered the restaurant and slid onto a barstool beside McCall.

The bartender came over.

"I just want some water."

The bartender brought her a glass of water and moved off again.

"I can't stay long," Helen said. "I have to meet with the attorney general about Tom. Also some Homeland Security officials."

"Is your job at the UN in jeopardy?"

"No. They believe me that I had absolutely nothing to do with Tom's treason."

She took the small bottle of her meds from her Tory Burch bag, shook out a pill, and took it with a swallow of water.

"Fucking pills. Language, sorry. Josh was always picking me up on swearing."

"Go on," McCall said gently.

But Helen couldn't go on. She looked down at the bar, then finally raised her eyes to McCall's face. "You tried to tell me the truth. I didn't believe you. So many innocent people would have been killed by Tom's craven cowardice. Including his own mother. How do I reconcile that to myself?"

"You don't. You just have to deal with it."

"Your colleague Mr. Kostmayer could have killed Tom, but he chose not to."

"He made a split-second decision. It was the right one."

"I don't know if there's anything I can do now for Tom. Except deal with the guilt."

"Lean on your daughter, Rebecca. She loves you very much."

Helen nodded, still looking at him. "If I have to call on you again for help, will you be there for me?"

"Yes."

Tears were in her eyes, but they didn't fall. "Because that's what the Equalizer does, isn't it? Evens the odds against you."

Helen Coleman slid off the barstool, kissed McCall gently on the cheek, then walked out of the restaurant. He watched her disappear into the crowd on Forty-Seventh Street.

No matter how he played it out in his mind, McCall knew he'd failed Helen and her sons.

When McCall walked into Dolls nightclub, three FBI agents were manhandling the DJ, Abusaid, from his spot spinning records. Another federal officer was packing up Abusaid's laptop computer. McCall had made a discreet phone call to the FBI before he arrived. Melody was watching all this, looking gorgeous in her shimmering blue dress. Another DJ quickly sat in so the loud music didn't miss a decibel.

Melody looked at McCall. "I told you Abuse's sexual preferences were for young girls between the ages of twelve and sixteen. I talked to one of the FBI officers. He said they found child pornography on his laptop for dozens of illicit sites. Truly disgusting. I guess they've been watching him since the nightclub changed hands. Good riddance."

"You left a message for me?"

Melody took McCall's hands in hers. "I never got the chance to thank you for saving my life with Blake Cunningham."

"You could have said that on the phone."

"Not the way I wanted to say it." Melody actually blushed. "I'm finished early tonight. I could meet you at your place, wherever that is."

McCall was a little taken aback. He remembered when Andel, his *angel*, had stood in the shadows of his room at the Hotel Leonardo in Prague after he'd barely survived the fight with Jovan Durković. She had looked at him in the same way. With lust, gentleness, and concern. McCall had never seen her again. Not that he couldn't have flown to Prague to find her, but he wouldn't do that. Her memory was ephemeral, like a dream. McCall kept two beautiful women close to his heart. Elena Petrov, a Company agent, had died in Control's arms on a mission. Serena Johanssen, also a Company agent, had been killed by Jovan Durković before McCall had killed him. There'd been sexual tension between McCall and Tara Langley, but McCall had known that wasn't going to come to anything substantial. When he had put Tara on the flight back to Minneapolis with Emily Masden, he knew he'd never see her again.

But maybe Melody was different. Maybe there *might* be a way for her to be a part of his life. If he allowed her to be.

"I'm living at the Liberty Belle Hotel on West Sixty-Sixth Street. I'll be there in a couple of hours. Here's a spare key to my suite, 1728. Let's have a drink together."

Melody's smile would have lit up half of Broadway. She took the key, slid it down her cleavage, since there wasn't any other place she could have put it as far as McCall could see, then she moved out onto the dance floor.

McCall walked out of Dolls nightclub.

He hadn't seen the elegant man sitting on the far side of the dance floor with its gyrating crush of bodies moving in the psychedelic lights. He wore a dark blue three-piece suit, a red silk tie with chess pieces on it, a slim gold bracelet on one wrist. His dark hair was long and wavy.

He wore the silver demon-claws skull on his right hand, and the silver band next to it, which was inscribed REMEMBER THAT YOU MUST DIE.

The elegant man finished his gin and tonic and made his way through the nightclub out into the street.

Linda Hathaway was sitting at the bar in Bentley's when McCall walked in. Sherry, the Asian hostess, gave him a hug. Then she escorted a party of six toward a table. McCall moved to the bar. Amanda was waiting for a tray of drinks. Gemma was standing, ogling her black gothic makeup with awe. Norman Rosemont sat on the barstool beside Linda, looking relaxed and happy.

Gemma asked Amanda, "Can I do my makeup like yours?"

"You don't *wear* any makeup," Linda said pointedly. "You're *three*."

"But can I try it?"

"You'll have to ask your mom," Amanda said. "I was six when I started getting into goth. My mom freaked out, but it grew on her. Thanks, Laddie," she said, taking the tray of drinks from him. She smiled at McCall. "Hi, Bobby." Then she rushed back into the fray.

Linda stood up at McCall's arrival, a little nervous. "I have to be at work in an hour, but you said to meet you here. What a great place! This is my friend Norman Rosemont."

Rosemont looked sheepish. "Mr. McCall and I have met."

"Really?" Linda turned back to McCall. "Norman turned out to be our landlord, can you believe that? When he saw the conditions we were all living under, he went to bat for us, but then the building almost burned right down to the ground!" Linda reached out and entwined her fingers in Rosemont's hand. "He was a hero! He saved Gemma's life!"

"No, no, that wasn't the way it happened," Rosemont said, embarrassed for the umpteenth time.

"That's the way I heard it," McCall said.

"Norman is putting us all up at the Liberty Belle Hotel until we can move back into a new building," Linda said. "He came with me for some moral support tonight." It was obvious to McCall that more than casual affection had sprung up between her and Rosemont.

Behind the bar, Andrew Ladd came over to them, looking quizzically at McCall. "What can I do for you, Bobby?"

"This is Linda Hathaway. She's working at a diner called the New York Minute in Chelsea. The clientele, to quote a police detective friend of mine, are 'a little above pond scum,' but she can't afford to work anywhere else."

Laddie was way ahead of this. He smiled at Linda. "We're hiring servers and bartenders right now. Fill out the application and you can start tomorrow. I know the New York Minute diner. They wouldn't care if you gave them an hour's notice."

Linda looked from Laddie to McCall, astonished. "Just like that? I mean, I *do* have restaurant experience and . . ."

Laddie shrugged. "If Bobby says you need a job, that's good enough for me."

McCall turned back to Linda. "You'll like it here. Nice people, good crowd." He started to move back through the restaurant.

Norman Rosemont hustled to intercept him. "I don't know what you had to do with turning my life around, but it's clear to me that *someone* did, and Sam Kinney won't talk."

"He's an old spy. They don't talk much."

"That lunch at the Russian Tea Room where you showed me those terrible bites on Gemma's arms and legs. I didn't give a damn about it. I didn't frankly care about anything. But I was very wrong."

McCall looked over at Linda Hathaway, who was sitting in a booth filling out her job application with Amanda's help.

"I'm just trying to tell you . . ." Then the irritation dissipated from
Rosemont's voice. He held out his hand. "Just thanks."

McCall shook his hand. "Sometimes you have to step back to look at
where you are."

"And what about you, Mr. McCall? Can you do that?"

"It doesn't work that way for me."

McCall walked out of Bentley's.

It look James Thurgood Cameron four days to try to put his life back together. Matthew Goddard had disappeared from the intelligence complex
in Virginia. No one knew where he had gone. Control ascertained that
Peter Wintrop, a high-level spymaster whom Control knew by reputation,
had taken charge of The Company. He was one of the first calls Control
made. Control made several discreet calls and found out that the colleagues he'd known in The Company had been fed a carefully documented
lie. That Control was out of the country on a highly classified mission in
the Middle East, a cover that must not be broken. He must not be contacted in any way. The staff and the higher-level officials at the Company
had signed agreements saying that James Cameron *didn't exist.* Two of
Control's colleagues who had wanted to know what the hell was happening had disappeared. Control knew that meant they'd been eliminated.
Records at The Company had been deleted. No trace of James Cameron
would be found . . . by *anyone.*

The rogue Company assassins who had been brought in to protect the
insidious terrorist plot had been well camouflaged. They had reported only
to Matthew Goddard. Once Control had talked to Peter Wintrop, these
rogue assassins had been searched for, but not found. Control knew that
most of them had been taken out in Texas. The three Croatian agents who
had kept Control a prisoner in the house in Virginia, Tom Renquist, the assassin whom McCall had killed in London, the blond twins, all had been
eliminated.

Control was certain that their sole purpose had been to protect the
three bothers—Tom Coleman, Dr. Patrick Cross, and Bo Ellsworth—so that
the plot against the United States could be carried out. Control and Gunner
were trying to piece together how Tom Coleman had come to fight with the
Insurgents in Syria. That intel had been carefully protected. Documents that

were just now being discovered pointed to Matthew Goddard as the head of the conspiracy. Control didn't know what had fueled Goddard's hatred of his own country. It was more than money. It was obviously a deeply held belief, fueled by the Jihadists who were at war with the United States. Matthew Goddard was now a high-profile traitor that all of the intelligence agencies, and NATO, were trying to find.

Control moved his wife, Jenny, and his two teenage daughters, Kerry and Megan, from the rented house they'd been living at in Denver, Colorado, back to Washington, DC. They were going to rent a colonial house just outside DC in Easton, Maryland, on the Chesapeake Bay, where they would again have anonymity.

When Control flew in to DC, he was picked up by Jason Mazer, a Company Control. He had gone to ground, as McCall had surmised, when Matthew Goddard had started his witch hunt for Control. Mazer had kept a low profile until Control called him.

Mazer drove Control out to his house in Arlington, Virginia. A FOR SALE sign was on the front lawn. Control walked up the flagstone path to the porch and looked through the windows. No furniture was in the hallway, in the living room, or in the kitchen. Control walked around the line of butternut trees to the McMansion on the right. It also had a FOR SALE sign on it. Control walked onto the front porch and looked in the windows. No furniture, no paintings, the stillness of dead air. Control met up with Jason Mazer as he walked back from the house on the left.

"Also for sale."

Control looked at the modern farmhouse he'd lived in for years. It was time for him to make a new beginning. He climbed back into Mazer's BMW, and Mazer pulled away from the cul-de-sac. Control would be investigating the people who McCall had said were living in the three houses. But he knew they would be long gone.

Control had called Emma Marshall in London. She was relieved to hear his voice. Control had asked her if she would consider returning to the United States, to The Company. She had said, "Oh, God, yes, please!" and that she had been considering matricide if she had to go on living with her seventy-six-year-old mother in Camberley for much longer. She would pack her things and see him in Virginia.

Control walked into the Company complex of buildings on the morning of the fifth day. He asked for a pass at the security guard's desk in the lobby of his building and was given a new one. He took the elevator to the sixth floor, walked down the corridor, and opened the door at the end. The Company offices looked the same to Control as the day he had walked out of them. There were some new people he hadn't seen before. He saw a couple of shadow executives, who acknowledged him, who had been apprised that he had returned safely from a highly classified mission.

Emma Marshall jumped up from her desk when Control walked in. It had been vacant since Samantha Gregson had mysteriously disappeared.

"Good to have you back, sir."

Control noted that Emma's white blouse was undone almost to the waist, her skirt was a mini, and her eyes were mischievous.

Some things weren't supposed to change.

"Good to be back."

Control walked into his office. The furniture had been moved back to where he remembered it. A photo was on his desk of Jenny, Kerry, and Megan. His in-box was full. His laptop was on the desk. Control sat down and said, "It's too bright in here."

Emma knew that her boss liked it moody, and she subdued the lighting. She brought him a Starbucks Guatemala Antigua coffee and told him he needed to respond to several messages immediately. Then she closed the office door.

A small card was on Control's desk. He opened it. It said, *Welcome home,* and was signed *Robert.*

Control sat back and took a deep breath. There would be extensive meetings at the Pentagon, the CIA, and Homeland Security about the aborted attacks on American soil. Reports would be written and committees formed and intelligence data gathered. Control would be called to the DIA, the NSA, and the White House.

For James Thurgood Cameron, it was good to know that he *existed* again.

CHAPTER 51

Megan Forrester was doing a fashion shoot in the Pierre Hotel on East Sixty-First Street. Lights were set up at one end of the lobby with its black-and-white-checkered marble floor. Crew members were tweaking trims and a second AD was grouping extras. McCall found Megan at a makeup table being fussed over by three assistants, getting ready for the next shot. She was wearing a stunning Pamella Roland laminated-lace trumpet gown with a velvet waistband. Megan looked up at McCall's approach, a little fearful, McCall thought. Obviously she had not fully recovered from her ordeal. The makeup girls and hairdresser continued their feverish activity. McCall spilled the turquoise mother-of-pearl buttons onto the makeup table.

"These came off the shirt you were wearing a couple of weeks ago in an alleyway off Essex Street." McCall had a diamond earring in his other hand. "And you dropped this in that same alleyway."

Megan was suddenly wary and self-conscious. "Were you there that night?"

"No. I picked up the second earring from a person of interest the police are talking to." He dropped the other diamond earring into her outstretched palm. "Better to have the matching set."

Megan dropped the earrings onto the makeup table. "Thank you so much. These were a gift from my mother."

"Have a good shoot."

McCall turned to leave.

"Who are you?"

But McCall had already moved through the ornate lobby and out into the street.

McCall knew Melody had already entered his hotel suite because he was assailed by the scent of her perfume. The curtains at the windows were open, moonlight shafting through them. Otherwise the suite was in darkness. Melody had kicked off her shoes and her blue dress had dropped right to the floor on her way into the bedroom. McCall was convinced again that she was wearing nothing else. The kaleidoscopic lights from the dance floor at Dolls had outlined her figure in perfect detail.

McCall took one more step toward the bedroom door before he sensed the danger.

Matthew Goddard's condescending voice said, "Turn around very slowly, old son, and please keep your hands out in front of you."

McCall turned. Matthew Goddard wore the same blue pin-striped suit with the red silk tie with the chess pieces on it. His features were lit by the moonlight. A thrill was in his eyes, as if this were something that *real* agents did in the field. He had always been an observer, the man who picked up the pieces after an aborted mission. Now he was directing the action, and he liked it. He held a Walther compact pistol in his right hand.

He wasn't alone.

Melody stood naked and unmoving beside him. Goddard had his left hand clamped on her left shoulder. The Walther pistol was pressed tight to Melody's neck. Both of them were standing at the low coffee table.

"Now reach into your right jacket pocket," Goddard rasped, "and take out your Glock 19 and throw it as far across the room as you can. This Walther will not move a millimeter from her neck."

McCall reached into his jacket pocket.

"Grip it by the stock."

McCall lifted the Glock 19 out of his jacket and threw it across the sofa to the far side of the room. He took two steps toward the coffee table. The silver demon-claws skull gleamed on Goddard's right hand, the silver ring beside it with its etching: REMEMBER THAT YOU MUST DIE.

"You and your mercenaries killed my men," Goddard said. "But did you think they were the only assassins working with me against the American government? There are a hundred of us, and the number is growing exponentially. This was just the first wave of patriots in the new world order."

"So you've been working for the Jihadists in Syria and Iraq?"

"We work for the forces who are ripping this world apart. These assassins are shadowy and untraceable. You won't find out anything about them. I'm sure Control has already put the best cryptographers in The Company to work to try to decipher the hieroglyphics on the back of the silver skulls."

Something caught McCall's eye on the coffee table. He didn't think it could be seen from where Goddard was standing, masked by a silver bowl of candies.

"Do they have any significance at all?" McCall took another step toward the coffee table.

"You'll never find out," Goddard said in his singsong rasp. "It's not a code that can be broken."

McCall became aware that Melody was moving slightly. Her hand had traveled down her body until it was below her breasts. McCall couldn't see in the intermittent moonlight what she was doing, but her hand stayed at her navel. She gasped suddenly.

Goddard pressed the barrel of the Walther tighter against her neck. "Keep still!" he hissed.

Melody gave a little whimper of fear.

But it wasn't that.

It was in *pain*.

McCall realized what she had done. His eyes flicked back down to the coffee table, then back to Goddard's face. His eyes were feverish.

"There's a mystique about you, old son. You're a legend. But even legends fade away after time. Memento mori. Remember that you must die."

Things happened all at once, as time slowed down for McCall.

Melody reached up and stabbed something small and sharp into Goddard's wrist on her shoulder.

When he gasped in sudden pain, she half turned out of his grasp.

The Walther pistol wavered for a fraction of a second from her neck.

McCall picked up the slim throwing knife from the coffee table and threw it at Goddard's face with a flick of his wrist.

The blade went into his right eye.

Goddard fell back, firing the Walther into the air. He crashed down to the floor. McCall grabbed Melody and held her tightly. He looked down at Goddard's supine figure, the blade sticking obscenely out of his eye socket.

McCall gently took the sharp object from Melody's hand.

It was an open safety pin she had unfastened and slid out of her navel, which was bloody where she had tried to get the pin undone. McCall dropped it onto the coffee table.

"Is he dead?" she whispered.

"Yes."

"You're sure?"

"Yes."

McCall let her go. She walked a little unsteadily around the couch, picked up her blue pumps and her blue dress from the floor, and disappeared into the bedroom. McCall heard water running in the bathroom. He retrieved his Glock 19, returned it to his jacket pocket, and dialed his iPhone. When Kostmayer answered, McCall said, "I need a cleanup at my hotel suite, number 1728 at the Liberty Belle Hotel."

"Anyone else hurt except your target?"

"My date for the night is a little shaken up."

"Dating and you don't mix too well," Kostmayer murmured. "I'll bring Jimmy with me."

McCall disconnected. Melody came out of the bedroom in her blue dress. She had on her blue pumps. McCall moved over to her.

"Are you all right?"

"There was a little more bleeding. Those safety pins aren't supposed to be ripped out after you've got them in place. But I couldn't think of anything else to do."

"You did fine."

Melody looked in the shadows to where Matthew Goddard's body lay partially obscured by the couch.

"Why did he want to kill you?"

"It's a long story."

"Will you tell me when you can?"

"It would be highly classified."

"Are you a spy?"

"Not anymore. I'm going to take you home."

They left the hotel suite. McCall picked up a cab on Sixty-Sixth Street, and they took it downtown to Jane and Eighth Avenue. McCall wanted to escort Melody up to her apartment, but she shook her head. She was more composed now.

"Getting to know you could be hazardous to a girl's health."

"I could have told you that."

"But it'd be worth it."

Melody kissed him softly on the lips, then got out of the cab and ran up the stairs to her building. McCall gave her time to get up to her apartment. He saw the light come on at her third-floor windows. Then he told the cabbie to take him back to the Liberty Belle Hotel.

Samantha Gregson sat in the little breakfast nook in her Washington, DC, town house, sipping a glass of cabernet sauvignon. Her boss had not called her when he had said he would. That meant Matthew Goddard was dead. There was no other explanation.

Sam took another swallow of the cabernet and gazed out at the Capitol Building in the hazy drizzle. She knew what she had to do. She would get in touch with other members of the Memento Mori movement. She would find out what steps were being taken to bring the assassins together. Before then, Samantha Gregson made a vow to Matthew Goddard, a man she had worshipped, albeit from far.

She would kill Robert McCall.

When McCall got back to his hotel suite, Kostmayer and Jimmy had been there and gone. There was no sign of Matthew Goddard's body and no blood

on the polished wood floor. Goddard's Walther pistol had also been removed. McCall would call Control to tell him what had happened, but
that was all. He wouldn't allow himself to be drawn into the hunt for the
rogue Company assassins and what kind of a world conspiracy they were
protecting.

That's what Control and The Company were for.

McCall didn't turn on any lights. He poured himself a shot of Glenfiddich and sat on the couch in the moonlight and sipped it. He picked up his
iPhone. He had thirty-seven messages. All asking for his help. Some would
sound genuine. A handful would be legitimate victims who simply had nowhere else to turn. Such as Emily Masden and her mother, Laura, Linda
Hathaway and *her* daughter, Gemma, Melody Fairbrother, and Norman
Rosemont.

A chime denoted McCall had a text on his private cell line.

He accessed it.

The text had obviously been sent in haste:

Odds against me. Still a prisoner in NK. Come and get me and others.
Granny.

McCall stared at the text. Kostmayer had been wrong. Granny was still
alive. Somehow he had escaped and got a text through to McCall. Maybe
Granny had been recaptured, or maybe he had used a phone belonging to
one of the guards without his knowledge. No one in that North Korean
prison camp would have known McCall's private phone number except
Granny.

The Equalizer could not ignore this request for help.

He picked up his cell phone and called Control at The Company HQ
in Herndon, Virginia:

"I need to be in North Korea in two days," McCall said. "Solo mission."